# the book of joe

# the BOOK of JOE

## of JOE

jonathan tropper

delacorte press

THE BOOK OF JOE
A Delacorte Book / April 2004

Published by
Bantam Dell
A Division of Random House, Inc.
New York, New York

Book design by Glen Edelstein

Delacorte Press is a registered trademark of Random House, Inc., and the colophon is a trademark of Random House, Inc.

Library of Congress Cataloging in Publication Data

Tropper, Jonathan.
    The book of Joe / Jonathan Tropper.
        p. cm.
    ISBN 0-385-33741-8
    I. Title.

PS3570.R5885B66 2004
813'.54—dc21

2003055079

Manufactured in the United States of America
Published simultaneously in Canada

10 9 8 7 6 5 4 3 2 1
BVG

For my daughter, Emma Yetta Tropper, whose laughter and love renew me on a daily basis, and in memory of the great lady whose name she bears, Yetta Tropper, who never found a room she couldn't light up simply by entering.

# Acknowledgments

Thank You

To my family: My wife Lizzie, who tolerates my creative mood swings, takes the kids on Sunday adventures so I can write, and who never doubted I would find the right home for this book. My parents, who supported and encouraged my writing long before I gave them any reason to. Spencer and Emma, who fill my every day with the perfect chaos of their love, and without whom this book would have been finished so much sooner.

To Simon Lipskar, my fantastic agent, my sounding board and my literary conscience. He gets excited on my behalf and he gets pissed off on my behalf and it's great to have someone like that, because it's no fun at all to be excited or pissed off by yourself. Thanks also to Maja Nikolic for handling the foreign markets, Daniel Lazar and everyone else at Writers House for taking such good care of me.

To Kassie Evashevski, my very cool film agent at Brillstein-Grey, for giving me four of the most thrilling and surreal hours of my professional life.

To Abby Zidle, my dream of an editor at Bantam Dell, who is frightfully educated but delightfully lowbrow when the moment demands it, and an absolute pleasure to work with. Thanks to all the folks at Bantam Dell for getting behind this book in such a big way and making me feel so welcome.

To Kelley Ragland, who edited *Plan B*, my first novel, and whose valuable input helped improve this one.

# acknowledgments

To Alan Arrick Stone, rest in peace, who passed away much too young on July 7, 1992, and to Steven Stone, who, on an ill-advised nighttime drive through a snowstorm from York, Pa. to New York City, shared his memories of Alan's final days with me. We ended up getting hopelessly lost and having to call AAA, but the stories stayed with me and bits and pieces of them found their way into this novel.

To Aari Itzkowitz, for staying unemployed just long enough to proofread the first draft of this novel, despite the conspicuous absence of Winston Churchill or a major world war in the story.

To all the devoted friends and family members who never stopped asking after this book. Here it is. Now please, just leave me alone.

# the book of joe

# book ONE

Now a life of leisure and a pirate's treasure
Don't make much for tragedy
But it's a sad man my friend who's livin' in his own skin
And can't stand the company
—"Better Days," Bruce Springsteen

It's a town full of losers
I'm pulling out of here to win
—"Thunder Road," Bruce Springsteen

# one

Just a few scant months after my mother's suicide, I walked into the garage, looking for my baseball glove, and discovered Cindy Posner on her knees, animatedly performing fellatio on my older brother, Brad. He was leaned up against our father's tool rack, the hammers and wrenches jingling musically on their hooks like Christmas bells as he rocked gently back and forth, staring up at the ceiling with a curiously bored expression. His jeans and boxers were bunched up around his knees, his hand resting absently on her bobbing head as she went about her surprisingly noisy oral ministrations. I stood there transfixed until Brad, sensing my arrival, looked down from the ceiling and our eyes met. There was no alarm in his eyes, no embarrassment at having been caught in so compromising a position, but only the same look of tired resignation he always seemed to have where I was concerned. *That's right. I'm getting a blow job in the garage. It's a safe bet you never will.* Cindy, whose back was to me, noticed me a few seconds later and became instantly hysterical, cursing and shrieking at me as I beat a hasty, if somewhat belated, retreat. I was thirteen years old at the time.

It's entirely possible that Cindy would have handled herself with a bit more aplomb had she known that years later the incident would be immortalized in the first chapter of the best-selling autobiographical novel that I would write and, as with most successful books, in the inevitable movie that would follow shortly thereafter. By then she was no longer Cindy Posner, but Cindy Goffman, having married Brad in their senior year of college, and I think it's fair to say that this inclusion in my book did nothing to improve our already tenuous relationship. The book is titled *Bush Falls,* after the small Connecticut town where I grew up, a term I use loosely, since the jury's still out on whether I've actually ever grown up at all.

By now you've certainly heard of *Bush Falls,* or no doubt seen the movie, which starred Leonardo DiCaprio and Kirsten Dunst, and did some pretty decent box office. Or maybe you read about the major controversy it caused back in my hometown, where they even went so far as to put together a class action libel suit against me that never went anywhere. Either way, the book was a runaway best-seller about two and a half years ago, and for a little while there, I became a minor celebrity.

Any schmuck can be unhappy when things aren't going well, but it takes a truly unique variety of schmuck, a real innovator in the schmuck field, to be unhappy when things are going as great as they are for me. At thirty-four, I'm rich, successful, have sex on a fairly regular basis, and live in a three-bedroom luxury apartment on Manhattan's Upper West Side. This should be ample reason to feel that I have the world by its proverbial short hairs, yet I've recently developed the sneaking suspicion that underneath it all I am one sad, lonely son of a bitch, and have been for some time.

While there is no paucity of women in my life these days, it nevertheless seems that every relationship I've had in the two and a half years since the publication of *Bush Falls* has lasted almost exactly eight weeks, following the same essential flight pattern. In the first week I pull out all the stops—fancy restaurants, concerts, Broadway shows, and trendy nightclubs—modestly avoiding any high-minded banter concerning the literary world in favor of current events, movies, and celebrity gossip, which are of course the real currency in the New York dating scene, even if no one will admit it. Not that being a celebrated author isn't worth something, but stories about Miramax parties or how you hung out on the set with Leo and Kirsten will get you laid much faster and by a better caliber of woman. Weeks two and three are generally the best, the time you'd like to bottle and store, primarily due to the endorphin rush of fresh sex. At some point in the fourth week, I fall in love, briefly considering the possibility that this could be The One, and then everything pretty much goes to shit in slow motion. I waffle, I vacillate, I get insecure, I come on too strong. I conduct little psychological experiments on myself or the woman involved. You get the picture. This goes on for a couple of painfully awkward weeks, and then we both spend week seven in the fervent hope that the relationship will magically dissolve on its own, through an act of god or spontaneous combustion—anything to avoid having to actually navigate the tediously perilous terrain of a full-blown breakup. The last week is spent "taking some time," which ends with a final, perfunctory phone call finalizing the arrangement and resolving any outstanding logistics. I'll drop the bag and Donna Karan sweater you left in my apartment with the doorman, you can keep the books I lent you, thanks for the memories, no hard feelings, let's stay friends, et cetera, ad nauseam.

I know it bespeaks poor character to blame others for your problems, but I'm fairly certain this is all Carly's fault. Carly Diamond was my high school girlfriend, the first—and, to date, only—woman I've ever loved. We were together for our entire senior year, and loved each other with the fierce, timeless conviction of teenagers. That was the same year that all the terrible events described in my novel occurred, and my relationship with her was the lone bright spot in my dismally expanding universe.

If you want to get technical about it, we never actually broke up. We graduated high school and went to different colleges, Carly up to Harvard and me down to NYU. We tried to do the long-distance thing, but my adamant refusal to return to the Falls for our mutual vacations made it difficult, and over time we simply grew apart, but we never formally dissolved our relationship. After college, Carly came to New York to study journalism, at which point we embarked on one of those long, messy postgraduate friendships where you have just enough sex to thoroughly confuse the hell out of each other and ultimately, through a sequence of poor timing and third-party complications, fuck the life out of what was once the purest thing you'd ever known.

We still loved each other then, that much was obvious, but while Carly seemed ready to reclaim our relationship, I kept finding reasons to remain uncommitted. No matter how much I loved her—and I did—I was constantly comparing the timbre of our relationship with the raw beauty, the sense of discovery, that had attended our every moment when we were seventeen. By the time I finally understood the colossal nature of my mistake, it was too late and Carly was gone. Losing her once was sad but understandable. Carelessly discarding the second chance afforded me by the fates required such a potent mixture of arrogance and stupidity that it had to have been cultivated, because I'm fairly certain I wasn't always such a complete asshole.

I've never forgiven myself for the head games I played with her during her years in New York, wooing her whenever I felt her slipping away and then pulling back the minute I felt secure again. I allowed her unwavering belief in us to sustain me even at times when I didn't share it, leading her along with promises, both spoken and implied but never fulfilled. By the time I finally began to understand how badly I'd been using her, I had used her up completely. She left New York heartbroken and disgusted, returning to the Falls to accept a position as managing editor of *The Minuteman,* the town's local paper. Every time I think I've gotten over her, I find myself waking in the middle of the night, pining for her with such desperation that you would think it was only yesterday and not ten years ago that she left.

Since then not a day goes by that I am not haunted by a vague but powerful sense of regret, every woman I date serving as a reminder of what I allowed myself to lose. So in a way, it's because of Carly that I'm alone in bed in the middle of the night when the phone rings, its electronic wail piercing the insulated silence of my apartment like a siren. Generally speaking, when people call you at two in the morning, it won't be good news. My first thought, as I swim up through the dense wormwood haze of alcohol-induced sleep, is that it has to be Natalie, my borderline-psychotic ex-girlfriend, calling to scream at me. I don't know what damage I could have possibly done to her apparently fragile psyche in eight weeks, but her latest therapist has convinced her that she still has significant unresolved issues with me and that it behooves her, from a mental wellness perspective, to call me, day or night, whenever it occurs to her to remind me what an insensitive jerk I was. The calls started about four months ago and now come fairly regularly, both at home and on my cell phone, thirty-second installments of furious invective with abundant smatterings of vulgarity, requiring absolutely no participation from me. If it happens that I'm unavailable, Nat is perfectly content to leave her colorful harangues on my voice mail. She's always been drawn to radical therapy, much as lately I seem to be drawn to women who require it.

The phone keeps ringing. I don't know if it's been two rings or ten; I just know it isn't stopping. I roll onto my side and rub my face vigorously, trying to coax the sleep from my head. The skin of my cheeks feels like putty, loose and fleshy, as if the night's prior excesses have dramatically aged me. I went out with Owen earlier, and, as usual, we got supremely shit-faced. Owen Hobbs, agent extraordinaire, is my emissary not only to the literary establishment but to all conceivable manner of chaos and debauchery. I never drink except when I'm with him, and then I drink like him, voraciously and with great ceremony. He's made me rich, and he gets fifteen percent, which has turned out to be a better foundation for a friendship than you might think, usually worth the thrashing hangovers that always follow what he terms our "celebrations." A night with Owen inevitably takes the shape of a downward spiral upon which in retrospect I can identify only a handful of the spins and turns as I nurse my wounded body back into the realm where consciousness and sobriety rudely intersect. And while I'm still loosely ensconced in that precariously optimistic place where drunkenness has departed and the hangover is still mulling over its options, I nevertheless feel nauseous and off-kilter.

The phone. Without moving my head from where it lies embedded in my pillow, I reach out in the general direction of my night table, knocking over some magazines, an open bottle of Aleve, and a half-filled mug of water, which splashes mutely on the plush ecru carpeting. The cordless is actually on the floor to begin with, and when I finally locate it and hoist it up to my immobile head, cold droplets of spilled water seep into my ear canal like slugs.

"Hello?" It's a woman's voice. "Joe?"

"Who's this," I say, lifting my head slightly so as to move the mouthpiece somewhere in the general vicinity of my mouth. It's not Nat, which means some speaking on my part might be required.

"It's Cindy."

"Cindy," I repeat carefully.

"Your sister-in-law."

"Oh." That Cindy.

"Your father's had a stroke." My brother's wife blurts this

out like a premature punch line. In most families, such monumental news would merit a thoughtfully orchestrated presentation carefully constructed to minimize shock while facilitating gradual acceptance. Such grave news would probably warrant a personal delivery from the blood relative, in this case my older brother, Brad. But I am family to Brad and my father only in a strictly legal sense. On those rare occasions when they do acknowledge my existence, it's out of some vague sense of civic responsibility, like paying taxes or jury duty.

"Where's Brad?" I say, keeping my voice just above a whisper as people who live alone do needlessly at night.

"He's over at the hospital," Cindy says. She's never liked me, but that isn't entirely her fault. I've never actually given her any reason to.

"What happened?"

"Your dad's in a coma," she says matter-of-factly, as if I've asked her the time. "It's quite serious. They don't know if he's going to make it."

"Don't sugarcoat it, now," I mutter, sitting up in my bed, which causes pockets of violence to erupt among the trillions of neurons rallying like soccer fans in my left temple.

There follows a pause. "What?" Cindy says. I remind myself that my particular style of irony is usually lost on her. I take a quick emotional inventory, searching for any reaction to the news that my father might be dying: grief, shock, anger, denial. Something.

"Nothing," I say.

Another uncomfortable pause. "Well, Brad said you shouldn't come tonight but that you should meet him at the hospital tomorrow."

"Tomorrow," I repeat dumbly, looking at the clock again. It already is tomorrow.

"You can stay with us, or you can stay at your father's place. Actually, his house is closer to the hospital."

"Okay." Somewhere in my diminishing stupor, it registers that my presence is being requested or, rather, presumed. Either way, it's highly unusual.

"Well, which is it? Do you want to stay with us or at your dad's?"

A more compassionate person might wait for the shock to wear off before pressing ahead with the petty logistics of the whole thing, but Cindy has little in the way of compassion where I'm concerned.

"Whatever," I say. "Whatever's better for you guys."

"Well, it's usually a madhouse here, with the kids and all," she says. "I think you'll be happier in your old house."

"Okay."

"Your father's in Mercy Hospital. Do you need directions?" Her question is quite possibly a deliberate dig at the fact that I haven't been back to the Falls in almost seventeen years.

"Have they moved it?"

"No."

"Then I should be fine."

I can hear her shallow breathing as another uncomfortable silence grows like a tumor over the phone line. Cindy, three years older than me, was the archetypal popular girl in Bush Falls High School. With lustrous dark hair and an exquisite body sculpted to perfection in her cheerleading drills, she was unquestionably the most universally employed muse of the wet dream among the teenaged boys in Bush Falls at that time. I myself made often and effective use of her in my fantasies, fueled in no small part by what I saw in the garage that day. But now she's thirty-seven and a mother of three, and even over the phone, you can hear the varicose veins in her voice.

"Okay, then," Cindy finally says. "So, we'll see you tomorrow?"

"Yeah," I say.

As if it happens all the time.

# two

I left Bush Falls when I graduated high school and haven't been back since.

There's never been any compelling reason to visit my hometown, and about a million reasons to stay away. My father still lives there, for one, in the four-bedroom colonial where I spent the first eighteen years of my life, and it's been many years since we had any use for each other. Every year, usually around Thanksgiving, Brad calls, inviting me to come stay with him and Cindy, have turkey with the family. But I know he just likes to take the opportunity to feel noble. This is Brad, after all, my older brother by four years, who once sent me to the emergency room by jokingly bearing down on me in our father's weather-beaten Grand Am soon after he'd gotten his driver's license, as I stood innocently shooting hoops in our front yard. The car didn't stop quite where he'd planned, and I ended up with a broken wrist and a separated shoulder, which wasn't what I'd planned either. Later, he claimed that I'd darted out in front of the car without any warning. Whether or not my father believed him was irrelevant, because there was a big game against Fairfield the following night and Bush Falls was counting on Brad to lead the Cougars one game closer to a second state championship. My father would have thought it unseemly to punish the town hero.

Meet the family.

My mother, Linda, was a manic-depressive, diagnosed too late, who gracelessly killed herself by jumping into the Bush River Falls and drowning when I was twelve years old. I can sometimes remember her as she was before the onslaught of her insanity and the subsequent barrage of antidepressants that failed to ease the pain as they slowly choked the vitality out of her—a tall, soft-spoken woman with smiling eyes and an impish grin that always made you feel like you were in on some private joke together. When she kissed me good night, she called me Jo Jo Bear. Her laugh was infectious; her frequent tears a vexing mystery. Brad, my father, and I bobbed violently in the thrashing wake of her suicide, utterly incapable of relating to one another without her gentle feminine presence to corral us.

Ultimately, Brad and my dad found a common ground in basketball. Brad was a star forward for the Bush Falls Cougars, and in Bush Falls you could aspire to nothing greater. He led the Cougars to two state championship titles, breaking a busload of scoring records along the way. He fucked many cheerleaders. That was pretty much all there was to Brad back then, fucking and basketball. Not bad work if you could get it. But I couldn't, and thus Brad could not relate to me but simply viewed me with a mixture of bemused pity and disdain. As far as I was concerned, Brad was a moron, shallow and one-dimensional, and I wanted nothing more than to be him. My father, Arthur, had been a somewhat less spectacular player for the Cougars himself, and he never missed one of Brad's games, home or away. Afterward, they would discuss plays, relive highlights, and watch the UConn games.

If it isn't painfully obvious yet, I never made the team.

Our tragically diminished household had no use for an increasingly cynical kid with a spastic crossover dribble and no outside shot, and I grew to despise the exclusive nature of their devotion to the Cougars and all things basketball. The question of who was responsible for setting in motion this cycle of alienation and resentment is your classic chicken-or-the-egg conundrum, but either way the gulf between us continued to widen, and if my father ever attempted the daredevil feat of crossing it, his efforts were so minuscule as to be invisible from my side of the chasm. Brad was awarded an athletic scholarship to the University of Connecticut and left for college the same year I entered Bush Falls High as a freshman, leaving my father and me alone to fill the inexorable silence that gripped our house in a stranglehold.

I never planned on going back to Bush Falls; that much is obvious. Otherwise, I never would have written a novel that trashed everyone there so thoroughly. The truth is, though, I never actually believed I'd get it published. So I wrote a book about my hometown, about Carly and Sammy and Wayne and the terrible events of my senior year, liberated by the notion that it would never see the light of day. Then Owen Hobbs called me one evening and told me that it was "fucking brilliant." Not too many people can pull off using expressions like that. Owen can, because Owen is fucking brilliant.

Statistically speaking, it's damn near impossible to write a best-seller. It's also remarkably difficult to piss off an entire town. Overachiever that I am, I managed to accomplish both feats in one fell swoop. When it comes to alienation, I'm something of a prodigy.

So I never planned on going back to Bush Falls. But I never planned on my father having a massive stroke, either, as he played in his Senior Alumni Basketball League in the high school gym late one Friday night. According to Cindy, he'd been standing about three feet to the left of the top of the key, in what he called his sweet spot. He never missed from there. He went up for a jump shot and came down unconscious, sprawled out on the glossy hardwood floor. All the eyewitnesses, ex-jocks in varying states of decline, will forever after make a big deal out of the fact that the shot was good. Like that makes a fucking bit of difference. Sweet spot indeed.

# three

I hang up with Cindy and instantly feel the need to call someone. This is all too enormous to contemplate on my own, in the frazzled aftermath of my shattered slumber. My father is near death, and I'll be returning to Bush Falls after seventeen years. I hoist the telephone to my ear and draw a complete blank. Who the hell do I think I'm calling?

Determined to end my cycle of meaningless relationships, I've been experimenting with celibacy for the last six months, and, after a few false starts, I seem to have finally gotten the hang of it. This makes me two things: horny and pathetic. On any given day I might feel one or the other, but as I lie in the dark, nonplussed and alone in the vast, barren acreage of my king-sized bed, an optimistic purchase if there ever was one, it's pathetic by a country mile.

I try to think of a friend to call, and am appalled when I can't come up with any that aren't in some way linked to me professionally. After *Bush Falls* hit the best-seller list, I quit my job and moved from my one-bedroom walk-up on

Amsterdam to a three-bedroom co-op on Central Park West, and the metamorphosis from an aspiring writer to a successful one seems to have somehow left me friendless. It's all an indirect but no less acute manifestation of my fuck-you money.

That's what Owen calls it. The advance was one thing: seventy-five thousand, less his fifteen percent, of course, and then another thirty-eight percent or so to taxes. That left me with just under forty thousand dollars, which was certainly nothing to sneeze at, but hardly what could be classified as fuck-you money.

"Oprah no longer picks books," Owen told me one day shortly after the publication of *Bush Falls* as we sat in his office, brainstorming. "On the bright side, though, she never would have picked yours anyway. It has no long-suffering women, overachieving cripples, or epic journeys to a new spiritual consciousness." This hardly came as a shock to me. Frankly, I was still reeling from the surprise that they'd published the book at all, let alone paid me a seventy-five-thousand-dollar advance. "So what are we going to do to sell this book?" Owen said with a frown.

"Book tour?" I said.

"You're not a name."

"Advertising?"

"Same problem."

"So how does one become a name?"

"By selling many books."

"Okay. And how do we do that?"

Owen frowned at me from behind his desk. "Oprah."

"Oh, come on," I said. "People sold books before there was Oprah."

He nodded absently, lost in thought. "I have an idea," he said.

Owen arranged for Paperbacks Plus, Bush Falls's local bookstore, to receive a large quantity of first editions at no charge. He then sent one of his clients, who also happened to be a staff writer for the *New York Times,* to Bush Falls to seek out some of the people portrayed in the book and interview them. The resulting article, "A Town Exposed," combined with Owen's incessant badgering, was enough to get someone at the Book Review to pay attention, and *Bush Falls* received a full-page write-up the following Sunday. The *Times* review was all Owen needed to launch his publicity machine. Within a month my little novel had been written up in *People, Time, Entertainment Weekly, Esquire,* and a slew of other major magazines. *Bush Falls* made its first best-seller list about three months after it hit the bookshelves, and there was suddenly a dramatic increase in the number of digits in my royalty checks. When we found out we'd made the list, Owen actually jumped up onto his hand-carved Chinese cherrywood desk and danced a crazy little Owen jig. Then he flew off to Frankfurt and sold the European rights collectively for $250,000, and then went out to L.A., where he sold the film rights to Universal for five times that, and through it all the royalty checks continued to gain weight. Six months later, still on the list, I was sitting on more money than I could have expected to make in a lifetime of working in brand marketing, which is what I used to do before I got a life.

"You now officially have your fuck-you money," Owen announced gleefully over steaks at Peter Luger's. He'd transformed the reporting of my monthly sales figures into a casual dinner ceremony compliments of the agency, although if you did the math, I was the one who really paid. But I chose not to think of it that way, because it was fun to be important, to be a major breadwinner for the agency. Also, as I said before, I don't have very many friends.

"My fuck-you money," I repeated.

"You bet," Owen said, sipping at his wine. He's somewhat overweight at thirty-one, with stringy blond hair and a ruddy, freckled complexion. Exceptionally literate and flamboyantly aggressive, he's fast becoming one of the most influential agents in the industry. Something about his full, grinning lips, his baby face, and the way his fat bulges forcefully against the constraints of his expensive, custom shirts all contribute to a subliminal impression of secret, nihilistic excess. A Roman emperor between orgies.

"What, exactly, is fuck-you money?" I asked him.

He picked up two fries, dipped them into his ketchup mound, and tossed them into his mouth, their twin ends protruding briefly from his lips like the legs of the expendable cast member being devoured by a Spielberg dinosaur. "It's money," he told me between noisy, sloshing chews, "that allows you to say fuck you to anyone: your boss, your family, ex-girlfriends, whoever. Anyone you ever had to take shit from because you depended on them. You're your own dog now. You don't need anyone anymore."

I looked across the table at him. "So I break even."

"What do you mean?"

"Nobody needs me, either."

Owen made a mock sad face at that, then grinned wickedly and said, "*I* need you."

He was right about the money. It's purchased me my new apartment, my new Mercedes convertible—a CLK 430 Cabriolet—and its obscenely expensive parking spot, a ridiculously large home entertainment center, and an assortment of other predictable extravagances. And I was right about no one's needing me, a fact I usually manage to avoid with an elaborate array of scrupulously employed defense mechanisms. But confronted with the prospect of seeing my father and Brad again, and returning to Bush Falls after almost seventeen years, smoke and mirrors will no longer protect me from what I've really known all along: that I'm pretty much alone in the world. Me and my fuck-you money.

Have I mentioned my penchant for self-pity? It's part of my charm.

I roll slowly out of bed, feeling twice my age, pull on a T-shirt, and pad down the hall for a late-night snack of cinnamon toast and POWERade. There's no avoiding the imminent onslaught of my hangover, but I've recently discovered, in an enterprise born either of desperation or an abundance of free time, that POWERade laced with liquid Tylenol effectively softens the blow. I'm not looking forward to morning, but still, it seems a long way off. I turn on my absurdly large flat-screen television and watch an Australian dude hopped up on caffeine dive into a swamp with two large crocodiles, ostensibly to demonstrate the proper way this sort of thing should be done. Shortly after three A.M., my nerves jangling from the electrolyte rush of my hangover cocktail, I say screw it and call Owen. I figure I owe him fifteen percent of my sleepless night.

# *four*

All roads lead back to Bush Falls.

I'm not speaking metaphorically. Just about every highway leaving the island of Manhattan to the north can get you there. You can take the Harlem River Drive to the Cross Bronx Expressway, which becomes the New England Thruway, and ride that all the way up to Bush Falls. Or you can take the Henry Hudson Parkway to the Saw Mill to the Cross County to the Hutchinson River Parkway, then get on the Merritt Parkway, which winds its way in a serpentine trail through the southern half of Connecticut. From the Merritt you pick up I-91, which will take you all the way out to Hartford and just past it to the Falls: more highways, less traffic. Or you can combine the two routes by taking the Merritt and then switching to the Thruway via the I-287 interchange. Despite this veritable smorgasbord of highways, I haven't once, in the last seventeen years, seen fit to take any of them to Bush Falls.

I sit behind the wheel of my silver Mercedes the next morning, idling at the curb just outside the Kinney garage where it's usually parked, paralyzed by indecision concerning which route to take for the two-and-a-half-hour drive. It's a clear, room temperature morning, but the discerning eye will note a visible diminishment of exposed flesh on the women on their way to work. Summer is over, and I can't recall its even having arrived. I'm stalling again. I don't want to go. My father hasn't ever been there for me. Why should I now have to be there for him? It's not like he'll notice me anyway, what with him being in a coma and all.

But I know I'll go, for the same reason Brad calls me every year with halfhearted invitations to various holiday meals. Because that's what you do. When you have a younger brother living on his own in Manhattan, you call him around the holidays, bursting with artificial familiarity and contrived bonhomie. And when your father has a life-threatening stroke in his sweet spot, you shelve seventeen years of bad blood and drive out to be there. Not to necessarily help, or even offer support, but simply because it's where you belong. Blood will separate, if need be, but its call is primordial, and it won't be refused.

The Motorola V.60 mounted on my dashboard rings and I flip it open, activating the car's speakerphone. "Hello?"

"Misogynist!"

Natalie.

"You're a petty, whining, self-absorbed schmuck without a clue how to love or be loved. You'll never understand what it means to care for another person more than you care for yourself, and you'll die miserable and alone!"

I want to tell her that I'm miserable and alone now, but she's already hung up.

"You have a nice day too," I say softly, affectionately even, and, with a final, epic sigh, throw the car into drive and turn onto Ninety-sixth Street, toward the West Side Highway. It's a safe bet your world has gone to shit when an angry phone call from a bipolar ex-girlfriend will probably be the high point of your day.

It's nine-thirty A.M., still theoretically rush hour, but I'll be driving north, against traffic. Keeping one eye on the road, I reach absently into the messy heap of CDs scattered on the seat beside me, an eclectic assortment symptomatic of a vague and misguided effort to transcend my actual age. It's not necessarily that I'm afraid of aging; I just refuse to do it alone. And so, at thirty-four, I'm listening to Everclear, Blink 182, Dashboard Confessional, Foo Fighters, and a host of other contemporary stuff. My audio Rogaine. I've somehow managed to beat the odds and keep a full head of hair, but that's really beside the point. We're all going bald somewhere.

Besides, I come from the eighties, a neon, hair-sprayed decade from which very little music made it out alive. When was the last time you heard Men at Work, Thompson Twins, or Alphaville on a mainstream radio station? The music from my youth has aged poorly and is now like a joke out of context. You had to be there.

And yet my fingers continue to dig, past No Doubt and Ben Folds, until they locate an old copy of Springsteen's *Born to Run*. There are some things that do transcend time and age, and the Boss is one of them. I slide the CD in, and it instantly takes me back, in that way only music can, to my bedroom in Bush Falls, where I wore out the record on the Fisher stereo I'd gotten as an eighth-grade graduation gift from my father. That was about nine months after my mother died, and he was still handing out consolation prizes. The stereo had been his grand finale, and soon after that he retreated permanently to his den to get drunk nightly in the company of his old high school basketball trophies, leaving the house only for work and Cougars games.

As I drive through the tolls in Riverdale, I dial Owen's office number. His anal-retentive secretary, Stuart, answers in a crisp, officious voice. "Owen Hobbs's office."

"Can I have Owen, please?"

"Mr. Hobbs is in a meeting right now," he says automatically. "May I ask who's calling?"

"It's Joe Goffman."

"Oh, Mr. Goffman!" Stuart gushes, suddenly the epitome of warmth and graciousness. "How have you been? I didn't recognize your voice."

"That's because we rarely speak." Stuart is a typically arrogant gatekeeper, a self-important poseur Owen keeps around for the sheer amusement of it, and while I usually relish the way he can be instantly transformed into a shameless sycophant where I'm concerned, today I'm not in the mood. "Please tell him it's me."

"Of course," Stuart says, and I can tell he's miffed. "Everything okay?"

"Peachy."

The hold music is "Band on the Run," and Paul McCartney's voice comes pouring through my speakerphone with surprising clarity, clashing with the Springsteen on my stereo. I turn off the Springsteen at the same instant that Owen's scratchy voice replaces McCartney's, and thus we avoid a historical duet. "Hey, Joe." He sounds hoarse and groggy, which is at least partially my fault, since I kept him on the phone until close to five this morning.

"Sorry about last night. I hope I wasn't interrupting anything," I say, although with Owen you're almost always interrupting something. The man keeps his social life hopping with a frenetic, almost desperate intensity. It's as if he's worried that if he took one night off, the wild circus of his life would pull up stakes and leave town without him.

"I'd pretty much gotten my money's worth from Sasha by then," he says with a low snicker.

"Sasha?"

"A Romanian nurse, if I understood her credentials properly."

"I see."

23

Owen's brazen patronage of high-end call girls is legendary in the publishing industry. He is currently working his way through the "sensual role play" ads in the back of *New York* magazine, gleefully reporting to me after every encounter.

"You heading up to the Falls now?" he asks. "The Falls" is a term used only by the locals, and it's just like Owen to insinuate himself like that.

"As we speak."

"Well, I hope your dad's doing better."

"Thanks," I say, feeling suddenly guilty, as if I might be perpetrating a fraud of some kind by accepting sympathetic wishes on behalf of my father. "Did you get the pages?"

"They were waiting for me this morning," he says after the slightest pause. Owen is not a man typically given to pauses.

"Have you read them?"

"Some."

Given the success we enjoyed with *Bush Falls,* Owen has been eagerly awaiting my new manuscript, which I've been promising him for the last year. I actually finished it about six months ago but have withheld that information, since I'm not particularly thrilled with the finished product. The conventional wisdom about fiction, according to Owen, is that first novels are generally highly autobiographical works, and mine certainly does nothing to contradict that notion. It's the sophomore effort that confirms a writer's ability and relevance in the literary marketplace, because that's theoretically the work wherein he must truly harness his imagination and voice to create something from nothing. The publishing world is awash in blood from the slit wrists of all the one-trick ponies.

"You hate it," I say.

"No." I hear the unmistakable grind and click of his cigarette lighter. "There are actually some wonderful sections."

"There's a big 'but' hanging over that sentence."

Owen sighs. "I never had you pegged as a magical realist."

"I do it pretty sparingly," I object. "It's an atmospheric conceit."

"It's a pretentious distraction," Owen says dismissively. "Look at me, pushing the literary envelope! It doesn't work. Magical realism is not a movement or a technique. It's a novelty act, and the novelty's long gone. Readers will tolerate it from Marquez and Calvino because the *New York Times* tells them to. You're a Jew from Manhattan and no one's going to cut you that slack. It's bullshit."

"Why don't you tell me what you really think?"

"I think you're too good a writer to waste your time with experimental postmodernism."

I test the waters of his remark for patronizing levels and decide that he's being sincere. "Well, other than that, how are you finding the narrative?" *Other than that, Mrs. Lincoln, how did you enjoy the show?*

"Honestly, Joe, I think the subject matter is beneath you."

It's shocking, really, how with one sentence he is able put into words what I've spent six months trying to pin down to no avail. The novel—working title: *It Starts Here*—is about a kid who drops out of college to follow a Grateful Dead–like band around the country for a few months with a woman he's only just met. He's running away from his privileged upbringing, and she's fleeing an abusive husband and the law. Romance and chaos ensue amid the tie-dyed backdrop of the rock-and-roll bedouin culture. Not the most original premise in the world, but I really did start the novel with the best of literary intentions, meaning to tell a contemporary love story while examining the way in which people struggle against America's invisible class system. The spare combination of two main characters and their unique spin on a universal theme should have kept me focused on the story without being overly ambitious. But they made the movie of *Bush Falls* while I was writing *It Starts Here,* and there is no denying that the film perverted my writing. I was blocking shots instead of describing scenes, an entirely transparent and unacceptable practice when writing outside the milieu of courtrooms and serial killers.

"Listen," Owen says. "I'm barely into it, so this conversation is premature. Talk to me after the weekend."

"But we've ruled out loving it."

"Does it get better?"

"I'm not sure."

"Ah."

"Don't 'ah' me."

"Hmm," Owen says.

"So," I say after a bit. "What now?"

He coughs lightly. "Listen, Joe, you're a good writer. Blah, blah, blah. You don't have to prove anything to me. But I really don't want to talk about this until I've read it all. Then we can sit down and decide what it needs."

What it needs, I suspect, is to be taken out back and given the Old Yeller treatment. "And if it needs to be scrapped?"

"Then we'll scrap it," he says easily. "And you'll write me something else. Happens all the time."

"Is that supposed to make me feel better?"

"It's not my job to jerk you off. You want to feel better, go back to therapy. My job is to make you write better, and it's been my considerable experience that the worse you feel, the better you write."

"Wonderful," I say dejectedly. I don't bother to point out that I've been fairly miserable for the last six months and haven't managed to write a single sentence worth shit and that it positively terrifies me to think that I might be one of those poor slobs who have only one book in them.

Owen changes the subject. "So, you're going back to the Falls. Let me once again say wow. This could be interesting."

"I'm just hoping for quick."

"Well, keep me posted. I want to hear every last detail."

"Owen," I say. "Sometime in the future, you really should consider getting a life of your own."

He chuckles. "I had one once and discovered that they're overrated. Besides, I don't need one anymore. I have yours."

" 'Bye."

I hit the END button, turn the stereo back on, and step a little harder on the accelerator. The engine responds instantly with a deep, low growl. Within minutes I'm on the Merritt Parkway, luxuriating in the way the Mercedes chews up the dipping curves of the two-lane blacktop. I'm still in the formative stages of a love-hate relationship with the car. There's no denying that it handles like a dream, practically anticipating my every move. But on the other hand, everyone who can afford a Mercedes doesn't necessarily belong in one, and I'm becoming increasingly convinced that I fit into that category. The car embarrasses me, and I sometimes find myself grinning apologetically at passing motorists in Fords and Toyotas, as if those perfect strangers know I'm really one of them, out doing some unseemly social climbing. The sleek German design was never intended to house my petty insecurity.

The Parkway winds its way through the green Connecticut foliage, the outer edges of the leaves just beginning to glow red, signifying the approaching autumn. I sing along loudly to "Thunder Road" in an attempt to distract myself from the anxiety rising in me with each passing mile, but it's no use. I'm assaulted by a steady barrage of scenes from my past that flash by too quickly for proper identification but nonetheless leave me feeling vaguely disturbed. And then, as I'm passing Norwalk, Bruce begins singing "Backstreets" and, as if on cue, Sammy Haber emerges without warning from the back of my mind, striding purposefully across the stage of my brain in his checkered pants and that ridiculous pompadour. The image is so complete, so overwhelmingly perfect, that I feel my throat constrict and tears well up unbidden in my eyes. I take a deep breath, but the tears continue to come, blurring my vision, and I have to quickly pull over onto the anorexic shoulder of the highway, choking back an astonished sob as I throw the car into park.

Sammy. It takes just that one image of him for me to realize that I've been cheating my memory up until now, relating to him strictly within the confines of a literary character, unwilling to connect with him on a personal level. I thought I'd exorcised my demons by writing the book, but I now see that I've merely appeased them temporarily. And now I'm heading back to the Falls, where his ghost and others await me, and I'll have to deal with him and everything that had happened all over again, this time without the structured buffer of my pages and chapters to hold them in check. I shudder, wiping away the warm dampness on my cheeks as I wrestle my breathing back under control. Cars hurtle past me on the Merritt like missiles, their force gently buffeting my car as it idles on the shoulder.

There was a time when I wasn't like this, when I had friends and I cared. Sammy, Wayne, and me, three misfits who somehow managed to fit. And then things got all fucked up and we didn't anymore, but for a while there we had something. And beyond that, even, I had Carly.

Time doesn't heal as much as it buries things in the undergrowth of your brain, where they lie in wait to ambush you when you least expect it. And so, as the years passed, Sammy became little more than an exhibit in the museum of my memory, and Wayne was reduced to an enigmatic hologram fading in and out of perception. Only Carly persevered as a living fixture in my consciousness, stubbornly eluding any and all efforts to retire her behind the glass wall of memory, maybe because I had loved her as an adult or maybe because that was just Carly, whose sheer force of personality would never allow such diminishment. Whatever the reason, my every feeling and experience is still colored by a dim awareness of her, and wherever I go, she floats, ever present, in the

background. She's still such a part of my life, the pain is still
so fresh, that it's unbelievable to me that we haven't spoken
in close to ten years. Everyone always wants to know how you
can tell when it's true love, and the answer is this: when
the pain doesn't fade and the scars don't heal, and it's too
damned late.

The tears threaten to return, so I willfully banish all
thoughts from my head and take a few more deep breaths.
I'm suddenly dizzy from the panic attack I've just suffered,
and I close my eyes, resting my head against the warm leather
of my steering wheel. Loneliness doesn't exist on any single
plane of consciousness. It's generally a low throb, barely audible, like the hum of a Mercedes engine in park, but every so
often the demands of the highway call for a burst of accelera-
tion, and the hum becomes a thunderous, elemental roar,
and once again you're reminded of what this baby's carrying
under the hood.

# *five*

## 1986

Sammy Haber moved into Bush Falls the summer before our senior year, a baby-faced skinny kid, with sandy blond hair gelled to an audacious height, tortoiseshell glasses, and an unfortunate affinity for pleated slacks and penny loafers. He and his mother had moved up from Manhattan, where, it was whispered, they'd been forced to leave in the wake of some kind of scandal. The lack of concrete details didn't hinder the powerful gossip engine of the Falls, was actually preferable, since it left the field wide open for sordid speculation.

Lucy Haber, Sammy's mother, did nothing to dampen the gossip. She was wildly beautiful, with thick auburn hair worn long and free, wide, uncomplicated eyes, and stark white skin that offered a perfect contrast to both her hair and her impossibly full lips, which came together in a thoughtless pout. In her platform sandals, long, flowing skirts, and clinging tops with plunging necklines, she exuded a casual, bohemian sexuality as she ambled distractedly past the stores on Stratfield Road, humming to herself as she went. Connecticut mothers, for the most part, weren't big on cleavage when they grocery shopped. The Bush Falls aesthetic tended more toward Banana Republic blouses tucked neatly into Ann Taylor slacks. Cleavage, like the good china, was reserved for special occasions, and even then was displayed sparingly. But Lucy Haber seemed oblivious to the catty looks she received from the women she passed, or the appreciative double takes she garnered from the men. Everyone agreed that she seemed much too young to have a son Sammy's age, and it was undoubtedly her abundant sexuality that was responsible for that, as well as the mysterious troubles back in New York. There apparently was no Mr. Haber, which was, of course, perfect.

That summer, as I did every summer, I went to work in my father's display factory on the outskirts of Bush Falls. My father was one of the few men in town who were not directly employed by P.J. Porter's, the immense discount department store chain whose national corporate headquarters was based in the Falls. With over seven hundred retail outlets nationwide selling everything from apparel, cosmetics, and jewelry to furniture and major appliances, Porter's was one of the largest employers in Connecticut. Bush Falls had originally been developed as a planned community for the employees of the retail giant, whose corporate campus was situated on seventy acres just a few miles north of the town proper and housed over a thousand offices. Just about every family in Bush Falls had at least one member working for Porter's. It was well-known that Porter's preferred to hire from within the community, and they ran a highly successful summer jobs program with Bush Falls High School.

My father had originally worked at Porter's as a purchasing agent before going into business on his own, manufacturing store displays, and Porter's subsequently became his largest account, thanks to his friends there, who ordered all of their promotional displays and packaging from him. While he was no less dependent on Porter's for his livelihood than he had been when he'd worked there, he was now his own boss, a distinction of which he was immensely proud, and pleased to point out at every opportunity.

So while my classmates went to work as summer interns at Porter's, I took my place alongside the stooped Peruvian immigrants who comprised my father's labor force, operating one of the hydraulic vacuum presses. My job consisted solely of continuously loading four-foot-square styrene sheets onto the press and setting the aluminum molds beneath them before lowering the press and activating the heating bed and the hydraulic pumps that melted and sucked the styrene onto the molds. Then I would lift the press and pull off the hot styrene, now formed in the shape of the mold, cut away the excess plastic with a box cutter, and toss the raw piece into a cart, which would periodically get wheeled out onto the floor for assembly and finishing. It was sweaty, monotonous work, and I trudged tiredly home every afternoon with stiff shoulders, smelling of burnt plastic, reminding myself that at least I didn't have to wear a suit. As a point of pride, my father always paid me marginally better than Porter's paid its summer interns. "Your old man is not a spoke on someone else's corporate wheel," he would say to me from behind the scuffed aluminum desk in his small, cluttered office in the rear of the factory. "And there's no reason for you to be one, either."

Summers were always busy, as we desperately churned out product for the fall retail season, and that summer we were particularly inundated with orders. Because of this sudden increase in production and the pressure to meet delivery dates, my father leased a second vacuum press, which he installed directly behind the first, and asked me if any of my friends would be interested in operating it for the summer. My best friend was Wayne Hargrove, who had proven to be such good company over the years that I was willing to overlook his regrettable status as a starting forward for the Cougars. A tall, sinewy kid with a thick mane of blond hair and a perfect swimmer's body, Wayne was one of those guys who effortlessly navigated the vast complexities of the high school caste system by being genuinely unconscious of its existence. He seemed to lack the innate filtration system we all had that automatically categorized geeks, dweebs, preps, stoners, jocks, goths, and the various subcategories therein. It's generally those occupying the lower positions on the food chain that are occasionally unmindful of the social boundaries, and their trespasses will usually engender swift repercussions worthy of a John Hughes film. Wayne's jock status exempted him from such concerns, and he was consequently one of the most genuinely liked people at Bush Falls High. His wit, while sharp, was never cutting or caustic, and he possessed an infectious energy that seemed to breed goodwill wherever he went. I was jealous as hell of him, but never resentful, since none of it was a conscious effort on his part.

I tried insistently to convince Wayne to forget about his internship at Porter's and come work at the factory. Linguistic and social barriers prevented me from having anything more than a nodding relationship with my coworkers, who I was always convinced were mocking the boss's son in their indecipherable native tongue. Wayne's presence would be the perfect antidote to my isolation, and a diversion from the sheer boredom of the work.

"Thanks, man," he said as we walked home on one of the last days of the school year. "But I'm already gainfully employed."

"We get off at three," I pointed out.

"You wake up at the ass crack of dawn," he countered.

"This pays more."

He raised his eyebrows. "There are things in this world besides money."

"Such as?"

"Air-conditioning."

He had me there.

I came home later that evening and found my father eating a frozen dinner in the den, bitching to the professional athletes on his television. *He's got nothing left. For Christ's sake, send in a goddamn closer already. What do you bother having a damn bull pen for anyway?* I told my dad that Wayne wasn't interested in the job. "So ask someone else," he said.

"There's no one else I can think of."

He turned away from the television to look at me, an event that should have been heralded by trumpets it was so unusual. "You really have no other friends besides Wayne?" he asked, frowning incredulously. That was my father, sensitive to a fault.

"None that are interested in working in an oven," I said.

"It's a good wage."

"No need to convince me. After all, I wasn't given a choice."

My father appeared ready to retort when his head suddenly jerked back to the television as someone hit or slid or did something clearly more important than the second fruit of his loins. "Okay," he said, shrugging his shoulders. "If you really have no other friends . . ."

"Thanks for pointing that out once again," I said, but he was already submerged in his baseball fog. *The goddamn Mets might actually go all the way this year.* I stood there for another moment to verify that the conversation was truly over, and then, with a sigh, headed into the kitchen to forage for my dinner.

The first time I met Sammy, he was standing in my father's office, looking atrociously colorful in a brown cotton vest over a mint green T-shirt, gray Gap chinos rolled at the cuff, and black penny loafers, nodding nervously as my father frowned skeptically at his gangly form. "This is Samuel Haber," my father said dejectedly, as if pointing out a troublesome wart on his toe. "He's here about the press job." My father was a broad, hulking six foot three, thick Polish stock, with a square jaw set just beneath his perpetual frown, and a wrestler's neck that looked as solid as a tree trunk. Next to his intimidating bulk, Sammy looked like a twig.

"A pleasure," Sammy said, extending his hand and shaking mine crisply. "I don't have any friends yet, but if I did, they'd call me Sammy."

"I'm Joe," I said. Looking at his skinny frame and his hairless baby face, I understood my father's skepticism. I wondered how often, if ever, Sammy shaved. "I guess you're new to the neighborhood."

"Just moved in," he said. He turned to my father. "So, big guy, when do I start?"

My father's eyes narrowed to slits. He was not the sort to appreciate jocular familiarity from his own children, let alone a strange boy. Arthur Goffman didn't relate well to any boy who wasn't an athlete, as I knew so well from painful experience, and Sammy was definitely a whole other breed. I liked him immediately.

My father grunted. "Listen, Samuel, I'll be honest with you," he said, which is what he generally said when he was about to put you down. "That's a big machine, and you're a skinny little guy. If you can work it, the job's yours. But if you can't handle it, you'll just gum up production, and I can't have that."

"Understood. Understood," Sammy said, nodding emphatically. "Don't worry. I'm stronger than I look."

"You'd have to be."

"Good one, sir."

"And you lower those guardrails, you understand?" my father continued, before turning to me with a stern look. "You show him the guardrails and watch him lower them, you got it?" I nodded and he turned back to Sammy. "If you leave your arm on the bed when that press comes down, you'll be going home with a stump."

"Duly noted," Sammy said. "The management frowns on amputation." And then, lowering his voice theatrically, he added, "Thank you for the opportunity, big guy. I won't let you down."

My father stared at him for a long moment, trying to determine if there was some joke he might be missing. "Don't call me big guy."

"Understood, Arthur."

"Mr. Goffman."

"That was going to be my next guess."

My father sighed deeply. "Okay then, you're hired."

Sammy said, "Cool."


*"You lower those rails."* Sammy imitated my father's growl surprisingly well as I walked him over to the press. *"We can't have a severed arm gumming up production. Jesus! Was that guy toilet trained at gunpoint or what?"*

"Now might be the right time to tell you that he's my dad," I said, not sure whether to be offended or amused.

He stopped walking and looked at me uncertainly. "You're kidding, right?"

"Afraid not."

"Fuck me very much," he said emphatically.

I decided to go with amused. "Don't worry about it."

"No, really. I'm a schmuck. Sometimes in my efforts to win friends and influence people, I just make a complete ass of myself."

"Forget about it. It was a good impression."

"And for my next impression, a skinny putz with his foot in his mouth."

"It's really okay."

"I really am sorry. I'm sure he's a great guy."

I shrugged. "Not really."

Sammy studied my face intently for a moment. "Well, then," he said with a grin. "Fuck him if he can't take a joke."

Sammy's father was a music professor at Columbia University. His mother had divorced him because of his unfortunate proclivity for bedding his female students, aspiring musicians being highly susceptible to passion and therefore easy prey. I learned this and many other things about Sammy during his first few days on the job. Working side by side for eight hours a day, we got to know each other pretty well. Sammy was a huge Springsteen fan and would unabashedly break into song as he worked the press, bobbing his head to the beat, serenading the immigrant women when they walked by, oblivious to their averted gazes. "*Rosalita, jump a little lighter,*" he would sing out without warning. "Come on, Carmen—sing it with me! *Señorita, come sit by my fire.*" He was fiercely passionate about Springsteen and would often lecture me on the profundity of a particular song, reciting the lyrics and punctuating them with his own commentary. He was terribly concerned about the recent commercial success of *Born in the U.S.A.* "I'm not saying it isn't a great album, but it doesn't compare to *Greetings from Asbury Park* or *Born to Run.* And all these airheads dancing to it on MTV are totally clueless. He's singing about the plight of our Vietnam vets, and the youth of America are shaking their asses like it's Wham! or Culture Club." He punched the air with his finger for emphasis. "Bruce Springsteen is not Wham!"

The summer of 1986 was on record as the worst to hit Connecticut in over ninety years, a hot, bleeding ulcer of a season. The air was laden with a cloying humidity and the pervasive stink of melting tar as the sun beat down mercilessly on the streets and roofs of Bush Falls. The neighborhood vibrated with the combined hum of the hundreds of central air compressors, nestled in side yards, that ran at a fevered pitch day and night, serving to further raise the already blistering outside temperature. People generally stayed indoors, and when forced to venture out, they moved sluggishly, as if under a greatly increased gravity.

In the factory, Sammy and I toiled in pools of our own sweat, the heating beds from our presses adding a good ten degrees to the already sweltering temperature. We took our breaks outside, on the concrete stairs that ran down the side of the building to the parking lot, sipping lazily at cherry Cokes as the sweat evaporated off our bodies. "Have I mentioned," he said to me during one such break, "that we have a pool?"

I looked at him severely. "No, you haven't."

He grinned. "I meant to."

It was starting to look as if my summer might actually not suck after all.


The Habers had bought an old white Dutch colonial on Leicester Road, a remote, hilly street that worked its way up to the highest point in Bush Falls, but that wasn't the important thing. The large, marbleized pool that glinted like a kidney-shaped jewel in their sizeable yard was all that mattered. Through eight hours of cutting and pressing hot styrene in the scorching heat, it seemed as if the image of its cool blue waters was permanently tattooed on the insides of my eyelids. But Sammy's pool represented far more than a relief from the summer heat. There were other factors. My house, which had the added distinction of not having a pool, was hardly a desirable destination for me in those days. A gloomy silence had settled over the family in the years since my mother's death, and rather than working our way through it, we seemed to have buckled under its weight, like a house with a latent flaw in its construction. Conversation was rare, laughter an anomaly. At least Brad and my dad could talk basketball, once in a while even step into the

driveway for some one-on-one, which gave the illusion of familial ease, but that summer my brother was off on a cross-
country trip with some of his college buddies. That left just
me to watch my father come home, his expression grim, his
massive shoulders stooped from a general exhaustion that
went much deeper than a hard day's work. I considered offering to play some one-on-one with him, but never actually
did, so sure was I of the sardonic, condescending grin that
would alight instantly on his face, the ironically pointed arch
of his bushy eyebrows as he looked down to me and said,
"You?" It was my sorry fortune to know that my father preferred to sit in the dim, air-conditioned privacy of his den,
washing down his TV dinner with Bushmills in the nuclear
glow of the television until he passed out, over stepping outside to spend some quality time with the runt of his incon-
siderable litter.

Factory hours were seven to three, and with Wayne
working at Porter's until after six every evening, my afternoons stretched out before me with a bleakly comprehen-
sive lack of options. A girlfriend would have come in pretty
handy in those days, but in three years of high school I'd
proven to be remarkably inept in that arena, and sadly not
for lack of trying. The closest I'd come to sex up until that
point was the night of my eighth-grade graduation, when
Morgan Hayes had let me feel her up under the shirt over
the bra while she shredded my lips with her braces.

So it was a lonely, motherless, bored, and sexually frustrated teenager who accepted Sammy's invitation to sub-
merge himself daily in the cool waters of the Haber
swimming pool. And it was that same boy who discovered,
much to his hormonal glee, that Lucy Haber, Sammy's long-
limbed, ridiculously sexy mother, spent her afternoons al-
ternately swimming laps and sunning herself in various
two-piece swimsuits whose every fiber strained to contain
her glorious assets.

Sammy wasn't much of a swimmer. He went through the

motions briefly, as if to justify his inviting me over to swim, but he would always climb out after five or ten minutes, pull a towel over his skinny torso, and retreat to the air-conditioned house, where he would reconfigure the soaked strands of his pompadour and read music magazines. After the first few days of this, we settled into a comfortable routine wherein Sammy hung out in the house reading and I stayed in the pool, nursing a shameless submarine erection as I chatted with his mother. Lucy, so unlike any mother I'd ever met, seemed to enjoy having someone to spend the afternoon with, and quizzed me incessantly about my own life, occasionally digressing into stories about hers. As far as I was concerned, she could have been discussing quantum physics and I would have been equally transfixed, so caught up was I in the constant inspection of her lush lips, her trim, tanned thighs, and the droplets of water that trickled down her glistening chest and into the crevice of her miraculous cleavage as she sunned herself beside the pool. Her husband's repeated infidelities now seemed not only wrong but baffling and incomprehensibly greedy. What could he possibly have yearned for that he didn't already have? It was all I could do to keep my hand out of my swim trunks as I floated around the pool, basking in Lucy's company. I developed the habit of leaving my towel by the pool's edge so that when I eventually, regretfully climbed out, I could artfully hide the rampant monster in my trunks.

Showering at Sammy's house after swimming became a daily necessity, my lone opportunity to spank out my excess sexual tension. Afterward, Sammy and I would head into town in Brad's car, which I'd been grudgingly lent for the summer while he was away. We'd meet Wayne for burgers or pizza and then see a movie or hang out.

Sammy and Wayne had hit it off right away. I could see how Sammy's frenetic nature and constant chatter might rub some people the wrong way, but Wayne's steady, easygoing demeanor was perfectly suited for it. Sammy seamlessly merged into our rhythm like a traveling musician sitting in with the band, and we became a merry little threesome.

The days of that blistering summer were fused together like something mass-produced, each one identical to the one before and after it. Long, smoldering afternoons spent in masturbatory fascination with every languid movement Lucy made, each luscious curve and mysterious crevice, and nights hanging out with Sammy and Wayne. Even knowing everything that happened afterward, that was already happening, I remember how much I enjoyed that summer: a hazy, wet, shimmering eternity of thoughtless, menial labor, the splash and smell of chlorinated pool water, and Lucy's deliciously pornographic body. As far as summers went, you could do a lot worse.

# *six*

I thought that I'd recalled Bush Falls rather well when I wrote the book, but as I drive through the town for the first time in seventeen years, I realize that all I've had are superficial recollections, cardboard stand-ins for real memories that are only now finally emerging. The corporeal experience of returning is the trigger to long-dormant memories, and as I gaze around my hometown, I'm stunned by the renewed clarity of what I'd buried in my subconscious. Memories that should have long since crumbled to dust from seventeen years of attrition turn out to have been hermetically sealed and perfectly preserved, now summoned up as if by posthypnotic suggestion. There is a sense of violation in learning that, unbeknownst to me, my mind has maintained such a strong connection with the town, as if my brain's been sneaking around behind my back.

Bush Falls is a typical if smaller version of many middle-class Connecticut towns, a planned and determinedly executed suburbia where the lawns are green and the collars predominantly white. Landscaping in particular is taken very seriously in Connecticut. Citizens don't have coats of arms emblazoned above their front doors; they have hedges, fuchsia and pachysandra, flower beds and emerald arborvitae. A neglected lawn stands out like a goiter, the telltale symptom of a dysfunctional domestic gland. In the summer, the hissing of the cicadas, invisible in the treetops, is matched by the muted machine-gun whispers of a thousand rotating sprinklers, some dragged out of the garage after dinner, others installed beneath the lawns and set on timers. Soon, I know, the sprinklers will be put away for the season, replaced by rakes and leaf blowers, but for now they remain heavily in evidence as I drive down Stratfield Road, the main artery connecting the residential section of Bush Falls with its commercial district.

Even though everything looks pretty much as it did when I left, I know the Falls is suffering. P.J. Porter's went bankrupt five years ago, resulting in over a thousand lost jobs. While the majority of people in the Falls were able to find new jobs in Connecticut's then still-solid market, many of them ended up at Internet start-ups, only to be savaged by the overdue collapse of the whole industry at the end of 2000. Now the town is solidly immersed in recession, and every block has at least one FOR SALE sign planted on the front lawn. Even though the houses generally look well maintained and the lawns immaculate, there's a sense of desperation in this quotidian tidiness, as if now, more than ever, these carefully tended homes are nothing more than facades concealing unknowable and irreparable damages.

I turn left onto Diamond Hill Road and drive past my father's house, which concealed its own share of damage long before Porter's went belly-up. I slow down to take in the slightly sloping front lawn, at the top of which sits the square two-story colonial in which I grew up. The aluminum siding, a pale shade of blue when I was a kid, is now a dirty eggshell color, and the hedges growing beneath the dark picture window of the living room aren't nearly as tall or dense as I remember, but otherwise the house is exactly the same. I stop the car and take a deep breath, anticipating some sort of emotional reaction to my childhood home, and I come up empty. I haven't always been this dispassionate; I'm fairly certain of that. Is it a function of time and distance, or have I simply shed over the years what general sensitivity I once possessed? I try to recall a time in recent memory that I expressed any heartfelt emotion to another person, and can't come up with a single instance of sentiment or passion. Turning right onto Churchill, I'm troubled by the notion that while I wasn't looking, I seem to have become an asshole. This leads to a brief, syllogistic argument. The fact that I suspect I'm an asshole means I probably am not, because a real asshole doesn't think he's an asshole, does he? Therefore, by realizing that I'm an asshole, I am in fact negating that very realization, am I not? Descartes's Asshole Axiom: I think I am; therefore, I'm not one.

It is debates like this one, and the sneaking suspicion that I'm losing the overall capacity to give a shit, that led to my brief and ill-fated stint in therapy. One of the drawbacks I've discovered to being a fiction writer is that I seem never to fully inhabit the moment at hand. Part of me is always off to the side, examining, looking for context and subtext, imagining how I'll describe the moment after it's gone. My therapist, Dr. Levine, felt it had nothing to do with being a writer and everything to do with being egocentric and insecure, which I thought, true or not, was a pretty harsh judgment to arrive at twenty-five minutes into our second session.

"What's more," he informed me at the time, "your penchant for self-analysis—which is, by the way, another manifestation of your egotism—is further complicated by immense feelings of inferiority. You don't allow yourself to become fully engaged because deep down you feel undeserving of approval, love, success, et cetera. All of the things you crave."

"Don't you think you should get to know me better before making such categorical statements?" I said, somewhat put off by his remarks.

"Don't be defensive," he chided me. "It just slows down the process. You're not paying me to be gentle."

"I'm not being defensive."

"You sound defensive."

"That's because it's patently impossible to deny being defensive without sounding defensive."

"Exactly!" Dr. Levine said enigmatically, sitting back in his chair and scratching the ridiculous little goatee that made his mouth look suspiciously like a vagina. I wondered if he'd grown it for just that reason, being such a resolute Freudian and all. He pulled off his gold-rimmed spectacles and cleaned them absently with his necktie. Then, replacing them on his nose, he asked me the question that all therapists invariably fall back on when creativity fails them before the hour's up. "Tell me about your father."

"Oh, come on. You can do better than that."

"Don't you think it's a legitimate question?"

"Now who's getting defensive?"

"I am not—" He caught himself and flashed me a pitying smile. "Very clever, Joe. I'm sorry you feel the need to best me in these verbal jousts of yours. It demonstrates a lack of respect for me and my abilities as a professional." My therapist was actually pouting. "I wonder why you bother coming at all."

So I stopped coming.

Churchill curves around to the right, rejoining Stratfield Road just as it widens to two lanes in each direction and enters the town's retail district. Upscale strip malls and expansive parking lots appear on both sides of the road. The next five blocks are packed with stores geared toward meeting just about every manner of suburban need. Radio Shack, K·B Toys, Blockbuster Video, Carvel, Party City, Home Depot, Barnes & Noble, Super Stop & Shop, a CVS drugstore,

Coconuts Music, two jewelry stores, a plant nursery, and the Duchess Diner. On the last block, I see what used to be P.J. Porter's flagship store, now being torn down.

One block later, I turn right onto Oak Hill Road and pull into the parking lot of Mercy Hospital, a red brick two-story building that seems too cheerful and not nearly institutional enough to be a hospital. I deliberately take up two spots to prevent anyone from parking too close, an embarrassing habit I developed after buying the Mercedes. Parking lots are a breeding ground for door dings, the bane of the luxury car owner's existence. It occurs to me once again that I hate my car. It's like a high-priced whore. The minute you're finished with it, you want it to vanish without a trace.

A cool October breeze touches down on me like a benediction as I step out of the air-conditioned confines of the Mercedes. The sky is crammed with thick, dust-colored clouds, and the baby elm trees planted at exact intervals throughout the lot have their leaves turned upward in supplication. A small group of young doctors are taking a smoking break on the front stairs, which strikes me as somewhat blasphemous, like rabbis eating pork. I brave the gauntlet of their fumes, holding my breath until I'm through the revolving door, and follow the signs to the intensive care unit.

Cindy is looking bored, sitting with her twins on a bench in the hall outside of the ICU. All twins are cute. I've never seen an ugly set. It's as if there's some stopgap measure in place, biological or divine, expressly there to prevent the duplication of ugliness. And Brad's girls are way beyond cute. Between him and Cindy, these girls have hit the genetic mother lode. They're twelve years old, with their mother's dark flowing hair and creamy complexion, wearing identical plaid skirts and white polo shirts. Just from looking at them it's clear that as they mature, they will never worry about pimples or how fat their thighs and asses are. Like their mother, they will be perfect, until that very perfection becomes their ultimate flaw. They swing their legs back and forth together, linked at the foot, creating an almost perfect mirror-image effect.

"Hello, Cindy," I say formally. It's been twenty years since the fellatio incident, but it's still the first thing to pop into my head. Men tend never to forget things like blow jobs, even those that happened to someone else.

Cindy looks up. "Hey, Joe," she says evenly. She stands up and gives me a dry kiss on the cheek, and I find myself unwittingly appreciating her body, which, even after three children, is still lithe and toned. There is nothing you could point to that's changed in her face, other than perhaps the slight weathering of the skin immediately beneath her eyes, and yet somewhere a light has gone out. The structure is still in place, exquisite as ever, but the engine that propels it has been compromised, its powerful throb reduced to a dull, vacillating hum. Men will still notice her walking down the street, will hungrily catalogue her toned stomach and buoyant breasts, her lean, lightly muscled legs and the soft, heart-shaped curves of her ass, will get reprimanded by their wives or girlfriends for staring a bit longer than the legal time limit, and will mollify them by declaring that they prefer more meat on their women and other masculine lies, but it will end there. They won't take her home in their minds as they once might have, to superimpose over reality as they thrust their way to mundane, household orgasm. Cindy's beauty, while still intact, has become of the forgettable variety.

She steps back and points to the girls, who are eyeing me with wide-eyed curiosity. "You remember Emily and Jenny." She doesn't bother to indicate which is which, as if it really doesn't matter for my purposes—which is true enough, I guess. In their entire lives, I've actually seen them only a handful of times, on those rare occasions when Cindy and Brad visited New York. "Girls, this is your uncle Joe."

"Hi, Uncle Joe," they say in perfect unison, and then look at each other and giggle. It's the first time I've ever heard myself referred to as an uncle, and I shiver, feeling conspicuously empty-handed. Uncles are supposed to have magic tricks or silver dollars or candy, aren't they? The only uncle I ever had—my mother's brother, Peter—used to squeeze my shoulder, slip me five dollars, wink, and say, "Don't shit a shitter," even though I hadn't said anything at all. I routinely withstood the abuse, because it seemed like a small price to pay for five bucks. I consider giving each twin a twenty, but decide against it—wisely, I think.

"Hello," I say weakly. "Do you two always dress alike?"

"We aren't dressed alike," Emily or Jenny says with a smirk.

"Yeah, we aren't dressed alike," the other one concurs, and they giggle as one again. Clearly, I've stumbled upon some inside joke.

"Sorry," I say. "My mistake." For whatever reason, my apology triggers another paroxysm of laughter from the twins, who lean back on the bench, chuckling gleefully.

"Keep it down, girls," Cindy says, so habitually that I'm willing to bet she doesn't even know she's spoken.

"Where's Brad?" I ask.

"He's in there with him." She indicates the door of the ICU just as my brother emerges.

Most people decompose after they die, but for athletes and rock stars, the process begins years earlier. With rock stars, it starts in the face; just look at any picture of Mick Jagger taken in the last ten years. With athletes, it's the legs that are affected first. There's a walk aging athletes have, a slight side-to-side rocking motion, as if they're favoring each leg as they step onto it. The legs take bold strides with the memory of effortless muscled power, and then, as if suddenly remembering that those muscles have deteriorated, a slightly pigeon-toed foot comes down early, hitting the ground gingerly to cut the stride short. It's a reality check, reminding the legs that they can't afford to be as ambitious as they once were, because with those muscles now atrophied, their ruined knees won't withstand the abuse. The shoulders rock as well, hunching up slightly with each step as if in anticipation of an arthritic jolt of pain. There's an awkward grace to this walk, the paradoxical blending of age and youth. Bush Falls being the basketball town that it is, there are many men who walk like that. My father is one of them, and now, as Brad steps through the swinging door of the ICU, looking greasy and fatigued, I see that he's grown into the walk as well.

He comes toward me and says, "Hey, Joe."

"Hey." We fall into each other's arms and hug tightly. No, we don't, we never have, but it would be nice, I think, to be the kind of brothers who hug. Instead, we shake hands thoughtlessly, like flicking a light switch, and the reunion is complete.

"I'm glad you made it." I search his voice for the rebuke that I'm sure will be there, but fail to detect any antagonism in it. He seems to be utterly sincere, without inflection.

If you took my five-ten frame and stretched it out to six foot three, you would get something pretty close to Brad. There is no denying the shared DNA, but his has received the benefit of a rolling pin, rendering him long and wiry where I'm shorter and considerably denser. But we both have the same straight brown hair and dark eyes of our mother, and our father's square, Polish jaw.

"How's he doing?" I say, indicating the room.

Brad frowns. "No change."

"What do his doctors say?"

The frown deepens. "Not much. They should be along soon, though, and you can ask them yourself."

I nod and look again at the door to the ICU. "Why don't you go in and see him," Brad says, glancing over at Cindy and the twins. "I'll join you in a few minutes."

It takes a few seconds to locate my father through the morass of tubes and wires that have colonized his supine form, entering and exiting his limp body at every juncture. He is intubated through his nose and mouth, has an IV line descending into his arm, a catheter hose poking out from

**49**

under the blankets near his hips, and various wires attached to electrodes on his chest that feed unchanging data to the beeping heart monitor to the left of his bed. He lies there, dehumanized, like something out of Isaac Asimov, all of his deeply personal living processes now co-opted by the machinery, which breathes, farts, shits, and swallows for him, the tube in his mouth robbing him of even the illusion of expression.

I look above the tubing at his hair, which has changed from the jet black I remember to a charcoal flecked with silver highlights. There are small dark patches of stubble on his chin, forming like poppy seeds in odd patterns that remind me of Homer Simpson. My father lies in critical condition while his estranged son thinks of cartoon characters. His eyebrows have grown bushier, but I'm still able to locate the scar above his left eye, the badge of honor from the elbow he took in the '58 state championship game. He tells the story often, to anyone who will listen, about how they came back in the fourth quarter from sixteen down. With less than ten seconds to go, he went up for the tying layup, got elbowed in the face, and still managed to finish the play. They won on his foul shot, which he sank with blood dripping down into his left eye from the gash on his forehead, all but obscuring his vision. The story, and a grainy picture of his bloody visage, appeared in *The Minuteman,* a framed yellowed copy of which hung conspicuously in the den of our house.

There is no sound in the room save for the beeping of monitors and the steady, mechanical hiss of the respirator. I sit in the chair beside his bed, not sure what to do with myself. Small talk is clearly out of the question. If he were conscious, that would no doubt be my defensive weapon of choice, but the coma puts me at a distinct disadvantage. I consider talking to him anyway, the way they always do it on television, in a low, trembling voice fraught with emotion, exhorting the patient to just hold on. Because he will hear me. Somewhere in the haze of his coma, my voice will circulate through his benumbed mind, images of me will flash in rock video fashion behind his eyes, and some as-yet untried combination will open the lock on his brain and his fingers will twitch in mine as his eyes tentatively blink open, and his first word, uttered in a hoarse, dry whisper, will be my name. But I know I don't have it in me. His hand lies by his side on the bed, and I reach out furtively and wrap my own around it. It's much larger than mine, hard and callused on the edges, but surprisingly soft in the center, like a slice of toast pulled out of the toaster just as it begins to burn. I can't remember ever having felt my father's hand before. I squeeze it lightly. It doesn't squeeze back. I hear the door behind me and quickly retract my hand, like a shoplifter.

"Hey," Brad says, coming up behind me.

"Hey."

"How have you been?"

"Pretty good. And you?"

He sighs. "Been better."

"I guess so," I say. We both turn and looked at our father's unconscious form. Brad walks past me and gently straightens the blankets on the bed. He does it slowly, with a good deal of tenderness. As I watch him, it occurs to me that Brad is devastated. In my ambivalence over my own feelings toward my father, I've forgotten that he is someone else's father, and grandfather, and that he is loved. I turn away as Brad finishes straightening the covers, feeling ashamed and more than ever like an interloper.

Brad steps back from the bed and grins at me uneasily. "So . . ." he says.

"What's the prognosis?" I say.

"Pretty lousy. They don't know that he'll regain consciousness, and even if he does, there's no way to know what shape his brain will be in."

"How long do they think he can just hang on like this?"

"They don't know."

"They don't know much, do they?" I say.

I look at my father again. He seems drastically reduced, his frame smaller and his color duller than I remember. We've seen each other very infrequently over the years, and I haven't thought to age my mental picture of him. There is no way, in his current state, to assess the natural toll the last seventeen years have taken on him, to see how he's aged up until the stroke. It occurs to me that even though I am finally in the same room with him, I will probably never really see my father again.

Brad sits down on the windowsill, and I take the chair beside the bed, the vinyl cushion emitting a whistling sigh as my weight descends into it. *What happens now?* I wonder.

"How long do you plan on staying?" Brad asks after a bit.

*Staying?* "I don't know."

He nods, as if this is what he expected, and then clears his throat. "I'm glad you came. I wasn't sure you would."

"I had to come," I say vaguely.

He looks at me. "I guess so."

We sit quietly as the conversation limps off to wherever it is that conversations go to die.

"Where's Jared?" I say.

Brad frowns and looks away. "I told him to stop here on his way to school, but he's not what you would call reliable these days." Jared is Brad's son, my nephew, who by my calculations should be sixteen or seventeen by now. I figure this because he was fourteen when he ran away from home, took the Metro-North into Manhattan, and showed up at my apartment at ten-thirty that night, hungry, out of cash, and simmering with righteous anger at the unspecified offenses that had led to this defiance. We ordered in some sandwiches and I made him call his father. Then we watched Letterman, and the next morning I put him on a train back to Connecticut, and that was pretty much that. Brad left me a message the following night thanking me, but I was out, and although I distinctly recall wanting to call him back, I never got around to it.

"What's he, seventeen?"

"Eighteen," my brother says. "He's a senior." So much for my math.

"Is he captain of the Cougars?"

Brad looks away. "Jared doesn't play ball." Those four words, layered with the grist of untold tension and regret, indicate that my lame efforts at innocuous chitchat have nonetheless managed to zero in on what is clearly a sore topic, and I resolve from here on in to let Brad steer the conversation. Brad, though, seems perfectly content to sit back and crack his knuckles as he watches the drip of fluids in and out of the beeping and hissing mess that was once our father.

"I read your book," he finally says, effectively ratcheting up the tension a few notches.

"Really," I say. "Did you enjoy it?"

He frowns, considering the question. "Parts," he says.

I shrug noncommittally. "Well, that's something, I guess."

He looks at me thoughtfully, as if debating whether or not to say something. Finally he sighs and looks away. "Yeah," he says. "Your book made quite a little splash around here."

I wait silently for him to elaborate, but he appears to have said all he plans to say on the subject. Between us, my father suddenly shivers, his entire body vibrating in a wave from his chest to his toes. I jump up, startled, but Brad puts his hand out, beckoning me to relax. "It's okay," he says, leaning forward to fix the corner of the blanket. "He does that."

# seven

## 1986

In Bush Falls, the vast emptiness of suburban night led to all manner of delinquency and sexual advancement. We were bursting with the preternatural angst and boredom that coursed through our throbbing teenaged veins, keeping our blood at a constant simmer. There were only so many nights you could hang out at the mall, so many new releases to see at the Megaplex, so many cheeseburgers and tuna melts you could scarf down at the Duchess. Beyond that, all we had left was drinking, fucking, and random acts of senseless vandalism.

Sammy, Wayne, and I developed the habit of occasionally sneaking over the chain-link fence of P.J. Porter's vast corporate campus at night and hot-wiring the electric golf carts left charging overnight near the loading bay doors. The carts were used by executives to traverse the acres of perfectly manicured grass between the main building and the distribution center on the far side of the campus. Working there as an intern, Wayne had learned that in lieu of a key, all you needed to do was lift the driver's seat, under which the battery was cased, and use a paper clip to close the crude circuit and start the cart. There was something pleasantly surreal about piloting those silent carts across the grassy back acres of the Porter's campus in the dark of night. We would race each other all over the campus, first driving forward and then in reverse, or attempt half-baked movie stunts like jumping from one moving cart to the other. Afterward, we would hang out on the manicured bank of one of the artificial ponds that glistened in the shadow of the office complex, lazily skipping stones at the spotlit automated geyser that shot fifty feet into the sky from the pond's center, while we chugged discounted beer purchased over in New Haven with Wayne's fake ID.

We were sitting on the lawn by the pond one hot, muggy night, buzzed on beer, staring at the kaleidoscopic spray of the geyser, when Wayne suddenly got clumsily to his feet. "I'm too damn hot," he said. "I feel like I'm on fire."

"Just like the Boss," Sammy said, singing lazily in his high-pitched voice. "*At night I wake up with the sheets soaking wet and a freight train running through the middle of my head, only you can cool my desire. Whoa, oh, oh, I'm on fire.*"

"He's singing Springsteen again," Wayne complained.

"I thought we discussed this, Sammy," I said.

"You sound like the Bee Gees covering Springsteen," Wayne said.

"You guys know you love it," Sammy said good-naturedly.

"You manage to come up with a Springsteen quote for every possible occasion," I said.

"I can't help that. It's a function of his genius."

"Whatever, man," Wayne said, climbing drunkenly to his feet. "I'm still boiling." He pulled off his T-shirt, upon which was emblazoned the phrase BIG IN JAPAN in large black letters, and threw it to the floor. "I'm going for a swim."

"We can go back to my pool," Sammy said.

"Why bother?" Wayne kicked off his high-tops and waded into the pond and then, with no hesitation, plunged headfirst into the dark, shimmering water and swam out with long, powerful strokes toward the geyser.

"Drunken night-swimming," I said. "Now there's a brilliant combination."

"And god only knows what the hell's in that water," Sammy said disapprovingly. "Microorganisms, parasites."

"Radioactive nuclear waste."

"The Loch Ness monster."

"The Porter family's personal sewage."

"Come on, you guys," Wayne called to us from the pond. "It's beautiful in here."

"Isn't this how the *Jaws* movies always start?" Sammy said.

"Sharks don't live in ponds," I pointed out.

"That's exactly what the chick in the bikini says before she gets eaten."

Out in the water, Wayne had reached the geyser and was now clinging to some unseen piece of its apparatus, his form lightly obscured by the thick residual mist of the water's spray. I closed my eyes for a second, feeling bloated and dizzy from the cheap domestic beer we'd been guzzling. When I opened them, Wayne was gone. "Where'd he go?" I said.

"I don't know," Sammy said, craning his neck to see.

We shouted his name as we got to our feet, scanning the dark water for where his head would surely break the surface at any second. "Where the fuck is he?" I said, alarm like an icy balloon inflating in my belly. I looked over to Sammy, who was already pulling off his sneakers, and quickly did the same. We charged madly into the cold water, calling out for him between frantic strokes as we swam desperately out toward the geyser, which was much louder up close than I would have thought. I reached the center first and quickly performed an awkward surface dive, my outstretched fingers scraping bottom and coming away caked in grimy pond scum. I resurfaced, panting, and was about to try again when there was a loud whoop and Wayne suddenly came flying through the glowing geyser's spray above us, his knees pulled up to his chest, flecks of luminous water trailing behind him like a comet's tail. He flew through the air in slow motion, framed in the backlit water like some mythical god rising from the depths, before landing in a perfect cannonball between Sammy and me. He surfaced a moment later, pulling his wet hair out of his face and laughing at us.

"Asshole!" Sammy shouted, splashing at him with disgust.

"What the fuck's wrong with you?" I said, choking on a sour mixture of relief and pond scum.

"It was the only way to get you guys in the water," Wayne said, still grinning.

A furious splashing fight ensued as we tried unsuccessfully to dunk him, his long, sinewy arms easily fighting us off. Afterward, he showed us the small maintenance platform on the side of the geyser that had facilitated his ambush, and we took turns jumping and diving through the geyser spray into the pond.

I was the first to eventually climb out of the pond, my stomach churning spasmodically from the injudicious combination of beer and pond water I'd imbibed. I leaned against a large sycamore for a few minutes, taking shallow breaths until my innards succumbed and I vomited violently, the hot acid of my puke burning my throat, filling my eyes with tears. I pulled on my T-shirt and lay down on the grass, feeling unsteady and light-headed. When I opened my eyes a few minutes later, Sammy and Wayne were still in the pond, their voices echoing eerily across the water, muted by the soft rumbling of the geyser. I propped myself up on my elbows and could just make out their shadowy forms in the darkness, bobbing up and down in the thick mist that floated around them. Their outlines blurred as my drunken, weary eyelids began to close, and their profiles waxed and waned like a throbbing pulse as the world around me began to spin at a dizzying speed. Just before I passed out, their fuzzy silhouettes appeared to touch in a tentative embrace, but I'd barely noted the illusion when unconsciousness dispensed with the foreplay and hungrily consummated our union.

# eight

Time slows to a crawl in my father's hospital room. Try as they might, the seconds are unable to overtake the measured beeping of the heart monitor. The day is a run-on Henry James sentence that makes no sense, punctuated by small talk, bathroom breaks, and trips to the temperamental coffee machine down the hall. It is unclear to me whether we're waiting for our father to wake up or to die, but it's almost beside the point, as the machinery seems specifically engineered to allow neither but to simply sustain him in this mechanical purgatory. Cindy, who left to take the twins to school soon after I arrived, returns around noon to bring us some pizza. Having never been married, I'm not equipped to decipher the nature of the glances that pass between Cindy and Brad, quick, intense looks bursting with angry nuance. Brad leaves to walk her back to the elevators and returns looking troubled and even further deflated. Something is definitely going on there.

At around five-thirty, some imperceptible variation in the beeps and hisses of our father's life support systems apparently signals to Brad that it's time to knock off for the evening. He conducts a quick conference with the nurse on duty, and then we leave.

"Nice car," Brad says, getting into the passenger seat of the Mercedes, the leather farting impudently against his jeans.

"Thanks," I mumble self-consciously.

"Must have set you back some."

I groan inwardly. No good will come of this conversation. Mercedes dealerships should have a back room they take you to after you sign the papers in the showroom, with plush carpeting and sofas upholstered in the same rich leather used in the cars, where an instructor gives a small workshop, over gourmet coffee and muffins, on the social intangibles of owning a luxury car, the etiquette and so forth. For sixty-eight thousand dollars, it's the least they can do. Then maybe I would feel equipped to handle the predicament it is my fate to continually confront as a novice Mercedes owner. If I agree with my brother's assessment, I'm being patronizing. If I say "not really," I'm showing off. Until you have money, you think it's the answer to everything, and only once you have it do you realize that it's just a whole new set of questions, the only difference being that now you have to keep them to yourself, because no one's going to sympathize. I grunt something unintelligible and hope we can leave it at that.

"You hungry?" Brad says.

"I could eat."

There are only two places worth eating at in Bush Falls. One is the Duchess Diner, right on Stratfield Road, and the other is the Halftime Pub, a combination sports bar and pub frequented primarily by the many former athletes living in the Falls. The Halftime Pub has the added distinction of serving the best steaks in northern Connecticut.

"You want to get a steak?" I ask, since we're fairly close to

Halftime.

"Nah," Brad says. "I'm more in the mood for something light. Let's just hit the Duchess."

"Come on," I say. "My treat."

"You can treat me at the Duchess," he says, looking uncomfortable.

I can't remember a time when Brad preferred anything to a Halftime steak, but I let it go, reminding myself that when you haven't been around for seventeen years, it's probably prudent to operate under the assumption that things might have changed somewhat while you were gone.

The Duchess is decorated in classic Diner. The benches in the booths are upholstered in maroon vinyl, the tables laminated in a shiny, speckled Formica finish. Beyond the booths is a long bar with nine spinning stools for single diners, and behind that is the kitchen. If the place has changed at all since I left, the differences are too subtle for me to detect.

The waitress behind the counter is Sheila Girardi, who was a grade behind me in school and who played the lead in every school play and sang and danced in every talent show. "Hey, Goff," she says with a familiar smile. "Goff" has been Brad's nickname ever since junior high. Whenever Brad executed a particularly spectacular move or hit a clutch basket, the nickname would reverberate against the walls of the gymnasium in a vocal frenzy. "*Goff! Goff! Goff! Goff!*" I'd sit in the stands, cheering Brad on, dreaming of the day when it would be me to whom the frenzied cheers referred. But I never made the team, and no one ever shouted *Goff* for me. And so I remain Joe Goffman, which sounds as if it betrays just the slightest hint of failure. Meet Joe Goffman, the somewhat disappointing brother of the great Goff.

"Hey, Sheila. You remember my brother, Joe?"

"Sure," she says. "Hey, Joe. It's been a long time. How are you?"

"Pretty good. And you?"

"Great." Sheila was voted most likely to succeed as the next Madonna, and if she's at all bitter that the gods chose Britney

Spears instead, there's no trace of it in her expression. "Listen, I'm so sorry about your dad. How's he doing?"

"No change," Brad says, and steers us to a booth. As we make our way through the diners, I notice that I'm getting a lot of stares from the patrons, none of them particularly friendly. "I guess you're famous," Brad says as we slide into opposite sides of the booth.

"I guess so."

We look awkwardly across the table at each other, and I suddenly miss my father's unconscious form between us, which served wonderfully as a distraction. "So," I say. "How's business?"

He grimaces. "It's been tough for a while."

"Porter's closing must have hurt you, huh?"

He sighs deeply. "It sure didn't help matters, but the truth is, we were hurting before that." He leans back as Sheila brings us some water. She was pretty in high school, I remember, tall and winsome, and she's still quite attractive, but in a more rugged, plastic sort of way, her hair flight-attendant blonde, her teeth Texas white.

"I'll have a deluxe burger and a chocolate milk shake," I tell her.

"Just like your brother," she says, raising her eyebrows at Brad.

"Is that what you usually have?" I ask him.

He shrugs. "I guess so."

As she turns away to see about our food, I think I catch a quick glimpse between her and Brad, something knowing and flirtatious, something private. *Hello,* I think to myself, italicized and in a British accent.

I look sharply at Brad, who quickly looks away and says, "We're being fucked by China."

"China?"

"Yeah. Everyone's buying their displays overseas now, for half the price. You want to do business with the big boys, you'd better be manufacturing overseas."

"Isn't your quality better?"

"Quality is a twentieth-century concept." He takes a sip of his water and grins bitterly. "Here in the twenty-first, being the low bidder is all that counts. Doesn't matter that you're offering warehousing, fulfillment, installation, and a slew of other domestic services that the importers can't handle. If you're employing American labor, you're priced right out of the market."

"So, what are you going to do?"

"Right now," he says wearily, pulling himself up from the table, "I'm going to take a piss."

The food comes while Brad is gone. I grab a fry off my plate and look up just in time to see a grayish older woman approach me and hurl her milk shake in my face. No matter how many times you've seen this happen on television, you're still utterly unprepared when it actually happens to you in real life. On television it's usually wine or some other clear drink. The milk shake is thick chocolate, cold as hell, and ounce for ounce a much more effective choice.

"You bastard!" the lady spits at me as I shoot out of my seat, the thick, icy fluid oozing down my neck and under my collar. "You can't just walk in here!"

Words fail me, and all I can do is stare at her face, now crimson with rage, as I wipe my soaking face and hair with my hands. "You've got no right to come here, after the pain you've caused!" she shouts.

"Lady," I finally stammer. "What the hell's your problem?"

"You're my problem!" she shrieks, and I become conscious of how quiet the other diners have become. "You and that goddamn book of lies you wrote."

Just then Brad returns from the bathroom, his eyes wide with alarm. "What the hell's going on here?" he demands of me.

"Ask her," I say, grabbing some napkins off the table to wipe my face. The shake is becoming dry and sticky on my skin.

"What's the problem, Franny?"

*Franny?*

"I'm sorry, Brad," she says to him, her voice still trembling with anger. "But he's got a lot of nerve coming in here."

"You're not exactly lacking in that department," I point out. Brad impatiently waves his hand to shush me, and I'm twelve years old again.

"I'm sorry, Franny," my brother says soothingly. "I know how upsetting it must be. But my dad's in the hospital; I don't know if you heard."

"I hadn't," she says, turning to face him. "What's wrong?"

Brad tells her, his voice remaining steady and conciliatory as he gradually steers her away from me and toward the door. They speak for a moment or two, and she leans forward and gives him a quick hug. Then, with one last, baleful glare back at me, she exits the Duchess. Brad comes back, shaking his head from side to side, and suddenly notices the seven or eight diners sitting stock-still, staring at us with their mouths agape. "Show's over, folks," he announces testily, meeting each gaze one by one until they look away. "At least for the time being," he mutters to me under his breath as we sit back down in the booth. I feel my shirt sticking to me as I lean against the back of my seat. The milk shake seems to have dripped all the way down to my waist and is making inroads further south.

"Who the hell was that?" I say.

"You don't know?"

"I thought I covered that with 'who the hell was that.' "

"That was Francine Dugan. Coach's wife."

"Oh," I say, nodding stupidly. "I didn't recognize her."

"Does it make a little more sense now?"

"It does," I say. "Except for the part where you call her Franny and she hugs you. When did you get so tight with Dugan's wife?"

Brad looks at me. "I'm the assistant coach for the Cougars. I thought you knew."

"Since when do high school basketball teams need assistant coaches?"

Brad sighs. "They don't, really. But Dugan's getting up there, you know? He's almost seventy already. It's supposed to be a transitional thing. I assist him for a year or two, run the weekly practices, and do all the yelling and floor drills. Then he retires and I take over."

"You want to be the coach?" It's never occurred to me that Brad might be interested in coaching.

"It's a good job," he says defensively. "Decent pay and a great pension. That's a lot more than I could say for the display business these days."

Now that he says it, it makes perfect sense. High school stars are forever living in the past, as if no other part of their life before or after were as real as the four years they spent playing the game. The rest of their life is just the time after basketball, soldiers missing the war. I recall the tensions I intuited between Cindy and Brad back at the hospital. It isn't difficult to surmise that Brad yearns for those days, when he was the town hero worshipped by all, including his wife.

"So how long have you been the assistant coach?"

"Five years."

"That's a pretty long transition, isn't it?"

He sighs. "No shit."

"Dugan doesn't want to quit," I say.

"Bingo."

That makes sense too. If the Bush Falls basketball players are the town's shining knights, then Dugan is their king, universally revered. He is greeted everywhere he goes with "Hey, Coach," "Great game, Coach!" "Give 'em hell, Coach," or some variation on that theme. His special table is always waiting for him at Halftime, where he traditionally goes with his wife after every home game. The restaurant is typically packed with former Cougars, and he invariably receives a round of applause when he enters, no doubt waving it down with feigned embarrassment well after it peaks.

This kind of blind reverence affords him no small amount of power in Bush Falls, especially as his former players grow into positions of affluence in the community. Ex-athletes rarely leave their hometowns. Anywhere else, they would be just anyone else, an unthinkable fate after four glorious years playing for the most dominant high school basketball team in the region. The graduates from Dugan's basketball program are a fraternity unto themselves, and he is their sovereign leader, the nucleus serving as the single link to their glorious past. If an ex-Cougar needs a job, Dugan makes sure he gets one. If an ex-Cougar runs for local office, Dugan makes sure he gets the necessary votes. Because of his relationships throughout the Falls, Dugan is also a highly effective fund-raiser for Bush Falls High, which lends him significant leverage with the administration and the school board.

Not surprisingly, Dugan is an arrogant, manipulative son of a bitch. And in my novel, he is also a chronic masturbator, a habit I rather artlessly connected to his nightly obsessive review of game tapes. The coach in his boxers, watching teenaged boys run and sweat as he pulls and twists his way to violent, angry orgasm. It's pure fiction, petty and mean-spirited, but I've never felt an ounce of remorse for writing it, in part because I hold Dugan responsible for what happened to Sammy and in part, I guess, because I am petty and mean-spirited.

I look at Brad. "So you work for Dugan."

"That's right," he says pointedly.

"I imagine he wasn't too pleased with my book."

"You think?"

"His wife either, I guess."

"Seems that way."

"I'm sorry," I say to Brad, although I'm not sure I am. "I guess it couldn't have been too comfortable working for him when the book came out."

"He didn't take it out on me," Brad says evenly. Then, looking directly at me, he adds, "Most people didn't."

"Glad to hear it," I say, getting to my feet. "Are you done?"

"Yeah. But you barely touched your burger."

"It tastes like milk shake," I say.

# nine

Memory is never beholden to chronology. Even though I know my nephew, Jared, is now eighteen, in my mind he's still the scared fourteen-year-old I last saw that night in my apartment a few years ago. So when I come upon him stripped down to his underpants, rolling around on my father's living room couch with a girl in an equal state of undress, I am doubly surprised. The girl, upon hearing me enter the room, lets out a piercing shriek and dives gracelessly behind the couch for cover while Jared reflexively yanks up the tangled pile of clothes from the floor and pulls them onto his lap.

"Shit, I'm sorry," I say, spinning on my heel and quickly leaving the room. I seem oddly predestined to be continually interrupting my relatives in midcoitus. There's a pattern forming here that might merit future study: the observation of lovemaking rather than the making of love. Always the bridesmaid and so forth.

"It's cool," Jared says, and I realize that he's talking to the girl behind the couch. "It's not my dad." A minute later he joins me in the hall, pulling up his jeans as he walks. "Hey, Uncle Joe," he says. "How are you doing?" Now horny, naked teenagers are calling me uncle.

"Not as good as you, I guess," I say. He snorts and casually buttons his fly one-handed, then stands up straight and looks at me. He's grown significantly since I last saw him and is now over six feet tall, lean and broad like his father. He tucks his long dark hair behind his ears, the lobes of which are marred with a wide assortment of gold and silver hoops and studs. Seeing the earrings, and the small patch of hair just beneath his lower lip, I instantly understand the quiet frustration Brad expressed earlier.

"I'm sorry," I say. "I didn't think anyone would be here."

Jared runs his fingers through his hair and shrugs. "We were just . . ."

"Yeah."

"I thought you were my dad," he says. "I would have been totally fucked, man."

"From where I was standing, you looked about five minutes away from that anyway," I say.

He smiles at me. There's an easygoing manner about him, a relaxed cool. He speaks in short, soft bursts and exudes a charismatic intelligence. There are no outward signs of anger in him, like you see in so many teenagers with a laundry list of things to prove to the world, but only a slightly sullen impatience typical of his age, evidenced in the way his eyes distractedly wander around me without ever coming to rest. "I hope you're not pissed," he says.

"What red-blooded American teenager can resist an empty house?" I say. "It's practically your patriotic duty to be in here with a girl." I hook the strap of my duffel bag over the head of the banister as I did a million times before, a lifetime ago. The act, completely instinctive, sends a flutter through my stomach, and for the briefest instant I can smell my childhood again.

"What happened to your shirt?" Jared says.

"A woman poured her drink on me."

My nephew grins. "Chicks."

"This chick was upwards of sixty years old."

"Why did she do it?"

"She had her reasons."

"Hey," he says, absently rubbing his impressive abs. "I really liked your book."

I raise my eyebrows. "Well, that would put you in the minority in this town."

"Literacy in general puts you in the minority in this town," he says. It is, I think, an unexpected comment, coming from someone who moments earlier was dry humping the girl who is still hiding, naked and trembling, behind the couch in the living room. There is more to Jared than meets the eye. As if on cue, the girl now emerges, cute and colorful as a Gap ad in her green and blue striped crew neck and jeans, with negligible hips and those perfect high school breasts, not large but commanding attention by their sheer exuberance, like a pair of frisky puppies.

"This is Sheri," Jared says, pulling on the shirt she hands him. "My uncle Joe."

"Nice to meet you," I say.

"Hi," she says, staring at the floor. She won't be recovering from my untimely intrusion anytime soon.

"So, just by way of summary," Jared says. "You won't be mentioning this little incident to my dad."

"Your secret's safe with me." I think Jared might appreciate the irony if I were to tell him about how I discovered Brad and Cindy in the garage way back when, but most well-adjusted boys don't want to hear anything that even remotely connects their mother to oral sex, so I keep my mouth shut. "Besides," I say, "I think he's got more important things on his mind right about now."

"I guess so," Jared said. "If you're here, Gramps must really be in bad shape, huh?"

"It seems that way." His eyes widen with what looks to me like fear, and I realize that he and my father share a special relationship. I experience the same stab of jealousy that I felt at the hospital, watching Brad adjust Dad's blankets.

"Damn," Jared says softly.

There follows a brief moment of silence in honor of the things we're thinking but won't say, about death and its proximity to my father. We're interrupted by the electronic chime of my cell phone, which I snatch off my belt with the apologetic smile of an addict. "Hello," I say.

"You're a lying, egotistical son of a bitch," comes Nat's voice. I put my hand over the mouthpiece and look at Jared and Sheri. "I have to take this. Be a minute."

"Jared," Sheri says, chewing her lip. "I've got to go."

"I'll walk you," he says. "Later, Uncle Joe."

"I'll be here," I say, putting the phone back to my ear to catch the rest of Nat's remarks. ". . . used me, you asshole. And when you were done . . ." I watch Jared and Sheri from the living room picture window as they shuffle down the walk, his arm around her, their hips gently bumping. It makes me suddenly feel old and used up. Nat finishes and hangs up, and I close the phone and slide it back into the plastic holster on my belt. With a heavy sigh, I grab my duffel bag and head upstairs to my old room to get that part over with. Coming home, I think. It's never quite how you pictured it would be.

# *ten*

## 1986

At night, Lucy swam naked.

Not actually, although for all I know she really did, but in my mind, where every night she habitually doffed all constraints and plunged naked into the pool, swimming languidly then floating on her back in the hazy glow of the submerged pool lights. The fantasy was born, and no matter where I was or what I was doing, it played continuously in my mind. *She stands there on the diving board, luminous in her nakedness, and just before she dives, she sees me standing across the pool from her. Instead of being surprised, she flashes a warm, knowing smile full of seductive promise and then plunges into the water. I step in from the shallow end and am waiting for her when she surfaces. We stand there, the water just above our waists, and she says, "I've been wondering when you'd come." "I know," I say, and then she envelops me in her arms, and I feel those magnificent, bulbous breasts, hot and damp, pressed against my chest, and her warm lips open up over mine as she probes me with her tongue. Below the waterline, our groins brush lightly and then with greater force, and she pulls me deeper into the water to make love to me while in the background there's a radio playing Peter Gabriel's "In Your Eyes."* Cheesy as hell, but at the time it seemed as magical as the alluring concept of pool sex.

Pool sex, for Christ's sake. A tenuous, complicated coupling, more strenuous than pleasurable, where every move and thrust must be compensated for in order to maintain a precarious semblance of balance, and for all of that extra work, sensitivity in the vital areas is actually diminished rather than enhanced. This was not the popular view embraced by late-night cable television, but that very fact proves the point that pool sex is a primarily visual phenomenon. It looks much better than it feels. But for a seventeen-year-old virgin, pool sex felt just as good as all of the other kinds of sex I wasn't getting, just another entry in my expanding journal of the unattainable.

Aside from my immense sexual frustration, which threatened to cross the line into obsession on a daily basis, I was having a pretty good summer. To have two friends is to have something greater than the sum of its parts. Sammy's introduction into the mix meant that I now had a group. A crew. "The guys." I reveled in our easy camaraderie, in the running jokes and understandings that developed among the three of us as the summer progressed. Me and the guys. I developed a spring in my step, a quicker grin, a wider eye. I was suddenly, unaccountably happy.

And for as long as I could, I ignored the larger, unspoken thing that was happening ominously on the periphery, the stray secret looks and the nonverbal signals that I was inadvertently intercepting with increasing frequency. I was determinedly unwilling to rock the boat. We listened to Springsteen and watched MTV, drank too much beer and went swimming, raced golf carts across the Porter's campus in the dark of night, talked back to the screen at the

Megaplex, ate burgers and pizzas at the Duchess Diner, and very occasionally scored some weed from Niko, who ran the Sunoco station downtown. And somewhere, in the middle of it all, Wayne and Sammy became something far more than friends.

How long can you remain oblivious to a love affair going on right in front of you? It's all a question of determination, actually. On some level, I must have registered the furtive glances and knowing smiles, the disappearing hands in the movie theater, the quick, jerky redistribution of bodily masses when I entered the room suddenly, and the slow general thickening of the atmosphere surrounding my two best friends. But I clung steadfastly to my oblivion, determined to ride out this new insanity like a powerful virus. I naïvely believed it was nothing more than a bizarre behavioral phase, a rebellious experimentation they would outgrow.

This was 1986, after all, and we hadn't yet been trained to deal with this sort of thing. We knew about homosexuality the same way we knew about god; we'd heard it existed, but didn't necessarily accept the reality of it. We speculated about Michael Jackson's alleged use of female hormones, and Boy George's lipstick, and we labeled them fags, but we didn't really believe, deep down, that they truly were gay. It was all just marketing. There were widespread rumors about Andrew McCarthy, but he made out so convincingly with Ally Sheedy in *St. Elmo's Fire*, he couldn't possibly have been gay. We derided one another with terms like "cocksucker" and "faggot," but we never meant it literally. We took our cues primarily from Hollywood, and they, too, denied the reality. For the suburban boys we were, homosexuality existed on a purely conceptual plane, like algebra or the corkscrew shape of the universe.

So for a while I was able to pretend not to see what I saw, and remained convinced that the best policy was to treat it like a stray dog: as long as I didn't make eye contact, it would eventually go away. I needed badly to believe this, not only because the alternative was unthinkable to me but because these were my best and only friends, and I desperately feared losing them. Their homosexuality, viewed head-on, might have been offensive to my sheltered sensibilities, but even that paled in comparison to the suffocating loneliness I had known since my mother's inauspicious plunge into the Bush River.

So I knew, and they knew I knew, and without ever discussing it, we arrived at a collectively silent acceptance of the situation. It was amazing, really, how quickly it grew to feel normal in the vacuum of that hot, empty summer. It was understood that I might sometimes arrive at Sammy's to find Wayne already there, or that at the end of a given night Wayne might stick around at Sammy's for a while after I went home. Somehow I never made them feel the oddness of their relationship and they never made me feel that three was a crowd. I suppose we all had separate reasons for minimizing the magnitude of what was happening and maintaining the status quo. And the summer rolled along, unobtrusively gathering its own silent momentum as it went.

One night, while we were all hanging out in Sammy's pool, I stepped inside to get a drink and flirt a little with Lucy, who was curled up on the living room couch in a pair of hospital scrubs, reading a *People* magazine. "Hi, Joe," she said, lowering the magazine to look at me. "How are you doing?"

"Fine." I was still damp from the pool, and I shivered as the central air-conditioning freeze-dried the moisture on my skin. "I just thought I'd say hello."

Lucy smiled, a warm, kind smile that I thought might have betrayed the faintest amused hint that my infatuation wasn't at all lost on her. "You're such a sweetheart," she said. "How come you don't have a girlfriend?"

"I have a problem with commitment."

"How's that?"

"Nobody wants me to commit."

She laughed. "Oh, come on. A handsome guy like you?"

"Go figure," I said with a grin.

She sat up and I took note of how the line of her cleavage appeared at the bottom of her V neck. It was absurd, really, how a simple vertical line could set off such volatile chemical reactions in my nether regions. She considered me somberly for a moment, seemed about to say something, and then changed her mind, biting her lip thoughtfully. All of a sudden, she looked bone-weary. "I'm glad you and Sammy became friends," she said.

"Me too."

"No. I mean I'm glad he'll have a friend like you going into school." She looked over her shoulder and leaned forward, and I could now see where the line split, heading off in two symmetrical curves. An erection, at that point, would have been instantly visible, raising my wet swimsuit and announcing itself like a rowdy, unwanted houseguest. Lucy spoke in a light whisper while I prayed desperately for continued flaccidity. "He's always had problems in school," she said. "Kids can be remarkably cruel when they want to."

"It'll be okay," I said awkwardly.

"You'll watch out for him, won't you?"

"We both will."

I didn't like where this conversation was headed, and Lucy seemed to sense that. She nodded lightly and leaned back on the couch. "Don't tell him I said anything."

"No worries there," I said more emphatically than I'd intended, and she chuckled.

"Well, I don't want to keep you," she said.

"You and every other woman I meet."

"If I were fifteen years younger . . ." she teased.

"You'd be out of my league," I said, and she laughed again.

When I stepped outside, Wayne and Sammy were in the water, kissing deeply under the diving board, Wayne's muscled arm resting lightly on Sammy's scrawny shoulder. Their heads were rocking in a slight circular motion as their jaws worked rhythmically against each other. Sammy's hand came up and lightly brushed Wayne's face. My knees buckled, and I felt an overpowering urge to flee. I wanted to be the kind of guy who could come running out, yell *"Get a room!"* and launch myself in a wicked cannonball into the water right beside them. I knew that they'd appreciate the gesture, but I just couldn't do it. Knowing was one thing; witnessing the concentrated passion of their kiss was something else entirely.

I backtracked quietly and walked back into the living room, where Lucy was lying on the couch, smoking and staring at the ceiling with a troubled frown. "I think I'll hang out in here for a while," I said.

She stared intently at me for a small eternity, her expression a pained mixture of consternation and resignation, and then sat up, patting the spot on the couch beside her. "Have a seat," she said with a smile, stubbing out her cigarette in the ashtray on the coffee table. "I'll go get you a Coke." She moved around the couch and then stopped, lightly patting my bare shoulder, her hand lingering there for a moment. "Joe," she said from behind me.

"Yeah."

"You really are a sweetheart."

"Yeah." I didn't turn around, because I didn't want her to see me cry.


Labor Day crept in with the stealth of a cat burglar in the dead of night, and when we woke up, summer had been stolen right out from under us. The Habers' pool was drained, winterized, and covered, and so was Lucy, whose bikinis, to my eternal dismay, had been put away for the season. The first day of our senior year loomed totemic on the horizon, like an indecipherable storm cloud.

The night before our freshman year, Wayne and I had

broken into the fire stairs that ran down the back side of Bush Falls High and climbed up to the roof. We'd sat together, perched on the large white cupola that looked out over the front lawn of the school, smoked a pack of Dunhills, and meditated on the upcoming school year. That evening evolved into an annual ritual for us, modified only slightly the night before our junior year started, when Wayne replaced our customary Dunhills with a bag of marijuana purchased from the stuttering pump jockey at the Sunoco station. This proved to be an almost fatal lapse in judgment, when Wayne nearly toppled off the cupola, pulling me with him, our collective balance impaired by the weed. We ended up sitting there into the wee hours, clinging fearfully to the smooth plaster walls of the cupola until the stars above us stopped flitting around like a galaxy in desperate need of Ritalin. Afterward, we agreed that next year we would go back to using regular cigarettes.

I didn't expect Wayne to join me for our annual smoke, but that Labor Day, a deep melancholy having to do with the vague notion of time's racing ahead unchecked compelled me to climb up there on my own. Once safely ensconced on top of the cupola, I lit a cigarette and looked out thoughtfully over the town. Despite the addition of Sammy to my pitiful roster of friends, I was feeling more alone than ever. I leaned back, studied the stars and thought about my mother, wondered if she was looking down at me, and felt bad about her seeing me in such a sad and lonely state, if she was.

There was a light scuffing sound of fabric against stone, and Wayne heaved himself up next to me with a light gasp. "What the fuck, man?" he said, breathing heavily, his blond hair plastered to his forehead with sweat. "You couldn't wait an extra ten minutes for me?"

I smiled, and lit him a cigarette from my own. "I didn't think you were coming," I said.

"Well, you're an asshole," Wayne said, accepting the cigarette. "Tradition is my middle name."

"I thought it was Howard."

"Remarks like that could lead to a nasty fall, if you catch my drift."

"Sorry."

"So," he said, holding up his cigarette in a toast. "Senior year."

"Senior year," I said, remarkably glad that Wayne had come, that we were hanging out again like the old days. It somehow made it seem possible that as weird as things had gotten, everything could still return to normal.

Wayne took a long drag on his cigarette and appeared to consider me thoughtfully for a few moments. "Joe," he finally said. "You're still my best friend."

"I know."

"Good."

We sat in companionable silence, looking up at the night sky, the abundance of unsaid things floating in the smoke-filled air between us. If there was ever going to be a time to discuss everything, this was it. "Wayne," I said tentatively.

"Don't say anything, man," he said, smiling sadly. "I'm fucked up enough as it is. If I have to talk about it, I think I'll go insane."

"Okay," I said, and then performed a loud, hyperbolic sigh of relief that made us both laugh. Below us, a plump skunk appeared on the school lawn, scurrying around with its nose to the ground as if searching for a contact lens. I followed the skunk's movements while Wayne lit two more cigarettes for us.

"Our last year of high school," he said, inhaling from both cigarettes at once before handing me mine. "It's all downhill from here."

"If this is as good as it gets, kill me now," I said.

Wayne grinned. "You should ask out that girl, Joe."

"What girl?"

"That Carly what's-her-face."

"Carly Diamond," I said. I'd been nursing a quiet crush on

her for the last half of our junior year, something I'd confided to Wayne on more than one occasion.

"She's cute," Wayne said. "You should go for it."

"Maybe."

"What's the problem?"

"We've only talked once or twice," I said. "How do you go from a few casual conversations to suddenly asking someone out?"

"But that's exactly when you have to do it."

"I feel like we should know each other a little better first, so it's not, like, out of the blue."

"Wrong, wrong, wrong," Wayne said. "This very time, when you know each other but your relationship hasn't been defined, is your window of opportunity. Girls divide guys into friends and potential boyfriends. You have to get yourself into the right category from the get-go. You do it your way, you'll end up being friends, and there's nothing harder than trying to switch categories once that happens. She'll end up talking to you about all the other guys she likes, in which case you're better off being rejected from the start."

"Thanks," I said. "But I think my way makes more sense."

"And you've certainly got the results to back it up," he said, smiling as he flicked his ashes over the edge of the building.

"Fuck you."

"Sorry, I've made other plans."

We smoked in silence for a while, watching as the scattered lights in the surrounding houses slowly went out. The hangnail moon took refuge behind a cluster of gray clouds, and I shivered as a slight chill took hold of the night. *This is what it feels like when time speeds up,* I thought.

Wayne turned to me, his expression earnest as he stubbed out his cigarette. "We should get tattoos," he said.

# eleven

I went in for rock posters in a big way back in the ninth grade, which is obviously the last time I redecorated my bedroom. Above the pine Workbench dresser in the corner hangs an enlarged poster of the painted girl from the cover of Duran Duran's *Rio* album. Beside the window, which looks out over the front door, is a poster of The Cure. On the far wall, above my bed, there was room for both Elvis Costello, peering inquisitively over his Buddy Holly glasses, and Howard Jones, relaxed and smiling under his hair spray, photographed sometime in the five minutes before synthesizer pop was laughed off the music scene. I seem to recall having had edgier taste in music, but I suppose that's just one more adjustment I'll have to make to my compromised memories. The young, bearded Springsteen sweating over his guitar on my bathroom door cheers me up for a second, even though I probably hung it there more for credibility than anything else.

On the door to my room, held up by thumbtacks, its white border ragged and torn in countless places from random human contact, is a *Star Wars* poster, just like in the song by Everclear. I hum the words softly to myself. *"I want the things that I had before / like a* Star Wars *poster on my bedroom door."* You have to question the originality of your life when it can be captured perfectly in the lyrics of a rock song.

Sitting on top of the dresser is my old Fisher stereo. I press the large silver power button, and the console lights up with an amplified squawk. I watch in awe as the phonograph arm rises automatically and swings over to the turntable, upon which spins an old 45. There is no reason it shouldn't work, and yet I'm surprised when it does. It's plugged in behind the dresser, and I remember struggling with the dresser to move it out far enough so that I could reach the outlet. It seems unbelievable to me that something the kid who would grow into me had done back then has remained intact until now, as if waiting for me to return. We are suddenly connected, he and I, as if by some cosmic warp in the time continuum, and I see him with perfect clarity, can feel his fears and thoughts suddenly running through my brain, his younger humors flowing through my veins, and for the briefest instant, through some act of molecular recall, I am him again. My thigh muscles falter and I sit down quickly on the bed. My bed. Through the speakers comes a scratchy rendition of Peter Gabriel singing "In Your Eyes," and I have to smile.

I use the hall bathroom, and my hand remembers that the flusher must be yanked up before being depressed, a plumbing quirk that has not been repaired since my childhood, because with my father living alone in the house, the hall toilet has basically gone unused. For a moment, I try to imagine a set of circumstances that might have led my father to use the hall toilet, but I cannot. Between the downstairs powder room and his own master bathroom, he'd have had no reason to come down this way, and Arthur Goffman is not the sort of man inclined toward whimsical changes of scenery when it comes to taking a dump.

I return to my room and walk over to the double windows that overlook the front yard, absently fingering the white plastic grille. My father had installed the grille because the pigeons kept mistaking the large window for open air and crashing into it. I can vividly recall the nauseating sound of those bone-jarring collisions jolting me out of my sleep in the early-morning hours. I would creep hesitantly to the window and look down to see the bird on our front stairs, dazed and shivering from the sudden, inexplicable crash. Usually they recovered after a few minutes and took to the air again on an erratic flight path, shaken and none the wiser for their bruising experience, left only with the vague and uncomfortable notion that the air will occasionally coagulate without warning and knock them out of the sky. Every so often the crash was fatal, and I was forced to remove the dead pigeon with one of the red snow shovels from the garage and inter the bird in a shallow, unmarked grave behind the hedges. The second time I buried a pigeon with a crushed skull, I vomited profusely and was sick for hours afterward, prompting my father to grudgingly install the grille, muttering under his breath about my fragile constitution.

The doorbell rings, and eager as I might be to continue my fond reverie of bad hair bands, pulverized birds, and my insensitive father, I clear my head and run downstairs to open the door.

The pale, lingering shipwreck of a man standing on my father's front porch, in baggy jeans and an old Cougars jacket, turns out to be Wayne Hargrove, but it takes a few beats before I recognize him. His once-thick blond hair has thinned to a few colorless wisps that float disconnectedly around his scalp, and there are dark shadows under his eyes, which are gravely sunken in their sockets. He is terribly thin in an angular way, with the stooped shoulders and protruding elbows and overall sense of diminishment that belong to a much older man. Implanted on the pasty diaphanous flesh of his forehead and neck are the small merlot-colored clusters characteristic of Kaposi's sarcoma, as if further proof of his terrible condition were needed.

"So the rumors were true," my old friend says, leaning against the door frame with familiar ease, as if it were yesterday and not seventeen years ago that he used to pop over whenever he felt the urge. "The prodigal son has returned."

"Good news travels fast," I say with a grin, shaking his hand. I can feel his bones, brittle and loose, shifting under his clammy, paper-thin skin as they yield to the pressure of my grip.

"News of any kind travels fast in this town," Wayne says. "No one knows that better than the town faggot."

We study each other for a moment or two.

"It's good to see you," I say.

He smirks, and a hint of the old Wayne, young, cocky, perennially amused, briefly flashes across his drawn face. "Aren't you going to tell me how great I look? How kind the years have been?"

"I was just going to say, you must give me the name of your dietitian."

Wayne's laugh is a strong and unfettered thing, and I congratulate myself on my direct approach. "Can I come in?" he asks hesitantly, and I see a subtle change in his expression, a quick flicker of doubt, as if he thinks he might very well be rebuffed. In that instant I catch the faintest whiff of the isolation and bigotry he's no doubt suffered as Bush Falls's only confirmed homosexual.

"That depends," I say. "Are you mad at me?"

"I promise not to spill any drinks on you, if that's what you mean."

"You heard about that."

"Tongues are wagging," he says, raising his eyebrows dramatically as he steps into the entry hall and looks around. "Wow. Time warp."

"Tell me about it," I say. "My bedroom is like a shrine to the eighties."

"I'll bet."

He asks after my father, and I give a summary of his condition and the generally pessimistic prognosis. He listens attentively, fiddling in his shirt pocket for a cigarette and a matchbook. He lights the match in the book one-handed, a trick he perfected back in high school, and takes a long, greedy drag on the cigarette. "Cigarette?"

"Yes, I know," I say, and we smile at the old shared joke. "Should you be smoking in your condition?"

"Most definitely." He arches his eyebrow cynically in what strikes me as a particularly gay manner: stately, self-deprecating, and slightly feminine. I wonder if he had these mannerisms back in high school and I was just oblivious, or if he'd cultivated this demeanor in the years after he left the Falls, living out in Los Angeles, working odd jobs, and auditioning for an endless stream of sitcom pilots. We'd stayed in touch sporadically, writing sarcastic letters to each other, documenting our latest, separate failures. At some point during my senior year at NYU, a routine HIV test Wayne took came back positive and his letters stopped coming. Only recently, in a rare conversation with Brad, had I learned that Wayne had moved back to the Falls, and more than once I'd resolved to give him a call, but predictably never did.

I look into Wayne's creased face and ravaged eyes, my throat constricting in an involuntary spasm of acute sadness, and I think that he's very much like those pigeons I buried in my youth, flying along minding his own business when the air suddenly turned solid on him. "How long have you been symptomatic?"

"I think I just crossed the line between long enough and too long," he says with a rueful smile.

"You're living at home?"

"Yeah. Apparently, the AIDS alone wasn't enough to satisfy my masochistic nature."

"And how are the Hargrove seniors?"

"Vindicated," he says with a sour grin. "My mother warned me there'd be hell to pay for my abominations."

Wayne's mother is a ball buster of a woman who embroiders obscure biblical verses on pillows and keeps an extensive collection of *Reader's Digest* magazines, which she weeps through every Sunday after church. Beside her, his father is practically invisible, a slight balding man who speaks in muted whispers, as if he's constantly afraid of waking someone up.

"Can I get you anything?" I say, although not having been to the kitchen yet, I have no idea what there might be to be gotten. Beer and Gatorade have always been my father's beverages of choice, but I suspect he still does his shopping one day at a time.

"No, thanks," Wayne says. "I actually came here to get you."

"Really? What for?"

"To go drinking," he says as if it should have been obvious. "As unfortunate as the circumstances might be, this is still a homecoming, a reunion of sorts. We owe it to ourselves to get hammered."

I look at his fragile form skeptically. "You're going to get hammered?" I say. "That can't be good for you."

"Oh, come on," he says with a frown. "Look at me, will you? It's a bit late to be implementing a policy of abstinence, don't you think?" There's a new quality to Wayne's speech, something I don't remember from our youth, a sharp thread of resigned bitterness woven into his wit.

"Is it really that bad?" I ask, and then quickly correct myself. "I mean, is the disease really that advanced?"

"The final countdown." The remark and its accompanying expression reveal the first crack in his veneer of jocularity. We share a sad, comfortable silence, feeling the textured close-

ness of old friends soberly acknowledging tragedy together. I
let out an audible sigh, wishing that I were by nature a more
expressive person, and Wayne sighs as well, probably wishing
he didn't have AIDS at all.

"I'm really sorry, man," I say. "I don't know what to say."

He nods and pulls open the front door. "You can think of
something en route."

We step outside into the muted pastels of suburban twilight. The cicadas have gone to sleep, the crickets have yet to
strike up the band, and I pause on the porch for a moment,
breathing in deeply the scents of freshly mowed lawns and
cooling blacktop and the faintest trace of honeysuckle. I am
suddenly awash in a confounding wave of nostalgia for my
youth and the house in which I'd grown up.

"You forget something?" Wayne says from the stairs.

"A lot," I say, perturbed.

His smile conveys telepathic understanding. "Welcome
home, my friend." He points to the Mercedes. "I take it this
obscene status symbol is yours?"

"Afraid so."

"Excellent," he says, pulling open the passenger door.
"Let's see what she can do."

At Wayne's behest, I drive out to Pinfield Avenue, a deso-
late stretch of back road that winds its way quietly around
Bush Falls, and floor it. The Mercedes growls with mythic energy as I push the needle up past ninety. In the passenger
seat, Wayne opens his window completely to let in the angry,
whipping wind, closing his eyes with a smile as it buffets his
head, blowing the clinging remnants of his hair behind him
comically. "Oh, come on!" he shouts above the combined din
of the engine and the wind. "You can do better than that."

I shake my head at him and step down harder on the accelerator. The needle creeps up past one hundred, and we can
now feel every dip and pebble in the warped pavement of the

old road. I tighten my grip on the wheel, thinking to myself that no good can come of this. In the passenger seat, Wayne appears even more depleted, and I find myself worrying irrationally about the pressure of the wind on him, as if it might pull his gossamer skin right off his flimsy bones. "Faster," he says.

"You're not even wearing your seat belt."

He turns to me and smiles ironically. "It's one of the few perks of my condition," he says, and then, affecting an exaggerated Mexican lilt, shouts, "We don't need no stinking seat belts!"

The trees rush by us in a haze of green as the Mercedes' tires churn against the blacktop. The needle now hovers at 115, which is, to the best of my recollection, the fastest I've ever driven. We shoot through the night, Wayne and I, two lost, lonely souls, vibrating in our seats like pistons as we hurtle over the road on borrowed power, the air desperately parting and diving out of our path in the xenon glare of our low beams. And maybe it's not about speed exactly; maybe it's about time, and trying to catch it, to overtake it and just slow everything the fuck down for a little while.

"Faster!" Wayne bellows jubilantly. "You pussy!"

"You're really a terrible influence on me," I say.

"Come on," he exhorts me. "What are you so worried about?"

As if on cue, we hear the growing wail of a police siren behind us an instant before the flashing lights appear in my mirror. "Busted," Wayne says, unable to conceal his glee.

"Shit." I brake heavily. "I hope you're satisfied."

Wayne leans forward to check his side-view mirror. "I think we can take him," he says earnestly, a wild look in his eyes.

"You can't be serious."

"Come on. Live a little."

When I slow down, Wayne goes into a pout, staring out

the window like a petulant adolescent. "Fine. Be that way," he mutters.

I frown at him as I pull over, the police car coming to a stop about ten yards behind me. "It's Mouse," Wayne says.

"What?" I lean over him to rummage through the glove compartment for my registration.

"From high school. Mouse Muser."

"No way." I peer through my side-view mirror as the cop approaches the car.

"Afraid so."

Dave Muser, the starting point guard for the Cougars during my tenure at Bush Falls High, was nicknamed Mouse because of his small stature and the frenetic manner in which he scurried around the court, distributing the ball among his teammates. In most cases, finding out that you've been pulled over by an old classmate might be a relief, but obviously this isn't most cases. Mouse, along with Sean Tallon, had been instrumental in terrorizing Sammy Haber back in high school, and in my novel I portrayed him as a truly grotesque character, even shorter and uglier than he was, more of a mascot than a friend to Sean and his henchmen. Mouse's father was the sheriff back then, and apparently Mouse has gone into the family business.

I roll down my window. Because of his diminutive height, Mouse's face is only slightly above eye level, and a cursory glance reveals that he's changed very little in seventeen years. With its primitive, jutting forehead, squinting eyes, and acne-scarred cheeks, Mouse's face suggests that sometime in his past, his progenitors might have been given to swimming a little more than they should in the family gene pool. "Well, well," he says with a nasty grin. "Look who we have here."

"Hey, Mouse," I say. "How've you been?"

"No one calls me that anymore."

"I'm sorry, um . . . Dave."

"It's Deputy Sheriff Muser, as far as you're concerned," he

says, and there is no mistaking the naked hostility in his voice. "You have any idea how fast you were going?"

"Not really."

"Hey, Mouse," Wayne calls from the passenger seat. "How's it going?"

Mouse looks past me and grimaces when he sees Wayne. "Hey there, Wayne," he says, clearly uncomfortable. "I didn't see you." Wayne's coming out was a first for a former Cougar, and his ex-teammates had vociferously denounced and shunned him, no doubt fearful of casting doubt upon their own proclivities through association.

"Do you think maybe you could cut us a break, just this once?" Wayne says. "A last courtesy for an old teammate?"

"If you'd been driving, I'd have considered it," Mouse says with a smirk. "What with your illness and all." He pronounces the word *illness* like it's in quotes, as if it's nothing more than a silly euphemism. "But this guy," he continues, pointing disgustedly at me, "has got no breaks coming from me, or anyone else in this town." He straightens up and turns back to me. "License and registration, please."

He strolls back to his car to run me through his computer, no doubt hoping the car will turn out to be stolen and my license a phony. "Mouse became a cop," Wayne says, smiling.

"I know that now," I say.

Ahead of us, an oncoming Lincoln Town Car slows to a crawl. As it passes us, the driver's tinted window comes down, and I find myself looking into the coal black eyes of Coach Dugan. He stares at me as he passes, his face expressionless, and I hate myself for the icy fear that nestles in my belly when our eyes lock, the tremor in my hands as they grip the lifeless steering wheel. Although he achieved evil of exaggerated proportions in my novel, I've forgotten how powerful his presence can be in reality.

Mouse waves eagerly to the coach as he drives by, then comes back to my window and hands me two summonses.

"That first one's for speeding. The second is for the broken taillight."

"I don't have a broken taillight," I object, still shaken from my fleeting glimpse of Dugan.

"Sure you do."

I step out of the car and we walk to the back of the Mercedes, where Mouse steps forward and casually kicks in my left taillight with the heel of his boot. He grins up at me like an evil troll.

Through my open car window, I can hear Wayne laughing his ass off.

# *twelve*

## 1986

School started, and Wayne and Sammy's relationship went underground, which was fine with me, since that made it easier to pretend it didn't exist. I still hung out with both of them, but they scrupulously avoided being seen together without my nullifying presence. After a while, through a regimented lack of scrutiny, I was able to convince myself that nothing else was happening between them after school, that the events of the past summer had been a fleeting madness, unable to survive the glaring, fluorescent reality of the high school hallways. I internalized this new, airbrushed version of reality with a minimum of effort, because the truth was that I had better things to think about. After three years of languishing in a social wasteland, I had scored my first real girlfriend.

In the unrestrained pageant of tits and ass that paraded through the halls of Bush Falls High on a daily basis, Carly the BOOK of JOE

Diamond's quiet prettiness generally flew below radar. Sub-
tlety is lost on teenaged boys, who are instantly riveted by
smooth, slim legs and tight, round bottoms under short
skirts, lively breasts straining against the fabric of form-
fitting shirts, long, shining hair, and glistening skin. Carly's
lithe frame was concealed in loose-fitting blouses and baggy
jeans, her thick chestnut hair cut short and close. Her high
cheekbones, flawless ivory skin, and impossibly round hazel
eyes with specks of yellow glinting in their irises were there
for all to see, but there was an overall sense of things being
held in check, of beauty controlled and refined by a keen intelligence. Naturally, she was completely overlooked by
most of the boys in our class. But not by me, which may very
well have been the greatest achievement of my high school
career. I had no singular skill to distinguish me from the
huddled masses, was lacking that strategic extracurricular
specialty to list on my college application; my unique accom-
plishment was simply having the anomalous wisdom and
foresight to register Carly's more mature beauty, to sense
the passion and smoldering sensuality behind her quiet
grace and easy smile.

It began simply enough, with Carly sitting next to me in
homeroom that year. We became morning buddies, casual
friends who started every school day together. And soon I
began looking for her throughout the day, living for the special smiles she flashed at me when we passed in the hallways,
feeling strangely possessive. I began studying her face when
she wasn't looking, entranced by the simple perfection of
her features, the flawless surface of her silken skin seemingly
without pores. More than once she caught me looking at
her, and her knowing smile encouraged me. I began walking
her home after school, our arms lightly brushing as we
walked, and eventually I summoned up the courage to take
her hand in mine. It didn't take long for hand-holding to es-
calate into short, careful kisses and then much longer,
deeper, open-mouthed kisses that ended only when we

93

needed to come up for air, our inexperienced tongues hungrily tasting each other. By mid-October we were virtually inseparable, fused together in a perfect symbiosis of rampant hormones and deep passion, which can feed harmoniously on each other for that rare period of time between childhood and adulthood, before they reach cross-purposes and begin mercilessly devouring each other.

Nineteen eighty-six was a fine time to be a teenager in love. Unemployment was down, the stock market was up, and people were generally optimistic. We listened to happy European synth pop: Depeche Mode, Erasure, A-Ha. The boys tucked the bottoms of their stonewashed Gap jeans into their high-top Nikes, gelled and cut wedges into their hair, and tried in vain to incorporate the moonwalk into their limited dance repertoires. The girls teased their hair high with mousse, wore iridescent skirts with matching eye shadow, fishnet shirts off one shoulder, and anything they saw in Madonna's videos. Things were so peaceful, they had to send Rambo back to Vietnam to look for action. We had no Internet or grunge bands to dilute our innocence with irony, no glorified slackers or independent films to make darkness appealing. Happiness was still considered socially acceptable.

Carly and I took long walks every day after school, stopped for pizza or ice cream on Stratfield Road, danced at parties on Friday night, and went to the movies on Saturday. We logged countless hours on the phone every night, lying in our respective beds, relishing the private universe that was expanding daily around us. Sometimes at night we lay on our backs in her yard, our fingertips touching as we watched for shooting stars. We fooled around in my father's Pontiac parked down by the Bush River Falls, the source of the town's name as well as its universal make-out spot, our impassioned kissing and petting progressing in tantalizing baby steps, each new plateau a delightfully sensual revelation making us feel that much more grown-up and that much more connected. As we lay together shirtless in the backseat of the car, the windows fogged, the leather upholstery sticking like cellophane to our sweating bodies, our groins conjoined, pressing and grinding through our jeans, kissing and tonguing each other with unrelenting urgency, it was easy to believe that what we had was all we'd ever need.

Things weren't going nearly as well for Sammy, who had inevitably caught the eye of the predatory duo of Sean Tallon and Dave "Mouse" Muser. Sean, with his patrician jaw, platinum crew cut, and dark, narrow eyes that glinted with just the faintest hint of malice, was a notorious bully who remained largely undisciplined either because of his status as a starting forward for the Cougars or because his father was rumored to work in some capacity for Frankie the Shoe, a local gangster of some repute. With Mouse's status as starting point guard and son of the town sheriff, the two were virtually untouchable, roaming the halls of Bush Falls High with a rowdy elitism, like young nobility granted diplomatic immunity from the rules of conduct that governed the rest of our plebeian asses. Sean was clearly the leader, while Mouse, a fireplug with the face of Australopithecus and a wit that relied heavily on bodily fluids, hovered manically in the background, the remora swimming behind the shark, snacking on the floating debris from its carnage. Sammy, with his colorful wardrobe and penchant for singing aloud as he walked the halls, might as well have had a bull's-eye tattooed to his forehead.

Sean in particular had a finely honed sadistic streak when it came to his weaker peers, and he zeroed in on Sammy almost immediately. Less than a week after school had started, Sean and Mouse found Sammy in the boys' room, fine-tuning his pompadour. "Look how pretty," Mouse said. "Pretty as a picture," Sean agreed. "Let's hang him up." They pulled on the rear waistband of Sammy's underwear, tearing the elastic from the cotton and yanking it up over his head as he struggled in vain. Wedgies were a routine rite of initiation for entering freshmen, and one in which Sean conscientiously partook almost daily in the first month of a new semester, but having it done to you as a senior was particularly humiliating. They left Sammy hanging by his belt and underwear waistband on the back hook of a bathroom stall door, where he remained, tears of pained frustration dripping down his face, until he was discovered and cut down by some freshmen who mistook him for one of their own.

"Why do you think it is," he said morosely when I came across him in the cafeteria later that day, "that no matter where I go, guys like that seem to find me?" I frowned sympathetically, feeling guilty, as if my not having been able to prevent this inevitability reflected a secret collusion with Tallon and his crew or, at best, an endorsement of the inherent system that put Sammy at such risk.

"You've met our resident assholes," I told him. "They go after every new kid. It's a territorial thing, like dogs pissing in their yards. They did their thing and it's over. I would just stay out of their way."

Sammy looked up at me, tears forming behind his glasses. "I've spent my entire life avoiding the Sean Tallons of this world," he said bitterly. "And somehow they always seem to find me. It seems to be my destiny."

"That's bullshit," I said.

Sammy remained unconvinced. "We'll see," he muttered.

A few days later in a crowded bathroom, Sean pulled Sammy away from the urinal in mid-piss, causing him to urinate all over his shoes and pants. "If you want to see my dick that badly, just ask," Sammy reportedly shouted at his attacker. "It will save you the trouble and me the cleaning up." Sean was utterly unaccustomed to this sort of slur on his unimpeachable character, and Sammy got a punch in the face and his head dunked in the toilet for his trouble. Indeed, most of Sean's attacks on Sammy did seem to depend on undressing him to some degree, but it would be years before I recognized this as possibly significant.

That afternoon, Wayne and I cut history and sneaked up

onto the roof for a smoke. It was drizzling lightly, a misty spray that licked at our faces as we lit up. "You heard about Sammy?" I said.

Wayne nodded, frowning as he blew the smoke out through his nose.

"You can say something to them," I said. "They'll listen to you."

"It'll just make things worse," he said.

"That's a cop-out," I said, getting annoyed. "If they were hassling me, you'd put a stop to it."

"It's not the same," Wayne said defensively. He sighed miserably, staring out at the thunderheads amassing on the horizon. "He brings it upon himself," he said softly. "Why does he have to act like such a . . . fag." The word rose in the air before us, baring its fangs like a dragon, challenging us to brave its snot-encrusted flames and enter its lair.

"He is who he is," I said. "Just because you defend a guy, that doesn't make you—"

"Doesn't make me what?" Wayne said, daring me.

"Nothing," I said.

"You think I'm a homo, Joe?" he said, glowering at me. "You think I'm gay?"

I considered the question carefully. "I don't know what to think."

"Well, I'm not," he said hotly.

"Fine."

"What do you mean, fine?"

"I mean fine."

He stared at me intently for a minute, then nodded slowly and took a long drag on his cigarette. "Fine," he said.

As far as I could tell, after that Sammy and Wayne stopped speaking altogether.

A few weeks later, Sean and Mouse grabbed Sammy between periods and pulled him into the yearbook office, where they pulled down his pants and attempted to photo-copy his naked ass for posterity. Sammy put up a fight, and they ended up breaking the glass plate as they forced him to sit on the machine. His cuts required sixteen stitches, and it was two weeks before he was able to sit comfortably again.

The principal of Bush Falls High was Ed Lyncroft, a portly, doddering, ridiculous little man who desperately craved ap-proval from students and faculty alike. On those occasions when he addressed large segments of the student body, he did so in a stammering, self-effacing manner, as if to say he was in on the colossal joke that was him. His well-documented excessive use of a cloying brand of aftershave and his penchant for peppermint candies did nothing to negate the conventional wisdom that he was a raging alco-holic who laced his ever-present coffee mug with generous amounts of whiskey.

Lyncroft's spineless demeanor rendered him fairly useless as a disciplinarian and made it easy for someone like Dugan to manipulate him. So it was after a quick consultation with Dugan that Lyncroft suspended Sean and Mouse for two days and demanded a written apology to Sammy from each before they could return to school. Dugan also made sure it was understood that despite their suspension, Sean and Mouse would still be allowed to attend basketball practice after school. After all, the season was under way, and why should everyone else on the team be made to suffer?

When I knocked on Sammy's door that evening, Lucy opened it, looking uncharacteristically glum, her eyes slightly red from crying. When she saw that it was me, though, she smiled brightly, and I shivered with secret delight. "Hi, Mrs. Haber. I came over to see how Sammy's doing," I said, which was only partially true. Mostly, it was an excuse to see Lucy, whom I hadn't seen since the school year began.

"Please, Joe," she said wearily. "I've told you a thousand times to call me Lucy."

I did, and it felt subversively intimate.

"It's sweet of you to come see him," she said. "But I don't think he's really up for a visit right now."

"Is he in a lot of pain?"

She looked at me, a deep hurt etched across her face. "He's humiliated," she said simply. "What those boys did to him . . ." Her eyes filled with tears again, and she turned away from me. "I need a smoke." I followed her into the kitchen, where she sat down and shook a cigarette out of a package lying on the round pine table. "That boy has never bothered a living soul," she said, absently curling her lower lip as she projected a stream of smoke upward. "And yet wherever he goes, something about him seems to inspire this cruelty." She paused to take another drag on her cigarette and then rested her head on her palm. I was both alarmed and terribly excited to discover that she was crying. She looked up at me standing idiotically beside her, reached out to grab my hand, and pulled me into the seat next to her. "You have to help him, Joe," she said, her eyes beseeching me. "You have to look out for him. There's just no one else to do it." I nodded mutely, feeling a powerful stirring in my loins. I was on a first-name basis with a beautiful older woman who was now holding on to me as she cried. What further intimacies lay ahead?

"I'll try," I said to her, squeezing her hand. She leaned forward to hug me, and I brought up my hand awkwardly to her shoulder. Her smells were a combination of lilac shampoo, a soft perfume with a citrus scent, and the cigarette still burning in the hand behind my left ear. As she spoke, her lips inadvertently brushing my ear, I tried to inhale her entire essence. "Be my hero, Joe," she whispered to me. "Take care of my boy."

She pulled back and smiled at me, her hands still on my shoulders, and I saw a flicker of something in her eyes, an amused recognition of my intense longing. I had a sudden, intuitive flash that maybe Lucy's seductive touch was not accidental on her part, that she was offering something here. I felt my legs start to tremble, but then she let go and took another long pull on her cigarette.

"I'll try," I said thoughtlessly. I'd pretty much forgotten about Sammy already. I walked back to the front door ahead of her, taking great pains to hide the shameless proboscis protruding under my jeans.

# thirteen

The Halftime pub is all dark mahogany and weathered leather that practically glistens with testosterone in the dim glow of the alabaster light fixtures. The wood-paneled walls are covered with framed sports memorabilia, and the bar is a dark, hulking monolith that runs the full width of the room. The air is thick with the smell of things burned and burning yet: cigarettes, cigars, chickens being grilled, and steaks being broiled. Despite the strategic placement of ceiling fans, there is a hazy smokiness to the room, highlighted by the flickering blue-green light emanating from the numerous large-screen televisions mounted throughout the pub. The men who sit scattered in small groups are for the most part cast from the same mold, ex-Cougars coming together nightly to relive their glory days and revel in this fossilized fraternity that was once the defining core of their existence. Like veterans of a great war, they come together nightly to repeat exaggerated tales of triumphs on the battlefield.

It's hardly a desirable destination for a dying homosexual

and a universally despised author, but into this miasma of swollen, aging masculinity we walk, despite my repeated suggestions to Wayne that we go elsewhere. I'm still trying to pick up the threads of my confidence, which have come unraveled since my run-in with Mouse and my quick, silent brush with Dugan. With every passing minute, those two incidents seem increasingly portentous, and I'm beginning to suspect what I should have realized from the start, that appearing in public in Bush Falls might be a colossal mistake. Wayne, however, is having none of it, and he strides into the pub with all the swagger his brittle, emaciated legs can muster. I haven't yet come to grasp the full extent of Wayne's fervent desire to stir things up while he still can, but watching him walk through the pub, tossing off excessively loud greetings at everyone he knows, feigning oblivion to their carefully averted gazes and barely concealed revulsion, I'm beginning to get it.

Despite the dim lighting, I am able to make out a handful of familiar faces as I peer around the room. There's Pete Rothson, who knew every word to "Stairway to Heaven" and never tired of explaining its various, contradictory interpretations. Alan Mcintyre, who taught me that free stuff could be gotten simply by calling the toll-free numbers on candy bar wrappers and inventing complaints. My shoulder is actually tapped in greeting by Steve Packer, who, legend had it, once actually fractured his wrist jerking off, and could always be depended on to know every acceptable synonym for *vagina*. "Joe Goffman," he declares, pumping my hand enthusiastically and inquiring after the well-being of my testicles. "How they hanging?"

"Steve Packer," I respond. (*What's your middle name—Fudge?* the old joke went.) "Nice to see you."

Steve has apparently not gotten the memo that I'm to be shunned at every opportunity, an oversight Wayne corrects immediately. "What about me, Steve?" Wayne says. "Don't you want to know how mine are hanging?"

Steve does not. He fixes Wayne with a glare that says balls are a privilege Wayne has blatantly abused, and moves off to join his buddies in the back.

"Does it help?" I ask as we take our own table against the wall.

"What?" He catches my look. "Yeah," he admits. "A little."

"Okay. Then it's worth it."

He flashes me a grateful smile as he slides into his chair. "I was pretty naïve when I came back to the Falls," he says. "I don't know what I was expecting, but I was one of these guys, you know?" He indicates the breast pocket of his old basketball jacket, where his name is stitched in thin gold thread. "That's me, right? I'm still that guy."

"Sure," I say.

"Anyway, I was actually stupid enough to come here once or twice when I'd first gotten back, looking to shoot the shit with old buddies. . . ." Wayne's voice trails off and he sighs deeply. "Being gay is like taking a crash course in human nature," he says. "Your first real glimpse at the dirty underbelly of routine social interaction. A lesser person," he offers with a wry grin, "might well become one bitter fuck."

"I can imagine."

He leans back in his chair. "Anyway, long story short, they didn't exactly throw a welcome home party for me, and I pretty much went into hiding. Only recently did it occur to me that I'm a guy who doesn't have very much living left to do, and I'll be damned if I'm going to give up one second of it over these bastards. The virus might have me beat, but this sorry lot of fuckers?" He raises his voice, indicating the crowded pub with a vast wave. "Now, that would be tragic."

I smile and say, "Bravo."

"I'm not relating this to you in order to receive your accolades," he says haughtily, "well deserved though they may be. I'm just trying to explain to you that we are far and away the least popular people here, and if you're waiting to be served, it's going to be one hell of a long night."

"Gotcha." I stand up with a grin. "What are you drinking?"

"It doesn't matter," Wayne says. "It'll be going down too fast to taste."

An hour later I have a pretty good buzz going. Wayne, who takes miserly, birdlike sips at his shot glass, seems to be in good spirits too, and I surmise that at his current body weight, it doesn't take very much to get him plastered. As the time drags on and I listen to Wayne tell highly embellished tales of his travails in Hollywood, my prickly sense of exposure begins to wane, and I start to relax. Wayne wields his outsider status like a weapon, a neat trick that simultaneously empowers and insulates him, and I drunkenly vow to internalize this strategy for the duration of my stay in the Falls. Somewhere in the back of my mind, I realize that being in knocking distance of heaven's door gives Wayne a certain reckless courage that I don't possess, but I am nevertheless resolved to have a go at it.

"This place," Wayne says, "is right out of Springsteen." He nods his head and sings a line. *"Just sitting back trying to recapture a little of the glory . . ."*

I finish it for him. *"Time slips away, leaves you with nothing, mister, but boring stories of glory days."*

Wayne smiles. "Like Sammy always said, there's a Springsteen song for every occasion."

"I remember."

"People are staring at us," Wayne observes with a grin.

I kill another shot of vodka. "Fuck 'em," I say, or actually the booze does.

"Fuck 'em," Wayne repeats, lifting his glass in a toast and taking another baby sip from it.

Drinking always leads me to form dramatic resolutions in the area of personality modification, behavioral adjustments that seem obvious and easy without the weighty hindrance of sobriety. At this moment, I resolve to stay enveloped in a protective leather pocket of cool, ironic detachment, like Wayne, ready to unflinchingly handle whatever demons from my past lie in wait for me. I am absolutely confident that I can pull it off. Which makes it all the more surprising when I'm suddenly snatched by a pair of powerful hands and yanked violently out of my chair. As I stumble, I catch a punch in the ear that spins me around and knocks me onto my ass. I look up to find an older, bloated version of Sean Tallon standing over me, his face contorted with crimson rage, his fists clenched in front of him. "Hey, Sean," I say, getting uncertainly to my feet. "How've you been?" I'm working under the assumption that it will be too incongruous for him to hit me, once engaged in conversation. Obviously, I don't know shit about fighting, because it's the conversation that is incongruous. He hits me again, this time with a roundhouse punch that sails through my girlishly awkward, flailing block and glances painfully off the outside of my eye socket, simultaneously disproving my ill-conceived theory and sending me flying back into my table.

"Hey, dickhead," Sean says, advancing on me. "I've been waiting for you to show your sorry little ass around here again."

The delivery of dead-on one-liners is rare in the nonscripted world. Usually, they occur to you only afterward, at which point, of course, they're completely worthless. Consequently, I always feel an almost religious compunction to seize those opportunities where the serendipitous confluence of circumstance and wit occur, regardless of the outcome, which will almost always be bad. So I say, "You always did have a thing for little asses," and Sean kicks me in the stomach. As I fall back onto my table, I am rewarded for my verbal acuity by Wayne's snorting, appreciative guffaw and somewhat comforted by the knowledge that Sean was already beating me up before I impugned his sexuality.

By now we are the main attraction, my second public flogging in one day. Sean theatrically hoists a chair above his head, and with horror I see that he fully intends to bring it crashing down on me as I lie splayed out on the table. I wonder crazily if it will fly apart on contact, the way furniture always seems to do in the movies. My body involuntarily contracts into a fetal position, my eyes clamped shut, absolutely pathetic. There is a loud splintering sound, which I presume to be my bones yielding to the chair, but after a moment I realize that there is no pain and I open my eyes. Sean is doubled over on the floor, his arms folded into his belly, the chair lying broken on the floor a few feet from him. Standing between him and my sorry little ass, with his hand pointed commandingly at Sean, is my brother, Brad. "That's enough, Sean," he says in a low voice. "This isn't the time."

Sean slowly gets to his feet, rubbing the area just over his left rib cage and looking at Brad in disbelief. "You fucking hit me, Goff?"

"Just lay off, Sean," Brad says. "I mean it."

From behind the bar, Louis, the diminutive, weasel-faced bartender, calls out anxiously, "You guys want to take this outside?" He is instantly assailed with a boisterous barrage of *shut-the-fuck-up*s from the assembled crowd, who are not about to be robbed of an evening's entertainment.

"You're defending that piece of shit?" Sean says. "After everything he said about all of us?"

"I'm not defending what he did," Brad says simply. "But I'm not going to stand here and let you pound him."

Something in my belly catches and chokes at Brad's words, and I slowly roll off the table and onto my wobbly feet. Sean is now standing toe-to-toe with Brad. "Get the fuck out of the way, Goff," he says menacingly, wiping some spit from his mouth. "And let him fight his own battle."

"It's not going to happen," Brad says quietly. I am almost bowled over by the rush of gratitude and admiration that pours through me as my older brother stands his ground on my behalf. A lump forms in my throat, although that might be a result of the beating I've just taken. The air between Brad and Sean seems to visibly thicken and swirl as they face off, each one waiting for the other to end the stalemate. With a sinking feeling, I understand that there is no way for this to end peacefully. Egos and manhood have been stirred into the mix, in public no less. Blood is now mandatory. My battered face begins throbbing hotly.

"It's okay, Brad. I can handle this," I say, not because I can but because I'm an idiot who always feels the need to say something.

There is a chorus of approval from the crowd, anonymous calls for Brad to let his brother fight his own battles, et cetera, which I hope to god he won't heed. Brad flashes me a withering, skeptical look that borders on contemptuous, the same look I would have gotten from him years ago if I'd challenged him to a one-on-one. Normally that look would enrage me to the point of doing something recklessly stupid, but now I find it positively reassuring. Brad isn't going to let me get myself killed tonight.

"You'd better move it, Goff," Sean says, his voice husky with rage. "I have no problem with you, but if you don't step down, I'm going to put you down."

"Let's get on with it, then," Brad says.

Sean steps forward and Brad's hands come up in a defensive position, his brow fiercely furrowed with a grim sense of purpose, but before anything can happen, a booming voice shatters the pulsating silence, freezing both fighters in their spots. "What the hell is going on here?"

The onlookers part, and through them, in an unhurried, almost regal gait, strides Coach Dugan. The coach is a tall, imposing man with a high forehead and dark, glowering eyes. The hair beneath his ever-present Cougars cap has gone from gray to titanium white in the years since I last saw him, and his face is considerably more creased than I remember. Portions of his architecture now creak and sag under the weight of time, but he still exudes a powerful sense of grace as he makes his way through the respectful crowd, a general going through the motions of mingling with his troops.

"Tallon!" Dugan yells in a throaty voice. "Goffman! What the hell are you two doing?"

"It's not about him," Sean says, still frozen in his pugilistic posture. He points past Brad at me. "It's the brother."

The coach turns to look at me, his eyes burning twin holes in my skull. "*He* is no reason for two of *my* boys to come to blows," he says, not taking his eyes off me. "Now, the both of you, put your hands down and step back from each other." They look at him and back at each other, frowning with uncertainty. "Do it now!" Dugan growls. Brad and Sean drop their hands and take a few reluctant steps back from each other. All the while, Dugan's eyes remain fixed on me, his expression a combination of scorn and amusement. "Art Goffman's in a coma over at Mercy Hospital tonight, and I think it would be a hell of a nice gesture, a token of our collective respect for our friend and teammate, if maybe we didn't beat the shit out of his jackass son." He turns to the bar, where Louis stands, looking comically relieved. "That being said, Louis, I turn to you, as the owner of this establishment, to help keep the peace. There's a man here who, by his very presence, offends your regular clientele, and I think it would be in everybody's best interest if they didn't have to drink with him. We wouldn't want an unfortunate incident."

"What," Louis says nervously. "You want I should kick him out?"

The coach holds up his hands in a placating gesture. "It's your place, Louis, not mine. You run your business at your own discretion, and no man has any right to tell you how to do that."

Louis looks at Dugan for a minute and then turns to me. "I think you'd better go," he says quickly. "It'd be best for all concerned, you know." Dugan nods at him, beaming like a proud grandfather.

"Fuck you, Louis," Wayne says disgustedly. "Grow some balls, would you?"

"Why, so you can lick them?" someone in the crowd shouts, and the place erupts into malicious laughter.

"Who said that?" Dugan roars, and the crowd falls instantly silent again. "Who the hell said that?"

Brad turns to me and says, "Time to go."

I nod, and we head for the door, with Wayne trailing behind, cursing and spitting at everyone he passes.

"You had to go out and get wrecked, didn't you?" Brad practically shouts at me when we get outside. "You had to go and stir things up."

"Hey, he attacked me," I say weakly.

"He would have finished you off too," Brad says angrily, and then snorts incredulously. "You don't get it, do you? You can't go running around the Falls like you never wrote that goddamn book. You pissed off too many people."

"So nobody likes me," I say with a defensive shrug. "That isn't exactly breaking news. I don't see what you're so angry about."

Brad turns on me, seething. "I live here, you asshole. This"—he gestures around at the buildings—"is my home. I realize it's just literary fodder for you, but I have to face these people every day."

"No one asked you to butt in," I say. "If I want to go out and get my ass kicked, it's not your problem."

He looks hard at me, his face a twisted mask of complex emotions that will never be articulated. At least, I hope they won't be, because I don't know if I could stand hearing what Brad really thinks of me right now. At this moment I become aware of two things: that my older brother really doesn't like me very much and that I want him to. Brad exhales slowly, audibly, shutting his eyes and shaking his head from side to side. "I'm going home," he says tiredly. He turns and walks away, and I watch him go, disliking myself intensely and thinking that maybe an asshole does realize he's an asshole at some point after all. There just might not be anything to do about it.

I turn to Wayne, who's leaning against the window of the bar, looking terribly skinny and ragged. "You ready to go home?" I say.

"Nah. It's just getting good," he says with a grin, then steps into the street and vomits onto the curb.

# *fourteen*

Sobriety is best approached slowly, like a scuba diver emerging from watery depths, stopping to decompress every so often. Having the shit kicked out of you denies you that luxury, slamming you into the brick wall of sobriety all at once, which hurts like hell, placing into excruciatingly sharp focus your newly acquired bruises and lacerations. On the plus side, I feel perfectly capable of driving Wayne and myself home, which I do with exaggerated care, already picturing the gleeful, rat-faced smile on Mouse's face as he books me for driving under the influence, his mind already sprinting forward to how he'll tell the story in mock heroic tones over beers the next night.

There is a tightness in my throat, a warm blockage at the junction of my esophagus and chest, and I realize that I'm holding back tears. I wonder if I'm still in shock from the raw violence of Sean's unexpected attack or if there's something deeper going on.

In the passenger seat, Wayne lies back, a tired, satisfied grin plastered across his gaunt face. "That was fun, wasn't it?"

"I'm so glad that my public beating made for good entertainment."

"No blood, no foul," Wayne says.

"Excuse me—have you seen my face?" I pull the rearview mirror down and examine myself. I have a gash on my left temple where Sean's punch cut me, and the skin around it is swollen and turning purple. Somewhere in the melee, my nose started to bleed, and my upper lip is now caked with dried blood and feels as if it's been cemented to my nostrils. There is another bruise still forming on the back of my right jaw, an inch or so below the ear, and a disturbing clicking sound every time I open and shut my mouth.

"You got off easy," Wayne says, waving dismissively. "If Brad hadn't stepped in, they'd be pulling your vital organs out from under tables."

"Jesus," I say. "I don't know if you could have stood so much fun in one night."

Wayne laughs and leans against the window, his eyes closed. "Still, it was something, him standing up for you like that."

"That it was," I say quietly, the hot balloon in my throat threatening to burst. "So what's the deal with Sean, anyway?"

The deal, according to Wayne, is this: Sean spent the summer after graduating high school like many of his jock peers, playing playground ball all day and getting drunk and engaging in a variety of wanton destruction at night. At the time, he was dating Suzie Carmichael, a Cougars groupie whose famously endowed body had achieved a certain measure of underground fame and scrupulous documentation, both written and illustrated, on the boys' bathroom walls. One night, after countless beers, Sean was driving Suzie up to the Bush River Falls to screw in his car when he missed a turn and crashed head-on into a large ash tree at the side of the road. With the booze in his belly and sex on his mind, he was presumably driving at a fairly high speed. High enough, anyway, for the impact to uniformly crush Suzie Carmichael's legendary body and kill her instantly. She bore the brunt of the crash, as Sean had been instinctively turning away from the tree just before impact.

Sean emerged with bruises, lacerations, some cracked ribs, and two broken legs, effectively ending his college basketball career before it ever got started. Sheriff Muser called in some favors to quash the drunk driving charges, and Sean's father's shadier connections were called in to silence Suzie's grief-stricken parents when they objected. For a while, it was all any-one in the town could talk about, but like all small-town scandals, it ran its course and then faded into the multicolored backdrop of town lore. Without basketball, Sean could find no compelling reason to go to college, opting instead to stay in the Falls and further develop his burgeoning reputation as a mean drunk. He went into his father's demolition business, and there, at least, he seemed to find some measure of satisfaction, having always harbored a particular affinity for destruction. One night while getting sloshed at the Halftime Pub, an ex-Cougar named Bill Tuttle, who'd played a few years before Sean's time, in a cataclysmic lapse in judgment pointed out that Sean's team in its senior year had been responsible for ending the Cougars' unparalleled championship streak. It took four guys to pull Sean off of him, and by then he'd already cracked Tuttle's skull. The sheriff had no strings left to pull where Sean was concerned, and he ended up serving seven months of a three-year sentence for assault and battery.

"He said he found Jesus in prison," Wayne says with a smirk. "And apparently Jesus was advocating body art and weight lifting, because Sean just came back bigger and meaner than before. That was about five years ago. Since then he's had some other scrapes with the law, but he's still a Cougar, so he's gotten away with murder."

"I hope you're speaking figuratively," I say, raising my eye-brows. "About the murder part, I mean."

"I am, but just barely."

"Swell."

"You're fucked," Wayne says, nodding agreeably. "But this is boring. Have you seen Carly yet?"

I look over at him, but his eyes are still closed. "What does that have to do with anything?"

"We've changed subjects."

"Oh."

"Why not give her a call?" Wayne says. "She's definitely heard you're here by now."

"Since all of my other reunions seem to be going so smoothly," I say.

"I haven't hit you yet." He opens his eyes. "Turn right here, on Overlook."

"Why?"

"I'll show you."

I make the turn and drive about halfway down the block before Wayne orders me to stop. "This is where she lives now," he says in a hushed voice, pointing out his window at the small Tudor we're idling in front of.

"Is that right," I say neutrally.

"She runs the newspaper."

"I know."

"She's divorced."

That throws me. "I didn't know she'd gotten married."

Wayne nods solemnly. "Real asshole. Not from around here. He beat her up."

"No way," I say, my efforts at nonchalance falling by the wayside. Wayne's words hit me like a battering ram to the chest. "She'd never have stood for that."

"Well, she did the first time. The second time, she ended up in the hospital."

"Oh, shit," I say softly, feeling my eyes go wet.

"And then some," Wayne says.

Something in his voice clues me in. "You guys are close."

"Yup."

"So, she knew you were coming over to see me tonight."

"She was supposed to meet up with us. She must have had second thoughts." He turns to look at me. "I suppose that was for the best, seeing how the evening turned out."

"What . . . does she think of me?" I ask him hesitantly.

"She's utterly indecipherable when it comes to that," he says, closing his eyes again. "I think you'd better get me home, man. I'm starting to fade."

I let my glance linger for one moment longer on Carly's house. The knowledge that she's in there, that we are separated only by a few feet and the stucco and brick of her house, fills me with a nervous energy that makes me restless. The house is dark, but there's a faint glow from behind the blinds in one of the upstairs bedrooms. Carly's bedroom. She's curled up in bed, reading a book or watching television. What might she be watching? *60 Minutes?* The news? Or maybe something requiring no thought, like *Dawson's Creek* or a *Seinfeld* rerun? I wonder what she looks like now. I pull away slowly, executing a three-point turn to head back the way we came.

A few blocks before we get to Wayne's house, I hear a change in his breathing and turn to find him staring out the window, weeping quietly. I look back at the road, feeling like an intruder. He opens his mouth as if to say something, but all that emerges is a series of sharp, anguished sobs that rack his frail frame, and he makes no effort to wipe away the shockingly robust tears that run in slow motion down his face. "I know," I say impotently, reaching over to pat his bony, trembling arm. "I know, man." An ironic choice of words for someone who doesn't have a clue. In the intermittent glow of the passing streetlights, I see Wayne's face, wildly contorted in grief, his eyes burning in torment behind the cascading tears, the face of a sad little boy. We drive around like that for a while, through the dark, still streets of the Falls, heedless of street signs or direction, until his cries gradually subside. "It sucks," he says to me hoarsely, the words struggling to find a foothold in his short, heaving breaths. "It sucks like you wouldn't believe." I nod mutely, keeping my hand on his upper arm. After another few minutes he closes his eyes and falls into a fitful sleep. I drive around aimlessly while he sleeps, hypnotized by the rhythmic bumping of my tires against the road. After about an hour I look up, registering for the first time the alien territory stretched out before me, and realize that I've crossed the town line and am no longer in Bush Falls. As if I've been thinking, much as I did seventeen years earlier, that escape is actually a viable option.

I let myself into Wayne's parents' house with keys that I find in his jacket pocket and quietly carry him upstairs to his bedroom. He feels terribly light, almost hollow, sleeping in my arms, and I have a momentary vision of the virus, a pink, hairy, corpulent thing inside of him, throbbing and dripping ectoplasm as it devours him from the inside. I lay him down on his bed and slide off his jacket, wrapping him up in the cotton comforter that lies folded across the foot of the bed. On a collapsible bridge table next to his bed, I see a vast collection of prescription pill bottles and a pitcher of ice water, the cubes already half melted. Under the table are an oxygen tank and a breath mask, and on the other side of the bed a large air purifier hums. Other than these sad additions, Wayne's room appears pretty much as I remember it from high school. I locate two copies of *Bush Falls* in his bookcase and have just pulled one off the shelf when his mother comes to the door in a bathrobe. It is well past one in the morning, but it doesn't appear as if she's been sleeping. I remember Wayne once telling me that his mother reads the Bible into the wee hours every night.

"Who's there?" she whispers. Her gray hair is tied back in a tight bun, and her thin, colorless lips crinkle and purse as she squints into the darkness.

"It's just me, Mrs. Hargrove. Joe."

"Joseph Goffman?" she says, walking into the room. "What on earth?"

"I'm just bringing Wayne home," I say. "He needed a little help."

She looks down at Wayne, who hasn't budged since I lay him down, and seems about to move forward with the intention of straightening his blankets and then, as if she's thought the better of it, stops and remains standing where she is, her hands folded rigidly against her chest. "He has no business being out and about like that," she says with a frown.

"He just wanted some fresh air."

"Fresh air," she repeats, raising her eyebrows scornfully. Then she notices the book I'm holding. "So, you're a famous author now," she says in the same tone she might have used to say "So, you're a convicted pedophile."

"I guess so," I say.

"Well," she says disdainfully. "You won't find me reading that trash."

"If you haven't read it, how do you know it's trash?"

"I heard about it," she declares gravely. "And believe me, hearing was plenty."

"Well," I say, placing the book back on the shelf and heading for the door, "I guess that's my cue."

I head down the stairs, now noticing the crucifix and assorted Jesus artwork that occupies every available bit of wall space. Wayne's mother follows behind me, muttering something quietly to herself. As I reach the front door, she calls my name softly. I turn to face her. "Yes?" I say.

"I'm praying for your father," she says.

"And what about your son?"

She frowns and looks heavenward. "I pray for his soul."

"He's not dead yet," I say. "I think he could use a little less praying and a little more compassion."

"He has sinned against the Lord. He's paying the price."

"And I'm sure the Bible has nothing but praise for the woman who denies her suffering child a mother's love in his final days."

She flashes me a dark look, her eyes filled with the defiant righteousness of the dogmatically pious. "When was the last time you read the Bible, Joe?"

"You won't catch me reading that trash," I say. "I've heard about it, and believe me, hearing was plenty."

I need a Band-Aid. It's just past two-thirty in the morning when I finally stagger into my father's house, reeling and bone-weary from what feels like the longest day of my life. I locate some Neosporin and gauze wipes in the medicine chest in the downstairs bathroom, but there are no Band-Aids to be found, and the cut on my left temple is stinging and wet in the open air. Then I remember that Band-Aids were always kept in the medicine cabinet above the hamper in my parents' bathroom, and this simple recollection unleashes a flood of half-formed images from my youth that leave me disoriented and short of breath. I pause for a few seconds, waiting for the chaos in my belly to abate, and then head upstairs.

My father's bedroom hasn't changed very much, with its oak bedroom set and dirt-colored carpet, the faded velvet reading chair buried under stacks of old magazines and newspapers. My mother's dressing table sits in its place, her assorted moisturizers and perfume bottles still standing on the small oriental tray against the mirror, untouched for over twenty years. If I were to open the drawers of her dresser, I know I would find her blouses, scarves, and undergarments neatly folded and waiting for her. I know that because in the first few years after her death, I visited those drawers frequently, occasionally taking out one of her scarves to smell the lingering traces of her perfume. There is no reason to think my father has emptied her dresser in the intervening years. His house has become a tomb in which the solitary remains of what was once a family are preserved, untouched by time and the various other elements that ripped us to shreds.

Band-Aids are best applied by somebody else. There's

something about pulling off those white plastic tabs by myself that always feels pathetic, seems to emphasize the fact that there's no one in the world to do it for me. With a sigh, I lean into the mirror to plant the adhesive strip on my skull, and something reflecting behind me catches my eye. In the corner of the mirror, I can see the door to my father's bedroom, half closed, and on the back of it hangs a framed poster. I turn around and confirm, to my great surprise, that it's the poster from last year's theatrical release of *Bush Falls*. The artwork depicts a somewhat distant swimming pool framed in the bare spread legs and bikini-clad bottom of a woman standing with her back to the camera. Standing waist-deep in the water between those legs is Leonardo DiCaprio, who stares up at the unseen top half of the woman in goofy, exaggerated wonder. Beneath the photo, in a grand white script, are the words BUSH FALLS followed by the ridiculous tag line THE SUMMER JUST GOT A LITTLE BIT HOTTER. Owen laughed uncontrollably for a good ten minutes when he first saw the poster. "Oh, my Lord!" he exclaimed dramatically in the fake Southern accent he always trots out for just this sort of occasion. "That is just too precious!"

"It's cheesy," I complained, irked by his condescension.

"Deliciously cheesy," he corrected me, and then collapsed into another paroxysm of full-bellied laughter. I was less than amused, wondering what Lucy Haber would think when she saw that poster.

And now here it is, hanging inexplicably in my father's bedroom. I stare at it intently, as if I might somehow discern the meaning of its presence by forensic analysis. Why does a father hang up the poster of a movie based on his son's novel? The only answer that I can come up with, dumbfounding as it is, is pride. My father was proud of me. The town was in an uproar about the book when it first came out, the local papers filled with furious editorials and defensive denials from all involved in the events described. When the movie came out two years later, dozens of newsmagazines and entertainment tabloids reignited the hullabaloo as they came in droves to do stories on the town and track down the people behind the movie's twisted characters. I was viciously derided by every person who managed to speak to a reporter. Sheriff Muser even tried to organize a class action lawsuit against me. And in the midst of all that furor, my father, with whom I'd barely spoken in ten years, framed and hung the movie poster in his bedroom, where he could see it every night as he climbed into bed.

With mounting apprehension, I run downstairs and into my father's den. There, beside the trophy case and framed basketball awards, both his and Brad's, stands an Ikea book-case with glass doors, in which I discover fifteen hardcover versions of *Bush Falls* and another twenty or so paperbacks with the movie poster pictured on the cover. Lying on top of the bookcase is a wide, flat book, which turns out to be a scrapbook, the kind they sell in stationery stores. The binding cracks loudly as I open it with shaking hands. On each page, carefully centered and glued under the protective plastic sheets, are a wide assortment of reviews of *Bush Falls*, every-thing from the *New York Times* to *Entertainment Weekly* as well as *The Minuteman* and some other regional papers. On the top left corner of one of the reviews, I notice a small im-print that reads "VMT Media Services." He actually hired a clipping service to track my press. My legs become rubber, and I sit down hard on the small couch against the wall, still clutching the scrapbook in my hands. The couch smells of my father's aftershave and pipe tobacco. "What the hell?" I say out loud as a tear runs down my cheek and lands on the brown faux leather of the scrapbook. A second tear soon follows, and then a third. I stare at those three wet spots on the cover, won-dering what the hell they mean. Before I've come up with any-thing, though, sleep is on me like shrink-wrap, and the last thing I hear is the sound of the scrapbook slipping out of my fingers and landing with a gentle thud on the carpeted floor.

# fifteen

I get my first flying book at around eight the next morning. One doesn't instantly identify the sound of a flying book. The light, fluttering sound of airborne pages is followed by a jarring thud as the book caroms off the living room picture window and lands in the front yard. I roll off the couch in my father's den, nauseous and without any discernible center of gravity, and peer groggily out the living room window, expecting to see another dazed or broken bird lying bewildered on the lawn. Instead, I am greeted by my own face smiling pretentiously up at me from the dust jacket of a hardcover copy of *Bush Falls*, which lies facedown and spread open, the upper portion of the book's spine indented from its collision with the window. The street in front of the house is completely deserted.

There is the sound of soft breathing behind me, and I turn around to find Jared sleeping on the living room couch in jeans and a black T-shirt that says "Bowling for Soup." I don't remember seeing him there when I came in last night, although that can hardly be considered conclusive. "Hey, Jared," I mumble. Four beds upstairs, and we both slept on couches.

"Hey," he grunts back, not opening his eyes.

"You'll be late for school."

He opens one eye. "Doesn't really pay to go, then, does it?" The eye closes.

He'll get no argument from me. I head upstairs for a shower, pausing only long enough to doff my shorts and perform some spastic dry heaves over the toilet. The light hits my eyes like needles, so I shower in the dark, leaning against the cold tiles in an effort to wake myself up. The hot water pummels my scalp soothingly, cascading in torrents down my face and shoulders, and my mind wanders. I think about Wayne and then my father and the scrapbook I found last night. It's unbelievable to me that before yesterday they and the Falls were such a remote part of my life, distant memories more than anything else. Now they threaten to consume me, the protective barrier of the last seventeen years dissipating like a mirage.

I step dripping into my bedroom, feeling hungover and old, to find Jared clipping his toenails on my bed. "Look at you," he says with an inquisitive smirk, taking in my battered face and bruised ribs.

"You look. I'm too tired."

"You know," he continues disinterestedly. "Statistically speaking, blocking at least some punches in a fight will usually lead to a more favorable outcome."

"I'll take that under advisement."

There's another bang from downstairs, and we both look out the window to see a green station wagon disappearing around the corner. On the lawn there is now a second copy of *Bush Falls* splayed out fairly close to the first one. "What's up with that?" Jared asks, not concerned, just mildly curious, and then leans back to resume clipping his toenails.

My cell phone rings, and Jared picks it up off the night

table and tosses it to me. It's Owen, calling to see how things are going. I update him on my father's condition, and he clucks and murmurs in all the right places. "And how has it been otherwise?" he asks pointedly. "You know, your return to the Falls?"

"Pretty crazy."

"I knew it!" he exclaims gleefully. "Do tell, do tell."

I quickly relate all of the events of the past day, listening to Owen's delighted gasps while Jared watches me, listening raptly, smirking when I include the incident of his coitus interruptus. "So let's review," Owen says when I'm done, not even trying to conceal his merriment. "In the last twenty-four hours, you've returned to your hometown, where essentially everybody hates you, you've been reunited, however awkwardly, with your estranged family, you've walked in on a sexual liaison, gotten in trouble with the law, been assaulted on two separate occasions, and met up with an ailing friend and gotten drunk with him. Am I leaving anything out?"

I consider telling him about the flying books, but I haven't gotten my mind wrapped around that one yet, so I leave it out. "That's pretty much it," I say.

Owen whistles softly. "I wonder what you're going to do today."

"You make it sound like I planned all of this."

"*Au contraire, mon frère.* For the first time in god knows how long, it's spinning wonderfully out of your control."

"And what the hell does that mean?"

But Owen has to go. "Listen, I'm late for something. We'll talk later."

"Wait."

"What?"

"Did you finish the manuscript?" I ask hesitantly.

"It's interesting that you refer to it as 'the' manuscript," Owen says. "Most writers, passionate about their work, will always refer to it in the possessive, as in 'my' manuscript."

"What's your point?"

"It seems you're already distancing yourself from your work."

"Oh, fuck off," I say. "Did you read it or not?"

"I did."

"And?"

"I have," he says, inhaling as he searches for the right word, "issues."

"So I gathered," I say dejectedly. "What do we do now?"

Owen sighs. "Well, we could make some changes and I'm sure I could still sell it, but I'm not convinced your interests are best served that way."

I allow the implications of that to sink in for a moment. "It's really bad, isn't it?"

"You're a good writer, Joe."

"Oh, for Christ's sake. Just say it sucked."

"If I thought it sucked, I would tell you it sucked." Owen takes another deep breath. "Listen, we've discussed this. You know the second one's always a bitch. There's too much riding on it. It's almost worth writing just to get it the fuck out of the way."

"So we just forget about it and move on to book number three?"

"That idea is not without merit."

"And why won't book three be just as bad? I can't even figure out where this one went wrong."

"Ah, but I already have," Owen says grandly. "That's why you pay me the big bucks."

"Would you care to enlighten me?"

"I could, but muddling through on your own is a critical journey for you as a writer."

"You are so full of shit," I say, annoyed.

"It's true, it's true," he admits.

"Then what good are you?"

"That, my friend, is a whole other conversation," he says with a chuckle. "I'll call you back."

I snap the phone shut and toss it onto the bed in disgust. "Problems?" Jared says.

"Just the usual." I notice his T-shirt again. I know I'll regret it, but I ask anyway. "What's 'Bowling for Soup'?"

"A band."

"Never heard of them," I say. This doesn't appear to shock my nephew in the least. And there it is, out in the open for all to see. I am officially an old fart. "What kind of band are they?" I ask, determined to prove that I'm at least generally up to speed.

"Kind of a mixture of pop and SoCal punk."

"SoCal?"

"Southern California," he explains. "Take the punk rock from your generation, like the Ramones or the Sex Pistols—"

"They were before my time," I point out weakly.

"Whatever," he says. "Anyway, take that stuff, add better musicians and production values and better songwriting, and that's basically SoCal punk."

"Like Blink 182," I say.

"Like Blink before they sold out," Jared says, wrapping up his toenail clippings in a tissue and tossing it into the waste-basket behind me, and for a brief instant I hate him.

"Fenix TX?" I try.

Jared looks up at me, surprised, and I feel a little better. "You listen to Fenix?"

"Doesn't everybody?"

My cell phone rings again while I'm tying my shoes. "Could you get that?" I say.

Jared flips open the phone, and even from where I'm crouched across the room, I can hear Nat's voice shouting through the plastic. "Oops," he says with a grin, leaning forward to hand me the phone. I listen for a few more seconds, and then she hangs up. "Man," Jared says. "Does anybody like you?"

"You like me, don't you?"

He grins sadly at me and says, "I don't count, man."

\* \*

My arrival makes the front page of *The Minuteman,* above the fold, no less. Jared has retrieved the paper from its plastic blue mailbox at the edge of the driveway and now tosses it onto the counter in the kitchen while I'm mixing some Folgers into a mug. "You're famous again," he says with his trademark grin. "Controversial Author Returns" is the headline in the top left corner. Below it is a grainy reproduction of my book jacket author photo. With mounting unease, I sit down and read the article.

> After a 17-year absence, author Joseph Goffman returned to Bush Falls yesterday. Goffman's best-selling novel, *Bush Falls,* angered many residents here when it was released in 1999. The book was loosely based on a number of incidents alleged to have taken place in Goffman's senior year at Bush Falls High. Although the book is classified as fiction, the author's use of these incidents, as well as characters clearly based on well-known residents of the Falls, caused a great deal of controversy when the novel was first published. Many locals viewed the book as nothing short of libel, written with deliberate malice and the intent to damage reputations. The novel and its author were widely condemned in raging editorials in this newspaper and on local radio and television stations as well. The recent film version, starring Leonardo DiCaprio and Kirsten Dunst, has done nothing to assuage the collective anger felt toward Mr. Goffman.
>
> Coach Thomas Dugan was one of those singled out for a negative portrayal in the novel. "I don't care about what he wrote about me," commented Dugan at the time. "But the condescending, offensive way in which he wrote about our beloved team and its history, which has meant so much to so many of the good people of this town throughout the years, is unforgivable. He's insulted every boy who ever played for the Cougars, and all of the good people who support them."

"This is a guy who's gotten rich by lying about the people in this town," said Deputy Sheriff Dave Muser, a former classmate of Goffman's who feels he personally suffered from a negative portrayal in the novel. "It's a slap in all of our faces that he thinks he can just walk back into the Falls. He should know he's no longer welcome here."

Alice Lippman, whose women's book club meets monthly at Paperbacks Plus, was similarly outraged. "We selected *Bush Falls* when it first came out, and I don't think there was a single member of the book club who wasn't morally outraged by it. I hope I run into Mr. Goffman, so that I can tell him in person what an awful, destructive man he is."

Goffman's father, local businessman Arthur Goffman, suffered a stroke this past Monday while playing basketball in the Cougars alumni league. Although father and son are reportedly estranged, it is his father's condition that is presumably the reason for Goffman's return to the Falls.

There is no byline, and I wonder if Carly wrote the article. If not, as editor in chief she'd at least have reviewed it before it went to press. I scan the article carefully, searching for any slant, any choice of words that might render some clue as to what her attitude toward me might be, but I come up empty. I discard the paper and, for the first time since my return, really allow myself to think about Carly, something I've been deliberately avoiding up until now. I would be hard-pressed to conjure up the images of women I dated a few weeks ago, but reconstructing Carly's face on the canvas of my mind takes absolutely no effort.

And now, sitting in my father's kitchen, I recall easily the taste of her kisses, the expression on her face as I clumsily worked to undo the buttons of her blouse that first time, a delightful combination of naked desire and affectionate humor. I told her I loved her, my chest quivering from the absolute truth of it all, and she kissed me deeply and said it right back. We lasted eight months, barely a pinprick on the overall time line, but when you're eighteen, time isn't nearly as crotchety and relentless as it becomes soon thereafter, and eight months is nothing less than a lifetime.

I push myself away from the table and head outside, stepping over the battered copy of *Bush Falls* lying faceup on the front walk, resolved to leave the books where they've landed. I'm opening the car door when I see that sometime during the night someone keyed my Mercedes, a handful of nasty, jagged streaks that traverse the car door in a clumsy, serpentine path, decimating the paint job. I study the scarred metal for a moment, the indecipherable hieroglyphics of vandalism, then climb into the car, taking pains not to disturb my bruised rib cage any more than is absolutely necessary. I drive off, still thinking about how far I've unwittingly drifted from the boy I used to be and wondering at how little I have to show for it.

# *sixteen*

## 1986

Things quieted down for a while after the copy machine incident, but Sammy remained inconsolable. I didn't know
whether he was despondent over Wayne or still smarting
from an assful of Xerox glass, but he walked the halls between classes with a resolute glumness, his normally irre-
pressible smile nowhere in evidence. He no longer broke
into little spontaneous dance routines or serenaded people
with Springsteen lyrics. And while Sean and Mouse no
longer attacked him physically, they continued to taunt him
regularly. *Hey, cutie, how's your ass healing? Don't worry—you'll
be bent over again in no time!*

Sammy, for his part, seemed utterly committed to being
victimized, submitting to each new barb with a sense of
tragic resignation, a slave to what he perceived as his im-
mutable destiny. Something about his determined lack of
resistance, the stoic manner in which he embraced his

suffering, was taken as a challenge by Sean, who became obsessively determined to get a rise out of Sammy, to see him fight back. The two of them became helplessly entangled in a tragic cycle where Sammy's submission served only to enrage Tallon, escalating the level of his cruelty, which in turn caused Sammy to retreat inwardly even more.

Although I tried to be a friend to him, it wasn't very long before Sammy's predicament started to suffocate me. I resented him for so obstinately remaining a loser in the face of my best efforts to help him out. Besides, I had Carly now, and there was only so much time in the day, so much room in my brain. Later I would tell myself that there was nothing I could have done anyway, and that might have been true. Sammy seemed fatalistically determined to follow the course that was charted for him. But there was no getting away from the fact that as time went on, I deliberately saw less and less of him, simply because something in his abject misery made me feel inexplicably guilty, as if I were somehow responsible for his predicament, and I didn't want to be guilty or responsible. Things were finally going my way, and I would be damned if I wasn't going to enjoy myself.

I had a girlfriend and a best friend, which might not sound like much, but it was everything I'd ever wanted. The simple act of walking the school grounds during lunch holding Carly's hand, on display for all to see, filled me with an overwhelming sense of well-being the likes of which I'd never experienced. We would sit together in the cafeteria, stealing little kisses, occasionally sneaking into the deserted backstage area of the auditorium when kissing just wasn't going to cut it.

Wayne was leading the Cougars in scoring that year, and Carly and I went to every game, home and away, where we cheered him on comically, like rabid fans. It felt so good, sitting in the stands with Carly, laughing, screaming, hugging, and throwing high fives whenever Wayne scored, that I forgot how much I'd hated Cougars games up until that point. They no longer felt like a glaring reminder of my failure as an athlete, but just one more place to go and enjoy being a boyfriend. After the games, we'd take Wayne out for a victory dinner, and the three of us would hang out until closing time, giddy from victory, our voices hoarse from screaming and laughing. Later, we'd drop Wayne off and then drive down to the falls, Carly's hands already rubbing and grabbing at me as I drove, her tongue in my ear as she told me to get there already.

I'd always been under the impression that there were nice girls and sexy girls. Carly was an honor student, the editor of the school newspaper, and a favorite among the faculty at Bush Falls High. But she was also capable of grabbing my hand and sliding it down into her opened jeans and pressing up urgently against it, moaning without a trace of self-consciousness as she bit down on my lower lip hard enough to draw blood.

Carly spent the first half hour of homeroom every morning scribbling copiously in a worn leather-bound journal. She was terribly concerned with the general transience of things and the imperfect, random nature of memory. It was the one compulsion in her otherwise laid-back disposition, this notion that particular feelings and thoughts could be irretrievably lost to the vagaries of time and distance. "This is the age," she explained to me once as we walked home from school, "when we're the purest forms of ourselves we'll ever be. We haven't been complicated by everything yet. I want to keep a clear record of who I am, so that down the road I'll be able to see who I was. Maybe I can avoid losing myself completely."

Although I admired her larger consciousness, there was something vaguely troubling about it, as if she were an oracle discerning ominous portents to which I remained oblivious. "But you'll always be you," I said. "Won't you?"

She sighed, biting her lip pensively. "Things happen," she said. "Small things and large things, and they just keep changing you, little by little, until there's no trace of who you used to be. If I get lost, this journal will be like a record of who I was, a trail of bread crumbs to find my way back."

"In that case, could you keep track of me in there too?" I said. "It would be nice to know there's someone looking out for me if I ever get lost."

"But what if we're not together anymore?" she asked, ever the practical one.

"Then it will mean at least one of us is lost," I said. "Just get me a copy of that journal, and it will lead me right back to you."

She stopped walking and hugged me, pressing her forehead against mine, her eyes closed. "It would be nice if it really worked that way," she murmured.

"Stranger things have happened," I said.

"All the same," she said. "I think it'd be better if we just stayed together."

I kissed her nose lightly and said, "Deal."

# seventeen

Brad and I resume our awkward vigil over my father's bedside as if the previous night's events never happened. He takes in my battered face and bloodshot eyes, and I can see a sentence forming behind his eyes, but some internal censor, the sort I sorely lack, mercifully stops the words before they can get to his mouth. He simply nods and remains silent. We sip at our vending machine coffee, thumb through magazines purchased at the sundry shop downstairs, and take turns offering the odd, flimsy conversational gambit that invariably tapers off into an embarrassed silence, encased by the enduring clockwork hiss of the respirator. The nurse's periodic visits to exchange the full plastic catheter bag for an empty one or record my father's vital statistics are welcome breaks in the monotony, providing us with an outlet, however brief, for superficial inquiry and discussion. Brad arrived alone today, offering no explanation for Cindy's conspicuous absence, and I know better than to ask. If the past twenty-four hours have taught me anything, it's that everything is a trap.

At around one, Brad yawns and announces that he has to go check on something at the factory. He scribbles his cell phone number on the back of a magazine in case anything should happen and then heads out, brow furrowed, lost in his own cloudy ruminations. I am both sorry and undeniably relieved to see him go.

Brad's been gone maybe ten minutes when the door swings open and Coach Dugan steps into the room. Every organ in my body contracts at the sight of him. After last night's episode, his presence here is impossible to process, and I just sit up in my chair and stare at him.

"Joseph," he says, taking off his baseball cap as he enters the room.

"Hello, Coach," I say, hoping my voice doesn't sound as shaky as it feels. Dugan is one of those men whose very presence commands attention, even in a crowded gymnasium. In the confines of the hospital room, he is a giant, much too large and powerful for so small a venue.

He walks over to the bed and stares down at my father. "He doesn't look very good," he says. "What do the doctors say?"

"It's pretty bad," I say.

Dugan grunts. "He's a good man. And if he knows he's in a coma, I'll bet he's pissed about it. He deserves better than this." His words seem to contain a shadow of rebuke in them, but I can't quite pin it down. It's too weird to be engaged in a conversation with him at all. Dugan's deep, hoarse voice is designed to address teams and groups, and there's something overwhelming about being addressed by him on a personal level. "Where's Brad?"

"He had to run over to the office for a few minutes."

"You'll tell him I stopped by."

"Sure."

To my surprise, Dugan leans forward and plants a dry kiss on my father's temple. Then he straightens up and steps over to the door, pulls it open, and turns to me. "Sean Tallon can be a dangerous man," he says. "He's somewhat unstable. If I were you, I'd steer clear of him."

"A bit late for that, don't you think?" I say, indicating my bruised face.

The coach shakes his head and squints at me like I'm an idiot. "He's capable of much worse."

"Well then, I guess I owe you one for intervening when you did last night."

"I did that for Brad," Dugan snarls at me. "He has enough to contend with without Tallon sending him to the emergency room."

"It looked to me like he was holding his own."

Dugan gives me a withering look. "I forgot who I was talking to," he says.

"And who's that?"

"Someone who doesn't have a fucking clue." He steps out of the room, closing the door behind him. I'm not surprised to discover that even in the heavily air-conditioned room, I'm sweating slightly.

"Just you and me now, Dad," I say somewhat self-consciously, and sit back with an *Esquire* magazine. A little while later I move on to *Newsweek,* and then, somewhere in the middle of *Us Weekly,* I doze off. I dream about Carly, as I often do, something warm and sweet and ultimately sad, and wake up to find my father staring at me. I sit up with a start, my elbow upsetting the Styrofoam cup resting on the windowsill, which falls to the floor, splattering my Rockports and the cuffs of my khakis with tepid coffee. "Dad," I say, my voice still thick with sleep. "It's me, Joe. Can you hear me?"

There is no response, but his stare, while somewhat dull, appears to contain some fragile semblance of clarity. I grab his hand, so much bigger and rougher than my own, and give it a soft squeeze. The hand remains limp, but I now see that his eyes are opened wider, his thick eyebrows raised inquisitively in two congruous arcs. I reach over him, rising slowly on my feet, afraid of breaking the spell, and thumb the nurses' call switch repeatedly. His eyes never leave mine, even as I move, and when I return to the edge of my seat, there is a large, bulbous tear, trembling and bulging as it forms on the red membrane of the inside corner of his left eye. The tear achieves critical mass and descends in a lazy diagonal across his cheek, being absorbed into his pasty skin as it goes, until it finally fades just shy of his sideburn. "It's okay, Dad," I say dumbly. "It's going to be okay." I reach for the call switch again and press it frantically. "Just stay with me. Someone will be here in a minute." But even as I say it, I can see his eyelids starting to close again, his eyeballs rolling upward in his skull. "Dad!" I shout at him, but his eyes remain closed, which is how the nurses find him when they come scurrying in a few moments later.

Dr. Krantzler, the young, tired-looking resident who shows up soon thereafter, reviews the folded rolls of printouts from the EKG machine and seems utterly unimpressed. He quizzes me for a moment, his eyebrows never once falling from their skeptical perch. "I'm not necessarily saying you didn't see what you saw," he says, although that's clearly his implication. "But there have been no fluctuations on any of his vitals. And you did say you'd been sleeping."

"What does that have to do with anything?"

He smiles condescendingly and rubs his eyes. "It's not unreasonable to think that given the monotony of waiting and the emotional stress you're under, you dreamed you saw him open his eyes, or experienced a brief optical illusion. It's quite common, actually."

"I know what I saw," I say hotly.

"Well then," he says huffily, backing out of the room, "let me know if you see it again."

I call Brad's cell phone and he arrives twenty minutes later, slightly out of breath, despite my repeated disclaimers that medical science has not embraced my version of events. He looks at me intently as I retell my story, frowning and shaking his head in frustration. "Why didn't you call the doctor immediately?" he says.

"I rang for a nurse," I repeat defensively for what seems like the twentieth time. "I was scared to leave him."

"Did you talk to him?"

"Yes."

"Did he give any sign that he knew what was going on?"

"He seemed to be somewhat aware." I don't mention the lone teardrop that I witnessed. A section of my brain is still replaying that in a continuous loop, and it feels to me like something personal between my father and me. Besides, I'm starting to get pissed. Brad seems thoroughly convinced that things would have happened differently if he'd been here, as if it's a direct result of my general failings as a son that our father has slipped away for a second time. "Listen," I say. "He opened his eyes and he closed them. That was it. There was no time for me to do anything else."

"I should have been here," Brad says, shaking his head and turning away in disgust. My newfound ambivalence toward him is fast dissolving into the old, familiar resentment as I come face-to-face with the older brother I remember, arrogantly superior and egocentric.

"I'm sure the sight of your face would have made all the difference," I say sarcastically.

"At least it would have been a familiar face," Brad says bitterly.

And there it is. A day late, but perfectly timed just the same. "Nice," I say, heading for the door, my voice uncharacteristically thick and bending under the weight of some as yet undefined emotion. Brad snorts, but makes no effort to stop me.

I walk quickly down the hall, struggling to regain my equilibrium even as I feel the improbable tears coming. I find my way to an abandoned stairwell and sit down with my head in my trembling hands, wondering what the hell is going on with me. Things are coming apart inside me, tearing loose from their foundations and scraping my innards as they fall. I need a plan, something to give me direction, but I can think only as far as the parking lot, which is where I'm headed when I run into Carly in the lobby.

An old girlfriend is a gun in your belly. It's no longer loaded, so when you see her, all you feel is the hollow mechanical click in your gut, and possibly the ghost of an echo, sense memory from when it used to carry live rounds. Occasionally, though, there's a bullet you missed, lying dormant in its overlooked chamber, and when that trigger gets pulled, the unexpected gunshot is deafening even as the forgotten bullet rips its way through the tissue and muscle of your midsection and out into the light of day. Seeing Carly is like that. Even though we haven't spoken in almost ten years, it's an explosion, and in that one instant every memory, every feeling, comes flooding back as fresh as if it were yesterday.

She's carrying a small, elegant bouquet of tulips and baby's breath, and as soon as I see her, I know she's here to see me. She hasn't yet noticed me, and I have to fight the overpowering impulse to duck back into the stairwell and hide until my stomach stops its nervous acrobatics. Dressed in a white pullover blouse that's tucked into a short gray skirt emphasizing her trim waist, she looks pretty much as I remember her, the only change being her hair, which she always wore short and off her face. Now it hangs at a luxurious shoulder length, framing her face and somehow emphasizing its simple, graceful aesthetics. When she sees me, her tentative smile falters as she takes in my bruises and reddened eyes, still a bit raw from the absurd crying fit I just had. For a minute it appears as if she's ready to turn on her heel and flee, but she waves the bouquet at me, her face breaking into a small, wry grin as she approaches. There seems to be some genuine warmth behind her smile, and as I look at her, registering with satisfaction that her eyes still contain those little flecks of yellow, I feel a familiar flutter in my chest, a highly irrational burst of euphoria. Before I know what I'm doing, I step forward and hug her tightly.

I want the hug to last forever. I want it to be one of those intense, slowly building movie hugs that start out awkwardly but then, on some nonverbal cue, come into their own as the feelings behind them are suddenly released, and we just melt into each other, all the distance and bad feelings between us unable to withstand the epic nature of our universal connection. A nothing-matters-but-this-very-instant hug. Within a second or two, though, it becomes evident that this particular hug has maxed out at awkward.

Carly exhales softly, clearly taken aback, but recovers quickly and hugs me back. "You look great," I say, stepping back as I release her.

"You don't," she says, still grinning as she hands me the flowers.

We smile, and it's comfortable for a few seconds, just like old times, but then it gets weird, so I look away and thank her for the flowers.

"They're for your dad."

"Yes. Of course."

"Of course," she repeats awkwardly, and now I can feel every day of the years that we haven't been in touch. "How's he doing?"

"Not good," I say. Even under the auspices of a genuine medical crisis, the small talk is offensive to me, a yardstick for the immeasurable distance between us, pebbles dropped into a bottomless well while you wait to hear the faint splash from below. "I think of you," I say, my voice, so unreliable lately, tripping on the threshold of the last word. "A lot."

"I have that effect on many men," she says, and we smile, not at her joke but because of it.

"How have you been?" I say.

"Fine, I guess," she says, simultaneously shaking her head

and flexing her eyebrows at the abject worthlessness of the question. As if ten years could be encapsulated into short answer form. As if she would even want to try.

"I guess what I mean is, how are you. Really?"

"I'm good," she says. "Hit a few rough patches here and there. 'Ninety-eight was a particularly gruesome year, but these days I'm okay. And you?"

"Apparently, I'm a controversial novelist."

She laughs. "You, of all people, should know not to believe everything you read."

"Did you write the article?"

"I edited it. The first draft was . . . strongly worded."

"I can imagine," I say. "They're throwing books at my house."

Carly laughs. "That would be the book club. They met last night and decided to return their copies to you en masse. How many have you gotten?"

"Three or four."

"There'll be more."

"Hey," I say. "Did you ever get the one I sent you?" I'd sent her one of the first copies of *Bush Falls* to come off the presses.

"I did," she says. "I read the entire book that weekend."

"Oh. Good."

"I meant to call you afterward," she says, her voice trailing off.

I wave my hand dismissively. "I didn't expect you to," I lie. "I just wanted you to have one, from me."

"No, I really meant to. I was going through something then, something bad, and I don't know, nothing seemed very real to me at the time."

I nod as if I understand. "We should get together," I say. "Catch up and everything."

"Okay."

"Good. I'll call you tonight."

"Only if you want to," she says. "Don't feel obligated."

"I want to."

She considers me for a moment, and then shakes her head lightly, as if whatever she thought she'd seen has turned out to be a trick of the light. "Wayne has my number," she says. I look at her, nodding stupidly. I'm still not fully comprehending that after so many years of being canonized in my mind, this is really Carly again, standing in front of me, ever so slightly weathered but fundamentally unchanged.

"Well," she says. "I have to get back to work."

"Sure." I say her name as she starts to walk away.

"Yeah?" she says, turning back around.

I hesitate, unsure of what I'm going to say until the words are out of my mouth. "I still know you," I say.

Carly smiles, a genuine smile so heartbreakingly familiar it takes my breath away. "Joe," she says softly, "you don't know shit."

I watch the soft curves of her calves as she walks away, the smooth muscles beneath them flexing and extending with each step. I always loved her legs. She was glad to see me; I'm pretty sure of that. Of course, that doesn't really mean anything in the overall scheme of things, but maybe it does. Since I came back, my past has achieved a fresh, reckless immediacy and nothing seems completely out of the question. I sit down on one of the attached styrene chairs in the lobby, suddenly incapable of standing. What it all comes down to is this: I still love her.

Maybe.

# eighteen

I don't know where I'd been planning to go when I stormed
out of the hospital room after my argument with Brad. Probably I would have just cooled down in the cafeteria for a half
hour before going back upstairs to rejoin him. But after
speaking to Carly, sitting still to eat a soggy prewrapped tuna
sandwich is out of the question, and so is returning to the
silence of the hospital room to squirm in the harsh glare
of Brad's disapproval. Something lying dormant in me has
been stirred up by seeing Carly, and now I'm a pulsating
bundle of raw energy, twitching, antsy, and surging with
adrenaline. I am suddenly claustrophobic in the white, sterile
hallways of the hospital and feel as if I might start bouncing off the walls if I don't get out. I leave my cell phone number at the nurses' station and head outdoors, feeling strangely
keyed up. Later I'll get Carly's number from Wayne and give
her a call. We'll sit and talk, and eventually the strange-
ness will start to wear off and then . . . Well, I can't really see
past that, but it still feels exciting in an old, familiar way. In

the meantime, I decide as I climb into my car, I'll go visit Wayne.

The damp aroma of steaming vegetables and curry engulfs me as Wayne's mother lets me in with a mumbled greeting before retreating through the swinging door of her kitchen. Her frown makes it clear that I will not soon be forgiven for my borderline blasphemy the night before, and my counterfeit smile and cheery greeting make it equally clear that I couldn't care less.

Wayne is propped up in his bed on pillows, scrupulously smoking a preposterously fat joint when I enter his room. He looks pale and remarkably haggard, his eyes squinting deep in their sockets, his lips heavily chapped. When he smiles at me, his teeth look like large, jagged stalactites in his receding, colorless gums. I wonder if he's possibly lost even more weight since last night. "I really shouldn't have let you drink like that," I say, alarmed by his deathly pallor.

"You're not the boss of me," he says with a wan grin. "And besides, you're not looking so pretty yourself." I look pointedly at the fatty hanging loosely between his fingers. "For medicinal purposes," he says. "I shit you not."

I wheel over the leather desk chair and sit down at his bedside. "I don't want to be a nag, but don't you think you should be in a hospital?"

He frowns and closes his eyes. "They recommended a hospice," he says. "But I'm not going to lie in some white room, doped up on painkillers and antidepressants, waiting for the end. How would I know when I'd actually died?"

I nod sadly, for the first time fully comprehending how far along Wayne is. He isn't looking at a matter of years or even months. Weeks is probably more like it, or maybe even days. It must have taken a Herculean effort for him to get dressed and come over to see me the way he did last night, and I feel like an idiot for not having recognized the full extent of his condition. I should have driven him home and put him right back into bed. Instead, I took him out drinking.

"Have you seen Carly yet?" he says.

"Why do you always go right to that?" I say, although I've been waiting for him to ask.

"Because it's what matters."

"Other things matter too."

Wayne opens his eyes, takes a short drag on the joint, exhaling a thin gray plume of smoke as he sits up a little. "Here on the cusp of the hereafter," he declares with mock gravity, "I've been granted a certain wisdom, for lack of a better word. An ability to see things with a clarity I never before possessed. It's a parting gift, I guess. You won't be advancing to the next round, but here's a consolation prize, and thanks for playing. That sort of thing." He pauses to smile ironically at his analogy before continuing. "I suppose that not being weighed down with the normal, self-absorbed concerns over health, wealth, and the future, my brain is freed to finally see the greater truth in everything. Or in other words"—he pauses, giving me a sharp look—"what really matters."

"And what does really matter?" I ask, inhaling a whiff of secondhand ganja so strong it stings my throat.

He grins at me, not answering, and looks out the window. The sun hangs low in the purple sky over the roofs of the houses across the street, and the afternoon light is quickly fading into the soft pink hues of evening. "Do you remember that day we cut school and took the train into the city—you, me, and Carly?" he says.

I nod. "Sure. We went to the Central Park Zoo and then saw a movie."

"*Back to the Future,*" Wayne says, closing his eyes as he remembers. "We were the only ones in the theater."

I have a sudden, vivid flashback of Carly doing cartwheels down the empty theater aisle in the middle of the movie and then skipping back to our seats, her face flushed with excitement, as Wayne and I applauded. I'd forgotten about that, and, recalling it, I feel a hot lump in my throat. "We had

Kentucky Fried Chicken afterward," I say. "Brought a bucket of it on the train and stuffed our faces the whole way back." Wayne nods, smiling. "All that shit with Sammy was going on then," he says. "I was still in denial that I was actually gay. That was a tough year for me. I was scared and confused, and I had this big secret I didn't feel safe sharing with anyone. But that day we all had a great time, better than if we'd done it on a Saturday." He turns away from the window and looks at me. "The three of us laughed a lot that day. That's what I remember most. And that for one day, I completely forgot about my secret and just enjoyed myself, for the first time in ages."

I nod, feeling my eyes becoming moist. Sitting there with Wayne, I can actually recall the way that day felt, the sensation of it, and what it felt like to be me then. The crisp autumn air, the noise of Manhattan, the delightful, conspiratorial sense of being somewhere we shouldn't have been, the flush on Carly's cheeks from the cool wind as we walked through the zoo.

"That day mattered," Wayne says emphatically. "There were plenty of other days that mattered too, but not nearly as many as there should have been. I've thought about it a lot. What makes a day like that matter so much, and why there are so many less of them as we get older."

"And what's the answer?" I ask.

"It's simple, really. We were doing what we wanted to do, instead of what we expected ourselves to do." He leans back in his pillows and takes a long, greedy drag on the joint, shaking off the ash into a cup by his bedside. "I'm here to tell you," he says, his voice high and clenched from the herb, "that at the end of the day, which is where I currently reside, nothing else matters but the things that truly matter. This is nothing you didn't know before, but even though you know it, it doesn't mean you really know it. Because if you really knew it, you'd act on it, man. Shit, if I could go back now . . ."

His voice trails off, and he's quiet for so long that I think for a moment that he's fallen asleep, but then he leans forward and takes a deep breath. "I am now going to invoke a cartoon character," he announces solemnly.

I indicate the joint. "What's in that thing?"

"Don't fuck with me when I'm being wise, Joe."

"Sorry."

Wayne rolls onto his side to better face me. A smattering of gray ash falls from the tip of the joint and disappears into a fold in his comforter as he readjusts himself. "You remember the old Roadrunner cartoons, where the coyote would run off a cliff and keep going, until he looked down and happened to notice that he was running on nothing more than air?"

"Yeah."

"Well," he says. "I always used to wonder what would have happened if he'd never looked down. Would the air have stayed solid under his feet until he reached the other side? I think it would have, and I think we're all like that. We start heading out across this canyon, looking straight ahead at the thing that matters, but something, some fear or insecurity, makes us look down. And we see we're walking on air, and we panic, and turn around and scramble like hell to get back to solid ground. And if we just wouldn't look down, we could make it to the other side. The place where things matter."

"I understand what you're saying," I say. "But Carly and I were so long ago. People change."

"The things that matter don't change," Wayne says, turning the joint around and expertly placing its glowing tip into his mouth, what we used to call glow-worming. "The distance between you and them just gets progressively bigger. There's obviously still something between you two."

"Is that what she said?"

"I might be reading between the lines a little," he admits, pinching out the joint and tossing it into the cup. "But really, Joe, what the hell do you have to lose?"

We look at each other, and I can feel my eyes watering

again, although it might be from the weed smoke, which by now has permeated every corner of the room, filling the air like sweet incense. "I saw her today," I say. "At the hospital."

Wayne stares at me. "You asshole. How long were you going to let me lie here laying on all that bullshit before you told me?"

"You were on a roll."

"Fuck you," he says with a grin. "How'd it go?"

"I'm not sure. We said we'd get together."

He leans back in his pillows, looking pleased. "Excellent."

"It doesn't mean anything," I say.

"Of course not."

"Really."

"I know."

We smile at each other. "That was a great day, wasn't it?" I say.

"The best." He rolls onto his back, pulling up the blankets. "I need to get some rest," he says. "Come and see me tomorrow if you can."

"You bet," I say, getting up to leave as I consider the merits of what Wayne has just said. Maybe there is something to it, or maybe he's just stoned out of his gourd.

"Joe," he says. "Remember what happens to the coyote when he doesn't run off the cliff."

"What happens?"

Wayne's smile is crooked and ever so slightly crazed. "A fucking piano falls on him."

Downstairs, I find Mrs. Hargrove waiting for me in the living room. "I want to show you something," she says. I follow her through a set of French doors and into a den that is completely overrun with piled boxes, large and small, all unopened. A wide array of major Internet retailers is represented: The Sharper Image, Nordstrom, Amazon.com,

Circuit City, Brooks Brothers, Sears, L.L. Bean, Gap, and a host of others. I turn to Mrs. Hargrove, who is peering suspiciously at the packages, her forehead lined with deep creases of consternation.

"What is all of this?" I say.

"He buys things," she whispers to me as if revealing a dark family secret. "Day and night. He just orders things off that godforsaken computer."

"What for?"

"How should I know?" she snaps, her voice edged with hysteria. "Every day I get packages. And when they come, he doesn't want to open them. Tells me to just put them in here."

I stare in puzzlement at the jumble of cartons. There are easily forty or fifty of them, scattered in haphazard piles around the room. "Have you asked him about it?" I say.

"Of course I asked him," she practically hisses. "He has no answer. I don't think he even remembers what he ordered."

"I think this might be a symptom," I say. "Some form of dementia from the illness."

She gives me a frazzled look. "What am I supposed to do with all of this stuff?" She looks back at the boxes, haunted by them. "What in god's name am I supposed to do?"

When I leave a few moments later, she's still standing there like that, staring desolately at the roomful of unopened packages.

# *nineteen*

## 1987

Bush Falls was named for a pair of medium-sized waterfalls
that fed the Bush River in the woods just off Porter's Boulevard. There was a well-known urban legend surrounding
these twin waterfalls, concerning a couple of high school
kids who parked on the bluff overlooking the falls to make
out. As things heated up, the girl, in a fit of passion, dared her
date to prove his love by jumping over the falls, offering up
her virginity as the prize. Naturally, he immediately threw
himself into the swirling, frigid waters and was carried over
the falls. Here the versions vary, with some claiming he ac-
complished this feat in the nude, and others saying he was
fully dressed. Some accounts have him breaking his arm on
one of the large stones that protrude from the pool of water beneath the falls, and others have him emerging unscathed. These details, and others, have been argued through
the generations with all the ardor of a Talmudic debate, but

there is universal agreement as to the story's conclusion. He returned triumphantly to the car, drenched and shivering, where he found his girlfriend lying gloriously naked in the backseat, ready to fulfill her side of the bargain and warm him with the sweet, wet heat of her surrendered virginity.

Not surprisingly, the woods immediately surrounding those waterfalls remained the most popular make-out spot in town. If you were a girl who didn't intend to put out, you avoided the falls, because agreeing to go was an unspoken covenant that you would be forthcoming with your favors. If you were a guy who didn't plan on getting some action, chances were pretty good that you didn't actually exist. Every once in a while, one of the more daring boys, in a hormonal frenzy, would brave the falls again, usually having secured a similar promise from his date. The occasional fatality served only to heighten the excitement, and the rule that evolved over time was that if you happened to be there with a date when someone went over the falls, you had a moral and historical obligation if not to actually have sex then at least to step up your usual routine significantly.

This ritual and its contemporary bylaws were surprisingly well respected by teens of both sexes, enforced by an unspoken collective conscience, a social contract between teenagers more binding than any rules imposed on them by the authorities. Like playing spin the bottle in the fifth grade, it somehow lent an air of validation and provided a forum for communication in the otherwise awkward business of incrementally increasing the output in budding sexual relationships. Sex in the back of a car might be regretted later as something tawdry and a poor setting for the surrender of innocence. This was something the girls worried about much more than the boys, who would have been happy to have sex bent over in a stinking dumpster. But if it happened at the falls, you were a part of a sacred tradition, the next generation in a revered and enchanted history. There was a sense of destiny to it, as if the place was part of some romantic heritage, a sexual legacy for the teenagers of Bush Falls.

Carly and I lost our virginity there in the backseat of my dad's Pontiac on a cold January night, with the snow falling like a curtain over the fogged-up car windows and George Michael singing "Careless Whisper" on the car stereo. To this day, the opening bars of the sax solo instantly take me back to that night. Say what you will about car sex, but thirty million horny teenagers can't be wrong. *Wait, can you lift this leg a second? Put your arm over here. Is that okay? Wait, that's not it. Move it up a little. Oops, sorry. Wait, now it's good.* There was a good deal of awkward fumbling before we managed to achieve penetration, and just as I began getting into the rhythm, Lucy appeared unbidden, stretched out magnificently across my consciousness in her bikini, and I went off inside Carly like a volcano.

"I'm sorry," I said, blushing. "That couldn't have been too much fun for you."

Carly waved away my embarrassed apologies with a happy grin and kissed me warmly. "We did it," she said triumphantly.

"Did it hurt?" I asked.

"Not as much as they say," she said. "I always suspected that was just propaganda to keep us virgins longer."

I laughed and told her I loved her. She said it back, and before long we were at it again. This time I was able to last, bringing her to a loud, unrestrained orgasm.

"Mm," she said afterward, purring into my chest. "Much, much better."

"We aim to please," I said, feeling like a major stud even as I felt myself shriveling up like a prune inside her.

"You know," Carly said, curling up in my arms, "we're going to have to do this all the time now."

\* \*

Kids starting in with sex are like Columbus landing on the shores of the New World; even though there are millions of natives running around in full view, they still think they discovered the damn thing. We did it everywhere: in my father's car, her parents' Jacuzzi, my bed while my father was still at work, and once in a ladies' room stall at the Megaplex, which I don't necessarily recommend. There was no stopping us. For a while, everything was either foreplay or the afterglow, and life was beautiful. Then Wayne and Sammy made up, and everything went to shit.

Apparently, Carly and I did not have the market cornered on unbridled teen sex. Unbeknownst to us, Sammy and Wayne were heavily engaged in their own sexual coming of age, albeit a necessarily secretive one. They hadn't even told me they were speaking again. I found out like everyone else did, when Wayne's unsuspecting born-again mother stepped into his bedroom one night and interrupted him and Sammy in the steaming throes of naked passion. I never got the details on the ugly scene that followed, but it ended with Wayne's being kicked out of his house. He crashed at Sammy's for a few days, but when Mrs. Hargrove learned that he was living with Sammy, she stormed the Habers' house, demanding that her son leave with her at once and immediately accompany her to see her priest. Wayne refused to see his mother, and Lucy was ultimately forced to slam and bolt the door when Mrs. Hargrove's rage threatened to turn violent.

Elaine Hargrove stood outside in the bitter cold of that winter night for the better part of an hour, wailing insanely for her son and cursing Lucy and Sammy at full volume, until one of the neighbors finally called Sheriff Muser. He arrived ten minutes later and, after some heated negotiations, finally managed to coax the hysterical woman into the back of his car. He then knocked on Lucy's door and insisted on speaking to Wayne, who verified that contrary to his mother's claims, he was not being held there against his will. Muser drove Wayne's mother home, undoubtedly getting an earful from the distraught woman the whole way back, and recommended that Mr. Hargrove call the family doctor for a sedative. That evening the good sheriff advised his son, Mouse, that he didn't want him showering after games and practices with a homosexual. Mouse probably had the phone in his hand before his father had left the room, and by morning every kid in Bush Falls High knew about Sammy and Wayne.

When Carly called that night to tell me she'd heard the news from one of her girlfriends, I was stunned—and I already knew they were gay, which just goes to show how adept I'd become at the whole denial thing. My dad was still at work with the car, so I took my bike and pedaled frantically up the hill to Sammy's house, a sense of dread beating steadily in my intestines like the lowest keys on a grand piano. Sammy and Wayne were camped out in the den, watching *Cheers,* when Lucy let me in. She took one look at my sweaty, panicked expression, and her smile vanished. "Oh, no," she said, closing her eyes. For a minute it looked like she might faint, and I reached out to steady her. "He can't go through this again," she said, fighting back tears, and I thought, *Again?*

Since neither Wayne nor Sammy had seen fit to tell me that they were even friends again, they pretty much knew something was up when I didn't seem surprised to find them together. "What's up, Joe?" Wayne said awkwardly while Sammy stared at me apprehensively.

"They know," I said, still panting slightly from my frantic bike ride. "Everybody knows."

"Everybody knows what?" Wayne said, but I could tell he understood. No one said anything for a full minute, and then Sammy said, "Fucking Muser," and sat back, a look of abject misery on his face. On television, Diane kissed Sam and then slapped him across the face and the laugh track laughed.

"I just wanted to warn you," I said. "You know, before you showed up at school tomorrow."

"Fuck, fuck, fuck, fuck, fuck," Wayne said in a hushed voice, his face devoid of any expression.

"Wayne," Sammy said.

"Fuck!" Wayne shouted, getting to his feet. "I have to get out of here."

"I'll come with you," Sammy said, starting to get up.

"No," Wayne said. "I want to be alone." He grabbed his jacket from a chair in the kitchen and ran out the front door.

Sammy's eyes filled with tears. "You'd better go after him," he said to me. "This is going to kill him."

"What about you?" I said.

Sammy turned to me, the tears running unchecked down his cheeks, and gave me the most pathetic look I'd ever seen. "Everyone knew I was a faggot anyway," he said softly, and for a fraction of a second I felt a powerful urge to reach out and strangle him. Instead, I turned and ran for the front door, muttering a jumbled farewell to Lucy, who hadn't budged from where she stood in the front hallway, staring at the wall, a stricken expression frozen on her face.

When I got outside, Wayne was gone and so was my bike.

It took me a half hour to walk home, and when I got there, I was surprised to find my father waiting for me in the kitchen, with a frown on his face. It wasn't the frown that surprised me; it was the part about his waiting for me.

"I just got off the phone with Coach Dugan," he said slowly, absently clasping his massive fingers as he cracked his knuckles.

"Yeah?"

"He said Wayne Hargrove is a homosexual. Him and that kid who worked the press last summer."

"Why the hell would he call you with something like that?" I said.

"He's looking to verify it."

"Is the coach looking for a date?"

"You watch your mouth, Joe," my father said sternly. "The

coach has a whole team of boys to think of. This is serious business."

"This is no one's fucking business," I said.

He gave me a sharp look and then tilted his head slightly, as if a new thought had suddenly occurred to him. "Are you a homosexual?" he said, squinting at me.

"What's with the sudden interest in my sex life, Dad?"

"Just answer the goddamn question!" he yelled at me, pounding the table with his fist.

I leaned against the doorway and sighed. "Dad," I said softly. "I have a girlfriend."

He squinted at me in surprise. "You do?" he said a little too skeptically for my taste.

"Thanks for the vote of confidence."

"I just didn't know," he said, looking relieved.

"I can't imagine how it never came up in all those meaningful talks we have."

"What's her name?"

"Oh, please," I said, heading for the stairs. "Spare me."

"Where do you think you're going?"

"To smoke some crack. You see? There's something else you didn't know about me."

In the hallway mirror I caught a glance at him, mouth agape, staring dumbstruck at the back of my head, and I figured it would be a few more years before he attempted another conversation with me.

Wayne showed up at around one in the morning, throwing pebbles at my window. I went downstairs to let him in, and we tiptoed back up to my room. He collapsed on my bed, still shivering, his face taut and raw from the cold. "I can't get a handle on it," he said, bouncing up and down nervously on the bed as he blew into his hands. "It changes from minute to minute. Sometimes I think it's the kind of thing that will blow over after a few days, and sometimes I think nothing will ever be the same again."

I was sadly leaning toward the latter view myself, but didn't think he needed to hear that just then. "Maybe you shouldn't go to school for a few days," I said. "Let everything settle down first."

"They'll all be talking about it, whispering behind my back."

"What about Sammy?"

"Fuck Sammy," Wayne said vehemently. "This is all his fault anyway. I told him that my room wasn't safe, but he had to keep on going at it."

This was a little more information than I really needed at the moment. "Listen," I said. "You're the star of the basketball team. If an asshole like Mouse is accepted because he's on the team, certainly a guy like you—"

"Mouse doesn't fuck men," Wayne said pointedly.

"Mouse doesn't fuck women either, as far as anyone knows," I said, trying in vain for even a small laugh.

"This is bad, Joe," Wayne said, lying back on my bed. "This is a fucking nightmare."

"What do you want to do?"

Wayne covered his eyes with his forearm and exhaled slowly. "I just want to wake up, man," he said, shaking his head sadly. "I just want to wake the fuck up."


I was the subject of much intense scrutiny the next morning as I made my way through the eerie hush of the school yard and down the hall to my locker. Students stood in clusters, conducting whispered conversations that ceased abruptly as I walked by, their glances ranging from inquisitive to accusatory. Wayne had opted to hole up in my room for the day, and before I'd even made it to my locker, I knew he'd made the right decision. In the two minutes since I'd arrived the stares and whispers were threatening to suffocate me, and I could begin to imagine what it might feel like to be

Wayne today. Carly was waiting for me at my locker, and I almost broke down when she kissed me. "Are you okay?" she said.

"Not really."

"You want to cut out and go somewhere?"

I did, but I shook my head no. With Wayne and Sammy lying low, I felt like I needed to be there to scout out the situation for them. Also, there was no denying my selfish need to be seen going about my business in the midst of this scandal as someone with nothing to hide, lest I become thought of as gay by association. Carly took my hand and pressed up against me. "I think I'm going to need to stay close today," she said, and I felt my eyes go hot with tears. I kissed Carly's hair and squeezed her hand as we walked toward homeroom, and felt a sudden stab of anger toward Wayne and Sammy. Everything had been going so well; why did they have to go and fuck it all up?

I was summoned to Dugan's office in the middle of second period. Sean and Mouse were loitering in the hall outside his office when I got there.

"Is it true about Hargrove?" Sean asked, blocking my way to Dugan's door.

"Is what true?" I said.

"Word is he's a fudge packer," Sean said.

"I'm not familiar with that term."

"You know, a bone smoker," Mouse clarified happily. "A faggot."

"Wayne's no faggot," I said hotly.

"We have it from a pretty good source that your buddy's a butt pirate," Mouse said, flashing an evil grin. The guy was failing English, but when it came to gay slurs he was a regular thesaurus.

"What are you getting so excited about, Mouse?" I said. "You get off on talking about faggots so much, we can only imagine where you fit into the whole bone-smoking scheme of things."

Mouse's smile faltered, and he stepped forward menacingly, grabbing my shirt in his fists. "What do you mean?" he said through gritted teeth.

"Which word didn't you understand?"

He banged me against the lockers, hard enough to rattle my teeth. "Fucking asshole," he said.

"There he goes again talking about fucking assholes," I said to Sean. "Are you noticing a pattern here?"

Mouse punched me in the stomach, and he and Sean were pulling me up to hit me again when Dugan stepped out of his office. "What the hell is going on out here?" he yelled, his gruff, authoritative voice freezing us in our places. "You boys aren't getting into trouble on a game day, are you?" he said, addressing Sean and Mouse. "Or maybe you've forgotten that we play New Haven tonight."

"No, sir," said Sean, releasing me and stepping back, pulling Mouse with him.

"Then get your asses into class now," Dugan commanded, and I couldn't help but think this display of academic concern was somehow being performed on my behalf. "Idiots," he said, ushering me into his office with an apologetic grin as I sought to suck back in some of the wind that had been knocked out of me.

The walls of Dugan's office were lined with framed pictures of teams past. The shelving behind his desk contained a slew of championship trophies. On his desk, almost as an afterthought, was an old picture of the coach and his wife with their arms around two unhappy-looking boys with crew cuts and their father's dark eyes. Dugan stopped on his way around the desk and pointed to one of the framed team pictures. "There's your old man," he said. "Nineteen fifty-eight. Now, that was a hell of a season. My third year as coach, our first championship, thanks to your old man's buzzer beater." He sat down in his worn leather chair. "He ever talk about that game?"

"He may have mentioned it."

Dugan studied me like a taxonomist trying to pin down a phylum and species. After a moment he nodded slowly, having determined the best course with which to proceed. "I guess you know why I asked you to come here," he said gravely.

I shrugged. "Not really."

"I'm concerned about Wayne Hargrove."

"Then you should have called him in here."

"He's absent today," Dugan said. "I can hardly blame him, given the circumstances."

"What do you want?" I said, sounding as annoyed as I dared.

"I want to help. Wayne's one of my boys. Whatever silly, adolescent experimentation he may or may not have done is really not of any concern to me."

"What can you possibly do?" I said, suddenly hoping in spite of myself that maybe there was a light at the end of this tunnel.

"I can put an end to the rumors," he said, staring intently at me. "I've already met with the team and made it clear to them that Wayne is their teammate and they are not to tolerate anyone slandering or impugning his reputation."

I looked at him incredulously. "Your team is where this all started," I said. "It was Mouse who spread the word to begin with."

"The sheriff was . . . indiscreet," Dugan conceded. "But Mouse will apologize for starting such a terrible rumor, and the sheriff will back that up if I need him to. You and I will be the only two people who know the real truth, and that truth will never leave this room."

I thought about it for a minute. If the coach made Mouse apologize for the rumor, then maybe Wayne really had a chance. The whole thing was so unbelievable anyway, it would actually make more sense to everyone that it had been a stupid prank. "Why are you telling me this?" I said. "If you can really make this go away, why don't you just do it?"

Dugan's eyes bored into me. "I want Wayne in that game tonight," he said.

"The game." I nodded slowly as the full realization of what this was about dawned upon me. "Of course. You can't win without Wayne."

"This is about more than a game," Dugan said.

"Right. It's about the play-offs."

"I'm only looking out for Wayne's best interests," Dugan snarled at me. "This is not going to be easy. Mouse will not be happy about it, and the sheriff will be furious that I am making his son a scapegoat. I believe I can get them to understand the wisdom of my plan, but no one will believe it if he continues to hide."

"Bullshit," I spat back. "You don't want to lose your leading scorer right before the play-offs."

Dugan stood up suddenly, and for a moment I thought he might actually lunge across the table at me. "Wayne is one of my boys," he said slowly, towering over me menacingly. "I look after my boys. That's what this is about."

"Really," I said, getting to my feet. "Then tell me this. If Wayne doesn't play tonight, will you still do it? Will you still help him out?"

The heat from his stare threatened to singe my eyebrows, but I maintained eye contact. "If any one of my boys skips a game," Dugan said softly, "he's no longer one of my boys."

"That's what I thought," I said, and turned to leave.

"Listen to me, you little shit," Dugan roared at me. "If you think this school is going to reach out and embrace a faggot, then you're an idiot. He'll become an outcast. I am offering the only chance he's got to be able to show his face around here again. It's not your decision to make."

I turned back to face him. "You're right," I said. "I'll tell him about your offer, and I hope he takes you up on it."

"That's the first intelligent thing you've said since you got here," he said, sitting back down slowly.

I looked at him with contempt. "Didn't anyone ever tell you that it's just a fucking game?"

"Sure," he said, leaning into the pressed wood of his desk with a nasty grin. "That's the universal slogan of losers. I'm surprised they haven't given it to you on a T-shirt yet."

Cougars games were always well attended, but that night it was standing room only at the Bush Falls High gymnasium. It appeared as if the entire school had turned out to see if Wayne would play. The air was charged with excitement as the crowd chanted for their team to emerge from the locker rooms. When the Cougars came sprinting out onto the court, Wayne was the second-to-last one in line, and he seemed to falter for a second when he took in the size of the crowd, but he put his head down and jogged resolutely out to the half-court line, and someone threw him a ball. He sank his first warm-up shot, a jumper from the top of the key, and there were scattered cheers. I tried to catch his eye from where I sat with Carly in the bleachers, but he was determinedly not looking around at the spectators, his face grimly expressionless.

That night, Wayne scored fifty-two points, a new league record, in a performance that no one in the capacity crowd would ever forget. He ran the floor like a demon, weaving through the defense as if they were moving in slow motion. Like a wild beast suddenly freed from its cage, he tore up and down the court with a passion and fury that left even his own teammates in the dust, shaking their heads in wonder. Carly and I screamed until we were hoarse, laughing and hugging each other every time Wayne made another incredible move on his way to the basket. The cheers grew with each additional basket, but if Wayne heard them, he gave no outward sign.

With less than a minute left to play and the game safely

won, Wayne signaled to Dugan that he needed to come out. He walked over to the bench to a rousing round of applause and grabbed a towel to wipe his face. Then, while the final minute was played out, Wayne turned his back on the court and finally looked up into the bleachers, where, after a few seconds, our eyes met. We grinned at each other for a moment, and then he gave a quick nod and a short wave and disappeared through the locker room door just before the final buzzer sounded and the gym erupted into a wild cacophony of cheers and applause. I didn't know it right then, but that brief wave was Wayne saying good-bye. It would be many years before he was seen in Bush Falls again.

Later that night, someone jumped Sean Tallon in the parking lot of the Duchess Diner, where the team had gone to celebrate their victory. Sean showed up to school a few days later with a broken arm and the right side of his face still mangled and swollen. He never said a word about the incident, but I could tell by the way he looked at me that Wayne had taken a short detour on his way out of town, to leave a last, parting gift for Sammy.

About four weeks later, Sammy went over the falls.

# twenty

For the last two days, the scattered fragments of my past have been popping up like Starbucks franchises, so I shouldn't be surprised to come home and find Lucy Haber waiting for me on my father's front porch. Still, it throws me for a moment. She's wearing sandals with platform soles, a long, clinging skirt with a daringly high slit, and a silk blouse with a scoop neck. From where I stand in the street beside my car, it appears as if she hasn't aged at all, and only as I get closer do I notice the faint worry lines beneath her eyes and at the corners of her apprehensive smile. The lawn has acquired a few more copies of *Bush Falls* since morning, and I almost trip over one of them as I make my way up the walk, unable to take my eyes off Lucy. "Hello, Joe," she says, her voice lower than I remember it.

"Hi, Lucy." I come up the stairs, and we maneuver awkwardly from aborted handshakes to a clumsy, poorly timed hug. She feels firm and lithe in my embrace, not at all like a fifty-year-old woman should feel, and in her hair I smell the same intoxicating lilac-scented shampoo that overwhelmed me as a teenager.

"I heard you were here," she says, stepping back to look at me. "I thought I'd pay you a quick visit."

"I'm glad you did," I say, although the jury's still out on that. I let her into the house, jingling my keys loudly in case Jared and his friend are at it again, but no one is home. I wonder what the hell I'm going to talk to Lucy about. "Would you like a drink?" I offer.

"I'm fine," she says, looking around the foyer with mild curiosity.

"You sure?"

"Yes." She steps into the living room and peers closely at the family pictures on the coffee table. Lucy Haber in my childhood home is like a rare astrological phenomenon, the convergence of planets with unforeseeable aftereffects. "How's your father?"

"Not too good," I say, sitting down on the couch. After a moment she joins me there, the cushion beneath me shifting as it registers her weight. The love seat that sits perpendicular to the couch would have been the more logical and appropriate destination, I think, and I'm confused, maybe somewhat concerned, and, let's not deny it, aroused by her choice.

"I'm sorry to hear that," Lucy says. "Were you in some sort of accident?"

"What?"

Her fingers graze my face as she traces the gash near my temple. Maternal? Sexual? Oedipal? The options run through my head like a quiz show. *I'd like to poll the audience, Regis.* Lucy's touch instantly sets off the low hum of internal machinery in my lower belly, generating waves of heat that spread quickly downward. I hope to god the trembling in my thighs isn't as noticeable as it feels. "I got into a fight," I say. "One of my more expressive critics."

She nods, her fingers lingering for another moment before

leaving my face. "I would imagine you have no shortage of those here."

"Are you one of them?" I ask nervously. It is this exact moment I'd envisioned when I tried to convince Owen to let me remove the lustier pages concerning Lucy from the novel. Now here we are, transplanted into my nightmare/fantasy, and I am utterly exposed, my obsession no longer a secret from her. This knowledge alone wouldn't be so bad, but she knows that I know, and I know that she knows I know, and this extra loop of awareness causes my bowels to clench with terror.

"I was really moved by your novel," she says, her lower lip trembling. "You showed me a whole new side of my son, one that as his mother I never got to see." She reaches over and squeezes my hand. "I can't tell you what a precious gift that was."

I am flabbergasted. It's a testament to my prodigious egotism that I've never even considered how Lucy might feel about the characterization of Sammy in the book. I've only ever been concerned with my own salacious confessions. "I'm glad," I stammer.

She nods and then laughs softly as she stops her tears neatly with the edge of her finger. Her nails are buffed and polished in ivory. "Sometimes, when I'm feeling lonely, I read parts of your book and it soothes me."

*Which parts?* I wonder. I study her face, still impossibly flawless and composed, her plump lips, so full of sensual promise, pressed outward in just the slightest pout, as if already anticipating the delicious, wet suction they can impart at will to your various parts. She sits back on the couch and smiles warmly at me, her teeth gleaming white, the beneficiaries of constant buffing from those phenomenal lips. I rack my brain for something to say, but my mind is a blank as the blood in my head, true to its liquid form, absconds to seek out the lowest possible point. "It's very good to see you, Lucy," I finally say.

She nods, smiling, and gets up to leave. "It's good to see you too. It brings back a lot of memories." I follow her back into the foyer, trying in vain not to stare at her ass. At the door, she turns around and takes my hand in both of hers. "You were a good friend to Sammy, Joe. That meant a lot to him. And to me."

"I tried to be," I say lamely, feeling every bit the horny hypocrite.

Lucy hugs me again, this time tightly, with the full length of her body pressed up against me. It is most definitely a different kind of hug from the first one, a loaded embrace. She does it suddenly, giving me no opportunity to contort my anatomy and create a discreet pocket for my arousal, which presses against her thigh like a red herring. She knows, I know she knows, and she knows I know she knows. Once again, our knowledge is a circle, spun around my unrepentant engorgement. She turns her head to press her lips against my ear, their gloss wet and against me, making me wish my ears had taste buds to identify what flavor she's wearing. I guess peach. "Come up to the house and see me," she murmurs. "I want to talk to you about your book some more."

"I will," I say, shivering at the crush of her lips on my ear, a hot flush spreading from the base of my neck. Half a year of celibacy will do that to you.

She steps back, her fingers brushing my arms as she lets go of me. "Promise?"

I do.


While editing *Bush Falls*, I was torn about whether or not to include the pages dealing with my obsession with Sammy's mother, worried that Lucy might one day read the book. "The minute you start editing your writing based on the consideration of how it might be received, you've greatly compromised the integrity of the whole work," Owen told me somberly.

"It is fiction," I pointed out weakly.

"The fiction writer is every bit as responsible for the truth as the nonfiction writer," Owen said haughtily. "Even more so, since he isn't constrained by factual considerations."

"That's a contradiction in terms, isn't it?"

"Only to an obtuse literalist. And anyway, it's entirely beside the point."

"The point being?"

Owen grinned. "Sex sells."


A short while after Lucy's visit, I'm in the shower when I frighten myself badly by letting go with a piercing, anguished howl that bursts angrily out of me, raking my throat before reverberating loudly against the tiles and frosted glass door of the shower chamber. That solitary cry opens the floodgates, and for the next five minutes I stand convulsing under the hot spray as my body is racked with powerful sobs that come from deep within my belly, clawing desperately through my esophagus to escape to open air.

When it's over, I step out of the shower, feeling light-headed and congested, and wrap one towel around my waist and another over my head and shoulders, which always makes me feel like a heavyweight fighter. The tissue disintegrates in my wet hands as I blow my nose, little sodden flecks of Kleenex mingling in my snot like guppies. I study myself in the mirror, not quite sure what I'm looking for, and then, when the steam has fogged up the glass, obscuring my face, I get dressed and go page Owen.

"I'm behaving oddly," I tell him when he returns my page.

I can actually hear him force his mouth shut against the comment he wants to make. "In what way do *you* feel you're behaving oddly?"

I tell him about my violent crying fit in the shower, and then back up to my tears in the hospital stairwell and in my father's den the night before. "Crying," he says, "is hardly odd behavior."

"It is for me."

"Listen, Joe, you obviously have a significant amount of unresolved conflict concerning your family and your past."

"No shit," I say, struggling to keep the impatience out of my voice. "But it's never reduced me to tears. How would you explain this behavior?"

"You mean, if I were a therapist."

"Right."

"Which I'm not."

"Whatever."

"Hell, I don't know," Owen says. "Therapy is a complex course of exploration and analysis. It's a perversion of the process to offer shotgun diagnoses."

"But you already have one."

"Of course I do. I'm just throwing up my usual disclaimer."

"Duly noted. Now lay it out for me. Do you think I'm having a nervous breakdown?"

Owen sighs. "You're not having a breakdown. I don't think you have it in you." Only Owen can make this sound like an actual character flaw. "Off the top of my head, I'd say that for many years you've been very lonely for the love of your family. It's probably a significant factor in the utter failure of all your other relationships. You're never satisfied, because no woman can fill the giant void left by your family. Now you're in your hometown, confronted with the family whose love you so desperately yearn for, and you can no longer contain your deep feelings of guilt, loneliness, and loss."

For a long moment there are just the sounds of our respective breathing over the phone lines as I consider what he's just said. "That sounds pretty much on the money," I finally say.

"I'd appreciate it if you would sound less surprised," Owen says. "Not for nothing, but I am probably the smartest and most insightful person you know, bar none."

"Thanks. What more could I ask for?"

"Drugs," Owen says. "If I could prescribe, now that would be something."

# twenty-one

Night comes quickly in the Falls, where streetlights are at a minimum, used only to light significant intersections. By the time I finish talking to Owen and step onto the front porch, it's dark out, the meager light radiating from porches and lawn lanterns barely making a dent in the thick shroud of suburban night. Somewhere nearby a dog howls inquisitively at a moon obscured by gray clouds, and in the distance there is the faint sound of a car speeding down Stratfield Road. There are approximately ten books arbitrarily strewn across the front lawn, the word apparently out as to what to do with your used copy of *Bush Falls*.

Jared is sitting on the steps, reading a worn paperback copy of *The Sirens of Titan* in the dim porch light. He looks up at me as I step out onto the porch and grins. "Hey, Uncle Joe." The uncle thing still rings discordantly in my ears, like a word continually repeated until it's shed all meaning.

"Do you ever actually go home?" I say.

"Not lately." His lips crease into a frown.

"You like Vonnegut?" I sit down beside him, my arrival momentarily dispersing the congregation of moths and mosquitoes worshipping in furious circles around the overhead porch light. We both spend a few seconds batting them away with lethal force, the survivors ultimately regrouping in frenzied congress under the naked bulb, reviewing their battle plan, discussing options.

"He's pretty good," Jared says. "I had to read *Slaughterhouse Five* for school, and I just kind of got into him."

I take the book from him and flip through it cursorily, finally coming to rest on the author's quirky inscription at the front. *All persons, places, and events in this book are real,* it reads. *No names have been changed to protect the innocent, since God Almighty protects the innocent as a matter of Heavenly routine.* Vonnegut has missed the point, I think. It's only for the guilty that names need to be changed.

I hand the book back to Jared, who slides it easily into his back pocket. He is wearing loose black jeans and a gray pullover jersey that hangs loosely over his lithe frame. "Where are you headed?" he asks me.

"Nowhere, really," I say. I intend to call Carly soon, but I'm still somewhat wobbly from my minor breakdown and Owen's subsequent long-distance head shrinking, and I need some time to regroup before I attempt to hold my own with her.

"You look like you could stand some fun," he says, getting up. "You want to come for a drive?"

"Where to?"

"It's a surprise."

I consider my nephew for a moment, listen to the three-part harmony of the crickets, and breathe deeply of the cool night air. "What the hell." I pull myself up to join him. Things seemed to be happening to me, gathering a subtle momentum all their own. Relinquishing my will and adopting the attitude of a carefree passenger feels like the way to go, is actually a relief.

"Cool," Jared says. "We should probably take your car."

"You have a car?"

"Nah. That's why we should probably take yours." He flashes me his trademark smirk and shuffles lazily over to the Mercedes, pulling his hair out of his face and tucking it behind his ears as he goes. I decide to overlook the fact that I've been invited along to wherever primarily because I come with wheels. When he reaches the car, he takes a moment to examine the disfigured door and the smashed taillight, whistling sympathetically, expressing the universal masculine sensitivity to marred beauty generally reserved for circumcisions and damaged imported cars. He turns back to me, eyebrows raised, holds out his open hand expectantly, and says, "Maybe I should drive."

"I heard it was Sean Tallon who beat your ass yesterday," he says conversationally as he pilots the Mercedes at dangerously high speeds through the shopping district of Bush Falls.

I pull on my seat belt. "Where'd you hear that?"

He ignores the question. "He's one crazy fuck, you know."

"So I hear," I say. "But what exactly does that mean?"

He shrugs and takes a hard right. "Probably that you shouldn't have fucked with him."

"Your dad didn't seem scared of him."

"Go Dad," Jared says sourly.

I look at my nephew thoughtfully. "What's the problem between you two?"

"This week, it's the earrings."

I start to say something, stop myself since it's none of my business, and then, typically, say it anyway. "You do realize that you're going through a stage right now, don't you. That in a few years you'll have outgrown all this rebellion bullshit and none of it will matter."

"Maybe so," he concedes, keeping his eyes glued to the

road. "But I still have to fight the good fight while it's mine to fight." He grins lightly. "You might say it's my job."

"Well, you certainly throw yourself into your work."

"Whatever," Jared says. "What's the problem between you and him?"

"Nothing that a few years of intense family therapy couldn't fix."

"Well, I think the boat's pretty much sailed on that one. What with Grandma gone and Gramps . . . you know."

I've never heard my mother referred to as Grandma before. It's never occurred to me that the title could be acquired posthumously, and hearing Jared say it is momentarily disorienting. I feel a chill in my belly, a pang of mourning so intense it renders further conversation impossible. We sit in silence for a few minutes until I see that we're headed out of town on Porter's Boulevard. "Where are we going?" I say. "The only thing out here is Porter's."

"Bingo."

"What the hell are we doing at Porter's?"

"You'll see."

P.J. Porter's corporate headquarters is a massive, sprawling five-story building whose exterior is comprised primarily of forbidding dark glass panels and burnished fieldstone, a monument to capitalism. The building is surrounded by acres of rolling, immaculate lawns and strategically placed ponds and fountains, as if it had been plunked down in the middle of a championship golf course. Adding to the overall sense of deliberate seclusion is a perimeter of forestry, roughly one acre deep, that has been deliberately left intact to surround the campus. This expansive, idyllic setting is either a grand testament to modern ergonomics or a corporeal manifestation of the grotesquely inflated collective ego of the Porter family in their financial heyday.

Jared drives past the main entrance, which is gated and locked, and we ride for another few minutes on a narrow road that winds its way through the trees until he suddenly pulls onto a dirt lane that runs into the woods. The lane ends at a gated section of the eight-foot chain-link fence that surrounds the perimeter of the Porter's campus. A group of kids suddenly materialize like ghosts in the narrow glow of the Mercedes' low beams, smoking, leaning against trees, and throwing rocks into the woods, looking like the Lost Boys waiting for Peter Pan's return. They disappear from view as Jared cuts the lights and parks in the forest between a Jeep and a Honda Accord. We step out of the car to join the kids, who all look to be about Jared's age. "What's up, boys?" Jared says, performing a number of multifaceted handshakes with a few of them as they eye me, the aging interloper, with unmasked suspicion. I count six of them, not including Jared and myself.

"Who's this?" a tall, beefy kid with dyed black hair and a blond goatee asks him.

"This is my controversial uncle Joe," Jared says, indicating me with a wave. "He's going to take Gordy's spot tonight."

"You the author?" another of the kids pipes up.

"I am," I say, feeling expressly older and suddenly self-conscious in my merino sweater and Brooks Brothers chinos. They are all dressed pretty much alike, in black T-shirts or sweatshirts, dark, baggy cargo pants, and sneakers. All of their faces are cluttered with the shrapnel of rebellion, as if a grenade of alienation has exploded in their midst, piercing every possible soft point of flesh—from earlobes and nostrils to eyebrows, lips, and tongues—with metal studs and rings.

"The author of what?" someone else wants to know, and a brief discussion of my credentials ensues.

"He wrote that movie about the Falls, man. Where that kid fucks his mother."

"He wrote the book, dipshit. Then they made it into a movie."

"Whatever, man."

"He fucks his mother?"

"It's the friend's mother, you tool. And they don't fuck. He just has a hard-on for her."

"Oh. That's okay. I have a hard-on for Jared's mother."

"Shut the fuck up, Mikey!"

"What, you don't think your mother's hot? Be honest."

"Bite me."

Having resolved all of these matters, the goateed boy, whose name I now know is Mikey, steps forward. "Yo, Jared, what's the deal with bringing a grown-up to the game?"

"He's cool," Jared says easily. "He won't tell. And it's just this once, since we need to replace Gordy."

They all consider me for a moment, frowning thoughtfully, and I feel like the class geek standing in a dwindling crowd, waiting to be chosen by one of the teams for dodgeball. Finally, Mikey steps forward and shakes my hand. "Okay, man," he says. "As long as you don't, you know, have a heart condition or anything."

"I'm good," I say wryly.

"Okay," Jared says, flashing me an approving smile. "Let's do it."

"It" turns out to be paintball. Mikey opens the back of his Jeep, and everyone clamors around as he hands out a slew of pneumatic air guns designed to look convincingly like cutting-edge terrorist weaponry. The boys are all business as they outfit their guns, speaking to one another in technical jargon about flip loaders, barrel plugs, hose kits, butt plates, and twenty-ounce $CO_2$ bottles. There is something almost professional in the easy familiarity of their references to cockers and beavertails, and if they were ever amused by the sexual innuendo in those terms, they've long since gotten over it. Jared hands me my gun, an Autococker 2000, and gives me a brief lesson in loading my vertical $CO_2$ bottle and feeding my cylindrical magazine of paintballs into the barrel.

He hands me a black knapsack containing a pair of goggles, extra ammunition, and $CO_2$ bottles.

Once everyone has a gun and gear secured to his body with Velcro and shoulder straps, they begin scaling the chain-link fence one by one, flipping easily over the top, and dropping down softly onto the grounds of the Porter's campus. I can't remember the last time I climbed a fence, and when my turn comes, I throw myself at it with a burst of physical intensity, determined not to embarrass myself by getting hung up or crushing my balls as I straddle the top. Once we're all assembled on the other side, we jog silently through the dense woods, which in the impenetrable darkness seem to go on forever. We fan out when we hit the large expanse of the back lawn, the titanium casings of the guns we clutch gleaming in the blue light of the moon. It's easy to imagine that we're a team of commandos infiltrating an enemy compound, and I feel a burst of childish adrenaline as we come over a knoll and I can make out the massive black structure of the office building looming in the distance.

I slow down as we pass the small lake where Sammy, Wayne, and I hung out so often that summer. I remember how Wayne looked flying through the spray as he jumped off the geyser's platform. Now the geyser is off, and the dark water lies still as a sheet of glass. In my head I hear the faint strains of Springsteen singing "Spirit in the Night," like an echo, and I feel something hot tremble briefly in my chest, but I don't stop running. This place is spooky enough; I don't need my own ghosts adding to the atmosphere.

This is clearly not the first time these kids have trespassed here, and they all move as one toward a loading bay on the far left side of the building. Two of them disappear into some shrubbery and return with crowbars, which they place under the rubber rim of one of the loading bay doors and force it up. The door moves smoothly on its rollers and we all file inside, the last ones in pulling down the door behind them. Jared now takes the lead, and we follow single file down a hallway and into a stairwell. We climb four flights and step out into an immense atrium filled with attached cubicles that extend across the width and breadth as far as the eye can see.

"They shut the place down when they went out of business," Jared explains to me as the other guys throw their gear down onto desks and begin loading and making adjustments to their guns. Apparently, silence is no longer required. "Everything is locked up while the lawyers fight it all out, so nothing's been touched."

I walk slowly through the continuous rows of cubicles, all still furnished with desks, chairs, computer terminals, phones, and fax machines. Many cubicle walls still have photos and posters adorning them, the accessories of low-level employees trying to forget that they occupy but one minuscule nook in the overall honeycomb. There is an atmosphere of apocalyptic desolation to the place, this once vast and bustling enterprise now a haunted corporate wasteland. As far as paintball goes, you couldn't ask for a better venue.

We split into two teams of four, Jared and I being paired with two kids, one named Grossman, chubby and riddled with acne, and the other simply called Tree, maybe an abbreviation or maybe because he is easily the tallest one in the group. The two teams head to opposite sides of the colossal atrium to hang their flags, then someone blows a whistle and the game begins. The next two hours are spent tearing madly through the labyrinth of cubicles, hiding, ducking, shooting, and screaming. Each game lasts roughly twenty minutes and ends when either all four teammates are "dead" or someone manages to pull off the far more difficult feat of stealing the opposing team's flag without getting shot. At first I am tentative, feeling silly and juvenile, but after my first "kill," I surrender to the primitive thrill of the game, losing myself in the adrenal haze of simulated battle. The paintballs, actually condensed gelatin caplets, sting painfully on impact, but the pain, too, is part of the rush. And there's no denying the added, illicit thrill that comes from the sense of real danger, as we are indisputably trespassers and vandals. The trappings of the ruined corporate civilization that comprise our battlefield add a surrealistic subtext to the game, giving it an otherworldly feel that, combined with the youthful battle cries reverberating off the high glass ceiling, is reminiscent of *Lord of the Flies*. Only when a time-out is called after the fourth game, and we all gather in the center conference area to rest, do I identify the alien sensation I'm feeling as fun.

Jared and I collapse into two desk chairs on wheels and pull off our goggles, resting our Autococker air rifles on our laps. We're sweating and breathing heavily, our clothing splattered with impressionistic splotches of blue paint. Our team's ammunition cartridges are labeled Red Virus, and in the faint glow of the exit sign above us, I now see that our opponents are splattered in red. The eight of us rest in the uncomplicated camaraderie of a platoon, catching our breath before we take the next hill.

"Hey, Mr. Goffman," Mikey says.

"Call me Joe."

"Joe. You did much better than I thought you would. You're in pretty good shape."

"Thanks."

"For an old guy," he finishes with a grin.

"Mikey," I say.

"Yeah."

"Suck my Autococker."

Laughs and guffaws all around at that one, and I experience a surge of adolescent pride at my quick wit.

"What about security?" I ask. "I can't believe they leave this place unguarded."

"Just two guards in the booth up front," Jared says. "They sometimes drive a golf cart around the property, but they never come inside."

"They're too busy watching TV," Mikey adds.

"We usually pick nights when there's a good ball game on," someone, I think Grossman, says.

"How do you know they never patrol the building?"

"It's just never happened," Jared says.

Naturally, it's precisely at that moment that the door to the stairwell flies open with a bang and two men in security guard uniforms come charging forward, shouting and waving flashlights in our direction.

"Oh," Jared says. "Shit."

"Freeze," one guard yells.

"Nobody move!" cries the other one.

Only I comply. The seven kids I'm with suddenly jump to their feet and, as one, raise their paintball guns at the two stunned men, who freeze in their tracks, mouths agape. "*You* freeze, motherfuckers!" Mikey yells gleefully. The guards stare in abject terror down the titanium barrels of seven Autocockers, and we all stay like that for a few seconds, suspended in a perfect Tarantino moment. Then a look of recognition comes over the face of one of the guards. "Wait a minute. Those are air rifles," he complains, as if we aren't playing fair.

Mikey lets out a bloodcurdling scream, and I watch in disbelief as the boys open fire, unleashing a spray of red and blue pellets on the two guards, the air rifles hissing and clicking like a new-wave percussion instrument. The pellets explode colorfully on the guards in a symphony of light popping noises, and they fall to the floor, crying out in anguished surprise as they curl up into fetal positions, arms wrapped protectively around their heads. "Let's move!" someone says, and we all begin backing toward the stairwell, maintaining a steady barrage of intermittent fire to keep the guards on the floor until we've made it. We fly down the stairs, shouting and whooping with savage glee, and I recognize one of the voices in the mix as my own. In a few moments we burst out of the stairwell and charge through the loading bay and out of the building, into the darkness of the Porter's grounds. The cold air is invigorating against my hot, sweating face, and I feel practically euphoric as we enter the welcome cover of the woods.

If you think climbing an eight-foot chain-link fence at full speed while wearing a three-pound air rifle and carrying five pounds' worth of gear in a knapsack is easy, you're mistaken. Or you're seventeen. I launch myself thoughtlessly at the fence, confident that I will fly over it in the slipstream of my fleeing compatriots, who have already effortlessly scaled it. I make it up and over the top with no problem, but on the way down the strap from my rifle gets snagged on one of the fence posts, and I'm slammed back into the fence, the strap flying off my shoulder and hanging me by my neck. I dangle there for a precarious instant, humiliated and dangerously close to death by hanging. It isn't my life that flashes before my eyes at this point, so determined am I even now to avoid clichés at all costs, but rather a clairvoyant glimpse of the bemused half grins and rolled eyes of family and associates as they read the news accounts of my ridiculous demise. It's then that Jared and Mikey finally notice my distress and jump to my rescue, hoisting me and freeing the strap from the fence post. As they pull me off, my leg becomes ensnared by a protruding clasp in the fence. There follows a loud tearing sound as my khakis rip from mid-shin to cuff, and I feel the hot slice of cold metal shredding my ankle. I'm proud that I don't scream, although with my windpipe only recently having been freed from the crushing rifle strap, I doubt I could manage much more than a hoarse croak anyway.

I limp gingerly over to the Mercedes, which Jared already has running, and Mikey helps me in, giving me a friendly shove in the shoulder as I fall back onto the seat. "Suck my Autococker," he says with a sardonic grin. "That was classic, man." He disappears into the night.

Jared throws the Mercedes into gear and drives us down

the dirt road. Just ahead of us, the furiously spinning tires of Mikey's Jeep kick up a small pebble that hits my front windshield with the force of a bullet. There is a sharp, cracking sound and a small circular chip appears in the German glass, just under the rearview mirror, with three or four spidery tentacles ambitiously extending in disparate directions. "Oops," Jared says.

"Just drive," I say. And as my burgling nephew steers us at high velocity into the night, my probing hand comes away sticky with blood from my wounded ankle, and through no easily discernible connection, it reminds me that I've forgotten to call Carly as I promised.

# twenty-two

I'm almost disappointed when there's no car chase. It's distinctly possible that the guards haven't phoned in the incident, swearing a solemn oath of secrecy rather than choosing to explain how a band of high school kids with paintball guns overpowered them. Whatever the case, we make good our escape and are soon parked in the woods overlooking the Bush River Falls.

I look at my nephew peering pensively at the churning waters. "Jared," I say. "I just want to be friends."

He laughs. "Was this the place in your time too?"

"My parents probably screwed around here too."

Jared fumbles through the many pockets of his cargo pants and, after a moment, triumphantly fishes out a slightly bent but wholly intact joint. "Join me?" he says, punching the dashboard lighter.

"Believe it or not, that's the second joint I've seen tonight."

"Good," Jared says, firing it up. "Then you're already primed." He takes two short tokes on the spliff to get it lit right, and then one long, meaningful drag, before passing it to me as he holds his breath. I am about to refuse, but the throbbing in my injured ankle is fast becoming excruciating and I think of something Wayne said earlier.

"Okay," I say, taking the proffered joint. "But strictly for medicinal purposes."

"Whatever floats your boat, man." Jared leans back and closes his eyes.

I take a long drag, coughing slightly at the acrid dryness of the weed, and then take another, this time pulling the herb down deeply into my lungs. I pass it back to Jared as I exhale, my smoke all but invisible in the darkness of the car. We pass the chubby joint back and forth a few more times and then lean back in our automatically reclining seats, turning down the roof so we can stare up at the stars. "I lost my virginity here," I say, apropos of nothing.

"No shit," Jared says. "Me too."

We enjoy a primitive male moment, high-fiving over our shared sexual triumph. I have a brief, vivid flash of Carly's milky white thighs as she pulled her skirt down her legs, smiling affectionately at my clumsy, sophomoric excitement. "Are you sure?" I asked as she pulled urgently at the waistband of my underwear. "I want this," she said. "I want it with you."

"I loved her very much," I announce to the universe swirling above us like a studio backdrop, vast and intimate, my sudden, piercing sadness amplified by the weed.

"That's nice," Jared says. "I just wanted to get laid already."


I open my eyes a short while later to discover that during my brief nap, our location has changed. We are now parked outside a large brick colonial set back on an impressive front lawn. "Where are we?" I ask.

"I just wanted to see something," Jared says, peering intently out his window.

I lean across the seat and look out over his shoulder. "What are we looking at?"

"Her." Jared points to a lit window on the second floor. A girl periodically passes in and out of the window frame as she moves around her room, getting ready for bed.

"Who's that?"

"Kate Portnoy."

"And she is . . . ?"

"Perfect," Jared says reverently.

"What about that girl from the house? Candi?"

"Sheri. She's just a friend."

"Some friend," I say wistfully. "I need some friends like that."

Jared smirks without taking his eyes off the upstairs window. "We have an understanding."

"Ah," I say. "And Kate doesn't know about Sheri?"

Jared sits back in his seat and looks at me, positively bereft. "Kate doesn't know about me."

I nod sympathetically, thinking I'd give anything to have the broken heart of an eighteen-year-old. "I'm hungry," I say.

We pull into the 7-Eleven and walk through the aisles, sipping at Big Gulps as we shop for munchies. "I never realized how many different kinds of potato chips there are," I say, stupidly overwhelmed. "How are you supposed to make up your mind?"

"You," Jared says with a grin, "are stoned."

"Could be. What time is it?"

"Eleven forty-two."

"Wow." It seems like it should be much later than that. I grab some Sour Cream & Onion Pringles, and Jared selects Funyuns. The cashier, a goth girl wearing pale makeup and too much black lipstick, rings us up indifferently. "Thanks, Delia," I say, reading her name tag. She has to call us back from the door to give us our change. "Sorry," I say. "We're a little stoned."

"How very clever of you," she says, munching on a Kit Kat. She seems so wise and sad to me at that moment that I want to sit down and ask her questions, learn her entire story.

We sit in the parking lot on the hood of the Mercedes, our backs against the windshield, washing down our chips with long, thirsty sips from our Big Gulps. When we're done, I hop off the car and let out a wail of pain when my right foot hits the ground. I pull up my torn pants and gingerly pull at the bloodstained remnants of my sock. My ankle is swollen and caked with too much dried blood to afford me a good look at the laceration. Jared lets out a low, sympathetic whistle. "You think we should go to the emergency room?"

"Nah, we'll sit there all night," I say. "It seems to have stopped bleeding. I'll just go home and clean it up."

On the way, though, I change my mind and instruct Jared to drive me to Overlook Road. "What for?" he says.

"You showed me yours; now I'll show you mine."

Carly's house is dark, which in my drug-addled condition seems to incriminate me. "I was supposed to call her tonight."

"It's past midnight," Jared says. "Call her tomorrow."

Some part of me knows this would be the wiser course of action, but another part, admittedly the stoned part, thinks that showing up in the dead of night is decidedly more romantic. And tonight I'm eighteen again. It's Jared and me, two young, throbbing hearts; stoned, lonely, and romantic to the end. Our yearning knows no bounds, our faith is endless, our testosterone coming out of our ears. Give us a chance and we'll love you fiercely with every cell in our bodies; give us the signal and we'll fuck you all night. Break our hearts, we'll weep and mourn and we'll be in love again inside of a month.

I climb out of the car and limp slowly up the front walk. "Not a good idea," Jared calls to me from the car.

"I know what I'm doing."

"All evidence to the contrary."

I ignore him and ring the bell. After a few seconds, I ring it again. Just as it's dawning on me what a terribly stupid idea this is, I hear the light tread of bare feet on carpeted stairs, and then Carly's at the door. She's dressed in blue boxers and a gray UConn T-shirt; her hair pulled back in a loose pony-tail, her eyes squinting and bleary as sleep and consciousness jockey for position. She looks, I think, quite beautiful.

"Joe," she says, not so much a greeting as a confirmation, in the same way the villain in a James Bond flick will note the sudden explosion in his underground nuclear facility and immediately say, in a carefully restrained European accent, "Bond." Because, really, who the hell else could it be?

"Hi," I say.

"What's going on?" she says, rubbing her eyes.

"I was supposed to call. I didn't want you to think I didn't."

"You didn't," she points out, momentarily confusing me.

"True." There follows a leaden silence as the handle on this particular conversation floats tantalizingly above me, just out of reach. "This isn't going very well, is it?" I say.

"I'm not sure what 'this' is, but I suspect you're right."

I'm suddenly exhausted. I turn away from Carly and sit down on her front step. I hear her hesitate behind me and then step outside, letting the screen door close with a hy-draulic hiss behind her. Score one for the home team. All things are possible. She sits down next to me, pulling her knees up to her chest.

"What do you want, Joe?" she says softly.

"I just—I don't know. I want to connect with you."

"And you thought showing up here after midnight would do the trick?"

"It seemed like the thing to do at the time." I find myself admiring her toes, which are short and thin and then open into little round bulbs at the end, like grapes, their nails painted a glossy crimson. "You have very pretty toes."

"Are you drunk?"

"No," I say. "Maybe a little high, though."

Carly nods. "Perfect."

Above us, the moon hangs like a fat blister on the heel of the sky, ready to burst in a spray of viscous white pus. I look at Carly and think I might cry. "I just wish I could get past all of this and just talk to you," I tell her. "You're the only person I want to really talk to, and I just can't seem to do it."

She nods again and leans forward and for one exhilarating instant I think she's going to hug me, but she only hovers in front of me, craning her neck as she looks down, and says, "Is that blood on your leg?"

Carly's guest bathroom is done in light pastels, pinks and blues, with impressionistic watercolor orchids on the wallpaper. Above the sink is a frosted Lucite shelf with scented soaps in the shapes of seashells and starfish. I know instinctively that she didn't decorate this room, that it was like this when she bought the house. It is far too delicate and refined a room to suit the base processes for which it is intended, and I'm sure that defecating in it would feel like swearing in a temple. I sit on the peach marble sink, and Carly sits on the furry toilet seat with my wounded leg planted between her smooth, hairless thighs as she dabs it gently with alcohol. I realize that this was my immediate motivation for having woken her up. I couldn't bear the thought of tending to my own wounds two nights in a row. "This is pretty deep," Carly says, grunting mildly as she works around the cut. "How'd it happen?"

"Climbing a fence."

"And what's that all over your clothing?"

"Paint."

She gives me an inquisitive look. "I was playing paintball," I explain.

"Oh." In the dissipating haze of the marijuana, her face

appears bathed in a soft golden light. "So," she says. "Tonight you played paintball, smoked pot, and hurt yourself climbing a fence."

"It sounds stupid when you put it like that," I say. "Out of context."

"Why don't you put it into context for me?"

I think about it for a moment and then shrug. "The context has temporarily eluded me. I guess I was trying to relive my youth a little."

"Like you were such a pothead in your youth."

"Well, maybe I should have been." This is of course the exact wrong thing to say, because it makes me sound like a bitter fuck. The correct response would be "I didn't need the weed because I had you," or something along those lines. It would be corny, overtly flirtatious, and would have earned me at best a sarcastic frown, but underneath it all it might have reminded her that she'd once loved me.

Carly tears open another alcohol swab with her teeth and continues scrubbing my bloodied ankle. "Can I be honest with you?" she says.

"As long as you're going to say something nice."

"Since you got to the Falls, you seem determined to make a complete ass out of yourself and absorb a good deal of bodily harm along the way."

"Could you explain to me how that was nice?"

"Some might say," she continues, easily ignoring me, "that you're doing it deliberately."

"And why would I do that?"

"I don't know," she says, turning back to my cut. She pulls out some gauze and tape from a drawer under me and begins carefully wrapping the cut. "Some misguided form of penance, maybe."

"That's a neat theory," I say. "But what's my sin?"

"Everyone's got something."

"What have you got?"

She considers the question. "I'm not sure," she confesses, biting on her lip thoughtfully. "But I know I've already done all the penance I'm going to do."

"I heard about that—your marriage, I mean. I'm sorry. I just—I don't know what to say."

"That's actually perfect," Carly says, standing up brusquely and lowering my now-bandaged foot. "Because we are so not going to discuss it."

"I'm sorry," I say again.

"Don't be."

"What should I be?"

Carly fixes me with a look in which bitterness and resigned warmth mingle awkwardly, like guests early to a cocktail party. "You should be going," she says.

Jared and I sit in a subdued silence on the short drive home, the last remnants of the weed diffusing from our bloodstream like bubbles from champagne going flat. I replay my conversation with Carly, trying to recall its exact tone, but it's already fading to fuzzy unreality. I still have no clue as to what she feels toward me, but I'm developing the strong suspicion that her ambivalence is probably not cause for uncontained optimism. We pull up to the house and Jared cuts the engine, leaning back as he hands me my keys. "So, how'd that work out for you back there?" he asks.

"Okay," I say. "Not too good. I don't know. Lousy."

"As long as you're clear on it."

"What about the window girl?"

"Kate."

"Kate. You think you'll talk to her anytime soon?"

"I don't know," Jared says. "As frustrating as it is, there's something nice about this stage."

"She doesn't know you exist. I don't think you can legally call that a stage."

"I know. But I haven't fucked anything up yet."

"Point taken."

We step out of the car and trudge across the lawn toward the front porch, two battle-weary soldiers back from the trenches, when Jared suddenly tenses up. "Busted," he whispers to me through his teeth. I looked up and follow his gaze to find Cindy standing on the porch, looking tired and mightily pissed. She takes in our ragged, limping, paint-spattered appearance with angry, disapproving eyes that burn with unbridled hostility when they come to rest on me. Her face contracts briefly as she sniffs, and I have no doubt that she can smell the weed on us. I steel myself for the inevitable tongue-lashing, but the night has one more surprise in store for me. Cindy comes down the stairs, nodding slowly as if I've done nothing more than fulfill her worst expectations.

"Hi, Cindy," I say to break the silence. "What's up?"

In a burst of intuition, I know why she's there before she says anything. My father's come out of his coma. It's a miracle, really; the doctors don't know what to make of it. The nurse just walked past his room and there he was, sitting up in his bed, looking slightly perplexed but no worse for wear. And when the respirator came out, he asked in a raspy voice for his sons, the plural form, meaning both of them. There will be recovery and awkwardness, occupational therapy, and halting discussions of our damaged past, recriminations and veiled apologies, but through it all a sense of renewal, a second chance. I will not shy away from it; I will let go my bitterness and my strong proclivity toward sarcasm and embrace this opportunity to be whole again.

Cindy holds my glance for a moment and then directs her gaze over my shoulder. "Your father's dead," she says.

Memories surface in a montage: my father teaching me to ride my new two-wheeler, then chasing me frantically when I suddenly get the hang of it and take off down our street, my mother and Brad laughing hysterically on the front lawn. My fourth-grade diorama project on Mount Saint Helens, when he stays up half the night with me trying to concoct the right mixture of baking powder and vinegar to simulate eruption from the crude papier mâché volcano I'd built. Helping me reel in a fifteen-pound striped bass on a chartered fishing boat on the Long Island Sound, cursing and shouting encouragement, then pounding my back in triumph when we finally land the sucker. Washing his car in the driveway and then turning the hose on Brad and me, chasing us around the yard and then tackling us so we all go down in a wet, muddy tangle of arms and legs . . .

But here's the thing. None of this ever happened. Or maybe it did. I can't tell anymore. I've spent so much time reliving and rewriting those years that I can no longer discern which vignettes are the result of which process. In my reckless anger, I've managed to fuck up a vital area of memory to the point where I will never again be able to isolate reality, and so whatever good there might have been has now been lost to rambling fiction. And the worst part of it is this: I think I did it on purpose.

# book TWO

One soft infested summer me and Terry became friends
trying in vain to breathe the fire we was born in
Catching rides to the outskirts, tying faith beneath our teeth
sleeping in that old abandoned beach house
getting wasted in the heat
and hiding on the backstreets . . .
With a love so hard and filled with defeat
running for our lives at night on them backstreets.
—"Backstreets," Bruce Springsteen

# twenty-three

The caskets all have names like Wilton, Exeter, Balmoral, and Buckingham, suggesting that the dearly departed will enter the afterworld as British nobility. Features include brass tone accents, hand-cast bronze handles, and tailored champagne crepe with matching pillows and throws. The higher-end caskets come with the patented Eterna-rest adjustable bedding system, and a number of caskets have artwork on their interiors, illuminated grottos with renderings of the Madonna or reproductions of *The Last Supper*. Only the acutely pervasive attendance of death prevents the whole business from crossing the line into comedy.

Brad is home, glumly working the phones, entangled in the myriad details involved in putting a body underground, so I've volunteered to pick out a casket, which turns out to be more complicated than I anticipated. I am now expected to choose between wood finishes and decorative trims for something that will be buried in the dirt almost immediately. And by the way, which features are most vital to a corpse?

The casket showroom, located in the basement of the funeral home, has the unreal feel of a sitcom set, with gleaming, lacquered caskets mounted on discreet black pedestals, all meticulously buffed to a showroom shine; a car dealership for the freshly deceased. In the air is the light smell of varnish and lemon Pledge. I make my way dazedly between the caskets, thinking it really doesn't matter which one I pick but still terrified of picking the wrong one. You can't go through life making as many wrong choices as I have without developing a certain wanton fearlessness toward decision making, but we are talking about eternity here, and it has me spooked.

My salesman, Richard, is obese and high-strung, with a frown of profound sympathy etched permanently into his features. I remember him from the neighborhood, a sad, chubby kid who could only ever manage to keep one side of his shirt tucked into his pants at any given time. He chases me nervously around the showroom, sweating and panting dangerously as he expounds on the virtues of the higher-end coffins, looking slightly pained when I bluntly ask for pricing, as if he finds the discussion of money vulgar and inappropriate. He works on commission, no doubt, which strikes me as being in poor taste, given the circumstances of his profession. The collective grief of Bush Falls will put his kids through college.

I finally settle on the Exeter in a mahogany finish, which comes to fifty-six hundred dollars before sales tax. I briefly consider haggling over price but decide that it would be a serious breach of etiquette, and besides, I just want to be gone from here already. Richard nods obsequiously at my choice and plants his considerable girth down at the laughably small black desk in the back of the room to write up the purchase. "There's also a sixty-dollar charge for refrigeration," he advises me.

"Excuse me?"

He looks up from his papers. "The body. We refrigerate it until the interment. It's thirty dollars a day."

"Oh, okay." I'm sorry I asked.

"And there's the seven percent Cougar discount."

"What?"

Richard looks up at me. "Your father was a Cougar, wasn't he?"

"He was," I say.

"He gets seven percent off."

"Lucky him."

Richard stands up from behind the desk, his chair letting out a hissing sigh of relief, and hands me my receipt. "Once again, I'm terribly sorry for your loss."

"Thanks," I say, thinking that at a ten percent commission he's just made six hundred dollars for fifteen minutes of work, so how sorry can he really be. But then again, after almost seventeen years of not speaking to my father, I've just picked out his home for all eternity, so I just shake Richard's fat, clammy hand and get the hell out of there.

The funeral is attended by a good portion of the Bush Falls community, who don't view my father's death as any reason to stop staring at me with eyes that range from clinically inquisitive to outwardly hostile as they mill about the greeting hall before the service. It's one thing to know that I am generally despised by the bulk of the population, but to have so many of them under one roof at the same time is another thing entirely. It feels like those childhood dreams where you show up to school and realize too late that you're not wearing any pants. The nakedness might be metaphorical, but the arctic frost in my intestines is inarguably real.

Looking around the crowd, I see that a significant percentage of the men are wearing their old Cougars team jackets in a show of solidarity for their departed teammate. Like firemen or policemen, they are here to bury one of their own, fallen in the line of duty, as it were. There is something oddly grand in this gesture, even if the faded jackets looked silly on the balding, fleshy, potbellied men who wear them over button-down shirts and ties. I know it's ridiculous, but I can't help bitterly observing that even in death my father has managed to remind me one last time of my exclusion from the privileged inner circle he and Brad inhabit as Cougars.

Thank god for Owen, who arrives from Manhattan in the obnoxious white stretch limo he has hired for the occasion. He strides purposefully into the hall, looking spectacularly and inappropriately dapper in a tan poplin suit, mint green shirt, and a speckled bow tie. For years, Owen struggled with whether his wardrobe should exude the sharp, clean lines of corporate confidence or the finer, softer dimensions of intellectual and literary perspicacity. Over time, his atrocious attempts to reflect this dichotomy yielded a dreadful, polychromatic style, which he'd ultimately embraced as an affectation. "I thought you could use some moral support," he announces grandly, basking in the stares he's generating. "But as I am famously bereft of anything resembling morals, you'll have to settle for my unmodified support."

"Thanks for coming," I say as he briefly embraces me. It's the first time he's ever hugged me. He smells like Old Spice and baby powder.

"Please," Owen says, stepping back to stare around at the gathering crowd with unconcealed curiosity. "How could I not?"

Wayne shows up looking shockingly healthy in his Cougars jacket and borrowed suit pants that manage to somewhat conceal his wasted frame. He gives me a light hug and we grin at my own borrowed suit, as if any further evidence of our alien status is actually necessary. "You too?" I say, indicating his jacket.

"I've always been a sucker for tradition," Wayne says with a smirk. "Except as it pertains to lifestyle, of course." I introduce him to Owen, who nods in recognition and hugs him suddenly and dramatically, Wayne patting his back in bemused surprise.

Carly arrives as the last guests are filing into the chapel for the service, and I realize that I've been waiting to see if she'll come. She walks over and kisses me lightly on the cheek. I was hoping for something a bit more dramatic: a lingering hug, maybe some tears. "I'm so sorry, Joe," she says. She is wearing a sleek black pantsuit with a white blouse opened at the neck to reveal a small triangle of pale flesh and the delicate protrusion of her collarbones.

"Thanks for coming," I say.

I want to say something more, but the sudden tightness in my throat makes it impossible. Carly squeezes my hand, her eyes wide and knowing. "I'll sit where you can see me," she says. I nod mutely, and she moves ahead of me through the twin doors into the chapel.

After that, everything is a blur. A rabbi reads some psalms in Hebrew, and then a parade of middle-aged men in faded Cougars jackets take turns at the podium paying tribute to Arthur Goffman, threatening to drown us in a deluge of basketball metaphors. Brad speaks last, dividing my father's life into four quarters and explaining what his contributions were in each one, and I want to stand up and shout that it's just a fucking game. But when he steps down from the pulpit, he looks teary and spent. I know that he loved our father, and for a moment, I feel deeply sorry for him. Then I go back to feeling sorry for myself.

Only a handful of cars accompany us in the procession behind the hearse to the cemetery, which is on the other side of town. Once there, Brad, Jared, and I are joined by three older men in Cougars jackets, buddies of my father's, in bearing the coffin to the grave, beside which lies a high mound of dirt and the telltale tracks of the backhoe that prepared the grave yesterday. We place the coffin on the two two-by-fours that cross the open grave, and as the gravediggers begin lowering the coffin, I realize with a jolt that I'm standing right beside my mother's tombstone. I turn to read the gray marble stone—ELLEN GOFFMAN, 1945–1983, BELOVED WIFE, MOTHER,

AND DAUGHTER—and then I'm on my knees, pressing my fingers into the grooves of the letters that spell her name, weeping uncontrollably while behind me, they cover my father's coffin with dirt, and then something hits my head, cool, smooth, and unyielding, the glazed marble of the tombstone, and maybe I pass out, I'm not sure, but I distinctly feel myself being carried, a live person borne over the scattered graves for a change, and the last thought I have is that I never thought of her as his wife before, and that wasn't fair because he lost something too, maybe even something larger than I did.

# *twenty-four*

**1987**

It took a while for me to believe that Wayne wasn't coming back. Every day I expected to pick up the phone and hear his voice, or walk into school and see him leaning against his locker in his team jacket, greeting me with his usual wry grin. I drove past his house daily, slowing down to peer intently through the curtained windows as if I might discern some clue as to his whereabouts. Mrs. Hargrove had installed an answering machine and taken to screening her calls, and my regular inquiries apparently didn't make the cut.

"I don't think he's coming back," Carly said gently to me one afternoon. It was one of the first warm days of spring, and we were sitting on the bleachers overlooking the football field during a free period, enjoying the freshness of the weather. Wayne had been gone for over a month.

"Of course he is," I said. "Why would you say that?"

She folded her fingers into mine and looked out onto the field. "Would you?"

I shook my head. "But where is he? I mean, you would think he'd give me a call or something. Just to let us know where he is. I'm supposed to be his best friend, for god's sake."

Carly leaned against me and kissed the side of my jaw. "He will when he's ready."

I rested my head on hers, kissing her scalp where her hair parted. "I wonder if he called Sammy," I said.

Since Wayne's disappearance, Sammy had devoted himself to a strict regimen of invisibility. His attendance in school became highly sporadic, and when he did come, he moved through the halls like a phantom, keeping close to the walls, slipping unobtrusively in and out of classrooms. His hair, no longer sculpted into a pompadour, grew long and lay flat against his skull, and he always appeared rumpled and slightly askew, as if he'd slept in his clothing. On those rare occasions when I did run into him, he offered short, perfunctory conversation, scrupulously avoiding eye contact.

I dropped by his house on a few isolated evenings, motivated less by friendship than by the possibility that maybe he'd heard from Wayne. But Sammy was sullen and uncommunicative, and after sitting in his room for ten minutes or so, the conversational well would run dry. "He's in trouble, Joe," Lucy said to me on one such night as she walked me down the stairs to my car. "I can't get through to him."

"Me neither," I said. "It's like he's pissed at everyone."

She leaned against my car, smoking a cigarette and shivering slightly in the cool night air, looking small and vulnerable. On the pedestal in my mind, she always loomed larger than life, and it was a revelation every time I noticed how much taller than her I was. It would be so easy, I thought, to just step forward and wrap my arms around her. "It's driving me out of my fucking mind," Lucy said, shaking her head. "He barely eats; he won't talk to me. I don't know what the hell to do about it anymore. I think I've been a good mother to him, you know? I mean, Sammy's no picnic, let me tell you." She blew out some smoke and then waved it away in quick, nervous motions. "And I know I'm nobody's idea of mother of the year; I have no illusions about that. I was just a little older than you when I had Sammy. Just a kid, really. I always said we were better off without his scumbag father, but I don't know. Maybe if he had a father . . ." Her voice trailed off, and she looked up at me with a sad grin. "I'm going a little crazy, aren't I?"

"It's okay."

"I'm sorry, Joe. I don't mean to lay this all on you. It's just—I don't know. I'm so frustrated."

In that moment I understood something new about Lucy. Until she'd given birth to Sammy, she'd sailed through life on the wind of her looks. Then she got divorced, and her life became filled with a new breed of tribulations that were largely impervious to her beauty. She seemed to feel unqualified to help Sammy, and despised herself for feeling that way.

"It's okay," I said again. "I just wish I could do more to help."

"Just don't stop coming here," she said. "He needs a friend so badly right now."

"He doesn't want me around. He barely talks to me."

She reached out for my arm and held it with both of her hands. "Don't stop trying, Joe. He'll come around. He always does."

"Okay," I said. "I won't."

But I did. I couldn't stop blaming Sammy for what had happened to Wayne, and every time I saw him staring forlornly into space, I was seized by a fury so raw it threatened to overwhelm me. I wanted to scream at him, pound him into a bloody pulp, and tell him how much I wished he'd never come to the Falls. I had offered him friendship, and he'd repaid me by shredding the very fabric of my life. On some level, I knew that I was taking a childish view of things, that there were greater and more complex truths in play here, but that knowledge did nothing to dissipate my anger.

"Stop hounding Mrs. Hargrove," my father said to me one night, sticking his head into my bedroom as he passed by on the way to his own. He was slouched and sweaty from work, his eyelids sagging with exhaustion. His chinos were worn nearly to transparency in the knees and frayed at the cuffs, and I felt a brief flash of intense sympathy for him. It wouldn't have occurred to him to buy some new pants without my mother there to tell him to do so.

"What?"

"That poor lady's been through enough. She doesn't need you calling her night and day and reminding her."

"I don't call her night and day," I said.

"Well, she practically attacked me in the parking lot at Stop and Shop and told me you were making her crazy."

"She was already crazy."

"You show some respect," he said sternly, stepping fully into my room for what had to be the first time since Reagan was elected. "If I found out one of my sons was a homosexual, I don't know if I'd handle it any better."

"Well then, take it from me," I said bitterly. "You wouldn't."

I saw the anger flare up briefly behind his eyes, but he was too tired to fight with me. "Wayne left of his own accord. If he really wanted to hear from you, he'd let you know how to reach him."

"You're glad he's gone," I accused him.

My father nodded. "Wayne needed to leave. It was best for everyone, including him. He understood that. And when you get a little older, maybe you will too." He turned to leave.

"That's bullshit," I said.

He stopped in his tracks for a second but didn't turn back around. "Just leave her alone," he said. "I don't want to have

this conversation again."

When he was gone, I punched my wall repeatedly until my knuckles were scraped and swollen, and then did it some more, the small streaks of my blood smearing like chocolate onto the flat finish of the ivory paint. He no doubt heard the racket but apparently didn't feel compelled to investigate.

A few days later, my father left for an overnight business trip and Carly came over to have sex in my bed. The luxury of making love in an actual bed without the constant fear of discovery inhibiting our every move was rare, and we never missed an opportunity to take advantage. We'd been going at it for something like two hours when the doorbell rang. "Who's that?" Carly said. I was lying on my back and she was lying on top of me on her back, her arms and legs spread precisely over mine. She liked to lie like that sometimes when we'd just finished, her goal being to have our bodies touching at as many points as was physically possible.

"No one," I said. "Just ignore it."

But the doorbell continued to ring insistently, so I slid out from under her and threw on some shorts. "I'll be back in a minute," I said.

"I'll keep your spot warm." She stretched out on the bed, affording me a full view of her naked body still glistening in the sweaty afterglow of our lovemaking. "Joe."

"Yeah."

"I love you."

"I love you too."

My smile faded when I opened the door to find Sammy sitting on my front stairs, fiddling with his car keys. "Hey, Joe," he said, standing up. "I didn't think you were home."

*Then why did you stay?* "How's it going?" I said.

"It's okay."

"That's good. What's up?"

"What's up?" he repeated, pondering the question. He was dressed in jeans and a blue windbreaker, his hair greasy and limp against his scalp, clearly lacking the benefit of a recent shower. On the edge of his chin and below his sideburns were small, asymmetrical patches of dark stubble, the first evidence I'd ever seen that Sammy was capable of growing facial hair. "I don't really know what's up," he said. "I was sitting in my room, listening to 'Bobby Jean' for like the millionth time, and I just couldn't breathe anymore. I had to get the hell out of my house."

"Why 'Bobby Jean'?"

"Have you ever listened to the lyrics?"

"Maybe. I don't know."

Sammy flashed his customary disdainful frown reserved for those philistines who didn't fully appreciate the complex beauty of Springsteen. "The song is about someone whose best friend leaves town without saying good-bye," he said. "You should listen to it again sometime."

"Maybe I will."

Sammy nodded, lost deeply in thought. "Joe," he said, "before all of this happened, we were friends, weren't we?"

"Sure."

"So why aren't we anymore?"

The naked directness of his question caught me off guard and I had to look away for a minute before answering. "I don't know. I've tried to stay your friend," I said, my words ringing false in my own ears.

"Do you hate me?"

"Of course not."

"Because I would understand it if you did," Sammy said. "I wouldn't agree with it, but I would understand it."

I sighed deeply. I didn't want to be talking about this right now. "I don't hate you, Sammy."

He looked into my eyes intently, trying to measure the level of truth behind my statement. After a few moments, he nodded. "Good," he said. "I don't think I could stand to be hated by you right now."

"Let me know when would be good for you," I said, belatedly flashing him an exaggerated smirk so he would know I was joking.

He smiled. "I will." He turned to go down the stairs and stopped midway, started to say something, stopped, and then looked up at me. "You know, I never meant to be like this," he said hesitantly.

"Like what?"

He smiled and waved his hand around to indicate himself. "Like this. A fag. Believe me, I tried like hell for a while not to be one. Even when we moved here, I still thought maybe in a new town where no one knew me, I could change." He flashed me a small, sheepish smile. "Obviously, I couldn't," he said. "And neither could Wayne."

"I don't think Wayne's really sure about what he is or isn't," I said, sounding a bit more defensive than I'd intended. "I think he's probably gone somewhere to work it all out."

Sammy looked at me for a long moment and then shook his head. "If Wayne wasn't sure, Wayne wouldn't have left," he said.

"Whatever," I said, and quickly changed the subject. I didn't need to hear Sammy speaking like an expert on my best friend. "Where are you headed?"

"I don't know," he said with a shrug. "I think I'll just drive around for a while." He looked up the stairs to me. "You want to come along?"

I almost said yes. Since Wayne's departure and Sammy's subsequent depression, I hadn't really had any friends to just hang out and be stupid with, and I realized that I missed it. But Carly was waiting, naked and primed, on my bed upstairs, and it was really no contest. "Maybe tomorrow," I said. "I'm kind of in the middle of something."

Sammy looked past me into the house and then grinned. "I should have figured." He turned and stepped into the street, heading around the front of his mother's Chevy.

"Sammy," I called out to him.

"Yeah?"

"I'll see you around."

He swung open the door and looked over the roof of the car at me. "Take care, Joe," he said.

The finality of his salutation struck me as somewhat odd as I made my way back upstairs, but I didn't have long to contemplate it, because when I stepped into my bedroom, I found Carly jumping up and down in the center of my bed, still magnificently undressed, and all thoughts of Sammy, like my blood, fled rapidly from my brain. "I got a little bored," she said sheepishly.

"So I see."

"Are you particularly attached to those shorts?"

"Not really. Why?"

"Because if they're still on five seconds from now, I'm going home."

I smiled and charged the bed, and for the next few hours the world faded to black and nothing existed beyond the universe contained within my four bedroom walls.

Later that night, after Carly had gone home, I pulled out my cassette of *Born in the U.S.A.* and played "Bobby Jean" on the stereo. Sammy was right. I'd never really paid attention to the lyrics, and it amazed me how well they articulated what I'd been feeling ever since Wayne had left town. Springsteen carefully avoided referring to Bobby Jean as male or female, leaving the listener free to associate as needed. When he sang the last verse, about Bobby Jean's being out on that road somewhere, on some bus or train, and how he wished he could have just seen him or her one last time, I began to tremble. *"I miss you,"* came the Boss's voice mournfully through my speakers. *"Good luck, good-bye, Bobby Jean."* He lingered on the name for an extra beat, and then Clarence's sax came on strong, wailing and rasping with a chilling despondence, and I sat down on my bedroom floor, rocking back and forth to the music, only aware after the fact that I had started to cry.

I didn't know yet that Sammy was dead when I got to school the next morning and found Carly giggling with some girlfriends near her locker. When she saw me, she excused herself and came running over to give me a kiss. "Hey, stud," she said, falling easily into step with me. "I had a lot of fun last night."

"What's all the giggling about?" I said, indicating her friends, who were still locked in an animated huddle.

"Cheryl lost her virginity last night," Carly said. "She was at the falls with Mike, and someone went over."

"Cheryl Sands was a virgin?" I said skeptically.

"Strictly in a technical sense."

"I see. So, did someone really go over the falls?"

"That's what they're saying."

"I miss out on all the good stuff."

"Excuse me, sir," Carly said sternly. "If I'm not mistaken, you got about five hours' worth of the good stuff last night, and you didn't have to wait for some moron to risk life and limb for you to get it."

"Which begs an interesting question," I said. "Who went over?"

Carly shrugged indifferently. "I don't know."

Nobody did. The buzz around school was simply that someone had gone over the falls the night before, and those boys that had been present were proudly embellishing tales of the sexual harvest they'd reaped in the face of this major event. Details were not yet available as to the identity of the daredevil or the outcome of his alleged plunge into the Bush River.

If news travels fast in small towns, it spreads at light speed in small-town high schools. We were all in our respective homerooms by the time Mouse arrived late to school, practically bursting with the news of Sammy's suicide, but somehow the information managed to permeate the very walls of our classrooms, carried like deer ticks through a network of hall monitors, latecomers, and students returning from bathroom breaks. "It's just a rumor," Carly whispered to me, placing her hand on my arm as I sat trembling in my seat. But I thought of the way Sammy had stopped by to see me that night, how strangely formal his good-bye had been, and I knew better.

Lyncroft's voice came over the PA system, as usual too loud and brimming with spit, announcing an immediate assembly in the auditorium. Everyone grabbed their books and bags and filed into the rapidly filling hallway, speaking in hushed tones as they went. I felt a cold sweat break out on my forehead and I knew that Sammy was dead. I also knew that there was no way I would be able to sit in a crowded auditorium and listen to our drunk of a principal confirm it for me. Carly had gotten a few steps ahead of me down the hall, and suddenly the effort of telling her that I was cutting out seemed too much for me, so I just took a quick left turn and walked purposefully toward the exit. I'd long since learned that teachers were far less likely to question you if you moved with authority.

I sat in my father's car in the parking lot, rocking back and forth and pounding on his steering wheel, screaming out a steady string of curses until my throat was raw. After a while I started the car and drove it toward Sammy's house. It was a warm, cloudless day, and as I drove through downtown Bush Falls, the utter normalcy of the streets began to override the insanity in my head, working to convince me that I was mistaken, that someone had simply spread a nasty rumor. It could very well have been that the assembly had been called over another matter altogether. With every passing block I became increasingly confident that Sammy was just cutting and that I would find him hanging out in his bedroom, probably brooding, but certainly alive. I would tell him about the crazy rumor and he'd grin and say, "They wish," and I'd tell him that I was taking the day off and see if he wanted to do something.

I managed to keep reality at bay in this manner for the remainder of my drive. Then I pulled onto Sammy's block and saw the cars from the Sheriff's Department parked outside his house, and the truth reasserted itself like a well-aimed kick in the crotch. I pulled over to the curb and sat there for about fifteen minutes until Sheriff Muser and a deputy emerged and climbed somberly into their car. Once they were gone, I got out of my car and quietly climbed the stairs to the Habers' porch. The front door had been inadvertently left open behind the storm door, so I could see down the long hallway and into the kitchen, where Lucy sat at the table, her head in her hands, crying loudly and steadily.

I don't know how long I stood there just watching her, rocked by the desolation of her wails and paralyzed by my own feelings of sorrow and guilt. I had just decided to leave when she happened to look up and see me through the storm door. I thought of running, even felt my feet turning in my sneakers, but her gaze froze me in my tracks. "Joe," she said softly, with no trace of surprise in her voice at having discovered me lurking on her porch.

I walked into the kitchen and stood awkwardly against the wall as she looked up at me, her eyes swollen into slits and raw from crying. "My Sammy's gone." Her voice was high and unsteady, like a young child speaking indignantly between sobs.

"I know," I said.

"He was all I had," she said, gracelessly wiping at the snot running from her nose with the back of her wrist. "And now I don't know what I'm going to do." This last sentence segued into a long, mournful sob as she buried her face in her hands on the table. I sat down and put my arms around her and she collapsed into me as if her bones had suddenly come loose in their rigging, her body convulsing against me with each new wave of tears. "Now I have nobody."

I wanted to tell her that she had me, but I knew that wasn't true anymore, so I just held her and said nothing. We sat like that for a while, suspended in our pathetic, futile symmetry, a motherless boy and a childless mother with no place in between to meet and nothing of any real value to offer each other. I left there feeling neither grief nor sympathy but only a burgeoning fury at my abject worthlessness and a growing certainty that the time had come for me to get the hell out of the Falls.

They'd pulled Sammy's body out of the Bush River early that morning. His car was found in the woods near the waterfalls, and although there were never any published reports of the circumstances of his death, I could imagine in vivid detail what had happened. Just as Carly and I were finishing our marathon sex session in my bedroom, Sammy drove his car up to the falls and parked. As all around him couples in parked cars clumsily groped and petted each other, Sammy stuck some Springsteen into his tape deck, maybe even playing "Bobby Jean" at the same moment that I was listening to it in my bedroom, and drank enough beer to blind himself to the consequences of what he planned to do. Eventually, he stepped out of his car and stared down at the waterfalls, the combination of darkness and alcohol obscuring the churning waters below so that they didn't appear particularly frightening to him. Then Sammy took a last, deep breath and hurled himself determinedly off the cliff and into the falls.

And maybe in that last moment it felt good to be so bold, to have made that decision. And for that brief instant of flight, before the waters angrily swallowed him into their tumultuous darkness, maybe he finally felt free. And maybe I just told myself that because I knew that if I'd simply chosen to go for that drive with him instead of staying home to have more sex, Sammy would never have jumped.

The rest of the year flew by in a blur. I went to school, hung out with Carly, and graduated, but I experienced it all from behind a gauzy veil of detachment, seeing everything and feeling none of it. It was like a switch in me had been turned off that day in Lucy's kitchen, and I became one step removed from my own life.

Sean Tallon made a crack about Sammy as he passed me in the hall one day, and without hesitation I punched him square in the nose, drawing a shocking spray of blood. He was more surprised than hurt, but he got over it quickly and pounded the shit out of me, bashing my skull in with the worn plaster cast on his broken arm while Mouse looked on, cackling hysterically. I studied my bruises in the mirror with an almost clinical interest, but I didn't recall feeling any pain.

Sean's broken arm, coupled with Wayne's disappearance, effectively crippled the basketball team. They had been easily knocked out of the play-offs in the first round, and for the first time in twenty years, the Bush Falls Cougars didn't go to the state finals.

About a week after Sammy's death, someone threw a large brick through Dugan's office window and trashed his trophy case. An investigation was launched, but the guilty party was never discovered. Looking back years later, I thought it was me, could sometimes recall the heft of the stone in my hand right before I threw it, but the memory was so vague and synthetic that I couldn't be sure. Maybe I just heard about it and wished it had been me.

# *twenty-five*

To err, as they say, is human. To forgive is divine. To err by withholding your forgiveness until it's too late is to become divinely fucked up. Only after burying my father do I realize that I always intended to forgive him. But somewhere I blinked, and seventeen years flew by, and now my forgiveness, ungiven, has become septic, an infection festering inside me.

I stay in bed for two days, sweating feverishly beneath my blankets, stomach clenched, thighs like jelly. I don't know if what I'm feeling is genuine grief or deep, paralyzing regret over not being able to grieve, but whichever it is, it isn't screwing around. I lie motionless, flitting seamlessly between sleep and wakefulness until they become all but indistinguishable. More than once, I dream I'm crying, and wake up with swollen eyes and a damp pillow.

My thoughts assemble before me in a ragged stream of semiconsciousness. I hate my life, and up until a few days ago I didn't even know it, and how can such a seemingly important fact have escaped my attention? Why has my father's death left me feeling so alone, when he hasn't been a part of my life in seventeen years? I'm an orphan. I repeat the word out loud, over and over again, listening to it bounce off the walls of my childhood bedroom until it makes no sense.

Loneliness is the theme, and I play it like a symphony, in endless variations. I've lived more than a third of my life, and am more alone now than I've ever been. You're supposed to make your way through life becoming more substantial as you go, the nucleus of your own little universe, your orbit overlapping the orbits of others. Instead, I've shed all those who cared about me like snakeskin, slithering angrily into my small solitary hole.

On the second afternoon of my self-pity fest, Jared comes by to see me.

"What are you doing?" he says.

Moping, sulking, crying, feeling sorry for myself. "Nothing," I say.

"You look awful."

"I'm having a bad life."

He nods, undeterred by my sarcasm, and tosses my clothing off the desk chair to make himself a seat. "Whatever. My father said to invite you for dinner tomorrow night, if you'll still be around."

"Why didn't he call me himself?"

"He did. I guess the wack job downstairs didn't give you the message."

I look at him. "What wack job?"

"Your agent, I guess. He's acting like he owns the place."

"Owen is downstairs?"

"I thought you knew."

"I didn't."

"He acts as if you know." Jared shrugs. "So that was some show you put on at the cemetery."

"I slipped," I say.

He stares at me intently for a minute and then frowns. "Just tell me: did you love him or not?"

I look up at my nephew. "He was my father."

"I wasn't questioning your genealogy."

"Listen," I say, but he waves me down.

"A simple yes or no will do."

"It's not a simple question."

He scowls at my equivocation, the uncompromising scowl of youthful conviction. "Make it simple," he says. "Boil it down to the basics."

I'm quiet for a long moment, but Jared seems prepared to wait indefinitely. "I can't," I say.

"Why not?"

"I just—I don't know."

He stands up and sighs. "How did you get so fucked up?" he asks me, not unkindly.

"It takes a high level of discipline," I tell him as he heads for the door. "And absolute commitment. It's like my own special super power."

He stops at the door. "So I'll see you tomorrow night?"

"What's tomorrow night?"

"Um, dinner, remember?"

"Oh, yeah. Sure."

He shakes his head and offers a sad little grin. "That is, if you can fit us into your busy schedule here."

A little while later I pull myself out of bed and crawl downstairs to find Owen sprawled out on the living room couch in a pair of my father's sweatpants and an undershirt, looking at Asian porno sites on his laptop. "Hey," he says by way of greeting. He sits up a little, and his white, hairless belly fat peeks out from between his undershirt and waistband like rising dough in a bake pan. Concentric circles of soiled paper plates, soda cans, crumpled junk food packages, and Chinese take-out boxes surround him like Stonehenge. Sitting there like that, a dough ball in the midst of his own refuse, he looks somewhat pitiful, and I have a sudden intuitive flash that the real Owen, the soft, unaffected one who hides behind the sharp wit and silly suits, is really just a sad and lonely little man. The spirited verbiage and outlandishness are the threads with which he constantly, desperately spins his protective cocoon, the only thing standing between him and the abyss. Or maybe that's just me projecting. "What are you doing here?" I say.

"Just holding down the fort," Owen says.

"You're doing a great job." I conspicuously eye the piles of litter.

"A man's got to eat."

I sit at the foot of the stairs, rubbing my face wearily. "Owen. Why are you still here?"

He smiles and folds his laptop. "I have a better question," he says, and then looks at me meaningfully. "Why are you still here?"

"I have some things I still need to work out."

"What things?"

"I'm not sure. I guess that would be the first thing on the list."

Owen nods and stands up, brushing an assortment of crumbs off his undershirt. "Well, to answer your earlier question, I stuck around to tell you something."

"What's that?"

"I'd like to tell you why your manuscript isn't any good."

"So now it's no good?"

"No. It was always no good."

"I can't stress enough how not up for this I am right now."

"Actually, you are," Owen says. "Your business is writing, but my business is writers, and of the two of us, I'm the one who's on top of his game right now, so it would behoove you to pay attention." He stares at me intently, daring me to contradict him. "*Bush Falls* came from inside you, from that place where good writers store the great narrative events of their lives. The problem is that since you left the Falls, nothing of any significance has happened to you. If I had to write the jacket copy for the book of your life, I'd be hard-pressed to come up with anything. Joe lives in Manhattan. Joe has maybe a little more than his share of what is doubtless highly conventional sex. Joe gets older. Joe gets depressed. That pretty much does it. You've had no great loves and no significant experiences. It's like you've been sleepwalking through the last seventeen years."

"Somewhere in there, I did write a critically acclaimed best-selling novel."

"So you did," Owen concedes. "The single remarkable event in your post–Bush Falls life was writing a book about the Falls. Do you see what I'm getting at here?"

"That I'm a big fucking loser?"

"Besides that. Listen. You've been gone from here for seventeen years, but really you never left. The things that happened here—with your friends, and Carly, and your father—they damaged you, and from that damage came your book, but you're not going to get another one out of it."

"Well, if you're right, what the hell am I supposed to do about it?"

"You're already doing it. You've been doing it since you got here."

"What exactly is it that you think I've been doing?"

Owen smiles. "Gathering new material."

"You're insane," I say. "This has been a nightmare for me."

"I know." He sits down next to me on the stairs. "You're in pain, and frankly I'm relieved to see it."

"And why is that?"

"Because, to paraphrase the late Bruce Lee, pain is good. It means that you're alive. And dead people, for the most part, don't write books."

"Fuck writing," I say angrily. "I have nothing. There's no one in my life." My voice trembles tellingly, and I take it down a notch for maintenance. "No one cares about me."

"That's not true."

"But it is," I say sadly. "And I never even realized it until now. What kind of colossal asshole must that make me, to have gone this far through life without having made a posi-tive difference to one fucking soul?"

"I care."

"You get paid."

"That just makes me care more."

I sigh. "Whatever."

"Wayne cares about you."

"Wayne's dying," I say, and immediately feel like a schmuck. Owen looks at me severely. "We're all dying. Just at different rates."

"Is this the first time you've tried to cheer someone up? Because, I have to tell you, you really suck at it."

"It's not in my job description." Owen slaps my knee as he gets up from the stairs. "Cheer yourself up. I'm going home."

I watch him gather up his laptop and a leather overnight bag, and then follow him to the front door. Unbelievably, the white stretch is still parked outside. "You kept the limo all this time?" I say. "That's going to cost you a fortune."

"Actually, it's going to cost *you* a fortune," he says with a smirk, heading out the door and down the steps before I can thank him for sticking around. I watch from behind the storm door as the absurd limo pulls away from the curb and meanders down the block. The sunroof opens and Owen's hand pops up, comically brandishing a half-filled wineglass. He'll be good and wasted by the time he gets home. For the first time I smile, feeling vaguely cinematic as I watch until the white of the limo is absorbed into the dusky Connecticut twilight. In the kitchen, my cell phone rings. I consider ignoring it, but then think the better of it. Like Owen said, it's time to start living again, to throw myself into the mix and begin sorting things out. Feeling suddenly and irrationally renewed, I pull the phone off its charger and flip it open.

"You're a fucking asshole," Nat says.

Owen has left a huge box in the kitchen. I open it to find a brand-new Dell Inspiron laptop, a handful of discs, and a hastily scribbled note from Owen. *Don't think about it. Just turn it on and get to work.* Fifteen minutes later I have the machine up and running on the desk in my bedroom, and I'm sitting pensively in front of it, its blank screen taunting me, daring me to try to fill it with something worthwhile. The idea of starting over from scratch is daunting, but not without appeal. I remind myself that I've done this before—to critical acclaim, no less—and allow my fingers to gently brush the smooth plastic keys of the laptop.

Over the last few days an idea has been forming, the bare skeleton of a story, and now I turn it around in my head, searching for the entry point that will get me started. *No one was more surprised when Matt Burns came home for his father's funeral than Matt himself,* I type, then pause for a moment before continuing. The sentence appears small and insignificant against the white expanse of empty screen, an unlikely springboard from which to launch an entire novel, but something in its conversational simplicity reassures me, and I begin to type some more, at first tentatively and then with greater confidence. Within two hours, I have three chapters done. It's a lyrical mystery I have in mind, about a son who returns home to investigate the suspicious circumstances surrounding his estranged father's death, excavating clues and his own troubled past as he goes. That's the basic idea, and even as I write the initial pages, I know that I'm onto something, that this is a book I can write from beginning to end. It's after nine o'clock when I finally stop typing and save my work, resisting the impulse to reread everything I've just written. It occurs to me that it's been over two days since I last showered, and I stink. I strip out of my sweats and head into the bathroom. For the first time since I returned to the Falls, things are starting to feel attainable again. I know this feeling is nothing more than the illusion of control brought on by my newly galvanized writing effort, but for now, all things being equal, I figure I'll take it.

# twenty-six

There's something about being wet and naked that always makes things seem eminently doable. I shower energetically, vigorously scrubbing off two days' worth of accumulated grime, and as I do, I am a congress of one, making sweeping resolutions by the handful. I will write my new novel. I will make amends with my family and work on becoming something resembling a brother and an uncle. I've already made some promising headway toward that end with Jared, even if it has involved some felonious activities. I will find a way to get past the awkwardness between Carly and me, and will find out if there's anything there to salvage. I will be a friend to Wayne and offer all the comfort and support I can. I am baptized in the faintly green foam of Irish Spring and Herbal Essences, ensconced in a lather of possibility.

I'm just stepping out of the shower when the doorbell rings. I quickly wrap a towel around my waist, the air invigoratingly cold against my wet skin, and run downstairs, still feeling a sense of elation at my newfound direction. And then I open the door and it's Lucy, looking flushed and somewhat breathless in a short skirt and a tight scoop-necked sweater, and things take a bit of a left turn.

"Hi," I say, stepping back to let her in.

"I'm sorry to barge in on you like this," she says. "I thought maybe you'd gone back home already." She pulls at a loose strand of hair that has become ensnared in her lip gloss.

"Nope," I say. "Still here."

She smiles awkwardly. "I'm sorry I didn't come to the funeral. I don't go out very much these days, and I just . . ."

"Don't worry about it."

Things seem to be moving in slow motion, because I have time to dwell on her every detail: the smooth lines of her face, the way her full, impossibly red lips seem to crush against each other where they meet, becoming an entirely new and delectable organ, her breasts straining against the dark fabric of her sweater, her smooth, tanned legs, and the soft curves of her thigh muscles where the hemline of her skirt bisects them.

We say a few more things to each other, but the sound of our conversation fades, seems to be coming from off in the distance, as we draw closer. I take a step back, clutching the towel at my waist with both hands, telling her that I'll just run upstairs and put some clothing on, but Lucy lunges forward and puts a restraining hand on my arm and says don't, and her voice is the radio signal and my anatomy the receiver, and I begin to shiver and say but I'm all wet, and she presses herself up against me, pulling my hand forcefully away from my body and guiding it up and under her skirt to the junction of her legs as she presses her lips against me and whispers so am I, and the towel hits the floor only a scant second before her skirt does.

We stumble up the stairs, kissing and clinging to each other with animal intensity, but once in my room she pushes me away so that I can watch her undress. She does it slowly, illuminated in the doorway by the soft light from the hallway behind her. And then, unbelievably, she is standing before me, unabashedly naked, as my eyes greedily drink up every inch of her magnificent body. Lucy has to be over fifty years old, but her body resolutely refuses to act its age. Her skin still shines with vitality, her breasts hang remarkably firm and full, her belly smooth and flat. You would think, after years of the fantasy, that the reality can't possibly measure up, but somehow it does. The odd imperfections, the dimples and creases and even a red birthmark in the shape of Italy just below her left hip, only serve as foils to her perfection, the exceptions that prove the rule. She walks slowly over to my bed and climbs onto it, stretching out on all fours, the upward curve of her age-defying, apple-shaped ass raised slightly as she turns to look over her shoulder and down her back at me. "Fuck me, Joe," she moans, lifting her upper body off the bed with her arms in a push-up so that through her spread thighs I can see the tips of her breasts grazing the rumpled sheets beneath her. "Fuck me hard."

I do. And she is warm and soft and wet and supple and smooth, and on some level it's how I've always imagined it. The soft roundness of her breasts in my hands, the cherry hardness of her nipples between my teeth, the taste of her tongue as it pushes its way into my mouth, seeking out my own, and the press of her moist lips on me. We kiss and lick and suck and stroke each other at a fevered pitch, not allowing even a moment's respite for rational thought to intrude, and when I enter her, she comes almost immediately, crying out and digging her nails into my ass as she pulls me deeper inside. Her quick finish is highly fortunate, because after six months of celibacy, I'm like an exposed nerve ending down there, and any demonstration of tantric endurance is out of the question. I follow a moment later, and as I heave with the last convulsions of my orgasm, I think of Carly and feel ashamed.

We lie absolutely still for a few moments, our mingled sweat and juices drying on us in the conditioned air and becoming sticky on our skin. Only as I roll off her do I realize that she's crying softly. I brush the hair out of her face and see tears streaming out of her eyes. I open my mouth to say something, but there's really nothing I can say that will matter, so instead I just lie on my side next to her, holding her against me as she sobs, until, after an indeterminate amount of time, she falls asleep. Once her breathing becomes slow and regular, I disentangle myself from her and go to the bathroom. My haggard, lipstick-scarred face stares back at me in the mirror as I urinate, and as I lean forward to study the jagged lines of burst blood vessels in my eyes, I find myself repeating the last thing Lucy said to me before we went to bed. "Fuck me," I say slowly, shaking my head at the face in the mirror. The face just frowns sadly back at me, disappointed that I can't come up with anything better.

Lucy is up before daybreak. I hear her furtive rustling as she moves quietly about the room, locating her discarded clothing. Once dressed, she comes over to the bed and kneels beside me, gently brushing my hair with her fingers. I would like to see the expression on her face, but I keep my eyes closed, feigning sleep. Finally, she leans forward and presses her lips softly to my temple. They are dry now, as if I've sucked all the life out of them. She rests them there for a minute before standing up and tiptoeing out of the room. I don't open my eyes until I hear her car engine fading in the distance.

# twenty-seven

A brief lesson in poetic justice: The first time I had sex with Carly, I thought of Lucy, and now, seventeen years later, I've finally slept with Lucy, and can't stop thinking of Carly, even with Lucy's fragrance still firmly ensconced in my nostrils, the taste of her still lingering on my swollen, chapped lips, her nakedness still tattooed across my eyelids, flashing in neon whenever I blink. I am the star in my own Shakespearean farce, never managing to sleep with one woman without wanting the other. The gods of sex and irony are playing hockey, and I am their unwitting puck.

I leave the house for the first time in almost three days, the sunlight harassing my constricted pupils as I drive the Mercedes into town. I try to think myself out of the perplexing cloud of distress that seems to have enveloped me in the aftermath of sex with Lucy, but the whole magically sordid evening defies perspective. I pull up to Wayne's house, but his mother tells me that he's still sleeping. Something in her manner, in the too quick pronouncement of this fact, makes me think she's lying, but she seems more on edge than usual and girded for battle, so rather than set her off, I tell her I'll come back later.

Once back in my car, I grab my cell phone and dial Owen.

"Congratulations on sleeping with your mother," he practically shouts with glee, prompting me to reconsider the wisdom of calling him at home so early in the morning.

"What?"

"Oh, come on, Joe. Your attraction to Lucy is a direct manifestation of your longing for the love of your own mother."

"Why can't it just be healthy lust?"

"It's just not that simple, given the complexities of your circumstances."

"I don't think you'd be saying that if you ever saw Lucy," I say.

"Well, you keep telling yourself that if you want," he replies smugly.

"What happened to not giving shotgun diagnoses?"

"Oh, come on, Joe. This one's a gimme."

I sigh. "Honestly, I'm starting to rethink this whole agent-as-therapist arrangement."

"There is a larger issue here," Owen says.

"Larger than mother fucking?"

He laughs. "Has it occurred to you that, oedipal issues aside, you're trying to fuck your past, as it were?"

"Come again?"

"It seems to me that you're subconsciously trying to correct past mistakes. Both your ridiculous ongoing phone relationship with Natalie and your sleeping with Lucy are part of a compulsive need you have to right past wrongs. You feel responsible for Sammy's death, and therefore that you wronged Lucy."

"Maybe I do feel somewhat responsible for what happened to Sammy," I say. "But how does sleeping with his mother erase that?"

"It doesn't, of course. But you would hardly be the first

man in history to think the answer to all his woes lies in his dick. All of your self-destructive behavior stems from this misguided need to fix your past. And the one person who it seems to me might represent real potential for the future— Carly—you've kept at arm's length."

"She hasn't exactly been giving me that come-hither stare."

"That may or may not be," he says as if he might have some inside information. "Carly represents something more than sexual to you, and you feel unworthy, of her and of the potential future she might offer, until you've somehow fixed your past, which I can tell you will remain unfixable, no matter how many people you fuck. Not that I'm discouraging it. Far from it. Fuck away, by all means."

"It's funny," I say. "All this crap happens to you and you think you're handling it okay, and then years later you realize that you weren't handling it all, and you hurt people and hurt yourself, and you've got so many things to make up for, you don't know where to begin."

Owen grunts, unimpressed with my latest epiphany. "Just go slow," he advises, turning serious. "Rushing into things isn't going to work, as evidenced by your decision to sleep with Lucy." As if any decision at all were even possible, once she'd walked, warm and willing, through that door. "You need to establish some distance."

"I've had seventeen years of distance," I say, impulsively flipping my phone shut, suddenly sick to death of talking about it. If I'm going to make a genuine effort to roll up my sleeves and get dirty here, it won't do to have our constant clinical analysis lifting me out of the fray. I pull over, wait for a break in the traffic, and then execute a quick U-turn, pointing the Mercedes in the direction of the editorial offices of *The Minuteman*. It's high time I got a little reckless, I think. Every once in a while you experience what alcoholics and addicts refer to as a moment of clarity, where the opaque veil of chaos falls away and the unarticulated cosmic rhythm of the universe seems suddenly within your grasp. I don't doubt that it will all turn out to be a load of crap as usual, but I nevertheless feel an overwhelming surge of optimism so powerful that it remains undiminished even as Mouse pulls me over, his siren wailing obnoxiously, to write me a summons for the illegal U-turn and, get this, driving with a broken taillight.

# twenty-eight

The offices of *The Minuteman* are located in a strip mall that's been converted into a small corporate park on Oxnard Avenue, just north of the center of town. I step through the glass doors and into a large open office area filled with the controlled din of enterprise—the plastic clatter of keyboards, the atonal electronic chimes of telephones, and, faintly in the background, some Lite FM refugee station for displaced artists like Phil Collins, Billy Joel, and Hall and Oates. In the center of the room, bathed in the fluorescent glow from light tubes in the drop ceiling, four reporters sit in oddly configured cubicles, typing urgently on battered gray computers. Two college-aged kids sit at aluminum desks on the periphery, looking cool and bored as they answer the phones and sort through mountains of papers and photos. In the far corner, two geeky-looking guys sit in front of oversized Macs, configuring digital layouts for the paper. The back wall contains three doors, all open, and through the one on the left, I catch a glimpse of Carly. As I make my way through the cubicles, a hush falls over the staff as they become aware of my presence, tracking my progress toward Carly's office with obvious interest.

"It's not going to work," Carly says when I enter the room. She's sitting Indian-style on the center of a worn oak desk, poring over a layout proof, her hair hanging over her face like a curtain.

"You haven't even heard my pitch yet," I say, and her head jerks up, her eyes wide with surprise behind the gold-framed spectacles that I had no idea she wore.

"Joe," she says, letting the proof slip out of her hands and onto the desk. "What are you doing here?"

"What's not going to work?" says a disembodied voice from behind Carly.

"The layout on page six." Carly addresses the speaker-phone, still staring at me. "I don't want to cut up the article for two lousy sentences."

"Then get editorial to trim fifteen words," comes the reply.

"Did you speak to them?"

"They told me to piss off."

Carly looks at me and grins apologetically. "I'll call you back in a minute," she says.

"Who's Joe?" the voice wants to know.

"Good-bye, Calvin," Carly says, hitting a button on the phone. "I'm sorry," she says to me, self-consciously removing her glasses. "What are you doing here?"

She's wearing a rust-colored stretch blouse tucked into dark pleated slacks, and she looks cute and compact on the massive desk. Her face, devoid of any makeup, looks more chiseled than I remember, bordering on gaunt, and I'm still getting used to the surprise of her long chestnut hair: straight, thick, and defiantly unstyled. "I thought I'd buy you lunch," I say, affecting a casual tone.

"It's ten A.M."

"We'll beat the rush."

She considers me thoughtfully for a minute. "What will we talk about?"

Carly's disarming directness, powered by the undercurrent of her incisive wit, was one of the qualities I always admired about her back when we were teenagers. But getting into the conversational flow with her now is like playing in a jazz combo, and I'm out of practice and my timing is off. "I don't know," I say. "We really haven't had the opportunity to catch up."

"It's sort of pointless, isn't it?" she says, rolling gracefully off her desk and landing in the worn leather chair behind it. The light from her desk lamp picks up the soft blond down on the side of her neck that disappears behind her ears into her scalp.

"Why would you say that?"

Carly rolls her eyes. "I mean, what will we really say? You'll tell me about being a big-time author, and I'll tell you about running a small-town paper and then we'll have a few awkward silences, which neither of us will be able to stand, so we'll say anything to fill them until one of us inevitably brings up the past, probably you, and you'll apologize for being such an asshole to me in New York and I'll say forget about it, it's ancient history, even though that's not how I really feel, and then I'll be mad at myself for not telling you, so I will, and then I'll cry and you'll think you made a meaningful connection when all you really did is make me cry. Again. And then you'll be off, back to your big life and terribly interesting friends in the big city, and I'll be here and everything will be just how it was before you came back, except now it will have this irritating little epilogue. And so I say again that it's pointless." She raises her eyebrows at me. "Don't you think?"

"That's one way of looking at it," I say slowly. "A neurotic and depressing way, but a way, I guess. May I rebut?"

"It's a free country."

I take a deep breath. "First of all, I'm sure it's interesting running the paper and all, but frankly I couldn't care less, and I'm not remotely interested in talking about being an author. I have no exciting friends or big life in the big city to get back to. As a matter of fact, I don't even have a little life there. You're probably right that the past will come up—how could it not—but I'm only interested in it as it pertains to the here and now. I was under the impression that I was avoiding the past for the last few years, but it turns out what I was really avoiding was the present and I'm firmly committed to not doing that anymore. There are good reasons for us to talk, to know each other as we are now, but I'm trying not to analyze them for the time being. I'm going on instinct here, which is something entirely new for me, and I promise, the last thing in the world I want to do is make you cry." I pause dramatically to catch my breath. "It's just lunch, for god's sake. It doesn't mean we're engaged or anything."

A small grin pulls at the corners of Carly's mouth, but she remains resolute. "I don't know if I'm up to dealing with this right now."

"I said that once, when I was about nineteen," I say. "Now I'm thirty-four."

"Jesus, we're old," Carly says wistfully, and I can tell I have her on the fence, her good judgment wavering in the face of my resolve.

"I can see you're conflicted. Let me make it easier," I say, sitting down in one of the chairs facing her desk. "I'm not leaving here without you."

She stares at me and I stare right back and something in the air where our eyes meet clicks. "Come on," I say. "How much damage could I possibly do over lunch?"

After a moment, Carly closes her eyes. "Oh, well," she says softly, more to herself than to me, and then stands up. She grabs her leather jacket off a coat tree and I follow her out of her office, back into the newsroom. If the *Minuteman* staff were interested in me before, they are now shamelessly gawking as we make our way back through the work space to the exit. "It doesn't take much to excite this crowd, does it?" I mutter to Carly.

"We reap what we sow," she says, opening the door and stepping out ahead of me into the parking lot. "You gave my employees the opportunity to read the vivid details of how you deflowered me in the backseat of your car. I would say you've earned your share of stares." I smile stupidly and try to ignore the traces of anger in her voice, like microscopic shards of shattered glass after a car wreck.

The sky is overcast; fat, dirty clouds hang low and thick like pollution over us, the air heavy with the probability of rain. "Your car looks like it was in a bar fight," Carly says, taking in the Mercedes' busted taillight and jagged scratches.

"We've both seen better days."

She looks across the roof of the car at me, wondering if my comment is inclusive of the car or herself. "Joe," she says softly, "I'm not sure about this."

"Come on," I say, trying to keep it light. "I plan on being especially witty today."

"Stop that."

"Stop what?"

"Stop trying to be charming."

"I'm not trying; I just am." Between us, a single pear-shaped droplet of rain lands on the soft roof of the Mercedes like a plump teardrop, and we both look at it, considering its potential for symbolism.

"Go easy on me," she says, opening the car door. "I don't exactly have my shit together these days."

"Who does?"

She climbs into the car, leaving me there to contemplate the lone raindrop on my own. I sigh deeply as it begins to drizzle, get into the car, and hope like hell that I know what I'm doing.

*  *

The staccato percussion of the rain on the roof of the Mercedes fills the awkward silence in the car, and the daylight has dimmed to a gloomy gray by the time we pull into the Duchess's parking lot. We run from the car to the restaurant, heads bent and shoulders hunched, our feet splashing through the mini rivers that flow down the flooded sidewalk. Once inside, I shake my wet hair and wipe my face with my hands, while Carly fusses with her blouse, which now clings provocatively to her chest in small, transparent sections that I will devoutly pretend not to notice. Sheila, the waitress who served Brad that strangely personal look a few days earlier, says a familiar hello to Carly and tells us to sit anywhere. Carly selects a window booth, and Sheila takes our orders immediately and disappears into the kitchen. We're the only diners there, which is fine with me, since it greatly reduces the odds of another unfortunate milk shake incident.

Carly moves her salad around with her fork, flipping, sorting, and rearranging the assorted vegetables into recondite patterns only she can discern. Every so often, when the leaves of her lettuce are properly aligned, she stabs at a particular section with her fork and brings it to her mouth. Eaten this way, a Caesar salad can last over an hour. It doesn't take nearly that long for us to run out of small talk. So for a while we sit in silence, watching through the window as the rain comes down in angry torrents. Finally, I look across the table at her and say, "So, ask me a question."

She raises her eyebrows, unsure of how to react. It was a game we played back in high school, usually after sex as we lay together basking in the afterglow. We wanted to know each other so thoroughly, and sometimes things didn't come up in general conversation, so Carly developed the habit of challenging me to ask her revealing questions designed to open up secret compartments in each other. She stares at me for a few more seconds before flashing a forced grin and putting her fork back down. "Okay," she says. "When are you leaving?"

"I don't know, but way to make me feel welcome."

"Come on, Joe. Why are you still here?"

"It's complicated."

"Why don't you give me the *Reader's Digest* version?"

I think about it for a minute. "My father's death has unexpectedly fucked me up. It only recently occurred to me that all those years I was hating him for not being there for me, he was grieving for my mother, and really, I should have been there for him. I let him down. I should have been there for Wayne and Sammy too—"

"You were," Carly interrupts me. "You were the only one who was."

"Physically, maybe," I said. "But what good did I do either one of them? I just kept hoping that the whole thing would go away on its own, that Wayne would wake up liking girls again, and most of the time I was too hot for you to care very much one way or the other."

"So it's my fault?"

"Of course not." I shake my head. "You were, by far, the greatest thing that ever happened to me, and now, seventeen years later, you still are, and that's either pathetic or wonderful, depending on how you look at it." I look away and clear my throat. "Um, how do you look at it?"

"As sad," Carly says neutrally, looking out the window. Not quite the reaction I'd been hoping for.

"Whatever," I say, feeling somewhat deflated. "I guess it's that too. But the point is, I feel like I've been angry for so long, and maybe I was because there was nothing I could do about it. But now it's like I've been given this chance, to be there for Wayne when he needs me, to help him see this through to the end. To become part of my family again, if they'll have me. And then there's you. . . ."

"There's me," Carly says, nodding her head bitterly. "The cherry on top of your psychotic little sundae."

"Excuse me?"

"You're unbelievable," she says, the volume of her voice

sliding up a few notches. "Everything back here, me and Wayne and this town, it has nothing to do with you anymore. You went off and hit the big time, and now you want to come back and shower your beneficence on all the little people who fell apart when you left."

"That's not it at all," I protested. "I'm the one who fell apart."

"Well, cry me a river," she says angrily. "News flash, Joe. Everything isn't about you. We all managed to get fucked up on our own. There was nothing you could have done about it then, and there's nothing you can do about it now. You think you have the market cornered on regret?"

"That's not it," I say, wondering how the conversation went haywire so quickly.

"Why don't we just cut to the chase here," she says, waving away my protestations. "What do you want from me, Joe?"

"Nothing."

"Bullshit. Try again. What do you want from me?"

Her eyes are cold and humorless, and looking into them, I experience the sensation of drowning, a careless swimmer who failed to heed the undertow warnings. "I just want the chance to get to know you again," I say. "I know we're not the same people we were, but underneath everything, you're still the only person I've ever really loved."

"So, what are you saying? You want to go out with me? You want to go on a date?"

"Why would that get you so mad?"

Carly nods slowly, her cheeks flushed with anger. "I look like such an easy bet to you, don't I? Your lonely, battered ex-girlfriend. You must have thought, after all I've been through, that I would just jump gratefully into your arms."

"That's not fair," I say, trying to manufacture some indignation of my own to neutralize hers.

"Fuck fair." She leans forward emphatically. "Look at me. Look at Wayne. When did fair come into the picture?" She stops for a second, fighting back her tears. "Things haven't worked out for you, and that's too bad. But you left, and then you used us all as props in your goddamn book. You don't get to come back here now and be the hero, Joe. I'm sorry, but you just don't."

I sit across from her in stunned silence, paralyzed in my seat. I had expected things to be awkward at first, and I'd been prepared to soldier through that, working under the basic assumption that Carly still had feelings for me, buried somewhere, simply in need of minor excavation. I hadn't counted on the possibility that she really might have no love left for me, that what we had once been is now completely dead to her. Suddenly, irrationally, I feel heartbroken. The rain beats manically against the window, and I feel the urge to run outside and dissolve.

Carly sits back in her seat, winded from her diatribe. If anything, she seems as shocked as me by the anger she's unleashed. I stand up slowly, reaching into my pocket for some bills. "I'm sorry," I say. "You were right; this was a big mistake. I'll take you back to your office now."

She looks up at me but makes no move to rise. "So that's it, then?" I can see the rage seeping out of her, the muscles in her face and shoulders slowly unclenching as she breathes deeply.

"That's it. Again, I'm really very sorry. You're right about everything. I don't know who the hell I thought I was."

Carly nods and then, instead of standing up, turns and looks out the window. "Ask me a question," she says quietly, all traces of anger now gone from her voice.

"What?"

"Fair's fair. Ask away."

I look at her in disbelief and then sit back down, looking at her reflection in the window. "Do you hate me?" my reflection asks.

"Yes," hers says. "Sometimes."

"Do you love me?"

She's quiet for a moment, and I can feel myself age a year

waiting for her answer. "Of course I do," she whispers, her voice barely audible over the pounding rain.

I nod, quivering imperceptibly as the news is circulated to my internal organs. I don't pretend to understand women. Or, rather, that's exactly what I do. Pretend. But sometimes it's apparent to me that it doesn't even pay to try. This is clearly one of those times, but somehow it comes to me, as if through divine prophecy, that I've made all the progress I'm going to at this juncture, and to push it would be a mistake. So even though there are a million things I want to say, I decide to wrap things up with one essential question. "Carly."

"Yes?" In the window, her reflection turns to face mine.

"Do you think you'd like to go on a date sometime?"

Outside there is a clap of thunder so powerful it rattles the window, and inside, Carly looks at me with the eyes of a stranger and says, "Maybe. I don't know. Ask me again tomorrow."

I'm following Carly out of the Duchess when the sound of the swinging doors behind the counter causes me to turn my head. Sheila has just walked through those doors to the kitchen and in the instant before they swing shut, I see a man leaning against a steel counter. His back is to me as they embrace, but just before the doors swing closed, I catch a quick glimpse of his profile, and although the angle is bad, I'm fairly certain the man is my brother, Brad.

# twenty-nine

I drive Carly back to her office with no idea at all as to how our lunch has gone, other than not as planned. She says a fast, awkward thank-you, keeping the eye contact to a minimum, her forced politeness ringing like a rebuff in my ears. As I drive away from the corporate park, a bruise-colored Lexus sedan falls in behind me. I had noticed the same car earlier, trailing us from the Duchess back to the *Minuteman* offices. I consider flooring it, fairly confident that the Mercedes is more than up to the task, but the foul weather and the growing pile of moving violations in my glove compartment convince me otherwise. Instead, I turn into the Mobil station on the corner of Stratfield and Pine, pull up under the protective awning, and step out to pump my gas. The Lexus hesitates for a second and then pulls in to the pump next to me. The door swings open, and I hear the nasal vocals and power chords of Green Day blasting over the stereo just before the driver cuts the engine. Sean Tallon climbs out of the car, looking like a movie in his cartoonish ankle-length leather raincoat and black motorcycle boots.

"Hey, Sean," I say, eyeballing his outfit. "What's Shaft wearing?" In situations that make me nervous, I often find it's best just to run my mouth like an idiot.

Sean jams his gas cap into the nozzle handle to keep his gas flowing, a brilliantly simple technique that has never occurred to me, and then approaches me, smirking at my little joke. "Goffman," he says. "You still here?"

"Afraid so," I say, tightening my grip anxiously around my own gas nozzle.

"I figured after your dad kicked that you'd have gotten the hell out of Dodge."

"Events have conspired to keep me here a bit longer."

Sean nods and leans against my car. In the last seventeen years he's packed on a layer of fat and disproportionate bulges of muscle that makes him imposingly bearish, and his complexion is cratered and raw, as if he washes his face every morning with steel wool. His once-proud nose has been broken, and its now-bulbous tip is stained with a thin network of winding capillaries. I didn't notice this physical depreciation in the dim lighting of Halftime—I was too preoccupied with getting the shit kicked out of me—but now, in the harsh light of day, I can see the tire tracks of a rough life are all over him. He pulls out a pack of cigarettes, lights one, and takes a long, hard drag, holding the cigarette dramatically between his thumb and forefinger. I strongly doubt that Sean ever misses an episode of *The Sopranos*. For a while he says nothing, and we stand beneath the shelter of the station while all around us it continues to pour. I look down at my feet, watching the odd patches of spilled gasoline form little rainbow-colored amoeba shapes on the rain-splattered pavement. My father is dead, I think apropos of nothing in particular, and feel a minor spasm in my belly, some heretofore dormant muscle suddenly clenching.

"I lost my temper in the bar the other night," Sean says, smoke bleeding out slowly through his nostrils. "I didn't know about your father."

"I see."

"I'm not apologizing," he says, folding his arms across his chest. "You deserved it. All that shit you wrote." He jams the cigarette between his lips and fishes through his coat pockets, eventually coming out with two crumpled pages that have been sloppily torn from a copy of *Bush Falls*. He studies the pages for a moment and then turns them over. "Here we go," he says, then clears his throat and reads aloud in a monotone. " '*It seemed to me that the hostility behind "Shane's" escalating cruelty toward Sammy far exceeded the norms of ritualistic school yard hazing and adolescent bigotry. Something in him was revolted by Sammy's clearly effeminate mannerisms, and only later did I come to understand that in Sammy, "Shane" saw the flesh-and-blood embodiment of the very sexual demons he was battling on a daily basis within himself.*' " Sean finishes and gives me a hard look.

"You bought my book," I say. "I'm touched."

"You haven't been touched yet," he says with a nasty grin. "But you will be soon, if you insist on sticking around."

"Are you threatening me?"

"I'm sorry—wasn't it obvious?"

"It's fiction, Sean," I say weakly. "Says so right on the cover."

"If by fiction you mean bullshit, then I agree with you," he says, pocketing the pages. "But calling it a novel doesn't change what you did."

"And what exactly did I do?"

"You called me a faggot," he says, tossing his cigarette butt to the ground. It fails to ignite the spilled gasoline and engulf him in flames, despite my fervent prayers. The nozzle jumps in my hand, indicating a full tank, and I place it back on the pump. "You made everyone in this town think twice about me." He straightens up, leaning off the car to face me. "You besmirched my reputation."

"Again," I say. "It was fiction. If you identified with the character on some level—"

"Cut the shit," Sean says. "You're trying my patience."

"So, what are you going to do, Sean?" I say, assuming a weary tone. "Are you going to beat me up again?"

He finishes pumping his own gas, replaces the nozzle, and roughly screws on the gas cap. "Get the fuck out of the Falls, Goffman," he says. "I mean today. I cut you some slack out of respect for your family. But it's only by my good graces that you can still piss standing up. You walking around town as if you're welcome here, as if you didn't write all that shit, is an insult to me, and to this town, and I can feel my self-control disappearing even as we speak."

"I appreciate the heads-up," I say, opening my car door. He steps forward and kicks it shut, his boot leaving a small dent just under the door handle. I add the dent to the mental damage report I've been compiling since my arrival in the Falls.

"Nice car," Sean says.

"Thanks."

"I've blown up nicer cars than this."

"Your parents must be very proud."

Sean gets right in my face. "Today, Goffman. I'm not fucking with you. I'll blow you up in your fucking car." He studies my face with a wide, nasty grin, delighted by my stone-faced reaction. Then he makes a gun with his finger, points it at my temple, and says, "Bam." In the execution of this universal gesture, most people bring down their thumb to signify the hammer's dropping, but Sean actually pulls his trigger finger, which I find much more threatening, since it seems to bespeak a genuine familiarity with the real thing.

He climbs into the Lexus, and I wait until he's driven off into the rain before getting back into my car, where I sing the theme to *Shaft* softly to calm myself down. *Who's the black private dick that's a sex machine to all the chicks? Shaft!* The clock on my birds-eye maple wood dashboard shows 12:05, earlier than I would have thought. It seems unlikely that I'll manage to stay out of trouble with so many hours left in the day.

# thirty

Wayne is fully dressed and sitting at his desk, looking through a photo album, when I arrive a short while later. "Hey," I say. "Looking good." He isn't, but I say it anyway. This is how we deal with the terminally ill. We establish a new standard and embrace it with manufactured cheer, as if the epic nature of death could be thwarted with a veneer of breezy compliments and light conversation.

Wayne grins and closes the album, looking haggard but resolute. "I have this theory that if I get dressed and do something, I stand less of a chance of dying that day."

"Makes sense," I say. "So what are we going to do?"

He stands up and begins pulling his basketball jacket on. "We're going to visit Sammy's grave."

I look at him for a moment. "You sure?"

"It's one of the items on my 'before I die' to-do list."

"I wish you'd stop talking like that," I say, helping him straighten the jacket on his almost nonexistent shoulders.

"I'm being heroic," he says. "Deal with it."

* *

The rain has stopped, and thick rays of sun are penetrating the gray cloud cover as we drive across town to the cemetery. "Look," I say, pointing out a sunbeam to Wayne. "When I was a kid, I always thought that was God, peeking through the clouds."

"That's not God," Wayne says. "That's the search party."

I nod dumbly. I generally avoid all discussions of theology, and with a dying friend this seems like a particularly wise policy.

"When I didn't hear from you after the funeral, I thought maybe you'd had enough," Wayne says.

"I'm still here." I bring him up to date on all that's transpired since my father's funeral.

"Jesus," he says. "Haven't we been the busy beaver."

"It's been a little intense."

"I can't believe you fucked Mrs. Haber."

"Me neither."

"How was it?"

"Unreal."

"I'll bet," he says with a nod. "And what about Carly?"

"What about her?"

Wayne gives me a fondly quizzical look. "You do realize that you were supposed to have slept with Carly and had the lunch with Mrs. Haber, don't you?"

"That would have been one way to go."

Wayne smiles. "Always the hard way."

"I've got to be me."

He reaches into my CD collection and picks out *Born to Run*. "In honor of Sammy," he says, sliding in the CD. We sit in silence, listening to the slow buildup of "Thunder Road" and Springsteen's raspy voice singing about hiding beneath your covers to study your pain.

Wayne waits in the car while I obtain a map with the coordinates of Sammy's grave from the lone woman working in the office. We drive through a maze of access roads until we reach the general area and park. Wayne has brought along a portable CD player, a bottle of wine, and two glasses. We sit on the damp grass beside Sammy's grave and Wayne pours us each a drink. "Sammy," I say, holding up my glass with a smile.

"Sammy," Wayne says, and we sip at our wine. He presses a button on the CD player and Springsteen comes on singing "Backstreets." "This was our song," Wayne says softly, closing his eyes as he listens to the music.

" 'Backstreets' was your song?"

"What's wrong with 'Backstreets'?"

"I don't know. Most of the couples I knew in high school had songs like 'Can't Fight This Feeling' or 'Glory of Love' or 'In Your Eyes,' you know? Romantic songs."

"We weren't romantics," Wayne says somberly. "We were desperately fucked up. And that's what 'Backstreets' is about." He pauses for a moment, nodding his head and swaying lightly to the music. "He's singing about these two guys who are trying in vain to breathe the fire they were born in. After all this time, that's still the best description of what we went through that summer, of what it feels like to be young and gay, that I've ever heard."

I try to pay more attention to the lyrics, which is hard, given Bruce's scratchy, mumbled delivery and the loud guitars and drums drowning him out at every turn. It doesn't sound like a song about gay love to me, but I guess we all hear what we want to hear.

"So," Wayne says, turning off the stereo when the song ends. "Would you like to say a few words?"

"I wasn't aware that this was a formal ceremony."

He hefts his glass at me. "Wine and music," he says. "It's either that or we're on a date."

I think about it for a moment, since Wayne seems intent on my saying something. "Sammy was a good and loyal friend," I start.

"He wasn't your dog Skip," Wayne interrupts me impatiently. "And besides, he's been dead for seventeen years. It's a bit late for eulogies."

"So what do you want me to say?"

"Just share your thoughts."

"My mind is a blank. You go first."

"Fine." Wayne sips thoughtfully at his wine. "For the longest time I blamed Sammy for my being gay. I thought that I could have gone either way but that he came along at just the right time in my adolescence to push me forever in that direction. I know that's a crock, but I hated him; even while I wanted him, I hated him for making me a freak. I thought if he hadn't come along, I would have eventually met some girl who turned me on. . . . I don't know. I was a kid, right?"

"We were all kids," I say.

"Anyway," Wayne continues in a dull voice, staring at Sammy's tombstone, "it feels like I've spent my entire adult life hating, first Sammy and then myself instead, for having been dumb enough to hate him for something that was so clearly not anyone's fault. Like the song says, we were just trying to breathe that fire." Wayne's voice breaks for a moment, and his eyes fill with tears. "Sammy," he says, "I've decided to forgive myself on your behalf, since you're not around to do it. I hope that's okay with you, and if it's not, tough shit. I guess you should have thought of that before you decided to kill yourself. And while I'm at it, I'll forgive our friend Joe for you as well. I'm not sure what for, but he seems to think he needs it."

Wayne takes another sip of his wine and then looks up at me with a weak grin. "How was that?"

I can feel my own eyes growing wet. "That was okay," I say.

Wayne leaves some flowers at the foot of the grave and we head back to the car. We drive in silence for a while, the car filled with the weight of our thoughts. "Joe."

"Yeah."

"Did you and Carly have a song?"

I'm about to say no when I suddenly remember. "We did. I can't believe I forgot it."

"What was it?"

" 'No One Is to Blame.' Howard Jones."

Wayne looks at me and we both smile. "That's a good song," he says softly, leaning his head back against the seat. "That's a good fucking song to have."

# thirty-one

I get home at around three to find Brad in the study, sitting back in the desk chair, smoking one of my father's pipes. "Hey, Joe," he says, looking up embarrassedly as I enter. He puts the pipe down on the ashtray and grins at me sheepishly. "Sorry. I just wanted to smell that smell again."

"You miss him a lot, huh?"

Brad nods. "I just can't believe he's gone, you know?"

"Yeah."

Brad shakes his head as if to clear it. "I wanted to talk to you about something. You have a minute?"

"Sure."

He looks across the desk at me, not sure how to begin. "Dad didn't have a will. I don't think he thought he'd ever die."

"Okay."

"Without a will, you and I are the legal heirs, entitled to an even split of all his assets, which are basically this house, the business, and an investment portfolio worth about two hundred thousand dollars."

I can see where he's going with this, and I'm determined to head him off at the pass. "Brad, I don't want any of Dad's money. I don't need it, and besides, you deserve it. I'm sure he'd want you to have it."

Brad nods and purses his lips. "It's just that we're struggling a bit, you know. The business is in the toilet, and I've got college for Jared to think about."

"Brad, really. Don't say another word."

But he's not done. "Cindy and me," he says. "We're having problems."

"Money problems?"

He shrugs. "I used to think that we were just stressed about money. But now I think it goes a lot deeper than that."

"Are you talking about getting divorced?"

"We're not really talking at all these days."

"I'm sorry to hear that," I say sympathetically. I wait for him to say more, but he seems stuck, which I completely understand. Brad is confiding in me, and I am suddenly terrified at the prospect of such intimacy even though I know it's a good thing, a path to better relations. I think we both feel like impostors, posing as the kind of brothers who speak to each other about meaningful things. I wonder if he'll talk to me about Sheila, how long it's been going on and whether it's a cause or an effect of his marital problems. If the conversation is headed that way, then, familial discomfort notwithstanding, I'm in. But Brad seems to have confessed all he's about to confess to me, and just sits back in the chair and looks miserable. I could ask, I suppose, could come right out and say I saw him through the swinging doors at the Duchess, grabbing her ass like a drowning man grabs a life preserver, but I suspect I'd better not.

Brad rests his head in his hands and rubs his eyes. "I don't know how everything got so fucked up. One day it's all fine, and then, I don't know. It's like I look at her, and she's still in there somewhere, but I can't get through, you know?"

"Yeah." I think of Carly and how I just want to freeze time, cancel all the rules and allow something else to emerge.

We look at each other for a moment. It's really beyond strange to be talking like this. We aren't suited for it. "Yeah," Brad repeats, and stands up. Apparently, he's had all the brotherly bonding he can take for now, and I think we're both relieved. Still, it's definitely a start, something we can build on in small increments. "Anyway. I didn't mean to lay this all on you."

"Hey, it's okay."

"Thanks for being so good about the inheritance."

"Forget about it."

He stops at the door. "Dad was proud of you," he says. "I know you probably don't think that, but he was."

"He told you that?"

"Nah," Brad says. "He'd never come out and say something like that. But I could tell it by the way he spoke about you. I inherited his business, but you left and made it on your own. He was proud of you for that."

I've just ceded the family fortune to him, and he's probably just saying that to return the favor, but even knowing that, I find myself moved by his effort. "Thanks for telling me."

"I'll see you tomorrow night," he says, extending his hand. We shake, an oddly formal gesture for so intimate a discussion. A hug would make more sense, but I doubt either of us is up to that.

Still, it's a start.


After Brad leaves, I get to work on my new novel, reveling in the ease with which the words come. The character of Matt Burns is beginning to unfold in my mind as if I'm discovering him rather than inventing him. He's an average guy, somewhat bowed under the weight of his own gradually diminishing expectations. He stuttered as a child and was ridiculed profusely for it, and even though he corrected the stutter years ago, he speaks in quick, economical bursts, as if terrified that it might start up again at any moment. Matt makes a living as a construction foreman. He's not particularly strong himself, but he's good with his hands. He's happiest when surrounded by the deafening cacophony of construction equipment. At all other times, the world feels too quiet, and now, as he begins looking into the odd circumstances surrounding his father's death, with conversation the only tool at his disposal, he feels uncomfortable and out of his element.

Matt proves to be my instrument, and I climb onto his back and ride him through the town, taking in the local flavor and meeting the secondary characters as we go. I write straight into the night, knowing that I'm going into excessive detail that I will later have to sift through and pare down, but I'm thrilled to finally be writing again, to be seeing everything with such clarity. I surge with the power of my creation, a god presiding over the formation of his universe. It's been far too long since I felt like a writer.

Sometime after two I fall asleep at my desk and dream that I'm at a party of some sort at Lucy's house. The yard is crowded with company, some dressed in formal wear and others in bathing suits. I'm in a bathing suit, so I make my way toward the pool, where Lucy sits in a lounge chair, sunning herself in a black bikini. "Hey, Joe," she says, smiling and waving at me lazily. "Look who's come back." I look up and see Sammy standing on the edge of the board, affecting a mock bodybuilder pose before jumping gracelessly into the water. But when he emerges, I realized that I was mistaken. It's Wayne, not Sammy, who now swims in powerful strokes across the pool. I call out to him, amazed that he seems to have regained his health, but he is too caught up in his swimming to hear me. I then step onto one of those frustrating dream treadmills where no matter how much I walk, I can't seem to get to the edge of the pool. "Wayne!" I shout. "It's me." He pauses in his strokes, treading water as he looks through the crowd, but despite my wild gesticulations, he can't locate me. Eventually, he shrugs and climbs out of the pool. Lucy gets up from her chair and hands him a towel, and they kiss, a deep, lustful kiss, which of course makes no sense. Then he turns and walks right by me, eighteen years old again, glistening and powerful and full of life.

"Wayne," I say. He turns and looks at me as if seeing me for the first time. There are droplets of water clinging to his ear-lobes and nose. "It's me—Joe." I'm confused and disoriented, but more than anything, I'm flooded with an overwhelming sense of gratitude that he isn't sick anymore, that we can go on being friends like in the old days. He looks at me somberly and nods slowly. "Joe."

"Yes."

He grins his old, cocky grin. "You have a phone call."

"What?"

"Just listen."

I do, and sure enough I hear a phone ringing. And as soon as the realization hits that the ringing isn't part of the dream, the dream vanishes and the phone wakes me up.

I'm sprawled at my desk, my face glued to my arm with drool, my neck stiff from sleeping bent over in my chair. The room is filled with the soft hues and shadows of indirect sunlight. I'm mildly bewildered at having inadvertently slept so deeply at my desk, and still haunted by the vivid images of my dream. "It's Wayne," Carly says when I pick up the phone, and I wonder foggily how she knows, since she wasn't in the dream at all.

"What?" I say, sitting up slowly. "Carly? What time is it?"

"It's ten-thirty," she says, her voice frantically urging me to get with the program. "Joe, Wayne's on the roof of the high school."

I'm trying to understand her, but it isn't computing.

"Could you say that again?" I use my fingers in an attempt to manually rub the consciousness into my brain via my eyeballs.

"Wayne's on the roof of the high school," Carly repeats impatiently. "We have to get over there."

"It's okay. We always used to climb up there. He won't fall."

There is a pause. "I'm not worried about him falling, Joe."

I stand up in my father's den, now fully awake. "I'm on my way."

"I'm already in my car," she says. "I'll pick you up in five minutes."

"You don't think he would really jump, do you?"

"No, I don't. But it would be just like him to want to surprise us."

The high school is already a mob scene when we pull up in Carly's Honda, the students milling about in an energized frenzy as the faculty make vain, halfhearted efforts at crowd control. In the meantime, sheriff's deputies are attempting to erect wooden sawhorses to cordon off the area directly below the building's cupola. A fire truck and a number of emergency vehicles are parked at random angles at the curb, and two local news vans with roof-mounted satellite uplink equipment have pulled onto the sidewalk, their crews hustling around the periphery of the school's front promenade as they try to capture the chaos for the evening news. Up on top of the building, lying back against the cupola and smoking a cigarette, is Wayne. He's too high up for me to make out the expression on his face, but he doesn't appear poised to jump.

The students are all staring upward in unmasked morbid fascination, talking and joking among themselves, thrilled by the unexpected drama and the resulting free period or two. Carly and I push and shove our way through the throngs of onlookers and then past the barricades, where Mouse stands in a huddle of emergency services workers, bullhorn in hand, looking tense and uncertain. "Dave!" Carly calls out to him. "Have you spoken to him at all yet?"

He looks up at her with a frown. "No press past the barricades," he says.

"That's Wayne Hargrove up there," she says. "Let us talk to him."

Mouse considers us dourly. "I know who it is. He doesn't want to talk. Now, get back there."

"Come on, Mouse, you know he'll talk to me," I say, which turns out to be a mistake, not only because I've accidentally called him by his old nickname but because he apparently hasn't noticed me up until this point. "You!" he barks, his eyes widening. "If you don't get your ass behind those barricades right now, I'll book you for obstruction."

I start to argue, but Carly pulls me back behind the barricades. I try calling up to Wayne, to let him know I'm there, but he's as oblivious to me now as he was in my dream earlier.

"What now?" Carly says, shielding her eyes from the sun as she looks up at the roof. She's wearing jeans and an avocado-colored blouse, her hair pinned loosely above her forehead by a brown leather barrette. This is no time to be realizing how lovely she looks, but as bad as the situation is, part of me is thrilled to be standing next to her like this, to be in it with her.

"This way," I say, grabbing her hand and steering her through the crowd. We work our way around to the side of the school, where we find another deputy guarding the path leading to the rear of the building and the fire staircase. "If we can get that guy to move, I can get up to the roof," I say. "Do you think you can create a diversion?"

"No problem," Carly says sardonically, ducking under the barricade without hesitation. Before I know what she's doing, she's taken off at a run across the side lawn toward the front corner of the school building. "Hey!" the deputy calls to her. "Stop!" Carly keeps running, and within seconds the guard has taken off after her. I hear her stop to inform him that she's a member of the press, but by then I've already crossed the lawn and made it into the stairwell. I take the metal stairs two and three at a time, feeling all James Bond as I make my way up to the roof.

I've just emerged onto the roof when I hear footsteps pounding up the stairs behind me, and I'm bracing myself for a confrontation with the deputy when Jared appears running up the last flight of stairs and joins me on the roof.

"Hey, Uncle Joe," he says, flipping his wild hair out of his face as we stand together, catching our breath.

"What are you doing here?" I say.

"I go to school here. Sometimes."

"You picked a hell of a day to stop cutting."

Jared shrugs. "Who knew?" He walks over to the edge of the roof and looks down at the crowd below with mild curiosity. "Be one hell of a swan dive."

"Why don't you go back downstairs."

"The view's much better from up here."

"Fine." I give up and turn to look up toward the cupola. "I'm going to talk to Wayne for a few minutes. You wait here."

"You bet," Jared says. "Good luck."

I've forgotten that the only access onto the cupola is from the front of the building, which means grabbing the concrete ledge at the base of the cupola and swinging my legs out into the open air before pulling myself up. If this somewhat risky move bothered me when I was a kid, I don't remember, but it certainly gives me pause now. One slip, and it's a good five-story fall onto the front promenade. Still, Wayne has managed it in his frail condition, so who the hell am I to back down? Before my hesitation can morph into paralysis, I reach for the ledge, the gritty edge of the concrete tattooing my fingertips, and swing my legs up onto the base of the cupola. The crowd below lets out a gratifying collective gasp.

Wayne sits leaning against the cupola, a cigarette in his mouth and another, just lit, between his slender fingers, dangled in my direction. "Hey, Joe," he says, nodding a casual greeting.

"Hey." I pull myself up and then squirm forward on my belly until I'm safely on the ledge. "How's it going?"

"Swell."

I take the cigarette and roll into a sitting position next to him, our feet dangling precariously over the side of the building. "Why don't I remember this being so dangerous back in the day?"

"Because we used to be immortal," Wayne says, still staring through his feet at the action below.

"That must have been it." I take a perfunctory drag on the cigarette. The smoke tastes stale and stings the back of my throat. "So," I say. "What's going on?"

Wayne nods as if he's been waiting for the question. "I woke up feeling especially strong today," he says. "And something told me that this very well might be my last day of being independently mobile. You can't begin to imagine what that feels like, knowing that this is my last day to simply climb out of bed and see the world, the sky, feel the ground beneath my feet, the wind against my face." He pauses to take a small, almost childish puff on his cigarette. "So, to make a short story even shorter, I took a walk, and here I am."

"I can't believe you managed to climb all the way up here," I say.

"I know, right? I wasn't sure I would make it."

"And how were you planning on getting down?"

Wayne leans forward and looks between his toes at the crowd below and then turns back to me, smiling ruefully. "Shortcut."

"Wayne, man." I'm at a loss. A couple of gray pigeons land to our right on the ledge, the jade green flecks in their plumage glinting like sequins in the sun. I've never thought of pigeons as colorful before, and I watch, fascinated, as they putter around for a few seconds in a quick, jittery ballet before flying off in a noisy burst of flapping wings.

"I'm tired, man," Wayne says. "I'm so fucking tired of getting up every day and putting on a brave face, trying to make it okay for everyone else that I'm dying." He grinds out his cigarette violently, his eyes welling up with angry tears, his dry lips trembling as he struggles to swallow the rage and terror frothing inside him like a witches' brew. It seems somehow incongruous that someone so near death, so desiccated, should still produce so many tears. "I'm fucking dying, man, and you know what? It is not okay. It's a fucking tragedy. I'm way too young to die. And I just can't keep cracking wise and acting like I've made my peace with the whole damn thing."

"Who says you have to?" I say just to say something.

Wayne fixes me with a droll look. "Come on, Joe. It's in the manual. Young people with terminal illnesses develop a whimsical, slightly sarcastic sense of humor about it to put everyone else at ease and to serve as shining examples of grace in the face of colossally fucked-up events. Don't you ever watch Lifetime, man?"

"Not really." I point to myself. "Not gay, remember?"

Wayne laughs. "Sorry. I forgot." He flicks his butt between his feet and over the ledge and we watch it fall. "I guess you could say I'm having a mid-death crisis. I mean, what the hell will my death actually mean? I was born, I got older, and now I'm going to die, and what the hell do I have to show for it? No kids, no significant other, no people I've enriched, no accomplishments. What am I leaving behind? I'm scared of dying, I won't bullshit you about that, but more than that, I'm immensely pissed at the realization that my entire existence has actually had no real purpose except maybe to serve as some sort of cautionary tale to others."

"Well, there are two possibilities," I say thoughtfully. "Either there is an afterlife, or there isn't."

"How profound."

"Fuck you. If you wanted a priest, you should have climbed up onto the church."

"Touché," Wayne says with a grin. "Please go on. I'm dying to hear this."

"As I was saying, if there is an afterlife and this world is but a waiting room, then the fact that you feel like you haven't done anything is really irrelevant, since there's more living to be done, albeit in a state we can't comprehend."

"And if there's no afterlife?"

"Then we're all headed underground anyway, just on different schedules, so what does anything matter?"

Wayne gives me a bemused look. "So what you're saying is, if there is an afterlife, then nothing here mattered, and if there isn't an afterlife, nothing here mattered."

"That's a gross oversimplification of a complexly stratified theological treatise."

"But that's it in a nutshell."

"I guess so. In a nutshell."

"So what does matter?"

"The little things," I say. "All that stuff you said to me the other day about me and you and Carly. Those moments are what matter. Don't you even listen to yourself when you speak?"

"I *was* stoned," Wayne says with a shrug.

He lights up another cigarette, nodding thoughtfully. We sit in silence for a few minutes, watching the ebb and flow of the swirling crowd below. From our vantage point, we can see drivers stopping their cars to gawk and people walking briskly through the streets toward the school. Nothing much ever happens in the Falls, and when it does, no one likes to miss it. More news vans arrive, as well as a handful of photographers. The quick flickering of flashbulbs makes the crowd sparkle like a diamond. I look for Carly, but we're too high up for me to spot her. I feel immensely sad, but also strangely liberated, as if I've been trying to feel sad for a long time but haven't been able to until now. "So," I say. "Are you going to jump, or what?"

"Nah."

"Why not?"

"I'm just not the jumping type."

"I agree. Can I help you down now?"

Wayne leans back and looks down at the crowd. "A few more minutes, okay?"

"Sure."

"Is Carly down there?"

"Somewhere."

"Joe?"

"Yeah."

"I don't want to go to a hospice."

"So don't."

"I was thinking maybe I should move in with you. You know, into your dad's place."

"That's a great idea."

Wayne nods. "I don't want my friends wiping my ass and stuff. I don't need to be remembered that way."

"I hope you won't be hurt when I tell you that we're not exactly lining up to wipe your ass. I'll get you a nurse."

"It'll set you back some."

"I can always sell my car."

There's a scraping sound and then a pair of hands appear on the ledge, followed by Jared's head. "Hey," he says with a grin. "What's new and exciting?"

From below there are cries from the crowd, and I realize that Jared's legs are dangling over the side of the building. "Will you get up here!" I say, pulling him onto the ledge.

"Who's this?" Wayne says.

"Jared Goffman," my nephew says, extending his hand for Wayne to shake.

"Brad's kid."

"That is my privilege," Jared says. "So, what are we doing up here, besides sitting on decades' worth of bird shit?"

"I thought I told you to wait by the stairs," I say.

"I'm a kid, I bore easily." He sits down against the cupola next to Wayne and lights up his own cigarette. "You're pretty sick, huh?" he says earnestly.

"They don't come any sicker," Wayne says.

"What are you, thirty?"

"Thirty-four."

"Damn," Jared says sincerely. "That's a real big bite out of the shit sandwich."

Wayne appears genuinely tickled by the idiom. I flash him a mock apologetic look. "You know what they say," I say with a sigh. "Youth is wasted on the young."

Wayne nods. "And life on the living." He turns to Jared. "Tell me one of your favorite things."

"What do you mean?"

Wayne looks out at the sky. "Tell me one of life's little treasures, a simple, thoughtless pleasure that you enjoy and then forget about." He fixes Jared with a grim look. "Keep in mind that if you say blow job I'll throw you right off this ledge."

Jared sucks thoughtfully on his cigarette. "Sometimes I pour some orange juice into a plastic cup and freeze it, like ices, you know? And then when you're sucking on it, you basically suck all the juice out of the ice, so that all that's left is this fairly tasteless chunk of ice. But some of the juice settles on the bottom of the cup, and as you work your way down to the bottom of the ice, every so often you can tilt the cup and get a swallow of pure, ice-cold juice, and it's just really sweet, you know?" He looks at us sheepishly. "Anyway, I know it sounds stupid, but you asked."

Wayne smiles and closes his eyes. A cool breeze blows against us, making him shiver noticeably. "That was perfect," he says. "What about you, Joe?"

I think about it for a minute and then say, "Phoebe Cates."

"Phoebe Cates," Wayne repeats skeptically.

"Who's Phoebe Cates?" Jared asks.

"She's an actress," I say. "Every guy my age was in love with her at one point."

"Because of the topless scene in *Fast Times at Ridgemont High*," Wayne says.

"Oh," Jared says, nodding. "I know who she is."

"It's got nothing to do with *Fast Times*. There's just something very pure about her. When I was a kid, she represented everything you'd ever want in a girl, and I would picture this whole incredible life I could have if I had someone like her. And now, whenever I see her on TV, I get this inexplicably happy, hopeful feeling, like all the dreams I ever had as a kid are still out there and can still be realized."

"Yeah," Wayne says. "But Phoebe Cates? I just don't see it."

"I don't see it either," Jared says, shaking his head.

"Well, you're gay, and you're a generation too late, so in the interest of time, I'm going to change my answer and go with the blow job," I say, and we all laugh. "So, are we going to get down now, or what?"

A comical hush falls over the crowd as the three of us stand up and make our way precariously off the ledge of the cupola, Jared going first and then helping me to guide Wayne down. Once we've made it to the safety of the roof, the crowd breaks into rowdy applause, cheering us like we're a rock band. *Thank you, Bush Falls! Good night! God Bless!*

Mouse is waiting for us at the top of the stairwell with another deputy and two paramedics. The paramedics step on either side of Wayne and usher him carefully down the stairs. The deputy pulls out some handcuffs, and Mouse arrests Jared and me for disorderly conduct and obstruction of government administration, since we'd apparently interfered with a police rescue.

# thirty-two

Carly has accompanied the ambulance to make sure Wayne is okay, so there's really no choice but to hang out in the holding cell of the Sheriff's Department with Jared until Cindy shows up to take him home. She stands outside the cell in jeans and a navy polo shirt that would fit a five-year-old perfectly, glowering at me while Mouse unlocks the door. "I'm sorry about this, Cindy," he says as he slides the cell door open. "They were interfering in front of a large crowd of students, so I couldn't just let them go." He looks at her obsequiously. "Would have sent a bad message to all those kids, you understand." Mouse's nervousness is palpable, and I realize that like many men his age in the Falls, he's grown up worshipping Cindy, and apparently still does. Even now he can't stop his gaze from repeatedly wandering from her face down to where her breasts are formidably outlined under her tiny shirt.

"I understand," Cindy says, still staring coldly at me. "It won't happen again."

I follow Jared to the door, but Mouse blocks it the minute Jared has passed him. "Where do you think you're going?" he says to me.

"Home?"

"I don't think so. You haven't been processed yet."

"You've got to be kidding me."

Mouse flashes me what is no doubt supposed to be a superior, predatory grin. "We're letting the boy off the hook," he says, closing the cell door again. "I haven't decided what to do with you yet."

"This is bullshit," Jared says.

"Shut up, Jared!" Cindy snaps at him, her voice low and trembling.

"We helped the guy down, Mom. We didn't do anything wrong."

"You interfered with a police rescue," Mouse says.

Jared looks down at Mouse coolly and says, "No one's talking to you, fuckface."

"Jared!" Cindy shrieks, grabbing him by the arm. "Not another word."

"Maybe you'd prefer it back in the cell," Mouse says, his face turning crimson.

"No!" Cindy says quickly. "We'll be going now." She yanks Jared down the hall toward the front offices, and Mouse follows behind, his eyes fixed intently on Cindy's ass. A moment later she returns alone and faces me through the bars. "Why are you still here?" she demands.

"Mouse isn't through fucking with me."

She frowns at the evasion. "Why haven't you gone back to New York?"

"You know," I say, stepping right up to the bars, "I've been asked that by just about everyone I know over the last few days. A less secure person might start to feel unwanted."

Cindy grins humorlessly, an ugly expression that thoroughly mars the flawless beauty of her face. One of the liabilities of such pristine beauty is the ease with which the slightest gracelessness shows, like muddy footprints on white carpeting. "You are unwanted," she says. "You've never shown any interest in this family before, and now the best you can do is act like a juvenile delinquent. Jared gets into enough trouble on his own. He doesn't need his big-shot, good-for-nothing uncle encouraging him."

"Wayne was up on the roof, and I went to help him," I say hotly. "Jared showed up on his own, and I told him to get lost."

She waves away my words with disgust. "You stayed away for seventeen years," she says, her voice lined with steel. "Do us all a favor and take your drugs and your condescending attitude and just go home already. You don't belong here."

Let the record reflect that I do not watch her ass as she turns abruptly on her heel and storms out of the room. I'm too busy trying to figure out if what I'm feeling at that precise moment is righteous indignation or just self-pity with a vengeance.

Carly shows up at around three and talks some sense into Mouse by threatening him with a series of editorials concerning the Sheriff's Department's questionable practices and apparently numerous inadequacies. By this point I'm in a deep funk, feeling supremely alone and universally despised. "How's Wayne?" I ask her as we walk down the steps of the Sheriff's Department. She's still dressed as she was this morning, but somewhere in her travels the barrette has been discarded and her hair now hangs in loose disarray over her shoulders.

"He's resting at home," she says, and then gives me a sideways look. "Did you two discuss his moving in with you?"

"Yeah."

"Well, I hope you were serious about it, because he's planning on doing it soon."

"Good," I say absently as we come to the corner. "Where's your car?"

"Still at the high school," Carly says. "Where's yours?"

"At home. You picked me up, remember?"

"Oh, yeah. God, that seems like forever ago."

We begin walking aimlessly up the block. "Time, in general, has been behaving oddly since I got here," I say.

"How so?"

"Well, I've been here for just under a week, but it feels like months already. And the days when I lived here, way back when, seem so much more immediate to me now than they ever did before, whereas the last seventeen years seem to have been reduced to this tiny area on the map of my life. Just a little yellow shading on the legend to mark my time away from the Falls."

Carly flashes me a funny, tender look that lasts for a few seconds. "You've been very unhappy, haven't you?"

"Not really." Then I think about it for a moment. "And by that I mean I guess so. Yes."

She turns to me and puts her hand gently against the side of my face, a gesture so loving and wholly unexpected that I nearly buckle under it and break down, but instead I just tremble quietly as the feeling washes over me. When my shaking becomes even more pronounced, Carly has to steady me with her other hand, placing it on the other side of my face. She cradles my head like that for a minute, staring at me intently as if she's taking measurements of my soul through my eyes. Then her own eyes mist up and she says, "Oh, shit," and her hands slide down my face in a caress as she steps forward and puts her arms around me. "Shit," she says again, crying softly, almost imperceptibly into my shoulder. I open my mouth to say something and then close it decisively in a rare display of restraint, not trusting myself to preserve the moment. Instead, I just bury my face in her hair and hold on to her as if my life depends on it.

*  *

We walk back to my father's house in companionable silence, our private thoughts mingling tangibly around us as we go, our bodies close enough to build up an electrical field that tingles like a bug zapper every time our stray limbs inadvertently touch. This thing between us, this invisible ball of anger and fear that's been floating ominously there ever since I arrived in the Falls, seems to have finally been vaporized, and in its place is a warm emptiness waiting to be filled. Given my recent success rate, I'll be damned if I'm going to be the first to attempt filling it.

Once we get to my father's house, we drive my battered Mercedes to the high school to get Carly's car. I pull up alongside her Honda and throw the car into park. School has already let out for the day, but a handful of kids are still hanging out in small clusters on the stairs or in nuzzling, groping twosomes perched on the hoods of cars. "God," I say. "Remember high school?"

Carly smiles. "Every day, lately. I have trouble remembering specific events, but I totally remember what it felt like to be so full."

"Full of what?"

"I don't know. Full of promise, full of dreams, full of shit. Mostly just full of yourself. So full you're bursting. And then you get out into the world, and people empty you out, little by little, like air from a balloon."

I think about her analogy for a few seconds. "So what, you just go through life being emptied of all vitality as you go, until none is left and then you die?"

"Of course not. You try like hell to fill yourself up with fresh air, from you and from other people. But back then"— she nods toward the kids outside—"it was so damn effortless to feel full, you know? All you had to do was breathe."

"I know," I say, nodding. "Even though my life in high

school pretty much sucked until you came along, I still woke up every day with the strength to get out there again, as if I believed at any moment things would change for the better."

Carly sighs, long and deep. "Oh, well."

We just sit there for a few minutes, watching the teenagers in front of us as if the windshield were a television screen, the two of us resting easy, buoyed by each other's silence instead of drowning under it. "This is nice," I say.

Carly combs the hair out of her face with her fingers and turns to look at me, her lips pressed together in an unintentional pout, and says, "You should kiss me now."

"I need some help," I tell Owen as I drive slowly back toward my father's house, still replaying Carly's kiss in my mind, running my tongue over the inside of my lips and cheeks to savor every last trace of her flavor, like the aftermath of a succulent candy. It's amazing how perfectly I've preserved the memory of her taste, making it feel as if it's been only days since we last kissed, instead of years. The minute the kiss ended, I was tempted to start another one immediately, but I managed to stop myself, somehow getting that making out wasn't called for here, that Carly required an attitude of careful restraint from me, even if I didn't fully understand why.

"Admitting you need help is the first step toward recovery," comes Owen's jocular voice over the phone.

"Seriously," I say, and then tell him that Wayne will be moving into my father's house with me.

"I understand. What do you need?"

"A nurse and a hospital bed for starters."

"I'll take care of it. What else?"

I realize that I have no idea. "I'm not sure. I've never really taken care of anyone before."

"Me neither."

I consider for a moment the sad fact of two intelligent,

successful men so clueless in matters of charity. "Are you thinking that we're a couple of empty, selfish pricks?" Owen says, and I have to smile.

"Nah," I say softly.

"Me too." He clears his throat. "Joe."

"Yeah."

"You're a good person."

"I'm an asshole."

"That notwithstanding."

"Well, do you think there's someone you could call about what else I'll need?" I ask him.

"This is America," Owen says. "There's always someone to call."

# thirty-three

I'm pounding away at my laptop later that evening when by some act of god I remember that I'm expected at Brad and Cindy's for dinner. At least, I suppose I'm still expected; I'm not sure. Perhaps the invitation has been rescinded in view of my earlier unpleasantness with Cindy at the sheriff's station. No one has called to cancel, but maybe this is one of those glaringly obvious situations that don't require a verbal confirmation. Hard to say, really. If so, showing up could be awkward—unpleasant, even. But not showing up when they're expecting me would be further confirmation of my wayward tendencies when it comes to family, the very perception I'm trying to change. And anyhow, when it comes to Cindy's shit list, I'm already number one with a bullet, so it's not like I can really do any further damage. And besides, Jared will be there.

Fuck it. I'll go.

Brad and Cindy live in a Dutch colonial about half a mile from my father's house. Emily and Jenny open the front door when I knock. They are dressed alike, in oversized Backstreet Boys T-shirts and black leggings, and perched on one of their wrists is an alarmingly large white bird with a hand-shaped feather emerging from the top of its head. "Hi, Uncle Joe," the twins say in unison, their voices just a half-tone off from each other, creating a spooky, alien effect that is enhanced by the bird. The twin holding the bird—let's call her Emily—turns carefully to lead me into the house while Jenny hand-feeds little biscuits to the bird, who snatches them jerkily from between her fingers.

"Hello, girls," I say rather formally, stepping into the house. There's something about addressing the two of them that makes me self-conscious, as if I'm being reviewed by a committee. I have no experience with adolescent girls, and these two in particular seem strangely jaded, like they can see right through me. The fact that they outnumber me somehow neutralizes the years I have on them, and they seem to know it. "Who's that?" I say, indicating the bird.

"Shnookums," says Emily.

"She's a cockatoo," says Jenny.

"She can talk."

"She can say 'How are you.' "

"And 'Oops, I did it again.' "

"Wow," I say. "Let's hear something."

The twins shake their heads and smirk at each other. "She won't talk for you."

"She only talks for us."

" 'Cause we trained her."

"And for Jared sometimes."

"Right. He taught her to say 'Hey, dickhead.' " They laugh together and it makes one sound.

The first thing I see as I follow the girls into the house is one of those museum-type living rooms that exist exclusively for display purposes. Plush white carpeting that has never known the tread of a shoe, Victorian couches that were clearly not designed with the human ass in mind, and a

Steinway baby grand lacquered to the point that you can actually see your reflection. The piano has probably never been played but serves simply as a platform for a slew of family portraits, all in gaudy electroplated gold and silver frames and carefully angled so that viewing them will not necessitate actually entering the room. This room is all Cindy, highly feminine and supremely forbidding. There is something tragic in the way Cindy has angrily and obsessively dedicated herself to the immaculate perfection of this room while her life and her marriage spin helplessly out of her grasp.

Across the large foyer is a family room with worn beige carpeting, sun-faded leather sectional couches, a fireplace, a La-Z-Boy, and a large flat-screen television upon which J. Lo is gyrating earnestly through an industrial-looking nightclub. Jenny and Emily take seats on the back of the couch, singing along to the video while caressing and fussing over their bird.

"Where's Jared?" I ask.

"In his room."

"Speaking to his girlfriend."

"Kissing through the phone." They make kissing noises at each other and laugh.

"And your mom and dad?"

"Dad's not home yet, and Mom's in the basement."

"Just follow the music."

My instinct is to go upstairs and find Jared, in much the same manner you would contact the embassy upon arrival in a foreign country, but tonight is all about reaching out to Brad and Cindy, so I locate the basement door right off the kitchen and head downstairs. I find Cindy working out to a Pilates tape in a playroom that's been converted into a miniature gym. While posters of Disney characters still adorn the walls, the space has been usurped by a treadmill, a stair machine, a rack of free weights, and a rubber mat on the floor, upon which Cindy now lies on her back, her legs and chest raised off the ground as she feverishly performs crunches along with the music emanating from the television. She is dressed in spandex shorts and a sports bra, her hair tied back with a bandanna, her face flushed and sweaty from her exertions.

"Hi, Cindy," I say from the stairs.

She doesn't miss a beat in her exercise but simply looks over to the stairs and grunts a greeting, evincing no self-consciousness at my intrusion of her workout, and with a body like hers, any such demonstration would be a laughable pretense. "Brad's-not-back-yet," she gasps, her words necessarily staggered by the up-and-down motion she is using to work her infomercial-quality abdomen. She can speak only on the exhalations, every time she rises in her crunches. There is a manic energy to her workout that seems to cross the line between rigid discipline and desperation, and against my instincts I experience a rush of sympathetic warmth for my sister-in-law, the sense that beneath her bitterness is simply a bewildered young girl who can't understand where her life went wrong.

"Brad's working late?" I ask, overtly casting my glance around the room to demonstrate my complete lack of interest in her glistening perfection.

"No," she grunts, now adding a left-to-right twist to her crunch, isolating yet another group of muscles in her lean trunk. "Fucking-his-waitress."

"Excuse me?"

"You-heard-me."

She finishes her crunches and flips over on the mat, hands pressed to the floor as she raises her upper body, arching her back to stretch out her flat stomach. "Are you sure?" I say quietly.

"There are no secrets in a small town. Everything is known; it's simply a matter of what people are willing to discuss."

I don't know if it's her casual revelation of Brad's infidelity or the contortions of her incredible body that have me off balance, but either way it takes me an extra beat to realize that she's just quoted the opening line of *Bush Falls*.

"I don't know what to say," I say.

She stands up, shaking off her arms and legs. "Join the club," she says. "Can you give me a hand with the mat?"

I help her to fold the mat and lean it against the door. Then she steps into a small alcove in which there are a washer and a dryer and, to my utter stupefaction, pulls off her sports bra and shorts. "He's been doing it for a while, I think," she says in a matter-of-fact voice as she tosses her sweat-soaked clothing into the washing machine and pours in a drop of detergent. "Not that he'll admit it."

"Well, maybe it's not true," I say, hoping my voice isn't betraying the instant panic her careless nudity has engendered in me. Am I being seduced? Is this her way of getting back at Brad, by having a go at his brother in their basement? I am ashamed at the momentary flash of excitement I feel beneath my horror at this possibility. She turns away from the machine to face me. "It's true," she says softly.

Confronted with my sister-in-law's head-on nakedness, I quickly avert my eyes to the postered walls, still seeing her breasts in the double spheres of Mickey Mouse's ears. "It's okay," she says, smiling dryly at my discomfort. "I work like hell on this body; someone ought to see it."

So it's not about seduction but simply exhibitionism. I am relieved and ever so slightly deflated by this realization. "That may be," I say, turning back to meet her glance. "But I'm quite certain that someone isn't me."

Cindy considers me for a moment and then shrugs, grabbing a lavender towel from the shelf behind her. "Suit yourself," she says, wrapping herself in the towel. "I'm going upstairs to shower."

J. Lo has been replaced by Britney when I come back upstairs to the family room. It's apparently the midriff hour on MTV. Jared is seated on the floor, his legs spread out in front of him, fiddling with an MP3 player while studying Britney's navel. The twins are still perched on the back of the sectional, playing with their bird. "Hey, Jared," I say, sitting down on the armrest of the La-Z-Boy.

"Did she show you her tits?" my nephew wants to know.

"What?"

"It's okay," he says. "She does it to everyone. Even me."

"Really?"

Jared nods, his expression inscrutable. "My friends love to come over."

"I'll bet."

Suddenly, the bird flaps its wings violently between the twins, and I instinctively jerk backward a little. "Can she fly?" I ask nervously.

"Of course she can," says the twin holding the bird. "She's a bird, remember?" To illustrate her point, she flings the bird up into the air, and with a squawk and a fierce flap of her wings, Shnookums takes flight in the general direction of my face. My hands fly up instinctively as I fall back off the armrest and into the seat of the chair. The bird spins away from me and settles on top of the television. The twins are laughing so hard they're in danger of falling off the couch, which at that moment I wouldn't mind at all. Cindy appears at the entrance to the room while I'm still sprawled across the La-Z-Boy in my defensive position, arms over my head, legs straight up in the air. She flashes me a tired, cynical look, as if I'm always doing this sort of thing, and then addresses the girls. "You two better get that bird back in its cage pronto," she says. "If it gets into my living room again, it's history."

Brad comes home, and he and Cindy retreat upstairs for a few minutes to scream and curse at each other while Jared and the girls watch television, their unblinking eyes glazed over in a practiced oblivion that's heartbreaking to witness. After a few minutes Brad comes down to say hello, and I accompany him into the kitchen, where he pulls a bottle of wine out of the Sub-Zero and starts rummaging through a drawer in search of a corkscrew. "Sorry I'm late," he says.

"Don't worry about it," I say. "Listen, Brad, maybe this was a bad idea. I can always come another time."

"It's fine."

"I don't know. Cindy seems to be upset."

"That's par for the course," Brad says, his expression grim.

Cindy serves up a dinner of overcooked chicken in marinara sauce that disintegrates wherever the tines of my fork pierce it, mashed potatoes, and a tossed salad that was dressed too long ago and is now soggy and fermenting. "Everything is delicious," I say. Jared, who has finally joined us only after being summoned repeatedly, raises his eyebrows incredulously at me. The conversation, or what passes for it, is stilted and awkward, and while I'm sure my presence is not without its own stultifying effects, I sense that dinner here is never a barrel of laughs. Brad eats resolutely and with great concentration, Jared with affected detachment, and Jenny and Emily giggle and whisper to each other in a secret twin language. "Oobo yoobo?" "Boobo wabo." "Yeah?" "Yeah." Cindy nibbles on some soggy lettuce and absently scolds the girls every few minutes for some minor transgression or another while I carve "save me" into my mashed potatoes. We go through the first bottle of wine in under ten minutes, and Cindy quickly opens a second.

"So, Joe," Brad says, "how long do you plan on sticking around?" Cindy perks up with obvious interest in my answer.

"I'm not sure," I say. "My plans are somewhat open-ended."

"I don't know why anyone would stick around this shit-hole a day longer than they had to," Jared says.

"Jared!" Cindy snaps at him as the twins gasp in delighted horror at his language.

"Watch your mouth, Jared," Brad says wearily.

"Sorry. This craphole."

The twins are like a sitcom laugh track.

"I used to feel like you, Jared. But you wouldn't believe how much you can miss a place you think you hate." That's me, affecting a guileless tone of open conciliation in a futile attempt to ease the tension at the table and perhaps begin smoothing things over between my only living relatives and me.

"Well, that's easy for you to say," Jared says. "I, on the other hand, have not yet written my revenge."

"My book wasn't for revenge."

"What, then?"

"It's complicated."

"You always say that. It's not so simple. It's complicated. Bullshit. You got back at all the people you were pissed at. There's nothing wrong with it, but let's call it what it is. Revenge."

"That's enough, Jared," Brad says, although not with much conviction.

"Oh, come on, Dad," Jared says, his face turning red. "You went apeshit when that book came out. You and Mom couldn't shut up about it."

"Now we're getting somewhere," I say, turning to Brad as if I meant for the conversation to take this turn. "I'm sure you were pissed when the book came out. So why didn't you say anything to me?"

Brad slowly puts down his fork and finishes the chicken in his mouth with slow, deliberate chews, dabbing at the corners of his mouth with his napkin to indicate that he will not be rushed. "Why didn't I say anything," he says, nodding resignedly, as if he would like to have avoided this discussion altogether but has been coerced into it. "One: because you and I rarely speak to each other. Two: because I probably didn't want to give you the satisfaction. But mostly—and I know you might find this hard to understand—because I'm an adult, Joe, and I have got much bigger problems to deal with than some stupid, mean-spirited book."

"That you do," says Cindy with a nasty grin before chugging down what I estimate to be her fourth glass of wine.

Brad turns to his wife, his expression a tired mixture of pity and disgust. "Don't you think you've had enough?"

"Not even close."

"Why are you mad at me?" I ask Jared in a whisper as Brad and Cindy gnaw at each other like two angry animals.

"I'm not mad."

"You could have fooled me."

"I'm just trying to draw their fire."

"From what?"

Jared sighs and looks at me. "From you."

Before I can ask him what he means, Shnookums comes flying into the dining room and performs a reckless dive into the chicken marinara, splattering the red sauce across the tablecloth as she flaps her wings in a frantic effort to correct her flight path.

"Brad!" Cindy yells as we all jump to our feet in surprise.

"Fuck!" Brad exclaims.

The bird spins around on the serving platter as if it's standing on a lazy Suzan, unable to take to the air again because of the saturation of sauce in its feathers. Cindy swats at the bird, missing completely but knocking over her wineglass, which spills onto the table, and the wine bottle, which hits the wood floor with a resounding thud. "Goddammit!" Cindy shrieks.

We all watch, mesmerized, as Shnookums finally extracts herself from the chicken dish and takes a few jerky steps across the table, leaving perfect red footprints on the tablecloth in her wake before coming to a stop directly in front of me. "Hey, dickhead," she says, and that pretty much wraps up dinner with the family.

After helping Brad and Cindy clean up the mess in their dining room, I am making my good-byes when I catch Cindy flashing Brad a meaningful look. "I'll walk you out," Brad says to me. I remember Jared's comment about drawing his parents' fire and wonder what's coming. We sit down on the front steps, and Brad gets right to it. "I need to talk to you about Jared."

"Okay," I say. "You know, I have to tell you, I really like him. He's a good kid."

Brad nods. "I know. But the thing is, he's also a bit of a discipline problem for Cindy and me. He skips school, he stays out all night, he's smoking pot."

"He's a teenager," I say with a shrug. "But I've been spending some time with him lately, and there's no question that he's a great kid. I don't think you have anything to worry about."

"I know you don't," Brad says pointedly. "And that's the problem."

"I don't understand."

Brad takes a breath and purses his lips. "Did you smoke pot with Jared?"

Uh-oh. "What?" I say.

"Cindy says the night she came to tell you that Dad was dead, you and Jared both reeked of it."

"Listen, Brad. I've been here for a week. Whatever Jared is into, he was into long before I got here."

"Just answer me. Did you or didn't you smoke up with him?"

"It was his stuff," I say lamely. "I just took a few puffs."

"Uh-huh, that's what I thought," Brad says, nodding. "Listen, it's like this: Cindy and I think you should go back to Manhattan. We don't want you hanging around with Jared anymore."

"That's insane. It was just a joint, for god's sake."

"You're just proving my point."

"Listen," I say. "Jared is going through a tough time right now. Things between you and Cindy are bad; he's confused about everything."

"You've been here for a few days, and now you're an expert on my son?"

"That's not what I'm saying. It may very well be the fact that I was a stranger to him. But either way, I'm the one adult he seems to be willing to talk to."

Brad looks up at me, anger blazing in his eyes. "You're not an adult, Joe. You're a thirty-four-year-old teenager. That's why Jared likes you. He doesn't look to you for guidance or wisdom. Your age just lends some credibility to his bullshit. And the last thing he needs is another pothead to get high with."

"I see," I say, standing up abruptly. "If you ask me, I think you're just looking for any excuse to keep Jared away from me because it makes you crazy that he relates to me and not to you. I'm sorry Jared couldn't be a ballplayer, Brad, but believe it or not, there can still be something worthwhile about a kid who doesn't play for the Cougars."

Brad remains sitting on the stairs, looking thoroughly exhausted. "You know why I wanted Jared to be on the team? Because I wanted him to feel a part of something, to learn what it means to be responsible to someone besides himself. That's something you've never understood, because you've never been a part of anything in your life. You've never looked out for anyone but yourself. It's so easy for you to sit there and be easygoing about his drugs and his delinquent behavior, because at the end of the day you have nothing invested in him. You're his little buddy. I'm his father, Joe, and as much as I'd like to be his buddy, I have a larger responsibility that you can't begin to comprehend, because you've never loved someone selflessly in your life."

"And how exactly does fucking Sheila Girardi contribute to your son's well-being?" It's a low blow, but I'm all out of high ones.

Brad stands up on the stairs, and for one scary moment I think he's poised to hit me. "Go home, Joe," he says, his expression one of acute misery. "You don't belong here."

\* \*

I'm a few blocks away when I hear the light tread of fast footsteps behind me. "Go home, Jared," I say as he comes alongside me, matching my gait.

"Hey."

"I'm not supposed to talk to you anymore," I say.

"I tried to warn you," he says apologetically.

"I know. It's okay."

"I listened to the whole conversation," Jared says. "He was really harsh with you."

"He made some good points."

"So, what, you're going to listen to him?"

I stop walking and turn to face my nephew. "Listen, Jared. I came over tonight because I had this idea that I could begin to mend fences with your folks, to become somewhat more connected with my family. But you know what I learned? That it's never going to happen, because you're all so disconnected from each other that there's really no family for me to reconnect with."

"So you're just giving up?"

"I'm rethinking my approach. Your father said that I don't know anything about selflessness, and he's right. I've been hanging out with you, talking about girls and music, smoking a joint, and you know who benefits from all that? Me. Because I get to feel like I have a family. But it does no good for you. You need a parent now, not a friend. And if there's one thing I am qualified to talk about, it's fucking things up with my father, so I'm going to give you the only advice I can: lose the attitude and let your father in. I know it won't be easy, but I can promise you that if you don't, you'll regret it."

Jared looks at me for a minute, then nods. "Okay. I'll think about it."

"Good. Now what's with the birdcage?" He's carrying a large white birdcage in which an agitated Shnookums is being jostled mercilessly from side to side as we walk.

"Much like yourself, Shnookums needs to keep a low profile for a little while where the folks are concerned. I had a meeting with my sisters, and we elected you temporary custodian." He smiles and hands me the birdcage.

"When do I feed it?"

"I'll come by and feed it."

"You're not supposed to hang out with me."

"Pay attention, man. I never do what I'm supposed to do."

"You want a bird?" I ask Carly when she opens the door.

She studies me on her doorstep with a whimsical smile. She's wearing Bush Falls High sweatpants and a tank top and chewing comically on a large raw carrot. "Who's that?" she asks.

"This is Shnookums. She's a cockatoo."

"Oh, my god, Joe. She's bleeding!"

"That's marinara sauce."

"Oh. Well, that's okay, then."

"I've had an interesting night."

"I don't doubt it," she says, smiling as she munches on her carrot. "And now you've made mine more interesting."

"I was on my way home from Brad's and I was passing by, so I thought I'd stop in for a minute."

"My house isn't on the way home from Brad's."

"Don't be so literal."

"Okay," Carly says. "I was just doing a little work. Would you like to come in? The bird can come too, of course."

"I want to, but I won't," I say. "I've got some work of my own I need to get back to."

"You're writing?"

"I am. Finally."

She nods. "So what can I do for you?"

"I was hoping that maybe I could kiss you again."

Her smile is the sun on my face. "I was hoping you could

too." She steps down to join me on her front stairs, and we're face-to-face. "I've got carrot breath," she says.

"I love carrots."

She grabs two small fistfuls of my shirt. "Whatever floats your boat, Romeo."

# thirty-four

It will take Owen another few days to pull together everything we need for Wayne, and Wayne tells me that's perfect,
because he'd like to spend another day or two in his childhood bedroom, looking through his drawers and shelves, re-
visiting his youth one last time. I suspect he's actually trying
to give his mother a little more time in the hopes that she'll
emerge from her religious stupor long enough for a genuine
good-bye, and while I understand this desire, I'm not optimistic on his behalf.

I don't bother shaving or showering or even brushing my
teeth when I wake up the next morning, but simply roll out
of bed and head straight downstairs in my boxers to get to
work on my manuscript. As I lay falling asleep the night before, Carly's kisses still lingering on my lips, I was awash in
ideas for the novel: plot points, character quirks, expressions,
and even whole paragraphs composed in my mind that I
want to get down before I forget about them. Writing without grooming somehow feels better, more conducive to the

whole enterprise, as if by neglecting all superficial considerations I will channel all my energies into the internal processes of creation. And so I sit, my breath stale, my hair a greasy mess, my skin stubbly and unwashed, and I feel, more than ever, like a writer. I imagine that Hemingway didn't mess around with aftershave and toothbrushes when in the throes of writing.

It's in this soiled state that I answer the doorbell to find Lucy Haber standing on my porch, clutching a copy of *Bush Falls* to her chest. She's applied her makeup with a heavy hand, and I find myself thinking for the first time that there's an element of desperation in her appearance, something that tries too hard for a woman her age, and then I feel ashamed for the uncharitable thought. My face on the back cover, looking up at me from her bosom, seems like an indictment.

"Did I wake you?" she asks, taking in my grimy appearance.

"No. It's okay." I find myself wishing that I'd at least thrown on a T-shirt.

"I thought maybe you'd come visit me," she says, looking highly uncomfortable. "Not that I blame you for not coming."

"I'm sorry. I just . . . didn't."

Lucy waves away my awkwardness. "It's okay. I don't want to make you uncomfortable. That's why I left so early that morning."

"I'm sorry," I say again. I seem incapable of saying anything else.

"I just thought you'd have left by now, and when I drove by and saw your car yesterday, I thought I would come by and say a proper good-bye."

"I appreciate that. Would you like to come in?"

Lucy smiles. "No thanks."

"I wasn't trying— I didn't mean anything by that."

"No. I know." She hands me the book and a silver Cross pen. "Will you sign this for me?"

"Sure," I say, taking the proffered book. "It's been a while since anyone's asked." I open up to the inscription page and write *Dear Lucy:* then pause for a few moments to compose my inscription. *You were my muse and my fantasy, and now I'm happy to call you my friend. Best wishes, Joseph Goffman.* She reads the inscription and smiles. "Give me a hug."

I hug her, the buttons of her blouse digging into my naked torso. There are no sexual intentions, but I think some people are capable of hugging only a certain way, and there's still an inadvertent erotic energy to our embrace, her hands on my bare back, her lower belly against my crotch. She pulls her head back and presses her forehead to mine. "I hope I haven't ruined the fantasy," she says, and in her eyes I can see this is a genuine concern.

"No way," I say. "You validated it beyond my wildest dreams."

"That's sweet of you to say." She leans forward and gives me a soft kiss on the lips. "Don't be a stranger, Joe."

"I won't."

She straightens up and I see that her eyes are threatening to tear. She smiles again, and I watch her go down the stairs to her car. Only after she's driven away do I notice Carly parked in her car across the street, observing the whole scene with a singularly perturbed expression. With a sinking feeling in my stomach, I wave to her. She waves back but makes no move to get out of the car, and her expression doesn't change. I am forced to walk down the stairs and across the street in nothing but boxers, shivering in the cool morning air, bouncing awkwardly when my feet encounter any sharp detritus on the street. "I know that didn't look very good," I say.

Carly nods. "Did you fuck her?" Her tone is one of neutral curiosity, as if the answer is of no particular concern to her one way or another.

"She just showed up now."

"I know when she showed up," Carly says. "Prior to that, did you fuck her?"

I sigh. "It was before anything happened with you and me." It's not that I necessarily buy into the notion that honesty is the best policy, but it is sometimes the most viable strategy, particularly when you don't have the time to come up with a credible alternative.

Carly's already nodding before I finish my sentence, the corners of her mouth straining against invisible weights that are pulling them downward. "Listen, Carly," I say.

"You don't have to explain anything to me," she says, her voice exaggeratedly rational. "There's no commitment between us. I'm happy for you. I mean, you've wanted her for, what is it now, twenty years? It's been well documented."

"Just give me a chance here."

"Congratulations. You finally bagged her, man."

"Can you please stop that?"

"No problem," Carly says. She violently yanks the gear shift and, with tires squealing, drives away, leaving me to cross the street gingerly in my bare feet, feeling a nakedness that extends far beyond my missing clothes. I am once again thoroughly amazed at how poor judgment and bad timing constantly manage to coalesce on my behalf, and always just as my life is starting to show some promise.

The writing is no longer happening, as can be expected, so I go upstairs to shower and get dressed. I am determined to not let things with Carly get derailed over this. The timing might be questionable, but I did not betray her. Chronology is clearly in my favor here, and I'm hoping that once Carly calms down, she can be made to see that. Surprisingly, she takes my call in her office a half hour later. "Hi, Joe," she says easily enough.

"Please don't be mad about this."

"I'm not mad," she says pleasantly.

"What?" This is an old trick of Carly's and one I've never fully understood. When she gets mad, she punishes the offending person by not allowing them the privilege of even witnessing her anger, for that would be the first step toward absolution. I was forced to navigate through the minefield of her hurt a number of times, both in high school and in our years together in Manhattan, and I now recall with clarity that when it comes to hurt and anger, Carly is like a Rubik's Cube.

"It's fine," Carly says. "It had nothing to do with me."

"So what are you saying, that we're okay?"

"We're as good as we ever were."

"Ah. Calculated word choice. Veiled references. Now we're getting somewhere."

"I don't know what you're talking about."

I take a deep breath. "I just want you to know that what happened with Lucy happened when I first got here, when there was nothing at all happening between us."

"Joe?"

"Yes."

"The minute you got here, there was something happening between us. You know it and I know it, so do me a favor and cut the bullshit. At least give me that."

"Okay," I say. I wonder if I should be encouraged that we've gotten past the feigned lack of concern much faster than I thought we would. "But what happened with Lucy happened once, and it would have been a mistake even if nothing happened between you and me, and it wasn't going to happen again regardless."

"That's too bad," Carly says dryly. "Now you'll have no one to kiss."

"You know I was completely yours the moment you kissed me."

"If you're expecting me to say 'You had me at hello,' you're in for a huge disappointment."

These frustrating conversations continue at odd intervals for the rest of that day and the next. Carly resolutely takes all of my calls while patently refusing my entreaties to meet in person. I have myself convinced that this will be a battle of attrition, but underneath it all I am terribly worried that she's working toward shutting me out permanently behind a wall of casual indifference. In between these seemingly futile calls, I struggle to shut out all distractions and maintain the momentum of my novel. The time has come for Matt Burns to visit the scene of his father's supposedly accidental death, at the foot of the waterfalls in the woods behind Norton's Textile Mill, where he'd diligently kept the books for the Norton family for so many years. I don't know when I made the decision to transplant the Bush River Falls into Matt's fictional upstate New York hometown, but now that they've become central to the story, I find myself at somewhat of a loss to come up with the exact mix of events, both romantic and sinister, that make the falls loom as the totemic centerpiece of the novel. I decide it might behoove me to take a drive out to the falls, to sit at the base of their deafening trajectory, become enveloped in the frigid shroud of their mist, and be inspired. If nothing else, at least it will get me out of the house for a little while.

It's a brisk, frowning October day, clear and cloudless, the Mercedes' leather cold enough to chill me through my pants in the two minutes or so before the seat warmer kicks in. I drive out to the falls, pulling off the road onto one of the plethora of dirt lanes that lead into the woods at the point where the falls descend into the Bush River. I leave my car in what I consider to be the approximate spot where once upon a time Carly and I engaged in the mutual surrender of our virginity, perhaps in the subconscious hope that I'll somehow stir the ghosts of our former selves to intervene with the fates on my behalf. Making my way through the underbrush toward the Bush River, I recall the slow, awkward nature of our lovemaking that night, and think that what is so often considered to be the loss of innocence is actually the height of it. I step out of the woods at the base of the falls and sit down at the edge of the large, thrashing pool into which both waterfalls noisily descend. Scattered along the banks of the water, as expected, are empty beer bottles, crushed cans, torn, faded condom wrappers, cigarette butts, and cracked plastic lighters, all the discarded equipment and residue of the ritualistic march of teens into sexual maturity. After a few minutes sitting in the cold, stinging spray of the falls, I decide it's time to move to higher ground for a more encompassing perspective.

I drive a little farther up the main road, past the Porter's campus, and turn onto the well-worn dirt lane that leads through the woods to the top of the waterfalls, a single path barely one car width, whose alliterative nomenclature has included such assignations as Randy Road, Skank Street, Titty Turnpike, Poontang Parkway, and no doubt a slew of others ascribed in more recent years. When I can drive no farther, I leave my car and walk the last twenty yards or so to the rusted guardrail that overlooks the waterfalls. Beyond this rail is a rounded outcropping of large rocks upon which the more reckless teens would often sit, drinking their illegally purchased beer and tossing their empties directly into the cascading waterfalls descending a scant ten feet in front of them. It is from this place as well that the legendary few who have gone over the falls did so. I climb over the guardrail and cautiously inch my way out onto the rock, scraping along on my ass as I go, until I've reached a relatively flat section, where I stand up with exaggerated care as in front of me the water rages furiously in its descent to the river below. This is spitting distance, as close to the falls as one can humanly get without being in them, and the combination of their deafening noise and residual spray, instantly covering me with a layer of cold moisture, is disorienting, making me feel unbalanced even as I steady myself. It's both frightening and exhilarating to stand in such proximity to this powerful force of nature, and it's also surprisingly soothing to be perched on this high promontory, in solitary communion with the falls.

"Hey, Goffman." The voice alone, so unexpected, is enough to cause me to lose my balance, and for the briefest instant I feel my center of gravity slide precariously forward before I right myself by jerking back slightly while lightly flailing with my arms for counterbalance. "Hey, Sean," I say. "What brings you here?"

He's leaning casually against the guardrail, dressed in his leather coat and black jeans, finishing off a cigarette. His presence here is startling, to say the least, and for the briefest instant I find myself entertaining the unlikely notion of a coincidence. "I was driving by and I saw your car turn off the main road."

"You saw me turn off," I repeat skeptically.

"Looked like you were coming to relive old times, so I figured, who better to relive them with than me?"

"Have you been following me, Sean?"

"Maybe." He takes a last drag on his cigarette butt and flicks it expertly past me, where it vanishes instantly against the backdrop of the falls. He moves off the railing and steps out onto the rock, grinning and shaking his head incredulously. "You're some piece of work, Goffman. I tell you to get out of town, and the next thing I know, you're on TV, hanging from the roof of the high school. For a guy who's supposed to be gone, you sure have some funny ideas about how to keep a low profile."

"And believe it or not, I've been trying to do just that," I say, uneasily watching his approach, torn between my desire to play it cool and my instinct to bolt for the safety of the rail before he gets too far away from it. I take an uneasy step or two in his direction, but he's moving faster and more comfortably along the rock's pitched, craggy surface, and within seconds he's reached me, looking over my shoulders at the waterfalls. "Look at that," he says. "Pretty amazing, huh?"

I half turn to look out over the falls with him, thinking it probably pays to humor him with conversation, and choose my moment to make a run for the guardrail. I just need one step on him, two at the most, and I'll be home free. "This is where your friend Sammy bought it, huh?" Sean says over the din of the falls. I remain steadfastly silent, looking into the thrashing water, unable to see the bottom from my vantage point. "Your mother too, if I'm not mistaken. What is it about you that makes so many folks in your life choose death by drowning?" He stares at me, waiting to see if I can be baited. "You might want to think about that."

"It's certainly food for thought," I say, feeling my legs go weak as I peer over the edge of the falls. It's easily a four-story drop, and in mid-October the water will be just this side of freezing. And landing in the water at all is contingent on avoiding the large cone-shaped rocks that jut out from beneath the swirling waters like the horns of a giant submerged beast.

Sean points to a spot somewhere in the woods below. "I was parked down there the night Sammy offed himself," he says, a genuine look of wistful nostalgia crossing his face. "With Vicki Hooper. You remember Vicki Hooper?"

"Vicki Hooters," I say.

"That's right," he says with a chuckle. "Vicki Hooters. Tits like fucking watermelons. They were something, all right." He pauses, relishing the memory. "There were a whole bunch of us parked there that night, messing around, and the word got out that someone had gone over. Of course, we didn't find out until the next day that it was Sammy, you know? That he'd gone and killed himself. We just knew someone had gone over. I got myself a world-class hummer from Vicki Hooper that night, courtesy of your little buddy. You know, tradition being what it is around here." He turns and flashes me a malicious grin. "Anyway, I just thought you should know that I came when Sammy went." His eyes are wide, daring me to react.

"Vicki Hooper was a skank."

Maybe I see the windup, I'm not sure, but I definitely miss the punch, which doesn't return the favor, connecting with my chin with the force of a locomotive, and I crumple to the floor like a marionette cut loose from its strings. Not unconscious, but definitely somewhere in the neighborhood. Sean crouches down next to me, shaking his head and smiling. "Answer me something, will you?" he says. "You fucked Carly Diamond here too. That's a matter of public record, now that you gave the world all the juicy details in your book. So what is it that makes my girl a skank and yours not? A fuck is a fuck is a fuck, am I right?"

"Whatever you say."

I roll over and begin standing up. Sean speeds up the process by lifting me by my shirt and holding me up to face him, nose to nose, my back now to the falls, which sound ominously closer than they did a few seconds ago.

"You know the difference between us, Goffman?"

"Oral hygiene?"

Sean smiles and slaps my face, a stinging blow that makes my eyes tear. "Wrong answer." The correct answer turns out to be this: "Someone pisses you off, hurts or threatens you or your loved ones, you don't do a damn thing except write about it after the fact. It wouldn't even occur to you to take some action, to be a man. Your whole book was just you admitting you were too much of a pussy to stand up for yourself or your faggot friends back in high school. I make my living taking action. There's a building that needs to be destroyed or a mountain in the way of a road, I don't sit down at my computer and write a nice little story about it. I blow it up. Demolish it completely. And if somebody does me wrong, I do the same fucking thing." He tightens his grip on my shirt and takes a step closer to the edge. I think of how Carly grabbed my shirt in exactly the same manner yesterday when she kissed me, and feel a wave of sadness that momentarily overcomes my fear.

"So what happens now, Sean?" I say. "You're going to blow me up?"

"Nah. But right now I'm seriously considering throwing you off this rock."

"That's a relief. Because for a minute there I thought you were angling for another world-class hummer."

All of the color leaves Sean's face and he takes another menacing step forward. I can feel his breath on my nose even as I feel my heels reach the edge of the rock shelf. "You know what?" he says. "I think you want me to throw you off. I gave you every opportunity to leave town, and I think the reason you haven't left is because you're a crazy, suicidal fuck like your crazy, suicidal fuck of a mother. You're just waiting around for someone to put you out of your misery."

I look at his face, only scant inches from my own, and try to get a handle on just how much danger I might really be in. Despite our world of differences, Sean and I grew up together, were invited to each other's birthday parties when we were little, and played in countless games of playground basketball together until his position on the Cougars made it unseemly for him to play with boys of my inferior skill. We can certainly hate each other, maybe come to blows, but it seems to me that our common past precludes such radical violence as throwing me off a cliff, to certain injury and possible death. All my instincts tell me he isn't planning on actually throwing me over the falls. It's incumbent upon me to say something submissively conciliatory, something that will acknowledge his upper hand and give him the wiggle room to back away without a loss of face. "Sean," I begin. He shakes his head and casually pushes me off the cliff.

The speed with which I am suddenly airborne is blinding. One moment I'm standing there, breathing in his stale cigarette breath, and the next I'm flying over the falls. I hit the icy waters on my side, and for a few seconds everything is silent as the pressure from the waterfalls sucks me down into the depths of the river. Time loses all meaning, and then meaning loses all meaning and all that exists is the low, soothing throb of the waterfalls fifteen feet beneath the surface. Everything appears to me in varying shades of the same muted green, the rocks, the muddy floor of the river, the backs of my eyelids when I blink. There is no sense of panic, although on some level I know that will come when the shock wears off, but for now there's just the powerful sense of an elemental peace, and in this frozen instant I understand the desire to stay beneath the surface forever, to embrace the dark, undulating peace that seems to so easily and completely shut out all other considerations. I think I even briefly consider it. And then, with the same force with which they have sucked me down, the churning waters spit me out of their throat and up to the surface, where I gasp desperately for air, the freezing temperature of the water belatedly jolting me into paralysis as the current sweeps me along, numbing my legs and back as they scrape against the rocks and branches that lie just beneath the surface of the roiling water. The river widens as it curves and then empties into a second, shallow pool, where the current briefly slows, and I am able to get to my feet and stagger over to the water's edge, shivering uncontrollably but feeling ridiculously elated at being alive. Cold water drips down my body, and it's Sammy's greeting, my mother's embrace, and I'm overwhelmed by a euphoria so intense it's almost blinding. I am baptized and renewed, and it's as if all the purpose and balance, missing for so long from my life, have been divinely restored. Cheating death is a milestone, I think, a springboard for untold possibilities. Then the thick, brackish waters I've swallowed rise in the back of my throat and I vomit copiously, my body racked by spasms that continue unabated even after the last liquids have been purged from inside me. I fall to my knees in the dead, browning grass at the water's edge and then over onto my side, where I summarily succumb to a shivering state of semiconsciousness, my earlier euphoria gone.

An indeterminate amount of time later, a pair of hands rolls me onto my back and I look up to find one of Jared's friends peering down at me curiously. "Mr. Goffman?" he says.

"Mikey, right?" I grunt.

"That's right."

"What are you doing here?"

There is a hissing sound and then a soft pop and Mikey staggers back a step, a flash of red paint splattering across his sweatshirt. "Ah, fuck," Mikey says.

*I'm alive,* I think, and smile as I pass out.

# thirty-five

Wayne is studying his fingers again. He holds them up in front of his face, flexing and extending, opening and closing, pressing their dry tips against each other. He's become infatuated with the various parts of his body, fascinated with their unhindered functionality, which seems to fly in the face of his imminent death. "It just seems like such a waste," he says to me without looking away from his hands as I enter my father's den, which Carly and I have converted into a bedroom for Wayne. "They're still so . . . capable."

I rub the last bit of sleep out of my eyes and sit down at the edge of his hospital bed, the one that arrived in a large moving truck along with all the other equipment Owen sent. In typical Owen fashion, my agent had gone overboard, sending up enough equipment to outfit a small hospital.

"Look at this," Wayne says, lifting up his covers and peering beneath them. "I have a hard-on, for god's sake."

"Hmm. An erection and a perfectly good hand with nothing to do. Maybe I should leave you two alone for a little while?"

Wayne leans back against his pillow and grins, affording me a glimpse of his black, wasted gums, the mucus-colored teeth protruding from them like driveway gravel. Everything about Wayne is dying fast, but his mouth seems to be leading the charge. "My mother told me that it had been medically proven that jerking off could lead to blindness," Wayne says.

"It was nice that you guys could talk so openly about sex."

"I know, right? And what were Mr. Goffman Senior's thoughts on masturbation?"

"He said if I messed my sheets, I'd have to do my own laundry."

Wayne smiles and returns to the obsessive contemplation of his fingers. "It's just such a waste," he repeats sadly.

There's a knock at the door and Fabia, the stout Jamaican nurse who also arrived courtesy of Owen, steps in quietly and begins preparing some pills for Wayne. "I got to give you your bath now," she says in her thick, musical voice, her daily cue for me to take my leave.

"Where's Carly?" Wayne asks me.

"Still sleeping."

"In whose bed?"

I shake my head at him as I head for the door. "She's in Brad's old room."

Wayne shakes his head right back at me. "Joseph, Joseph," he sighs. "You're killing me."

I pause at the door and we look at each other seriously as the irony in his choice of words dissolves slowly into the room around us. "See you in a few," I say hoarsely, and leave the room.


Carly and I moved Wayne into the house the day after my ignominious trip over the Bush River Falls, from which I'd somehow emerged miraculously unscathed. Mrs. Hargrove glowered at us the whole time we were there, but raised no objection as we carried Wayne's things out. When we were walking Wayne out, Carly on one side and me on the other, he stopped us at the door and turned to face her, his eyes wet and his jaw quivering. "Good-bye, Ma," he said. "I just want you to know that I love you and I'm sorry for what I put you through." His mother nodded, and I was sure that she would break down right there and beg him to stay, but she just said, "I'll pray for you," and continued to nod mechanically until Wayne finally turned away and we headed down the stairs. He paused one more time, just before we got into Carly's car, to get one last look at his childhood home, and then we left. What must it feel like, I thought, to look at something, anything really, and know that it's for the last time?

I sat in the back with Wayne while Carly drove. As we rode through the neighborhood, Wayne stared out the window, determined to take in everything on what would surely be his last view of the Falls. From my seat behind Carly, I could see the small convulsions of her shoulders as she cried silently to herself. "It's okay," Wayne said softly, maybe to Carly or maybe to himself; it was hard to tell, since he was still looking out the window. "It's okay," he said again, and all I could think was *It's pretty much as far from okay as it can possibly get.*

Once we arrived at my father's house and safely deposited Wayne into the hospital bed and the aggressive care of Fabia, Carly and I worked together in silence to unload Wayne's things. We did not discuss our current state of discord at all, but she summarily disposed of her anger, the two of us instinctively understanding that we would not sully Wayne's final days with our trivial differences. I was forgiven by default, which left me with a vague sense of dissatisfaction, because with the process of making up having been circumvented, we were robbed of the fresh intimacy that comes with a hard-fought resolution. When we were done unloading the car, I stepped outside to find her pulling a small overnight bag from her trunk. "Don't give me any crap about it," she said self-consciously. "He's my friend too."

I nodded. "No crap."

Carly came up the stairs and stood in front of me. "He's very close," she said, speaking softly as though she feared Wayne might overhear from inside.

"I know," I said.

She nodded pointlessly, swallowing back her tears, and rested her head briefly against my chest. We stood that way in the dwindling sunlight for a full minute as a noisy fall wind tinged with the first steel hint of winter blew the auburn and yellow leaves in a circular dance across the sidewalk. "I'm glad you're here," Carly said.

That was two weeks ago. Since then, Carly and I have fallen into the pleasant routine of eating breakfast together every morning while Fabia bathes Wayne, who is adamant about our not being present to witness the less dignified necessities of his care: the sponge baths, the ass wiping, the emptying of bedpans. I don't blame him, and I don't mind one bit. So we sit in the breakfast nook, with its picture window overlooking the backyard. Often we eat in silence, watching the wildlife, which consists mostly of squirrels hurriedly humping one another and scurrying about in search of provisions, and the occasional stray cat sunning itself on the patio. The only sounds are the random groans of the perforated straw seat bottoms of the Workbench kitchen chairs we sit in, sagging under our weight. That sound, more than anything else in the house, conjures up images of my mother as clear as photographs. I sat in these chairs for the better part of my life, wolfing down Honeycombs and milk under her watchful gaze as she leaned against the counter in her bathrobe, sipping her coffee serenely from the *#1 Mom* mug I'd bought her in the third grade for Mother's Day.

Carly sits nibbling at her cinnamon toast with one leg pulled up, her chin resting pensively on her knee. There's a raw elegance to her pose, an easy grace that is as much a function of personality as posture. Sitting like that, in her faded jeans and gray hooded sweatshirt, she looks remarkably like she did in high school, the only deviation being the light shadows under her eyes, the drawn expression of someone who isn't getting nearly as much sleep as she should. Her gaze is fixed on something outside, and so I am able to watch her intently for a few seconds as I sift through the jumble of emotions she evokes in me, trying to isolate exactly what it is I feel for her, which is like untying a severely knotted rope, where all you end up with is more knots in a different configuration.

"What are you staring at?" she asks without turning to face me.

"Nothing."

She smiles at the lie. "Just checking."

"Can I confess something crazy to you?"

Carly gives me a suspicious look from the corner of her eye, clearly concerned about the direction of this particular conversational gambit. I am still finding her somewhat panicky reactions to me unsettling. The Carly I knew was direct and fearless, and the intermittent nervousness in her eyes now seems to indicate a depth of damage I don't fully comprehend. I consider the possibility that her asshole ex-husband is largely responsible for this transformation, but I wonder if I'm simply passing the buck because the alternative is too depressing to consider.

"What?" Carly finally says in a tone of advance regret.

"I have a great apartment in the city," I tell her. "I really do. But I've lived there for over three years and I haven't once stopped thinking of it as my new apartment. Living in this house, with you and Wayne, has been the first time since I don't know when that I've been waking up every morning and feeling at home. And I feel guilty as hell about it because of the whole premise of the arrangement. I mean, Wayne's dying and it's horrible in a million different ways, but at the same time, part of me is so grateful for this time we're all sharing." Carly has gone back to staring out the window, but I notice that her expression has relaxed, and a small, sad smile is curling the bottom of her mouth. "That's pretty self-absorbed, isn't it?" I say.

"Maybe." Her voice is a delicate pillow embroidered with butterflies. "But I know exactly what you mean. I feel the same way."

"I'm glad. That makes me feel better."

"It doesn't make you any less self-absorbed."

"I know. But at least I'm in good company."

We smile at each other like we've just shared an intimate secret, and the unguarded nature of her expression makes me tremble momentarily.

After breakfast I bring my laptop into Wayne's room and work on my novel while he drifts in and out of sleep. I've gotten into the habit of writing in his room because it makes me feel close to him, and I think he likes the idea of being in the presence of a work in progress, something that won't be finished until after he's gone, as if he'll somehow go on living through the pages of its narrative. My first novel was about Wayne. This one has no character remotely resembling him, and yet it feels as if every page is infused in some way with his essence. And those pages, I am pleased to see, are starting to add up to something substantial. I've been working on it for less than three weeks, and I already have over two hundred pages. What's more, I think a lot of them are keepers.

Carly has set up a temporary office in the living room and spends most of every morning on her cell phone, checking in with her staff and reviewing layouts and e-mails on her frighteningly large laptop. Whenever Wayne wakes up, she comes in and the three of us have long, streaming conversations about nothing and everything, reminiscing and telling stories about the lives we've led up until this point, as if our entire adult lives have been nothing more than filler until we could be reunited. We laugh a lot, sometimes strenuously, our combined laughter always tapering off into identical wistful sighs and averted gazes. It's just too hard to know how to feel. No one wants to dampen the mood, but the upbeat sounds of our conversations, reverberating conspicuously against our silences, can sometimes seem callous and disrespectful of the situation at hand. Is it better to laugh in the face of death, or cry? In the absence of any evidence pointing in either direction, we vacillate randomly between the two, hoping that the compromise we arrive at is serving Wayne well.

Later in the afternoon, Jared stops by to say hello. He's developed a liking for Wayne that borders on fascination, and has been coming every day to sit on the edge of his bed and listen to our conversation. Wayne, for his part, seems to relish Jared's company, often interrupting us in the middle of anecdotes to include Jared. "Wait till you hear this one," he'll say sardonically to my nephew as one of us starts to tell a story from our shared past. "I think you'll agree your uncle was quite the wanker."

I tell the story of the night Wayne and I, with nothing else to do, drove his car up and down a nearby stretch of I-95 that was home to a slew of gas stations, stopping at each one to ask for the bathroom key and then driving off with it. By the end of the night, we'd collected seven keys, which Wayne kept in his glove compartment so that we'd always have access to bathrooms when we were out driving. Wayne tells about the time the three of us went into Manhattan to see Elton John playing at Madison Square Garden. We paid eighty dollars each to a scalper on the corner of Thirty-third and Eighth, only to find, when we tried to enter the arena, that we'd been sold years-old soccer tickets. Wayne and I were thoroughly disgusted with ourselves, but Carly managed to somehow sweet-talk the ticket taker into letting us in anyway.

Carly surprises me by relating how she and I, desperate for a place to have sex, climbed the fence and infiltrated the Porter's campus one cool spring night and got naked on a picnic blanket. We were well into the act when the automatic sprinklers suddenly came on, soaking us and drenching our discarded clothing in a spray of freezing water. She cracks up Wayne and Jared by describing how we tried in vain to soldier on in spite of the continuous onslaught of the sprinklers. The fact that I'd forgotten about it shocks me into a thoughtful silence, and while the three of them laugh it up, I flash back to that night, the feel of the grass, and the smooth, slippery surface of Carly's soaked skin as we slithered hungrily over each other, reveling in our slickness and the sudden lack of friction.

"Joe?"

I snap out of it to find everyone looking at me, Wayne and Jared with amused grins and Carly with a funny, questioning look. "Should I not have told that story?" Carly says.

"What? No, no. It's fine," I answer too quickly, looking to put everyone at ease. "I was still finding blades of grass in my crotch two days later."

"Didn't all that cold water make it hard to maintain your . . . concentration?" Jared says.

"I was eighteen," I say. "I shouldn't have to tell you of all people that when you're eighteen and in love, there's just about nothing that can ruin your concentration."

Jared and Wayne snicker, while Carly holds my gaze for another few seconds before shrugging lightly and letting me off the hook.

While many of our group reminisces are from the time we shared back in high school, Wayne seems equally intent on sharing experiences from the years he lived in Los Angeles.

He tells us in carefree tones about his failed auditions, the slew of odd jobs he worked in order to pay his rent, and the occasional celebrity encounter. In all of these stories, there is no mention of any friends or lovers, confirming my suspicion that those were exceedingly lonely years for him. Beneath the surface of his narrative is a quiet deliberation as if, through all of those solitary years, he had comforted himself with the promise that at some point in the future he'd be in a position to share those years retroactively, and now, with the clock winding down, he is fulfilling that promise to himself.

After a while Wayne falls asleep again, and Jared goes upstairs to instant-message some of his friends with the computer in my father's room. "I'm sorry if I made you uncomfortable," Carly says. "We were telling stories, and it just popped into my head."

"No, it's fine," I say. "I had just forgotten about that night."

"So you're saying sex with me is forgettable?"

"Hardly. But I've been carrying so many different memories of us around for so many years, and I guess there's some sort of rotation. Some get pulled up more frequently, and others get buried under the bottom of the pile for a while, and you forget they're there."

"That's good to know."

"What?"

"That you've got piles too," Carly says, looking away from me. "I didn't want to be the only one."


I boil water and cook some spaghetti while Carly cuts a salad, and the four of us eat dinner together in Wayne's room. We all pretend not to notice that Wayne's food is going largely uneaten. Fabia will supply him with whatever nutrients he requires intravenously, until the time comes that he no longer requires any nourishment. While we're eating, Wayne seems to fall asleep, his eyes closed, his chest rising and falling with even, shallow breaths. Carly, Jared, and I continue to speak in hushed tones when, without any warning, Wayne opens his eyes and sits up in the bed. "I want to shoot a basketball," he says.

We all stare at him. "Say that again," Carly says.

"I don't think I've touched a basketball since high school."

"What, you mean that night before you left?" I say. "When you scored like fifty points?"

"Fifty-two points," Wayne says.

"That record still stands," Jared says.

Wayne looks at him sharply. "No shit?"

Jared nods. "No shit."

Wayne lies back on his pillow, lost in a moment's reflection. "I want to shoot another basket before I die."

"Maybe tomorrow, if it's warm enough, we can take you out to the driveway," Carly says dubiously.

"No. Not tomorrow, and not on some stupid backyard hoop. I want to do it in the gym."

"The high school gym?"

"Yes."

"It's past eight," I say. "The high school's closed."

Wayne frowns, and turns to look at Jared. After a moment, Jared grins and nods his head. "No problem," he says.

We take Carly's car, which she insists I pull up to the front of the driveway and leave running with the heater on for ten minutes before we bring Wayne down. Jared throws the wheelchair, which arrived courtesy of Owen, into the trunk while Carly and I help Wayne into a second pair of sweats and a large overcoat of my father's that I find hanging in the front closet. As we escort Wayne toward the front door, Fabia gets wind of what's going on, and her eyes fly open in alarm. "What in the hell you think you doing?" she yells at us. "That man, he cannot go outside, you know. It be the death of him!"

"It's okay, Fabia," Wayne says. "We're just going on a quick trip."

"You catch a cold, you dead," she says, planting her considerable frame between the front door and us.

"And what if I don't catch a cold?" Wayne says to her. "What then?"

Fabia looks at him for a moment and then nods slowly. "Okay," she says, darting into his room. "But you cover yourself with this." She brings out his comforter and drapes it over his shoulders. "One hour, you hear me? One hour."

"You got it," Wayne says, and we head out the door and down the steps.

I drive, Jared rides shotgun, and Carly sits in the back with Wayne. "How are we getting in?" I ask my nephew, who is humming along absently to the radio.

"Buddha will provide."

"Has it occurred to you that since I got here, you and I have fallen into the habit of breaking the law together on a regular basis?"

"What's your point?"

"I just wonder if your father's right. That I'm not being a good uncle to you, you know? A proper influence."

"Well, if it makes you feel any better, I was doing shit like this before you ever showed up."

"It does, thanks." I'm quiet for a moment. "Don't do drugs."

"Thanks for the revolutionary tip."

"And speaking of tips, always wear a condom on yours."

"Condom," Jared says. "Got it."

"Smoking causes cancer," Carly chimes in.

"Don't drink and drive," Wayne says.

This goes on for a little while. "Seriously," I say. "If we get into trouble again, your parents will have me shot."

"Chill. I do this all the time."

"You do what all the time? Hang out in the gym after hours, or breaking and entering in general?"

"Yes."

We park in the lot by the gymnasium, alongside three sets

of double exit doors. They are fire doors, the sort that can be opened only from the inside, by pushing in the waist-high access bars. "So," I say to Jared, cutting the engine. "What now?"

"Now we wait," Jared says. "He'll be here in a minute."

"Who?"

"Drew."

"Who's Drew?"

"The key master."

A moment later Jared's pager goes off. He pulls it expertly from where it's clipped to his unused belt loop and looks at the screen. "Drew," he says with a nod, pressing a button on the pager and returning it to his waist as he looks expectantly out the window. Moments later, a black Volkswagen Beetle speeds into the parking lot and comes to a screeching halt a few spots away from us. A sticker on the car's rear bumper reads I SELL COCAINE FOR THE CIA. Jared gets out and jogs over to the car. Drew turns out to be a tall, skinny kid with sideburns of Elvis proportions. He's dressed in baggy jeans that are kept from falling down around his ankles by some undetectable special effect and a black zip-up sweatshirt, also a few sizes too big. I recognize him as one of the boys from our recent paintball outing. He climbs out of the Beetle and he and Jared perform a complex handshake before walking over to the exit doors. On the way, Drew tugs on a thick silver chain that hangs from his belt loop and disappears into one of the gaping front pockets of his jeans, producing a comically oversized key ring. He inserts one of the keys expertly into the last fire door and pulls on the key after he turns it so that the door swings open a little, his manner indicating that it's not the first time he's done this. Jared leans a rock against the doorjamb and walks Drew back over to his car, where they execute another convoluted handshake before the kid gets back into his car and peels out of the parking lot. Jared saunters back over to our car and flashes us a thumbs-up. "We're golden."

I wrestle the wheelchair out of the trunk, along with a basketball, signed by the championship Cougar team of 1958 that we've liberated from my father's trophy case and pumped back up to regulation. I feel funny about borrowing the ball, but I reason that my father is gone and Wayne's still alive, and basketballs are meant to be played with, not to sit inactively in showcases. Besides, I'm pretty sure that Arthur Goffman would have understood Wayne's imperative to return to the scene of his past glory one last time, even if he would have frowned on my act of petty pilferage.

The waxed wood of the gym floor glistens pristinely in the dim orange glow of the exit signs and emergency lights as we wheel Wayne in, our footsteps echoing momentously in the cavernous room. Wayne's eyes are wide with excitement. "Can we get a little more light?" I ask Jared.

"Afraid not," he says. I now see that the two main fiberglass backboards are suspended thirty feet above us on either side of the court. "The switches for the lights and lowering the hoops are in Dugan's office, and no one can get in there but him."

"It's okay," Wayne says. "We can use the side baskets."

All along the gym walls, bolted into the elevated running track, are the standard white wooden backboards with orange targets and rims. These are the baskets everyone in the school uses except for the team. As a point of pride, Dugan reserves the use of the regulation-size, retractable fiberglass backboards for Cougars only.

Wayne pulls himself up into a standing position in front of the wheelchair and tosses off his comforter. Alarmed, Carly steps forward, but I catch her arm and hold her back. Jared helps Wayne off with his overcoat and then hands him the basketball. He stands in the half-court circle, spreading his fingers out and pressing them along the seams of the ball, closing his eyes and swaying from side to side almost imperceptibly, the way skyscrapers supposedly do. The room is filled with the kind of loaded silence particular to large, empty rooms, like the simmering instant before an explosion that never comes. "Man," Wayne says, his voice soft and tremulous. "It feels exactly the same. Like I could open my eyes and be eighteen again." I feel a hot pressure build up and lodge itself in my throat. He begins to dribble the ball, and the sound reverberates loudly in the empty gym. Even in Wayne's decrepit condition, devoid of any real strength, you can see the shell of his once remarkable athleticism in the way he bounces the ball back and forth in front of himself, his wrists loose, his fingers fanned out, and in the way he slowly moves toward one of the painted foul lines on the side, dribbling all the while. He stands at the line for a moment, studying the backboard, holding the ball up to his chest. "Let's see," he says, more to himself than to any of us. He bounces the ball four more times, bends his knees, and releases a foul shot. His form, even after all these years, is perfect, and it's a graceful shot, right on target, but three or four feet too short. "Air ball," Wayne mutters. "I don't believe I shot a fucking air ball."

"Move a little closer," I suggest while Jared grabs the rebound.

"Give it to me again," he says impatiently. "I just need to calibrate."

Jared tosses him a bounce pass, and Wayne sets up for the shot again. He bounces the ball four times, and I remember that this was his ritual back when he'd played too. This time he brings the ball up from down below his waist as he bends his knees and slightly arches his back. The ball sails over the front of the rim and drops through the net with a soft, satisfying swish. "There we go!" Wayne's voice echoes loudly across the gym.

"Nothing but net," Jared says, grabbing the rebound and tossing it back to Wayne.

Wayne smiles and takes a few more shots, sinking each one with an identical swish. "He's doing it with his eyes closed!" Jared says.

I step forward and see that this is actually true. Wayne looks at the basket between shots, but from the moment Jared tosses back the rebound, his eyes close in an almost rapturous bliss. "Foul shots are aimed with the body," he recites. "Not the eyes."

After a few more shots, Wayne suddenly lists to the side, and Carly and I jump forward to help him back into the wheelchair. His faced is bathed in a sheen of sweat that shines in the meager light just like the polyurethane finish on the gym floor, and his brow is furrowed with exertion, but his smile is ear to ear. "I've still got it," he says, hoarsely jubilant as Carly lays the overcoat on him like a blanket.

"Yes, you do," I say. "You ready to go home now?"

"Nah," Wayne says, brushing his head with his sleeve. "Shoot around for a few minutes. I just want to rest and then take a few more shots."

I pick up the ball, walk over to the top of the key, and put up a shot. It hits the back of the rim and bounces off to the left, where Jared catches it. He pulls it into his chest and releases a powerful line drive of a shot that swishes forcefully through the hoop, snapping the net with authority. "Nice shot," I say, feeding him the rebound. He dribbles back and off to his right and then puts up another shot from behind the three-point arc, with the same powerful, practiced motion. Swish. Impressed, I toss him the ball again and then watch, dumbfounded, as he sinks another six shots in a row. "I thought your father said you didn't make the team," I say.

"I never tried out." Jared grabs my pass and launches another perfect shot from long range. "It's something of a sore point with my dad."

I catch the rebound and hold on to the ball. "Why didn't you try out?"

He shrugs. "Couldn't be bothered."

"Did you think you wouldn't make it?"

He walks over to me, snatches the ball from my hands, and

sprints toward the basket, dribbling. As he approaches, he tosses the ball lightly against the backboard and leaps into the air, catching it as it comes down, then swinging his arm around in a windmill and jamming the ball violently through the hoop.

"So it's not a confidence thing," I say.

"Not exactly," he says sarcastically as the ball rolls slowly away from him and comes to rest at Wayne's feet. "Every now and then Dugan still calls me into his office for his why-you-should-be-a-Cougar seminar."

"So, why not, then?"

Jared scratches his head and looks at me. "You know in your book, how you wrote about not fitting in with my dad and Gramps because they were all about ball and you weren't? Well, I was all about ball in junior high and when I first got here, on junior varsity. I was the best one on the team, and my father just loved it. But it got to the point where it was all he ever talked about with me, and it was non-stop, man, you know? I mean, my whole relationship with my father was just basketball. Anything else I did, anything else that I was interested in, he could care less. As long as I was the star of the team, that was all he gave a shit about." Jared pauses and looks around self-consciously, suddenly aware that Carly, Wayne, and I are listening raptly. "Anyway," he says, clearing his throat. "I decided that I didn't want to be all about basketball anymore. There were other things I wanted to do with my time besides going to practice and hanging out with the jocks. I figured my dad would have to find something else in common with me, although that sort of backfired, because it turns out we have nothing else in common."

For a kid who speaks as little as Jared, this is practically a speech, and the rest of us greet it with respectful silence. Jared walks over to Wayne and reaches out for the ball. "And that's my whole, sad story. Film at eleven." He catches a toss from Wayne and dribbles it back and forth between his legs.

"I guess I have more in common with you, Uncle Joe, than with my dad," he says to me.

"Except that you can actually play," Wayne points out, much to everyone's apparent amusement.

"Fuck you," I say good-naturedly while Jared and Carly snicker. "You want to go one-on-one right now?"

Wayne smiles. "Them's fighting words." He throws off his overcoat dramatically and pulls himself carefully to his feet, extending his arms to Jared. "Give me that ball, Junior."

Just as Jared tosses him the basketball, there is a high-pitched whine of scraping metal and the creak of hinges. We all look toward the far wall of the gym, where one of the doors has suddenly swung open, casting a triangular shaft of light across the gym floor. Standing silhouetted in the light from his office is Coach Dugan. His features are obscured in the shadows, but there's no mistaking his chiseled profile. "Who is that?" he says, stepping out onto the floor.

"Busted," Jared groans under his breath.

"Hey, Coach," Wayne says sheepishly. "How's it going?"

Dugan squints across the gym in his direction. "Who's that, Hargrove?"

"Yes, sir."

"What the hell are you doing here, son?"

"I just wanted to feel the old hardwood under my feet one more time."

Dugan looks around at the rest of us, his expression becoming particularly grim when he gets to me. He seems about to say something, but then he turns around and disappears back into his office, the steel door slamming solidly behind him.

"Busted," Jared says again, heading for the doors. "Big-time. He's definitely calling the cops."

"What should we do?" Carly asks, giggling giddily in spite of herself. "Should we run?"

I think about it for a second. "Let's."

Wayne sits back down in his wheelchair, and we begin

quickly heading for the exit doors when we're stopped in our tracks by a loud clicking sound and the whir of unseen electricity. Seconds later, the gym's sodium lights begin audibly popping on, row by row, their soft electric hum filling the room. We stand in their purple glow, gazing around incredulously in the growing illumination, and I see that Wayne is smiling. "Look!" Carly says, pointing upward.

"Well, I'll be damned," Wayne says, his voice thick with emotion. At first I don't understand what they're talking about, but then I look a little higher and see the fiberglass backboards, the ones reserved for Cougars only, sliding slowly, almost majestically down in their grooved path until finally settling simultaneously into their game positions.

Jared lets out a whoop and turns Wayne's wheelchair around, running back downcourt toward one of the newly lowered backboards, and Carly chases them, dribbling the ball much too high in the exuberant and deliberate manner of an uninitiated female. I'm touched by Dugan's gesture, and then pissed at myself for being touched, because does he really think this one kindness, this one minuscule act, can make up for everything, and then I think, *Is it really any different from what I've been trying to do since I got to the Falls*, and I answer that *Yes, it is different, because he's an asshole*, and then I remember that I am too.

I move to join them at the far end of the court but find myself suddenly frozen in place, a potent wave of largely unformed emotions overwhelming me. It feels like my blood is being heated before it's circulated, threatening to melt my veins. What paralyzes me is the sudden, certain realization that I'm standing in the exact spot where my father fell in his last conscious moments. I look at the top of the key and mentally count the paces to where I stand, confirming that I am in fact standing in the right spot. "Come on, Joe!" Carly calls to me from the other side of the gym. I use two fingers to brush away the hot wetness that has suddenly formed on my cheeks, and then I shake it off and step decisively out of Arthur Goffman's sweet spot.

Now that the lights are on, I can see that the ink from the ancient signatures on my father's basketball has been rubbing off onto our sweaty hands and comically splotching our faces where our ink-smudged hands made contact, making us look like quite the wild bunch. We stay for around a half hour, Carly, Jared, and I shooting around while Wayne sits in his wheelchair at the foul line, a happy smile on his face. Every so often he stands up and we toss him the ball for one or two perfect foul shots.

Later Jared is handily defeating Carly and me in a loose two-on-one when I happen to glance at Wayne in his wheelchair. He's sitting upright and absolutely still, his eyes wide and unblinking. "Wayne?" I say, stopping in mid-dribble. He doesn't reply; gives no indication that he even hears me. "Wayne!" I call again, this time a little louder. "Oh, my god," Carly whispers, and I feel her nails dig painfully into my forearm, denting it like clay. "Is he . . . ?" The two of us approach him apprehensively as if in slow motion, the basketball slipping out of my grasp and bouncing noisily off to the side. "Wayne?" I say again, this time softly, the sound of my own voice ringing hollow in my ears. I feel Carly's arm trembling against my own. We're a step away from him when he blinks and grins. "Just a little gallows humor," he says.

Carly collapses into me with a gasp, and behind us, Jared hoots hysterically and claps his hands.

On the short drive home, Wayne announces that he wants to be cremated so that we can do something meaningful and dramatic with his ashes, like they did with Debra Winger's in *Terms of Endearment.* "You remember that?" he says. "Shirley

MacLaine is just sitting there, carrying that urn around, trying to figure out what the hell to do with those ashes. That's what I want. For the two of you to come up with something meaningful and dramatic for my mortal remains."

"You want to at least point us in the right direction?" I say.

"I've already offered to be incinerated," Wayne says. "Jesus, do I have to do everything?"

Once home, after depositing Wayne safely with Fabia, I'm headed for the shower when I see Carly through the open doorway of Brad's room, sitting on the bed, still dressed in the jeans and sweatshirt she wore for our earlier excursion, looking thoughtfully at her ink-smudged hands. "What's up?" I say.

She lowers her hands and looks up at me. "More than forty years ago those boys signed that basketball, trying to preserve something that was meaningful to them. They knew even then, from the second they won that championship, that time was making it less and less relevant with every passing minute. Their names stayed on that ball for over forty years, and then, in a matter of an hour or so, it was all over my hands, and yours, just another brick in the crumbling wall of their posterity."

I step into the room and lean against Brad's old desk, with its Led Zeppelin and Rush stickers frozen in time under the glass blotter, along with pictures of Brad and Cindy in their prime, clutching and groping at each other with what then must have been simple young lust but what now seems like something infinitely more desperate. "I'm not sure what you're getting at."

"Did you really forget that night in the field, when the sprinklers went on?" she asks me, her expression frank and unyielding.

"I don't know. I'm not sure if I'd forgotten it, or just hadn't thought about it in so long that it felt that way."

She nods. "Either way, I guess it amounts to the same thing. We all try to hold on to the good things from our past. Especially when the here and now doesn't measure up. These jocks . . ." She holds up her hands again. "It's almost like they knew it would never get any better for them than it was right there. And for me, it was the time I spent with you. And for the last seventeen years, that time was the ball in my trophy case that I could look at every day and find some measure of comfort, of happiness remembered."

"For me too."

"I know," she says. "But memory is imperfect at best. And if that's all you've got, then what do you have when it's gone?"

I walk over and sit down beside her on the bed, holding up my own hands demonstratively. "Just some dirty hands."

She presses her palms against mine and we slowly fold our fingers into each other's. Small, charged things fly back and forth between us at harrowing speeds. "I was just on my way to take a shower," I say.

Carly nods. "You want company?"

In the shower, we scrub each other softly with washcloths, the water coming off us dark with the ink of the 1958 Championship Cougars team. We watch the stained water swirl around the drain at our feet until the color gradually fades and the water regains its normal clarity. Satisfied that we've washed off the last traces of the past, we drop the washcloths ceremoniously to the floor, our hands and mouths being more suitable instruments to the business of becoming reacquainted in the here and now.

My fingers encounter a small, knob-shaped dent in Carly's chest, just above her left breast, and they stay there, rubbing it questioningly, until she looks up at me, water dripping down her face and over her lips in thin rivulets from the overhead spray of the shower. "He hit me with a toaster oven," she says neutrally. A tiny puddle of water is collecting in this unplanned crevice, and I lean forward and suck it out, my tongue exploring the smoothness of the small site where her bone has been permanently compromised. Then I pull her tightly against me and we cling to each other directly beneath the showerhead, its unrelenting spray enveloping us in a soft hissing curtain. "When I hold you like this, I can't feel it," I say into her wet ear.

"Me neither," she says, opening her mouth against my shoulder and biting down.

I carry her, wrapped in a towel, back to my room, where I spread her out on the bed and unwrap her carefully, like packaged pottery. I lie on top of her and we spend a long while stroking and kissing each other, but Carly holds off on taking me inside her. She wants it to last like this for a while, like it did when we were kids, when heavy petting was an end unto itself and not simply the means by which the sexual wheel was greased. Then, sex had been a far-off and mythical prize, but now it's just the last part of the whole act, and she doesn't want to get there so fast. Eventually, though, the mounting heat from our friction will not be denied, and we're faced with the pragmatic choice of acting our age or making an unseemly mess. Afterward, I turn on my old stereo, and we listen to Peter Gabriel sing about getting so lost sometimes, the sound of the phonograph needle on dusty vinyl hissing like rain through the speakers. Carly lies with her head on my stomach and we listen to the music until we fall asleep. We're still lying in that position at around three in the morning when Fabia raps loudly on our door and tells us that we had better come downstairs right away.

Wayne lies propped up in his bed, eyes closed, thin beads of perspiration coating his forehead and upper lip. "What's up, Wayne?" I say, sitting down on the edge of the bed. Carly moves around the bed to sit on his other side. Fabia stands at the foot of the bed, looking highly agitated. Wayne's eyelids flutter open, but he can't quite get them to stay that way, and they flicker erratically, as if some internal motor is shutting down, which of course it is. With considerable effort, he manages to achieve eye contact with me for a few seconds before his lids collapse again. "Joe," he whispers, and his voice sounds distant and muted, as if I'm hearing it straight from his throat without its passing through his mouth.

"Wayne," I say. "We're here."

He nods, and I think I can see his blood through his skin, slowing to a crawl in the veins of his forehead, barely propelled by the waning pump of his heart. "I think it's time," he says after a minute. Something thick and wet has entered his voice, drowning out the very end of each syllable. "It's so strange. I thought I'd be more afraid."

We have entered a movie, the death scene. He will reveal a secret, a long-kept indiscretion, a buried treasure, a child given up for adoption at birth, the name of the murderer, a clue to be followed up on. Carly reaches forward and runs her fingers lightly over his brow, wiping away the droplets of sweat that have begun to trickle down his face. He opens his eyes again and focuses briefly on her. "Tell the truth," he whispers. "You guys got it on tonight, didn't you?"

Carly smiles, even as her eyes begin to fill with tears, and nods. "We did," she says softly.

Wayne smiles. "Thank god." Reaching out with a shaky arm, he gently brushes his fingers against the dampness of her face, then brings them to his parched tongue, closing his eyes as he tastes her tears. For a few minutes he just lies there, his chest moving in small increments as the frequency of his shallow breaths increases. I can tell that the simple act of breathing is becoming difficult for him. He opens his mouth to say something else, but this time all that comes out is an unintelligible wet noise, and the effort seems to further weaken him. "It's okay," I say, my voice high and wavering. "Just try to relax." I feel my own chest heave in a short series of autonomic convulsions, then feel Carly's steadying hand on my shoulder. "It's okay, Wayne," I say again.

After another minute or so, he opens his eyes again. "You'll dedicate your book to me." It's a question, but he lacks the vocal power to raise it at the end.

"Of course."

"Make me sound noble."

"I will."

"But not uncool."

"Noble and cool. You got it."

Carly leans forward and kisses his forehead. A moment later I do the same, his skin hot and salty against my lips. By the time I sit back up, his eyes are closed again, but his lips have formed a weak smile. His mouth moves once or twice after that, but no sounds come out.

Death starts at his face and works its way down, like someone closing up shop, turning off the lights as he goes through the building. First Wayne's eyes stop flickering, and then his mouth closes, his lips coming together in a mild frown. His chest continues to rise and fall lightly for another half hour or so, the movement becoming increasingly harder to detect until it becomes clear that it's stopped. During this time, Carly and I sit in silence on either side of him, gently rubbing his arms to keep him company. At the very end, Wayne's legs lock together in a quick, surprising spasm, and Carly lets out a small shriek in spite of herself, quickly bringing her hand up to her mouth the way a little kid will when she's said something she knows she shouldn't have.

# thirty-six

You can have all the sex you want, make declarations of love until you're hoarse, but all it really takes to feel like a couple is arriving together to a formal function, dressed appropriately, walking in step. I take an extra second to revel in this feeling as Carly and I ascend the stone steps of Saint Michael's Church for Wayne's funeral, to breathe it in and exhale it through my pores, knowing that such consciousness is fleeting and that it inevitably gets processed in the same thoughtless manner as oxygen.

The sky is a violent, ominous gray, the air humid and thick with the threat of an approaching storm. It's perfect funeral weather, and I know it would have appealed to Wayne's sense of drama. "I don't get this at all," Carly says as we approach the tall, forbidding doors of Saint Mike's. "Why would Wayne ask for a traditional funeral mass? He hates the Church."

"I don't think it has anything to do with the Church," I say, pulling on the wrought iron door handle and entering the church. "He's doing it for his parents."

"Maybe. But still, this doesn't feel like him at all."

It's been three days since Wayne's death, and we are still doggedly referring to him in the present tense, unwilling to allow his inevitable shift into the past to occur.

We are the first ones here, and the sound of our footsteps on ancient stone tiles echoes in triplicate off the high arched ceilings of the foyer. We walk through a low arched doorway and into the church proper, making our way through the rows of empty pews to the front of the sanctuary, just below the raised altar. I gaze around the cavernous chamber, taking in the stained glass windows, the exposed wooden ceiling beams, the molded crucifixes that adorn the ceiling on either side of the vast iron chandelier. "Do you know what?" I say. "This is the first time I've ever been in a church."

"Really?" Carly says. "This is actually my third time. One wedding and one funeral."

"Aren't we the heathens." We're speaking in hushed tones now, even though it's just the two of us in the vast chamber, two neophytes overcompensating with exaggerated deference.

"We're not heathens. We're lapsed Jews."

We sit down in one of the forwardmost pews, the wooden bench creaking under abused vermilion upholstery that has absorbed decades of baby puke and the discarded remnants of illicit candies and gums. "Nothing like being in a church to make you feel the Jew in you," I say.

Of course, it's not as if the Goffmans have ever been devout practitioners of Judaism anyway. The only time I can recall seeing the inside of a synagogue was on the occasion of Brad's Bar Mitzvah. He stumbled through some blessings over the Torah in the Reform Temple on Churchill, and then we had a party. There were little matchbooks and mints with his name on them, the table centerpieces were miniature basketball hoops with Styrofoam basketballs, and there was a seedy-looking DJ with a perm, still languishing in denial over the death of disco. I suppose that if my mother hadn't died before my thirteenth birthday, I would have had a Bar Mitzvah too, but she did, so I didn't. According to Jewish tradition, as I understand it, this means I've never officially become a man.

The doors swing open behind us, and we turn to see Wayne's parents enter, escorted by Father Mahon, a burly, amiable priest who's been with Saint Mike's for over thirty years and is known to Catholics and heathens alike for his theatrical, old-school umpiring style in the Bush Falls Little League. Another two couples that I don't recognize but presume to be relatives from out of town follow the Hargroves down the aisle. I nod in greeting to Mrs. Hargrove and am perfectly content to leave it at that, but Carly steps forward and shakes her hand somberly, leaving me no choice but to follow suit. "Mrs. Hargrove," she says, "I am so sorry. We loved him so much."

Mrs. Hargrove nods and then looks at me, her eyes aggressively probing mine like a retinal scan, daring me to evince the slightest glimmer of judgment. Her hand is limp and dry in mine, a small dead animal wrapped in tissue paper, and I nod once and recite a perfunctory condolence. Wayne's father's handshake is hard and clammy, and he holds on for an extra second, forcing me to look him in the eye. "Thank you, Joe," he whispers, his voice hoarse and unsteady and, I realize now, so much like Wayne's. "Thank you for everything."

His eyes well up with tears, and for one terrifying moment I worry that he's going to pull me into a grieving embrace. Mrs. Hargrove, clearly not happy with the direction this is taking, clamps her hand firmly on his arm and leads him forward toward the front row. "Pull yourself together, Victor," she admonishes him. "For heaven's sake."

Brad and Jared join us a few minutes later. Brad is wearing suit pants and his Cougars jacket, and Jared is wearing a navy suit without a tie. He's pulled his hair back behind his ears in a miniature ponytail for the occasion, and his eyes look slightly puffy, as if he's been crying. Brad drops Jared off at our pew and then steps forward to offer his condolences to Wayne's parents. When he walks back to our seats, I see him discreetly brush a tear from the corner of his eye and feel another one of the inexplicable rushes of affection for him that have been catching me by surprise ever since I got to the Falls. "Hey, Joe," he says, leaning over to shake my hand, "I'm really sorry." We haven't spoken since that night at his house, and he must know that Jared and I have still been spending time together, but if he's still upset with me, he's keeping it well concealed.

"That's a nice gesture," I say, indicating Brad's basketball jacket. "Wayne would have appreciated it."

Brad shrugs. "It's a tradition."

A few more random guests file in over the next few minutes. I recognize Paul Barrow, Wayne's doctor, and Dave Sykes and Stan Rydell, two guys who'd been in our class back in high school, and a small assortment of men and women who are either colleagues of Mr. Hargrove's or fellow parishioners.

Wayne had requested a small ceremony for just family and a few friends, so after a quick whispered conversation with Mrs. Hargrove, Father Mahon ascends the altar and starts flipping through his prayer book. I remember how Father Mahon used to do a little dance when he called a strikeout, lifting his knee high into the air and then lunging forward with his fist as he yelled, "Steerike three!" I look over at Brad and see that he's smiling. He turns to me and mouths the words *steerike three*. I nod and we smile, like brothers.

Two solemn men in matching mustaches and black suits wheel the casket down the aisle and bring it to a stop at the front of the sanctuary. Wayne was adamant in his refusal to be embalmed, and thus a closed casket is the only real option, which is fine with me, and judging by the relieved expressions on Carly's and Brad's faces, I think they feel the same way. Only Jared frowns and seems mildly disappointed, having come with the intention of glimpsing his first dead body, of confronting death and his own notions of mortality.

Just as Father Mahon is about to begin, there is a sound from the back of the church and we all turn as one to see Coach Dugan come striding down the aisle, his weather-beaten basketball jacket on over a white oxford and a wine-colored paisley tie. He walks to the front of the room and holds a brief, quiet discussion with Wayne's mother. After a moment she nods, and Dugan steps to the foot of the altar and conducts a shorter discussion with Father Mahon. Apparently, Dugan's jurisdiction extends to the church as well, because the priest nods and smiles, and Dugan turns and walks back up the aisle. Our eyes meet for a second, and I'm surprised to see him nod in a friendly manner. I nod back and then feel like an idiot when I realize that I've inadvertently intercepted a smile intended for Brad.

"I know that Wayne requested an intimate ceremony," Father Mahon announces. "But there's been a slight . . . wrinkle. I explained to the coach that this service was intended just for family, and he pointed out—rightly so, I think—that by broadening our definition of the word family, we can accommodate this change without the danger of doing Wayne any disservice. As a matter of fact, I'm sure he would have been quite pleased."

"What's going on?" Jared whispers to me.

"You got me."

"Look," Carly says.

We turn to the back of the church, where Dugan has propped open the double swinging doors, and suddenly a virtual parade of men in blue and white Cougars jackets begins filing through the doors. Their ages run the gamut, from men in their sixties to kids who are probably on Dugan's current roster. The older men walk with the same peculiar gait my father owned, each step informed by bowed legs and ruined knees. They have their funeral faces on, grave, awkward expressions that bespeak a deep-seated discomfort, not with death itself but with being in the presence of the bereaved. The younger boys look uncomfortable but grimly determined, and you can see the fire of Dugan's instruction in their eyes. Gradually, amid the sound of groaning floorboards, creaking benches, and the deep rumble of their collective shuffling, the current and former Cougars fill the pews until the church is at capacity. Standing by the back doors, overseeing this somber procession, is Coach Dugan, his expression impatient and severe, as if he's ready to inflict forty laps around the church on the entire squad if they don't get it done right the first time.

And now the entire rear of the church is a standing sea of blue and white, and however contrived the whole thing might be, there is something grand and majestic in it, something undeniably real, and it works. I look at Jared and Brad sitting to my right and see that they're both wiping away tears. On my other side, Carly's eyes have welled up as well, so I feel a little better about my own constricted throat and the abundant wetness on my cheeks. I take Carly's hand and pull her into me. "He would have liked this," I whisper.

"I know." She squeezes my hands and sniffles, wiping her tears softly against my blazer.

Father Mohan clears his throat to begin the service, but his voice breaks at the first syllable and he has to take a minute to collect himself. He has no sooner done this than he is interrupted by a loud wail as, in the front pew, something in Mrs. Hargrove that can bend no more finally snaps, and she collapses against her husband in a fit of hysterical weeping. I'm glad for Wayne and hope that wherever he is, he can see that his mother has finally broken through. I feel my own chest spasm involuntarily and Carly cries into my shoulder while Jared breaks down and leans into Brad's embrace. Wayne's voice, unbidden, suddenly speaks up in my head. *Now this,* he says enthusiastically, *this is a funeral.*

# *thirty-seven*

We exit the church into an epic thunderstorm, the rain descending in thick sheets, furiously battering the steps of the church and swallowing both light and sound, lending our surroundings the grainy, muted texture of a newspaper photo. In the movies, black umbrellas would sprout everywhere in a funereal manner, but here they come up red and yellow as well, bright, deliberate globs of color superimposed on the subdued gray hues of the day.

The six of us who have been selected by Wayne as pall-bearers descend to the foot of the stairs to wait at a discreet basement door, where we will meet the casket and wheel it over to the waiting hearse. The pallbearers are Brad, Jared, Victor Hargrove, a nondescript uncle, Coach Dugan, and me. I am somewhat taken aback by this posthumous show of respect for Dugan, and experience a twinge of indignant rage toward Wayne over his apparent forgiveness of the man, abandoning me to cling alone to my vestigial anger.

There isn't very far to bear the pall, but with both hands

on the casket, there is no way to hold an umbrella, and in the minute or so it takes us to wheel Wayne from the basement door to the curb, we all get effectively soaked. The hearse stands idling at the curb, its driver and a second attendant standing by the open back door with a matching set of professionally sorrowful expressions. I picture them in some back room, trying out these expressions on each other, maybe even naming each variety, and then bursting out laughing. They step forward to help us guide the casket onto the steel tracks in the car, giving us hushed directions like stage cues, and I feel the lump in my throat shudder and dissolve into hot liquid as Wayne is transformed into cargo.

We stand in the rain watching as the hearse drives away. There will be no procession, since its destination is the crematorium in Noank, two towns over. Carly and I will go there tomorrow to pick up Wayne's ashes. Between now and then, we'll try to figure out what to do with them. There is a tap on my shoulder and I turn, expecting Carly but instead find Dugan, stooped under a compact blue umbrella. "Goffman," he says. "I'd like a word with you."

A reflexive shiver runs through me, but I face him and even manage some guarded eye contact. The skin around his eyes is cracked and chapped, the hardened folds of skin lining up to form deep crevices, but the eyes themselves, dark and intense, still command your attention. "Thanks for what you did in the gym the other night," I say, not so much to thank him as to vent some of the nervous energy pouring into my chest cavity. "It meant a lot to Wayne."

He dismisses my remark with an impatient frown. "I had some long talks with your father when your book came out," he says with no preamble, his eyes squinting forcefully, his face burnished with a wet sheen from the rain. "We talked a lot about Wayne, about the extent to which we might have mishandled the situation back then. Art was hurt by your book, but he thought you made some good points, and he was proud of you."

I nod and comb my soaking hair back with my fingers.
"Thanks. I appreciate that."

"I thought the book was a load of horseshit," Dugan continues without missing a beat. "The malicious work of one
miserable son of a bitch looking for someone to blame."

I nod again and attempt a sardonic grin, but I can feel it
coming out wrong, my facial muscles all out of whack, reflecting frayed nerves instead of confident wit. "You'll understand if I don't ask you for a blurb on my next book jacket."

"You're an asshole, Goffman."

"Well, it's always a pleasure to hear from my readers," I say,
searching desperately through the sea of umbrellas for Carly
to come rescue me.

"I'm an asshole too," Dugan says. He produces a cigar
from his jacket pocket and lights it with a gold butane lighter
that bears the embossed logo of the Cougars. The lighter is
not standard issue, but clearly a gift, and I find myself idly
wondering what other Cougar paraphernalia Dugan has accumulated over the years: neckties, shirts, pocket watches,
gold pens. He blows out a few puffs, and we both watch the
smoke float out from under the shelter of his umbrella and
fade quickly like a ghost between the raindrops. "Nothing
wrong with being an asshole as long as you do it responsibly."

"So I'm doing it wrong?"

"You wrote a lot of shit in that book to cut me down personally." Dugan looks right into me, daring me to contradict him.

I shrug. "If the shoe fits . . ."

He grimaces, an expression somewhere between a grin
and a sneer, nodding as if to say he'd expected as much. "I'm
not going to say you weren't right about some of the things
you said. But the problem was, you threw in all that other
perverted crap and character assassination, and whatever
truth you might have had there was buried under it. If you'd
just written it straight, people might have been able to accept
what you had to say. But you showed no respect, so you just

pissed everyone off and you lost your credibility." Dugan takes a deep breath, and to my immense surprise, I see his jaw trembling. "Not a day goes by that I don't regret the way I handled Wayne's situation," he says. "I didn't think I was doing something wrong at the time, but that's no excuse. One of my boys was in trouble, and I let him down. It took me a while to understand that, but I know it now."

A fat lot of good that does now, I think angrily, but don't say it. Anything I say at this point will come out wrong, or it will come out too right, and either way it will blow up in my face. So I just look up at him, trying to discern from his expression what this conversation is truly about.

"When he came back to town, sick like he was, I couldn't shake the notion that somehow, in some way, I might be to blame, that if I'd handled it differently back then . . ." Dugan's voice trails off and, impossible as it seems, he appears to be fighting back tears. "Wayne must have hated me for a long time. But I guess dying slow gives you time to think things through, and he decided that he didn't want to leave this world looking back in anger, so he forgave me. I've been teaching basketball for going on fifty years. When you teach anything for that long, you get so used to teaching, you kind of forget how to learn. But I'm going to learn something from Wayne's death, and that is that holding on to anger is a waste of fucking time. It's a waste of life."

Now there are actual tears in his eyes. After all these years, Dugan and I are sharing an Oprah moment. Later, I know I'll come up with a million things I would have liked to say, things that would have assuaged various aspects of the anger and guilt I've been harboring protectively for all these years, but the only part of me that seems to be operational for this historic meeting are the muscles in my neck that enable me to nod.

"Anyway," Dugan says, clearing his throat and looking over my shoulder, "I'll tell you the same thing I told your father. We make mistakes. They don't make us. If they did, we'd all be royally fucked, especially a couple of assholes like us."

I grin at his last remark, and finally find some words to say, even though I'm not sure I possess the conciliatory feelings to match my tone. "You could learn a lot from an asshole."

Dugan smiles at that, and it's the first time I've ever seen him do it. "I guess so."

I watch him walk away, still chomping on his cigar. From behind, his age is considerably more apparent, in the stoop of his posture and the sag of his crumbling shoulders under his basketball jacket. Later, I'll replay this conversation and be somewhat unsure of what exactly transpired. Is it my forgiveness or his own we've just been negotiating? But at this moment, I felt vaguely satisfied that a rapprochement of sorts has been reached, and a long-raging battle has been ended. I don't like him any more than I did before, but maybe I hate him a little less, and I guess that's something.

When Carly finds me a few minutes later, I'm still standing in the same spot, staring up into the rain. "You're soaked," she says, pulling me under her umbrella and wiping at my face with her fingers. The underside of her umbrella has a reproduction of the Sistine Chapel's ceiling. "I always wondered who bought these things," I say.

"What was that all about?"

Her eyes are black and smudged with ruined mascara, and she looks like a little girl who's been playing with her mother's makeup. I kiss her cheek and we press our foreheads together. "Nothing," I say. "I don't know." I am suddenly exhausted, and want nothing more than to just climb into bed with her and sleep the wet chill out of our bones. Carly hugs me, and it's a good, tight fit, and at some point we finish crying, although, with the constant spray of the rain on our faces, it's impossible to tell exactly when.

# thirty-eight

Wayne and I used to lower the basketball hoop in my drive-way to about eight feet every so often so that we could prac-tice our alley-oops, tomahawks, and reverse dunks. Over time, this practice led to a gradual loosening of the bolts that fastened the hoop to the backboard, so that whenever the ball made contact with any part of the basket, there was a dis-tinct rattling sound. It's been many years since I heard this sound, but sitting in the study, writing my novel, I recognize it instantly, and step outside to find Brad shooting around, still dressed in the suit pants and loafers he wore to Wayne's funeral earlier that day. "Hey," he says when I step out onto the porch. "Want to shoot around a little?"

I step down to the driveway and catch his pass. "Sure." The driveway is still wet from the earlier rain, and the ball is cov-ered with a film of wet grit from the blacktop. I take a step closer and put up an easy bank shot, too close to qualify for courtesy, but Brad tosses me the ball anyway. We shoot around in silence for a few minutes in the fading daylight, the only sounds the chirping of the crickets and the hard leather slap of the ball on damp pavement.

"That was something today, at the funeral, huh?" Brad finally says. His tone is casual, but his posture is weighted with purpose.

"It sure was," I say, and take another shot, which hits the front of the rim and lands right in Brad's hands. He tosses in an underhand layup, grabs his own rebound, and dribbles out to take an outside shot. He still handles the ball with complete authority, and when he launches his shot, there's no question that he'll sink it.

"I said some things to you the other night," he says as I grab his rebound.

"All justified."

"Still, I feel bad about the way we left things."

"Don't. I have no one in my life to kick my ass when I'm out of line. I think I needed it."

I toss him the ball, and he stares at it with a thoughtful frown, as if he's never taken the time to actually look at a basketball before. "I'm leaving tonight for a trade show in Chicago. I'll be gone for a few days, and when I get back, I'll be moving out of my house and into this one." He walks over to the steps of the house and sits down. "I didn't know how much longer you planned on hanging around, but I wanted to say good-bye in case you were leaving, and if not, I just wanted to warn you that you'd be getting a roommate."

"I guess I'll be heading back to the city fairly soon," I say, sitting down beside him on the stairs.

He nods and clears his throat. "This thing with Sheila," he says. "It only happened after Cindy and I had already fallen apart."

"It's none of my business."

He casts a sideways glance at me. "Let's pretend for a moment that it is."

"Okay," I say. "Are you getting divorced?"

"I don't know."

"Are you in love with Sheila?"

"Hard to say."

"Well, then."

"What about you and Carly? How's that going?"

"Remains to be seen."

Brad looks at me and smiles. "I guess we have more in common than we thought."

"Who knew?" I smile back and nod. He pats my back and we sit there staring at our shoes, two brothers on our dead parents' stairs in the gathering dusk, a little lost, a little found, looking toward the future and wondering which it will ultimately be.

# thirty-nine

The next day, Carly and I drive up to Noank to pick up Wayne's ashes, which are waiting for us at the receptionist's desk in a typical brass urn. We spend the drive home trying to figure out what to do with them. "We could spread them over the falls," Carly suggests.

"Maybe," I say. "But as someone who recently took that plunge, I don't exactly recommend it. What about the lake at the Porter's campus?"

She shakes her head. "There's been talk around town that they're going to put up a new mall. Your lake is probably the future site of an Old Navy."

"Since when do news editors listen to rumors?"

"We're the ones who start them."

"So much for Porter's, then. Wayne can't spend eternity in Old Navy."

"What about the high school gym?" Carly says. "He loved playing ball so much."

I nod, but the practicalities of spreading ashes indoors troubles me. I picture them landing in undignified piles on the wooden floor, only to end up in the murky depths of a custodian's mop bucket. Besides, I suspect there are laws about this sort of thing. "I think it needs to be outdoors. Remember in *Terms of Endearment,* how they flew out behind Jack Nicholson's convertible? It was like they were flying up to the sky and out into the ocean, being dispersed into everywhere at once. I think that's what appealed to Wayne."

"Well." Carly lifts the urn and sets it carefully on her lap, her fingers tracing the bends in the brass as she speaks. "You've got the convertible, so we're halfway there."

"I guess so. We're an act in search of a venue."

We drive in silence for a few minutes, and Carly leans her head against my shoulder and lets her hand fall lazily into my lap, softly stroking my thigh. "I'm tired," she says softly, her lips just inches from my ear. Despite the sadness of the day and the morbid nature of our current expedition, the combination of her breath in my ear and her hand on my thigh doesn't take very long to stir my anatomy.

"You keep doing that, and sleep won't be an option."

She smiles and slides her hand slowly upward, pressing down as she brings her lips to my ear. "Home, Jeeves," she whispers.

We leave the urn in the car and hurry inside, groping each other like a couple of teenagers.


We have sex repeatedly, loud, reckless, passionate, dirty sex, with a violent urgency that was absent in our earlier reunion. Wayne is gone and, with him, my last excuse for staying in the Falls, and it's as if we're trying to push past all of the questions and doubts that have been attending us up until now and somehow fuck our way into a new understanding of our situation. It doesn't work, sex being more of a question than an answer to people in our position, but we go at it with great industry nonetheless. If we're going to remain clueless, I can't think of a better way to do it.

After our third go-round, Carly collapses into a deep sleep, and I throw on some jeans and a T-shirt and go downstairs to watch the rain, my body still delightfully sore from our prior exertions. I'm exhausted but at the same time strangely invigorated. The thing in me that had been cracking ever since I got to the Falls finally shattered when Wayne died, and now I can feel the first, vague stirrings of something new being configured in its place, equally breakable but as yet untouched. I pull a folding chair out onto the front porch and watch as the rain finally tapers off into a thick wet mist that hangs in thick curtains around the porch lights. The obscured moon lends the night a spooky timbre, and I imagine Wayne's ghost hovering somewhere in the mist in front of me, invisible and light as air. "Hey, man," I say, "how are things on the other side?" The lone cry of a neighboring dog is the only reply I get, but it feels good to be speaking to Wayne anyway.

A short while later the front door swings open and Carly emerges, dressed in some old sweats she must have found by rummaging through my drawers. She has pillow hair and sleepy eyes, but she still looks radiant in the soft glow of the porch light. "Hey," she says.

"Hey."

She grabs another folding chair off the wall and sits down beside me, pulling her knees up to her chest and looking out into the rain, her expression inscrutable. I reach for her hand and cradle it in both of mine. We sit in silence for a little while, listening to the sounds of each other's breathing. "Joe," she says, "this is insane. I mean, are we really going to try to do this?"

"I want to," I say, realizing as I do how true that is. "I'm still in love with you."

She gives me a sharp look. "I'm not ready to hear that from you right now. I don't know that I'll ever be."

"It's the truth."

"That doesn't matter. I'm not the same person I was. I'm fucked up." I give her a sideways glance. "I am," she says. "You haven't even scratched the surface."

"I find that most people worth knowing are fucked up in some way or another. Take me, for example."

She smiles sadly and touches my face tenderly. "It's never going to work."

"Come on," I say. "What's the worst that could happen?"

At the curb directly in front of the house, my Mercedes bursts loudly into flames.

The concussive force of the blast knocks us both backward, flipping us onto our backs as the chairs collapse. Upstairs, my bedroom window shatters, never again to knock unsuspecting pigeons out of the sky. We crawl onto our knees to see that the car has been transformed into a bright fireball, the flames reaching a good twenty feet into the sky. Car alarms go off and lights go on up and down the block. The heat from the fire licks savagely at our faces, and our arms go up in matching defensive postures as we watch in stunned silence while the car burns. On the lawn, a number of copies of *Bush Falls* have been ignited and burn in isolated little fires all their own.

"What the hell?" Carly says, raising her voice significantly to be heard above the roaring flames.

"Sean," I say incredulously. "He actually went and blew up my car."

"I don't believe it."

"Well, this isn't the book club's style."

A moment later the door opens behind us and Jared emerges, much to our surprise, pulling up his jeans as he goes, his hair in a tangled mess over his face. "What the fuck?" he asks.

"What the hell are you doing here?" I say. I had no idea he was in the house.

"I'm always here. What happened to your car?"

"What does it look like?"

"Looks like it blew up."

"Then you know as much as I do."

The door swings open again, and a cute blond girl steps out wearing Jared's T-shirt and, as far as I can see, nothing else. "This is Kate," Jared says. I recognize her from the night Jared pointed her out through the window. "No way," I say. Jared just smiles and shrugs at me.

The flames have subsided somewhat by then, and the four of us sit down on the stairs to watch the car disintegrate. "You know what?" I say. "I really hated that car."

"It didn't suit you," Carly agrees, leaning against me.

"It would have suited me just fine," Jared says morosely.

Carly suddenly jumps to her feet so fast that I worry a stray ember has burned her. "Look!" She extends her hands, and we now see that the air all around us is saturated with a million small particles drifting down from the sky like a dusting of snow. "It's Wayne," she says.

"What?"

"Wayne's ashes. They were in the car."

We step down into the front yard, arms extended, palms upward, to allow as much surface area as possible for Wayne's ashes to land. A moment later Jared joins us, looking up to the sky in wonder. Kate remains on the porch, watching us with only partially concealed disgust. The three of us stand, spinning slowly with our arms outstretched as all around us Wayne descends in slow motion, coloring the air white. Awakened neighbors stand on their porches, watching us with varying degrees of alarm. Carly sticks out her tongue and catches an ash on it, then smiles at me. "He's everywhere." She waves her arms up at the sky. "He's the air itself."

Some ash lands on my own outstretched tongue and I swallow it, then turn to face Carly, whose hair is now white with the falling ashes. "You look like an angel," I say.

"I feel like one."

"Listen. It looks like I'm going to need a lift back to Manhattan."

She stops spinning. "Yes, you are."

"Come spend some time in New York with me."

Carly looks at me for a long while. "Maybe."

"Maybe?"

"Maybe is the best I can do right now."

Off in the distance, the first shrill wails of the approaching fire trucks can be heard piercing the night, and I know chaos is only minutes away. I walk over to Carly and wrap my arms around her, and we spin slowly in the firelight, dancing under the serendipitous canopy of Wayne's remains. "I can live with maybe," I say.

## About the Author

Jonathan Tropper lives in Westchester County, New York, with his wife and two children. He is also the author of *Plan B*, and is at work on another novel for Bantam Dell. *The Book of Joe* is currently in development at Warner Bros. Studios.

Jonathan Tropper can be contacted through his website at www.jonathantropper.com.